D0014807

THE PERÓN NOVEL

TOMÁS ELOY MARTÍNEZ

THE

PERÓN

NOVEL

Translated by ASA ZATZ

PANTHEON BOOKS   NEW YORK

To Susana Rotker

First American Edition

Translation Copyright © 1988 by Asa Zatz.

All rights reserved under International and Pan-American Copyright
Conventions. Published in the United States by Pantheon Books, a
division of Random House, Inc., New York, and simultaneously in
Canada by Random House of Canada Limited, Toronto.
Originally published in Argentina as *La novela de Perón* by Editorial
Legasa. Copyright © 1985 by Tomás Eloy Martínez.

Library of Congress Cataloging-in-Publication Data

Martínez, Tomás Eloy.
  The Perón novel.

  Translation of: La novela de Perón.
  1. Perón, Juan Domingo, 1895–1974—Fiction.   I. Title.
PQ7798.23.A692N613   1988   863   87-43058
ISBN 0-394-55838-3

Book design by Jennifer Dossin

Manufactured in the United States of America

CONTENTS

If the reader prefers, this book may be regarded as fiction. But there is always the chance that such a book of fiction will throw some light on what has been written as fact.

Ernest Hemingway,
Preface to A Moveable Feast

As you know, we Argentines are noted for believing that we always have the sole truth. Many Argentines come to this house trying to sell me on a different truth as if there were no other. What can I do? I believe them all.

Juan Perón to the author,
March 26, 1970

THE PERÓN NOVEL

1
GOOD-BYE, MADRID

Again, General Juan Perón dreamed he was walking toward the entrance to the South Pole and that a pack of women were blocking his way. When he awoke, he felt as though he were outside time. He knew it was June 20, 1973, but that meant nothing to him. He was in a plane that had taken off from Madrid at the dawn of the longest day of the year and was flying toward the night of the shortest day in Buenos Aires. His horoscope had predicted for him an unknown misfortune. What could it be if the only misfortune he had not already experienced was the desired one of death?

He was in no hurry to be anywhere. He was comfortable that way, suspended from his own feelings. And what are feelings?

They are nothing. As a young man he had been told he was unable to feel, that he could only act out feelings. He needed only something sad, a bit of compassion, and that was enough for him: he would pin it over his face. His body was always off elsewhere, beyond reach of the pain of the heart's fervors. Even his language had become interlarded with words not his own: "lad," "haste." Nothing had ever belonged to him, least of all himself. In all his life, there was only one home he'd enjoyed—Madrid in the last few years—and now he was losing that, too.

He raised the window shade and was able to make out the sea below: Nowhere Land. Above, yellow strands of sky shifted lazily from height to height. It was five o'clock by the General's watch but up there on that moving point in space, no time could be exact.

His secretary had kept him confined to his compartment so that he would feel fresh on arrival and the crowd waiting for him would see him as he used to be, the Perón of the past. The compartment had four seats, taborets, and a small dining table. From the shadows, he observed his wife, leafing through a picture magazine. She was tiny as a bird and had the virtue of seeing only the surface of people. The General had always been terrified of women who went deeper, forcing their way through his non-feelings.

Shortly before lunch, his secretary took him for a stroll through the tourist section, which was occupied by his retinue of a hundred courtiers. He recognized almost no one. The names of governors, congressmen, union leaders trickled into his ears. "Ah, of course," he greeted them. "I'm relying on all of you. Now, don't abandon me in Buenos Aires." He stretched out his hand this way and that until a sudden pain stabbed him in the pit of his stomach forcing him to stop and catch his breath. "It's nothing, nothing at all," his secretary reassured him.

"It's nothing," repeated the General. "But I'd like to be left alone."

His wife wrapped a blanket around his legs and tilted the seat back so that the General's sluggish bloodstream might revive his spirits.

"Daniel is such a good man! You see, Perón, what a helpful person God has sent us?"

"Yes," granted the General. "Let me sleep now."

Although the secretary's name was José López Rega, the first time he felt on a somewhat intimate footing with the General, he asked very seriously to be called Daniel, the astral name under which he would be known to the Lord on Judgment Day. He looked like a neighborhood butcher: squat and brash. He lit like a fly on conversations without the slightest concern for the reaction of the persons involved. In the past, he had tried to be ingratiating. Now, he reveled in his offensiveness.

As Perón napped in his seat, López tried several times to gauge the air density in the alveoli of the General's lungs. He penetrated to them mentally and followed the dilatory and labored course of the air currents from one alveolus to another. On encountering a stertor at the diaphragm, the secretary became alarmed and decided to mount guard on the arm of the General's seat and by the force of his will help the air to circulate. Meanwhile, the General's wife, bored with rereading an article in *Hola* about a wedding in Seville, slipped off her shoes and lost herself gazing into the steel landscape through which the plane was imperceptibly moving.

The instant the secretary noticed the General's eyelids flutter open, López made him stand and walk in the aisle. He folded the blanket, straightened the back of the seat, and pulled one of the taborets close to the window.

"Sit here," he ordered, "and loosen your trousers."

"What time is it?" the General wanted to know.

The secretary shook his head as though he had heard a question asked by a child. "Who knows? Two o'clock, maybe. We'll be crossing the equator soon."

"Then there's no turning back." The General sighed. "What you predicted is coming true, López . . . that I'd drop my carcass on the pampas one of these days."

Two months earlier, when the military regime had recognized the Peronists' election victory and become reconciled to allowing them to take over the government, the General had begun preparing for the return to Buenos Aires. Hundreds of telegrams importuned him: "Return at once to the fatherland, to your home."

"My home?" The General had smiled. "The only home in Argentina is exile."

That year, spring had come early to Madrid. Toward the end of March, when he opened the door to his bedroom balcony, the smell of frying food and pigeons entered from far away, enough to set his entire body to savoring the past. He stretched out his arms and, suddenly, there it was: the cooing of the crowd. Thousands of pigeons quivered at the ritual greeting: *"Compañeros!"* and cheered him, waving photographs and placards. Beyond, between the rose beds and the turrets of the pigeon lofts, next to the Guardia Civil sentry box yawned the mouths of the Anglo-Argentine subway, construction of which was begun in 1909 almost under his very eyes. Hadn't he once walked those mud flats, trailing behind Grandmother Dominga, when they were pursuing the providential scholarship that would allow him to enter the Colegio Militar?

The General's imagination always refused to go beyond this point, to go any further into the past. He began to feel melancholy over what had not even happened yet—I will lose Madrid, and I will be too old to get around by myself in the house they have given me in Buenos Aires. And in the emptiness of his heart he discovered that he had had time to be happy only when he was without a country.

During those days in March he was gripped by a premonition that he should not leave. Every time he thought of Buenos Aires, his center of gravity shifted from his liver to his kidneys and his insides began to throb. He said that those were ill omens, and the way to exorcise them was to watch a John Wayne movie on TV: the dust of Westerns that no Buenos Aires dampness could reach. His hands would get tangled up in towels and tablecloths, and even after all the linens had been packed up for the trip, his body continued clinging to the auras they had left.

Amidst such disturbances the final weeks passed. The General's daily regime included six or seven interviews, all of which involved his acting as arbiter in one factional squabble or another. He would write a letter or two, make phone calls, if not to the doctor in Barcelona who was treating his prostate then to the veterinarian (the General's family of poodles required constant care). And when he felt like taking a walk along the Gran Vía, as had been his custom, he was no longer allowed to. If God the Father were to let Himself be seen on the streets—they dissuaded him with his own epigram—people would ultimately lose respect for Him.

After Peronism had won out in the elections, his secretary relieved him of all administrative details. López was the one who decided whom the General should receive and who could never see him again, even if they had been used to meeting with him almost daily. In either case, the secretary's decision would be based on whether the person emitted a good or bad aura, which to him was

6

as clearly recognizable as an odor. At night, he sorted the correspondence, destroying the unimportant messages, so that the General's time would not be wasted. Frequently, all that survived his scrutiny were the electric bills and announcements of sales at Galerias Preciados (of great interest to the General's wife).

Every dawn the crowing of cocks awakened the General. He would be relieved to realize that the time had not yet come, that the date of departure was still a long way off. This recurred so frequently that the arrival of June 20, 1973 went almost unnoticed.

It was late, past 4:30, when the first cockcrow was upon him. The General screwed his eyes up tight and complained, "Now that damn day is here and I haven't had time to get ready." He rose slowly and, through the balcony door, watched the mist between the hills. After switching on the radio, he tried, as usual, to tune in a news broadcast. He got only some strange voices and music, but couldn't fix on them; it was as though they were being transmitted into other ears.

The secretary burst into the room, still in his undershorts, turned off the radio, and snapped his fingers. "Up! Up! Time to get up!" The General backed off all the way to the bed. He felt a sudden spell coming on and wanted fresh air. He was pale. His flesh had sagged over the years and now he looked like a sponge slowly sinking in water. I'm swamped, they're going to have to take me this way, he said to himself. Then, he noticed that the pain he felt was not coming from his body but from a sinister bright spot that slowly climbed the slope of the plateau.

His wife came in with the breakfast tray. "No butter, no rolls," the General ordered, involuntarily lapsing into a Spanish accent. "Just some peppermint tea. The good-byes upset my stomach."

He groomed himself carefully and put on a blue suit. He soaked his handkerchief with the perfume he had been using ever since the time he knew Evita and which always reminded him of the words with which she had first approached him: "You smell the way I like, Colonel—Condal cigarettes and peppermint drops. The only thing that's missing is a touch of Atkinson's." The next day they exchanged bottles of lavender water and Cytrus perfume. "Just as if we were sweethearts," she had joked, fully intending that it should come true. But the words with which Eva won his heart were different, impregnated with scents so heady that memory could no longer bear it: "Thank you for existing."

7

Standing next to the still-unmade bed, his feelings frozen again, the General heard the trucks pass, carrying the trunks and the zealous secretary to the airport.

"What shall I wear?" His wife startled him, speaking as she undid her curlers. "Look, I kept out these three dresses."

"You're going to have to put them all on, my girl. Buenos Aires is so far away that even the clothes get tired before they arrive."

At 6:30 a.m., hand in hand, they went downstairs to the porch. They were greeted by applause and exploding flashbulbs from the sidewalk, beyond the fence. Reporters called out for a statement, asking the General for just a word, anything, in return for all their days of waiting. But his wife and he only raised their arms and said good-bye.

Generalissimo Franco, in ceremonial uniform, was waiting for them in the Moncloa Palace courtyard. Three months before, he had finally deigned to receive Perón after so many years of ignoring his requests for an audience and not reciprocating his Christmas greetings. But on that occasion, as now, he had marched out to meet him with an escort of admirals, noblemen bearing standards of the Napoleonic wars, and a contingent of Moorish guards from Morocco. He held his hand out to the General so limply that Perón could grasp only the first phalanges.

"What's happened to Franco?" Perón couldn't help muttering as he stepped forward. "He's only three years older than me and he looks like they took him out of a jar of formaldehyde this morning."

At the same time, the Generalissimo was commenting to his aide, "Just look at what exile has done to the man! My age, and he's already a ruin!"

On June 20, however, the two approached one another curious to see what new adversities had eroded their powers. They were surprised to find that everything had remained much the same. They signed protocols of friendship and departed in single file for Barajas Airport. The highway was dotted with blue and white pennants wishing the travelers a safe journey. A squad of Hussars mounted guard in a semicircle at the head of the runway. The Generalissimo noticed the name of the plane: "Ah, Betelgeuse, the dying star . . . An astronomer whom I went fishing with pointed it out to me in the sky over Galicia. But I couldn't make out a thing. There were thousands of stars right in the same spot. 'There it is,' he insisted. 'Betelgeuse is almost a thousand times larger than the sun!' But as far as I was concerned . . . nothing!"

"It was my secretary, López, who thought of naming it that, because Betelgeuse changes intensity every five years, like the destiny of people. When we get to Buenos Aires, I'll send you a present of a telescope."

They approached for the embrace, each feeling that the other might well crumble. Franco proffered a cheek.

"Consider this your home, General."

"If only it were!" Perón replied.

The plane had barely disappeared above the ocher aridity of Castile when the General asked to be left alone and drifted off to sleep. His wife removed his shoes and set about thumbing through the morning papers. The flight was so smooth and the half-light so soft that when they closed their eyes, they could imagine they were still in their bedrooms in Madrid, lulled by the turbines that sounded more than anything like the gargling of an elderly aunt. The General awoke a little later, startled.

"What time is it?" he wanted to know.

"Nine-fifteen, now, in Madrid," his wife replied, "but in Buenos Aires, daybreak is still a long way off. Up here, a person doesn't know what hour it's supposed to be. You heard Daniel explain it. The plane is flying contrary to the direction of time."

The General wagged his head. "How the world has changed! God's order is being all turned around, my girl."

The plane made a stopover at the Canary Islands under a sun so glaring that the landscape blurred. The governor came aboard with ceramic flowers for the señora and a handful of medals that he hung around the nearest available necks. Then, standing on tiptoe, he delivered a speech that must have been intended for some other visitor since it extolled the General's victories in wars he had never been part of. The ceremony was routed when an army of flies invaded the plane and mercilessly attacked its occupants.

It was a long time before they finally took off. Late in the day, having suffered through a storm over Cape Verde, the General went to the lavatory. He looked in the mirror. There were swollen bags under his eyes and a sudden growth of gray stubble on his cheeks. He came out to get his shaving kit and the cotton balls for his dyes. Bloody gray hairs, he said. I must be feeling very sad for my beard to be growing like this.

Someone had left maps on his seat showing the routes of Aerolineas Argentinas marked in dotted lines, naval bases in the Antarctic, railway networks that had been out of service since 1955. He

9

opened a plan of Buenos Aires. With his forefinger he traced the freeway that ran from the factories in Villa Lugano to Ezeiza Airport, passing through housing projects, public swimming pools, and eucalyptus groves. He tried to imagine where the overpass was from which he would address the crowd. López had told him that close to a million people were waiting for him. Entire families had left their houses without even locking the doors, as if the end of the world had come. A famous singer, traveling back and forth over the highways to keep up the pilgrims' spirits, was exulting: "A mysterious ray enlightens us! It is the faith that moves mountains! God is with us! God is an Argentine!"

On passing from one hemisphere to the other, the plane entered such strong turbulence that its wings trembled. The pilots informed the General that the coast of Brazil was now in sight and invited him to the cockpit to see it. "I'm not in the mood," he said, thanking them. "All I ever got from Brazil was trouble and bad luck."

What he did want, however, was to have the few friends he still trusted brought in to visit with him.

"Call them for me right now," he told López. "It's late and we'll have to get ready soon."

He agreed that the secretary's daughter and son-in-law, who often amused the señora with gossip about movie actors, should be first. Raul Lastiri, the son-in-law, was a small-time operator, adept at preparing a barbecue and picking up cabaret girls. Norma, the daughter, although twenty-five years younger than her husband, treated him with the authority of a mother-in-law.

Perón spied José Rucci, the diminutive chief of the General Confederation of Labor, through the curtains at the entrance to the rest rooms where he stood waiting his turn and chewing his nails.

Perón felt drawn to him. "Son," he called. The little man poked his head in. He had a bushy mustache that moved up and down in concert with his enormous Adam's apple, and his forelock was pasted flat with brilliantine. "Come have a seat. Is it true there are a million people down there? It'll be double that when we arrive. What if they suddenly stampede like horses?"

"Don't worry, General," Rucci reassured him with a self-satisfied grin. "We've taken over the airport and the entire area around the overpass. I have thousands of loyal boys posted along all the access roads. If necessary, they will give their lives for Perón."

"That's right, their lives for Perón." The señora awoke.

10

The General lowered his head. This produced a strange feeling. Every time he did it, time became water running out of his body. He lowered his head and by the time he raised it again many things had taken place that he couldn't remember, as though this evening had suddenly turned into tomorrow's.

An Italian came in, sat down next to the señora, and kept plying her with magazines and sunglasses. It was said that, before he died, Pope John XXIII had granted him his most intimate confidences. The General had personally heard this Italian joking over the telephone with cardinals of the Vatican congregations and talking, without intermediaries, to Mao Tse-tung and Pope Paul VI.

His name was Giancarlo Elia Valori and he had paid numerous visits to the villa in Madrid. Each time, he had pushed hard to obtain a decoration for a certain Licio Gelli, a banker friend of his, who was also on the plane to Buenos Aires. Gelli was a gloomy, taciturn individual. He smiled readily when speaking to the General but kept his distance, as though fearing contagion of some sort. Seduced by Valori, the secretary had guaranteed him the decoration. The General, however, hesitated. "The great Cross of the Order of the Liberator, Valori . . . ? Why does he want so much?" But the Italian insisted. "He got the Church on your side, Your Excellency. Get Gelli on my side."

Of all the displeasures and irritations the General had to put up with during the trip, none was more insufferable than the company of Héctor J. Cámpora, the President of the Republic. Over the past three years as Perón's personal representative, with no obligations beyond obedience, he had been loyal, discreet, wonderful. Sometimes, when evening fell, the General would reach to give him a few friendly pats, forgetting Cámpora wasn't there at all but in Buenos Aires. But once Cámpora began to feel in command, things changed abruptly. He began to take himself seriously in the part, became overenthusiastic. He was anxious to be popular, he loved being called "Uncle"—the leader's brother. The General felt a surge of anger every time he thought of this foolishness.

Fortunately, Cámpora had made himself scarce for most of the trip. He had tried to approach the General a few times while they were still flying over Spain. "Are you comfortable, sir? Is there anything I can do for you?" But the General rejected him. "Take it easy, Cámpora. Relax. Make the most of these last free hours and get some rest." They had eaten lunch together in silence. Relations

11

between them had been strained for nearly a week. There were moments when Cámpora felt like begging his pardon, but he did not know for what.

The President was sixty-five years old. His feelings could easily be read; every pleasure lit up his face like a candle. He was proud of his excellent set of teeth and the fine little mustache that glided above his lips. His manners were ceremonious and genteel, like a tango singer's. His carriage was buoyant, the shoulders more youthful than the rest of the body. But in the General's presence he became transfigured. Tremors coming from his heart caused him to stoop, making him look like a waiter with a napkin over his arm.

When Perón sent for him, Cámpora was feeling ill, upset. On entering the compartment, he noticed that the sun was in the señora's eyes and hastened to draw the curtain.

"What are you doing, Cámpora?" scolded the General. "Let the stewardesses take care of those things. And sit down; you've been socializing for hours."

The secretary ordered tea and cookies. There was a long lapse of silence, or confusion perhaps, until the moment the señora accidentally upset a pile of magazines with her foot. It was like a cue. Perón stood up. Cámpora, who had managed to relax, tensed up again. They all felt evening fall with perfect timing. The General spread out his arms with an expression of deep sorrow. "I'm amortized, boys . . . paid up. I have nothing to look forward to in life except firing my last rounds in the service of my country . . ." He sighed. His voiced changed pitch and became edged with sudden anger. "I receive alarming news every day from Buenos Aires . . . I hear about strangers walking into factories and with no justification whatsoever taking them over in the name of Perón, dispossessing the legal owners . . . I have been told they are harassing and beating up union members who have been most loyal to me in the name of a Peronism that has nothing to do with me . . . I have learned that they are even making telephone calls to generals in the middle of the night threatening their families . . . What madness is this? The extremists are infiltrating the movement everywhere, top to bottom. We're not violent, but we can't be foolish either. This can't go on! Disorder leads to chaos and chaos ends in bloodshed. Before we know it, we won't have a country anymore. There will be no more Argentina. When the military see all this

12

blundering they are going to start to conspire again. And rightly so. But I won't be there to hold them back. At my age, nobody sacrifices himself to die among the ruins. I warn you that Chabela and I will pack our bags and return to Spain at the first sign of abuse."

The secretary nodded emphatically, forming his lips in repetition of all the General's words. Unable to contain himself any longer, he broke in. "These tragedies occur because you are too kindhearted, because you don't want to give the guilty parties what they deserve . . ."

". . . and throw them out of the movement by the scruff of the neck," Rucci summed up.

"By the scruff of the neck," the General agreed.

It was at this moment in the story that it happened. The cockpit door opened and one of the pilots stepped out. In bewilderment, he pointed downward desperately, with his thumb. The words must have been almost out of his mouth, but when he became aware of the General's majesty poised over the group he didn't know what to do with them. He paused a moment, then swallowed. The secretary took him by the arm and went into the cockpit, closing the door behind them.

"Now, tell me what's going on," he urged.

"The Ezeiza control tower advises us to come in at another airport, sir." The radio whistled hysterically from the instrument panel. The copilot, also agitated, was replying to the information from the ground with long-drawn-out a's and o's. "It seems that the General's platform was attacked. There's a lot of confusion. People dead, hanged, trampled by the mob . . . The reports are horrible."

"Pass it on to the General just like that," López yelled, as he opened the cockpit door. Everyone turned around. Even Gelli, who was busy putting drops in his eyes, listened in astonishment.

The pilot had hardly begun to repeat the story when the señora said in despair, "Oh God! What atrocities have been committed?"

The Italian, Valori, holding out a perfume-soaked handkerchief, hastened to comfort her. The General, meanwhile, did not for a moment lose his equilibrium. He wanted to know if the pilots had made contact with Lieutenant Colonel Jorge Osinde, head of the reception committee, and what was the opinion of Vice President Solano, who must be under terrible pressure there at the airport.

Yes, they had done everything. "We received the first notification at 15:05 hours: a call from Colonel Osinde. It was a very confused report. Shouting could be heard . . . Somebody who did not identify himself called again at 15:23 hours to say that they were taking depositions from prisoners. It was thought to be a plot to assassinate the General."

The señora could bear no more and burst into tears.

"Relax!" Valori recommended hysterically.

"Now, what do we do?" The secretary confronted President Cámpora. "Let's see if something occurs to you for once in your life."

"At 15:32 hours, we spoke personally to Dr. Solano Lima," the pilot went on. "He'd just returned from inspecting the area and recommended bypassing Ezeiza Airport. He agreed with Lieutenant Colonel Osinde, who advised going on to Morón. The Vice President promised to call back. He wants to talk directly to Dr. Cámpora."

"And have they found out who started all this?" the General asked.

"They reported that they have, sir." The pilot read from notes. "A bulletin came in to the effect that at 14:03, approximately three thousand persons were advancing along Route 205 toward the platform, carrying placards of the FAR [Revolutionary Armed Forces] and the Montoneros. At 14:20, said persons attempted to break through the police cordons and invade the area closest to the platform right at the foot of the overpass, where there wasn't room enough left for even a mouse. The cordons stood firm, and the FAR started shooting. They were using Soviet-made sawed-off rifles. When the fire was returned, the shooting spread . . . We have received contradictory casualty figures: fifty, one hundred, five hundred. It seems there aren't enough first-aid squads and some wounded are being taken to hospitals in Lanús and Monte Grande. The most terrible . . ." The pilot was about to continue but held back. "The details are too gruesome for the lady . . ."

"Go ahead," she said, "what difference does it make now?"

"They found several men hanging from trees in Ezeiza. Young fellows beaten to death with chains are being dragged along the airport runways. According to the control tower, the people are going berserk and have taken justice into their own hands."

Exhausted, the pilot handed the notes over to the secretary and began to massage his throbbing temples with his fingertips.

14

"Here's a follow-up message from Osinde," López said. "Everything is arranged for us to land in Morón. He is waiting for orders direct from the General and nobody else."

"And what can I do from here, so far away, so helpless?" Perón complained. "Leave me alone a moment."

"Not possible," the secretary cut in. "There's no time. We're coming in to Buenos Aires."

The General squeezed his wife's hands. "I could see this coming. They've sowed the wind and now they're reaping the whirlwind."

"The whirlwind." She nodded.

The General closed his eyes and collapsed into his seat. "To come back to this . . . So sad!"

"So terribly sad," his wife repeated, wagging her head.

"Then, there's nothing to be done," the secretary decided. "There will be no ceremony in Ezeiza. Let them disperse the crowd at once. Get them out of there as best they can. We'll land at Morón."

President Cámpora felt that his moment had come. The General disliked his style of governing. Very well then, he would act as if he were Perón. He would exercise the power entrusted to him.

"No sir!" he countermanded the secretary. "We must proceed to Ezeiza. People have been traveling for days to see the General in person. How can we disappoint them? There's bound to be a way out . . . We've been in this airplane for over twelve hours. What's there to lose if we circle until the problem is resolved . . . ?" As he spoke, he began to feel himself a man without peer, incontrovertible, powerful, at last. He turned to the pilot. "I am the commander-in-chief of the armed forces, dammit! Advise Osinde to stand by for a message I am going to record right here to reassure the people. And if the General agrees, he will also speak. Yes, that's it, two messages. Have the radio stations notified to stand by to transmit them on a national hookup. We'll need only ten minutes, that's all. Have announcements made over the public-address system that the General and Uncle Cámpora will be making an appeal for peace. That will put an end to it. And we will be able to land in Ezeiza!"

The pilot turned to open the cockpit door with the intention of carrying out the order.

"You will call nobody," the secretary stopped him. "Don't even think of it. There are thousands of irresponsibles down there killing one another because one irresponsible up here has been giving them their head. The General's safety is not to be gambled with. If we land in Ezeiza, that mob will attack us. They're all sick, demented. Or aren't Osinde's reports clear enough?"

All eyes fixed on Perón, awaiting his word. An obscure force brought the group to their feet. Nothing happened. The General had fallen asleep. His wife was stroking his hair, with tenderness, perhaps.

"Daniel is right," she murmured. "Daniel is right . . ."

"Do as I tell you, Captain." The secretary raised his voice. "Or don't you know yet who gives the orders here?"

2
ARCA'S CREW

In his sleeping bag, stiff with cold, Arcángelo Gobbi has slept only a few hours during this night of horror. However, his will power is more than enough for him to stand up and thank the Lord for keeping him alive to see the Great Day. Reverently, he contemplates the General's photograph that the set designers have hung in the middle of the altar, where he stands guard above the overpass nearest Ezeiza Airport. When dusk falls, Perón will emerge from a helicopter and walk to the pulpit—suspended over the heads of the crowd—to deliver his sermon of return. Arcángelo will be beside him, among the honor guards. Now, he advances a few steps and stretches out under the photograph to look up at the sky. Day will dawn at any moment. If the wind were to dislodge the huge portrait of wood and iron, Arcángelo would be chopped into two exactly equal parts . . . an impossible death reserved by God only for the elect of paradise.

His assignment was to keep watch from 2 to 5 a.m. on the temporary shelters that had been set up at the Municipal Auto Raceway. Over 30,000 people were sleeping there, the women in the boxes, the men in tents flanking the track. Arcángelo was chilled to the bone by the time his relief arrived. "It's very windy," his companion warned him. "The wind is what kills you." The transistor radio announced the effective temperature to be 2°C.

By 5:15, he was back in his sleeping bag on the platform. Another half-dozen men were resting there, retired lower-rank officers commissioned, as he was, to protect Perón's life. Above and below the overpass, he knew, squads of Juventud Sindical (Union Youth) were patrolling with drawn revolvers. The night advanced sluggishly. At odd moments, a bass drum thundered a complaint. Arcángelo gradually relaxed inside the sleeping bag. All at once, he heard the Virgin calling to him and, in his dream, he ran to find her.

He had survived because God is great. His mother died of childbed fever soon after she gave birth, and his father had to leave him in the charge of decrepit old aunts who died off, also, of tropical diseases. The only recollections he had of his childhood were the heat in the sheet-metal shack next to the food market in San Miguel de Tucumán and the sight of sparrows expiring on the pavement under the merciless sun. He was alone most of the day while his father was at work operating a linotype at a newspaper plant a long distance away. His only outings were rounds of the various churches.

At nine years of age, Arcángelo could neither read nor write. Measles and diarrhea besieged him but no one took any notice. He cured himself as dogs do, licking himself and swallowing a little water. Not until neighbors called it to his father's attention that his son was being raised like a savage did the father begin to bring home bars of type metal with which the son learned the alphabet. Arcángelo could soon read fluently, but only while looking at his book in the mirror and seeing the words backwards. He was set straight when he had to learn his catechism.

He took catechism class twice a week in a Franciscan monastery where the outstanding students were rewarded with a cup of hot maté* and a roll. One day, one of the boys announced that he had dreamed of Saint Claire. The teacher asked him to describe the saint's face and crown. "I couldn't see her face because it was hidden by the sky," the boy answered, "but her crown was made of bloody pearls."

"You saw her exactly as she is," the priest said approvingly and sent the boy to the dining hall to eat chicken left over from lunch.

That same night, Arcángelo dreamed of the Holy Virgin. He saw her walking in a velvet cape, dressed as she is on the altar. At one point in the dream, she stroked his hair and smiled at him sadly. "Arcángelo, my dear Arca" were her only words. When he told his dream to the priests, their response was bitterly disappointing. Instead of rewarding him, they ordered him to write "I will never tell another lie" one hundred times in his copybook. But Arcángelo was not discouraged and had the same dream many times thereafter.

Toward the end of 1951, his father found himself without work and decided to move to Buenos Aires. They traveled for two days on a train that ran blindly through wastelands of dust. They covered their faces with wet paper and had to keep their eyes shut to protect them from being scratched by flying thorns. They woke up on the third morning to the sight of the horizon jammed with palaces and gardens. It was Buenos Aires.

A friend of his father's put them up at a little print shop in Villa Soldati near Riachuelo, and found work for both of them there. At night, they unrolled a cheap mattress and went to sleep by the burners of the linotype machines. They sweated streams. The air was so humid their lungs became waterlogged, and they had a permanent taste of lead in their mouths.

On Sundays, they accompanied their friend to the temple of the Basilio Scientific School on Calle Tinogasta, at the other end of the city. One could tell nothing about the place from the outside of the building. It was a house with a façade of crumbling stucco, an iron fence, a grimy garden. But inside, there were signs of God everywhere. Around the main hall, stands of candles illuminated photographs of spirits that were doing penance in the house. Don José Cresto, the evangelical director, explained to the newcomers

* Typical Argentinian infusion.

that these were all trustworthy souls and they need have no fear of them. A few months before, in June of 1952, Cresto had made himself famous by putting the power of his mind to work to protect two German aerialists who walked blindfolded on a wire stretching from the top of the obelisk to the roof of a building a hundred meters away.

The mainstay of the temple, however, was Doña Isabel Zoila Gómez de Cresto, who made good-luck charms out of mica from the Humahuaca and took charge of the collection plate, threatening with hell-fire anyone who gave less than fifty centavos.

It was necessary to pay close attention during Don José's sermons and trances because his speech, twisted by an impediment in ordinary conversation, then became quite incomprehensible: instead of "chaplain," he would say "apple chain" or "The lord is my shepherd" would come out "The herd is my lordship." However, a skinny girl with thin lips and splay feet like a chicken's was always there to come to Don José's rescue when he tripped over his words.

At the beginning of every month, Doña Isabel de Cresto gave a party at which she served meat pies and lemonade for a modest price. Sometimes, the followers brought around a phonograph and Antonio Tormo records. More often, they entertained themselves with song fests and recitations of the poems of Belisario Roldán. One day, they brought in a piano and at Doña Isabel's insistence, the skinny girl gave a rendition of Beethoven's "Für Elise." She played with such a will to please that every time she hit a wrong note, she would start the piece all over again from the beginning, shaking her head apologetically. On another Sunday, she dressed in native costume and danced a *chamamé* with Cresto but was unable to finish the number because the old man was so clumsy and arrhythmic that the audience couldn't restrain their laughter.

Arcángelo, fifteen years old at the time, fell madly, hopelessly, in love with the girl. She was almost twenty-four, and when asked if anyone were courting her, she would lower her eyes and reply, "No, nobody. I only like men who are settled down and when I find one it's always too late."

In the fall of 1954 the school closed for good. Many of the followers went over to the congregation of an evangelical pastor by the name of Theodore Hicks, whom they called "The Wizard of Atlanta." Instead of summoning up the dead as Cresto did, Hicks drove out sickness from the bodies of the living on a soccer field before the multitudes. Perón even received him at the Pink House "to find out what this is all about."

One Sunday at the end of July, Arcángelo went by himself to the temple on Calle Tinogasta. No sooner had he entered the room than he sensed the pungent aroma of spirits moving about freely. There was one in particular floating at a higher level whom the others greeted with much respect. Arca asked who it was. "The spirit of Don Carmelo Martínez," Doña Isabel replied, showing the man's photograph. Martínez, a worthy employee of the Mortgage Bank, dead for twenty years, had been invoked to say good-bye to his daughter. That was when Arcángelo discovered the girl with the thin lips praying at a prie-dieu in the shadows with her arms crossed.

"It's so long since I've seen her," Arcángelo burst out, involuntarily.

"Long!" said Don José. "A certain Redondo, an imperario, sired her to pour the tovinces with flamingos."

"Señor Redondo, a successful impresario, hired her as a flamenco dancer to tour the provinces," Doña Isabel translated. "For a month. Now, she's been accepted as a *bailaora* in Faustino García's zarzuela company, and next week, after the closing performance at the Teatro Avenida, she will be leaving for Montevideo and Bolivia."

"I sawfore it when she was wittle, Isabel's fame will be namous."

"Is her name Isabel, the same as the señora's?" Arcángelo inquired.

"No," replied Doña Isabel, "her real name is María Estela Martínez Cartas but she didn't like it and asked to borrow mine because it sounds more artistic."

That night, Arca's desire to see Isabel dance in the zarzuela was so intense that he hardly slept. He would wake up, his hands dripping perspiration from applauding so hard. It wasn't until the half-price, late-afternoon Thursday performance that he was able to afford a gallery ticket at the Teatro Avenida. The show turned out to be a fiasco for him. Isabelita was lost among the singers and being so skinny, was constantly hidden by the prop trees or the leading lady's tambourine. Arcángelo waited in vain for her appearance in the second act. It was the last he ever saw of her.

Nonetheless, it was the last happy day he had for a long time.

His father was notified that the government had expropriated the land where the print shop stood and that they would have to vacate immediately. As if that were not enough, nature herself became so upset that the trees began to smell of incense, and the maté plants sent up clouds of sulfur on contact with water.

One night, they heard General Perón on the radio declare war on the Catholic Church. Arcángelo's father did penance by kneeling on kernels of corn as he prayed to the Lord to bring the General to his senses, despite which Perón delivered an inflammatory speech a few weeks later on corruption of priests, permitted marriage annulments, and ordered houses of prostitution to be reopened.

The Gobbi prayers were of no avail in reconciling the General and the Church, but at least the prayers did bring about the miracle of finding them work. The neighborhood butcher introduced them to a printer on Calle Salguero and rented them a room in a tenement house near the National Prison.

It was there that Arcángelo began to dream of the Virgin again every night. Although he was still growing and his voice continued squeaking from time to time, he looked like an old man. He walked bent over, and his face was broken out with pimples. Strangest of all were his eyes, which showed no age at all. They gleamed like large empty lakes but were set so close to the bridge of his nose that when he looked at something, they did not seem to be focused anywhere.

Arcángelo had only to smile at women to make them feel threatened and turn their backs on him. Always sensitive to being slighted, he would get even by dreaming about them. As soon as his head hit the pillow, he would summon them up in his mind, where they would remain throughout the night immobilized in flexible iron bands, begging him not to slash their vaginas with a broken bottle nor to cut off their nipples with pruning shears. But Arcángelo was unmoved. One by one, he made each one pay for offenses committed when he was awake.

Then, all at once, the Virgin, too, began appearing in his dreams. Arca saw her descend from the altar, barefooted, the Child in her arms, and when he knelt to venerate her, she raised him tenderly to his feet and brought her tits close to him to suckle, saying, "I have too much milk and they are hurting me."

After a time, the Virgin appeared without the Child, the lower

22

part of her face muffled, dark rings under her eyes, and her enormous breasts shrunken to the size of small pears. Arcángelo awaited her, feeling such pity that sobs welled up from his entire body down to the soles of his feet. On one occasion when the Virgin approached to console him, he ventured to draw aside her veil. Although he didn't have the slightest doubt that it was the Holy Virgin of the altars, the features he saw in his dreams were those of Isabelita Martínez.

Months of turmoil now followed. The General was overthrown and fled to Paraguay. Doña Isabel de Cresto was stricken with an illness the doctors were unable to diagnose and Don José's sermons lost their power to attract the spirits. Even Arcángelo and his father had to force themselves to attend the services at Calle Tinogasta where life had deteriorated to such a degree that now the furniture smelled not of spirits but of mice and termites.

The Crestos received two letters from Isabelita Martínez, the first a melancholy postcard mailed in Antofagasta, the second, more cheerful, from Medellín, Colombia. Life had not been easy for her. Instead of going to Bolivia, she had traveled the coast of Peru and Ecuador with Gustavo de Córdoba's Spanish ballet. The theaters she worked in were so disreputable that the managers would often skip with the receipts after opening night. The performers had no choice but to go to work as waitresses in cheap barrooms to pay for their food and lodging. "We got so thin," she wrote, "that a German in Guayaquil offered us jobs as extras in a film about castaways from a shipwreck."

Finally, they were hired to dance tangos in Medellín at an anniversary celebration for Carlos Gardel. Being the only native Argentines involved, success was considered certain, so they spent all their savings on refurbishing their costumes. But there were only twenty people in the audience on opening night and four for the next performance. The reason was that eight films Gardel had made for Paramount were being shown dirt cheap at a theater only a block away, and, on top of that, the restaurant at the airport was featuring a Japanese singer who was causing a sensation with his imitation of the dead man's voice.

The company broke up then and there. "Left to our fate," Isabel related, "we didn't know what to do. Some of the girls went back to the bars. I didn't. I pawned my costumes and jewelry at the National Pawnshop and began looking for work teaching piano and flamenco in the hope of scraping together enough for the trip back to Buenos Aires. But the Almighty came to my rescue. A leading artist from the Caribbean, Joe Herald, took me under his wing. I joined his group as a second-string dancer. We go on tour as soon as rehearsals are over. After a week in Cartagena, we open in Panama. We do variety dancing, not flamenco, but are being treated so well that I couldn't be happier. Mr. Herald is like a father to me. He buys me so much food that I'm afraid I'll grow fat as a cow . . ."

With the help of Arcángelo, whose beautiful penmanship looked like printing, Doña Isabel sent Isabelita a long letter in which she recounted all the details of her sickness and lamented the godlessness that had befallen Argentina. She longed desperately for a reply. Don José would go out every afternoon to wait until the mailman came, and when he returned with empty hands, consoled his wife with the same refrain: "Isabel'll be famous. I sawfore it when she was wittle."

Arcángelo visited Doña Isabel faithfully from the time she took seriously ill. Seated at her bedside, he would hold her hand and tell her about the bats he had seen flying over the market in Tucumán. He was strongly tempted to confide in her about his encounters with the Virgin, but never dared.

Doña Isabel died in September, 1956, refusing to believe the turn of fortune that had transformed Isabelita's life. In the last stretches of her agony, Don José showed her a magazine photograph of the young woman, disfigured by overweight and a permanent, with General Perón at a hotel in Caracas. The caption read: "The mysterious secretary of the deposed dictator." Doña Isabel glanced at the magazine apathetically and decided that everything it said was a fabrication to inveigle readers. She then turned her face to the wall and refused to be bothered anymore with the follies of this world.

Her grave in the Chacarita cemetery, at the outset a showplace of offerings and wreaths with dedications, soon fell into neglect. Only Arcángelo and his father visited it now and then to polish the metal flower vases, but when the widower closed down the Calle Tinogasta temple and set off on a mysterious trip, they too lost interest in preserving those memories.

The print shop became the center of their lives. Most of the linotypists followed the Rosicrucian teachings by correspondence and Arcángelo convinced his father to enroll them both in the courses. Soon they grew familiar with the language of sounds and colors and with cosmological shifts.

Even toward the end of 1957, when work at the print shop became overwhelming, Arcángelo and his father, instead of resting, studied the doctrine. Before going to sleep, they would pore over maps of the heavens and note down the discoveries constantly being made at the observatory of the Rose-Croix University in California.

Worried that his studies would be interrupted by military service, Arcángelo brought along an amulet when he went for his medical examination. He was found unfit for service because of a spinal curvature. One of the medics reprimanded him for having come without his glasses. Arcángelo was surprised. Glasses? It was then that he learned that he was nearsighted in one eye and astigmatic in the other and therefore that his view of the world had always been distorted.

At the print shop, almost all the leaflets circulating in Buenos Aires at the time were entrusted to him: the electoral propaganda of Arturo Frondizi and Alejandro Gómez, Father Benítez's pamphlets in defense of the policy of turning in blank ballots, and even the secret orders of the leaders of the steel and textile workers' unions to members whose sections had been taken over by the government.

In March, 1958, another linotypist, also a Rosicrucian, came to work at the plant. Although he had a high-pitched voice and was hard of hearing, he had sung on the radio in New York—he claimed—before he became a corporal in the federal police. He was in regular correspondence with the disciples of the theosophist Eliphas Lévi and boasted of being an expert in the Cabala and alchemy.

This was José López Rega. Although mild-mannered in those days, he also carried a heavy load of vindictiveness. He spent his evenings playing cards at The Horsefly, a club in Saavedra where the members went about in pajamas and slippers. On Sundays, however, he was content to resume the role of husband and father. He would arrive at the club with a basket of beef innards and take over the shelter in the back yard that had the best shade. Without neglecting his fire, he played in pickup soccer games, always as right fullback. Toward evening, he would bawl María Greer boleros and Agustín Lara waltzes to the accompaniment of any willing guitar-thumper. And as his closing number he would burst out with the high notes of "Granada" at imminent risk of respiratory arrest.

His greatest pride, as he said, was to have reached life's mid-point beholden to no one. He was put to work at thirteen years of age as a laborer in a textile factory. To compensate for this harsh fate, he studied singing and declamation with a woman who gave classes in the neighborhood. In the summer of 1938, he found a berth on a merchant ship as an assistant cook and dropped from sight for six months. On his return, he reported that he had sung on WHOM, a Spanish-language radio station in New York, with such success that he was offered a contract at El Chico night club on 42nd Street. He was able to give only two shows, however, because his ship was due to leave.

One of the card players at The Horsefly who was studying at the British Cultural Institute, was determined to bring him down a peg. "Write down the name of that Yankee radio station for me," he challenged. López Rega wrote it correctly: WHOM. "Of whom are you talking?" asked the would-be maestro, in English, figuring he'd cornered him. To everyone's surprise, the linotypist came back with the mystifying riposte, also in English:" 'I knew six honest servingmen / (they taught me all I knew) / their names are what and why and when / and how and where and who.' Of whom am I talking?"

Arcángelo knew the rest of the story because José himself told it to him. Early one morning he found him in the paper-storage shed drawing planets around the star Vega and shading the purple depths of Betelgeuse with gray water colors.

"Such a big star, and it's dying?" Arcángelo asked.

"You've got the idea. But it's not dying by itself. I've started to kill it."

They became inseparable after that, and in recompense for Arcángelo's appreciation of his powers, López took him on as a disciple. Closeted in the paper shed at the end of the day's work, they studied the equivalences between scents, the signs of the zodiac, and the musical notes that correspond to each letter of the Lord's Prayer. Sometimes, López took Arca along to The Horsefly and granted him the privilege of sitting behind him while he played cards. During the bus trip, he would show him his notes for the vast compendium on esoteric astrology that he had begun to write, complaining that his wife—whom he called "Tiny"—often interrupted his thoughts with neighborhood gossip. "The poor thing doesn't realize," he said "that I don't belong to this world."

One night, while walking on Alberdi Plaza, a few blocks from the club, López confided that he had been in contact with General Perón and the departed Evita. Arcángelo listened to the story, unable to believe his ears.

"In 1946, the Supreme Powers assigned me the mission of watching over the two of them in the presidential residence on Calle Austria. The Voices instructed me that it was not necessary to see them more than once a day, and from a distance. I decided to incarnate in an ordinary policeman, which would make it possible for me to be on guard duty for eight hours in the booth at the entrance. I don't know what I did wrong but for a time I lost my powers. I was transferred to a judge's office where I put in five bad years. After my promotion to corporal, I went back to my previous post. By then, everything was a disaster. Evita didn't want to have relations with the General; all she cared about was looking out for the poor. She would be coming back from her work at five o'clock in the morning when he was getting up to go to his work. On top of everything, she had a fatal disease that was destroying her, but it was already too late for me to save her. On June 4, 1952, when Perón was getting ready to take the oath for his second term as President, I was on duty at the stairway to the bedrooms of the residence. Early in the morning, Evita gave orders to bathe and dress her to accompany the General to the Congress. Even though she couldn't stand on her feet, she kept the whole staff on the run. After a doctors' conference, they refused to give her permission to go out. But she was stubborn, and insisted. The way she cried tore your heart out. A little later, her mother, Doña Juana Ibarguren, stopped in to see her. 'Mom, convince Perón!' she said. 'After today, I don't care about anything anymore. I want to see my people for the last time and die in peace!' I heard Doña Juana say no, that it was cold outside and the wind was cutting like knives. When her mother left, the nurses locked the bedroom door. Evita threw a fit but eventually pure exhaustion quieted her down. Meekly, she complained, 'Why won't they let me see my people, my poor little people?' Then, the house was quiet . . ." Sitting on a bench in Alberdi Plaza, López recounted those events with an air of actually creating them, making them happen. "I exerted a tremendous mental effort to help her get better, but it was no use. I felt drained. For a moment I was afraid I was going to faint but I controlled the feeling and went up to the bedroom. I walked by a tall mirror and stopped to observe my body. I could see that outwardly it looked healthy and vigorous but the organs inside were all cobwebs and dust. I walked into her room. She was resting in the darkness. She felt my presence but was not alarmed. 'I am the representative of most high powers,' I said to her. 'Be easy in mind because today, together with the General, you will be receiving the blessings of the people.' She was intrigued. 'How?' Evita was very foul-mouthed. She began cursing out everyone. 'Those doctors . . . those half-assed little generals . . . Nobody will let me go out . . . !' I touched her. She used to be a beautiful woman but now there was nothing left of her but air. She weighed something like eighty pounds. I sensed that death was part of the Lord's immediate plans for her. 'Give orders for them to inject sedatives immediately into your ankles and at the nape of your neck,' I told her, 'and have them make you a corset of plaster and wire to hold you up for when you go by in the open car with the General . . .' She stretched her hands out to me. I pressed them. And after that day I never went back to the residence again."

"What did they say at the police department? What a story!"

"Evita never spoke about it. Maybe the Almighty erased it from her mind." López chewed on some leaves. He showed no feelings at all now. The sweat, the slippers, and the toothpick between his teeth went back to being what they always were. "I immediately applied for retirement. I tried to go back to singing on the radio and they even published a photograph of me in *Sintonía* presenting me as a potential movie actor. What can I tell you, kid? I had to give up those ideas. Who was going to put the bread on the table? With a wife and daughter you just can't allow yourself the luxury of being an artist. I hooked up with the Rosicrucians, opened a small linotype place, and when I sold it, I put the capital into the Salguero print shop. Now, as you can see, the Lord is with us."

As they walked toward The Horsefly, Arcángelo felt like telling López that he, in his way, had crossed the General's path, too, through Isabelita Martínez, the girl with the thin lips. But he decided to keep quiet that night because López Rega introduced him to the realm of astral symbology and on the following day spoke to him of books that changed his memory. Not until years later, after the secretary had gained the señora's full confidence, did Arcángelo venture to tell him the story in a letter.

How long ago was that . . . a whole lifetime? Night is dissolving in the distance behind the water towers. Stretched out on the platform, Arcángelo observes the turmoil in the sky. The images of Perón's two wives swathe him in all the sheets of which his mother had deprived him. The wind blows against Evita's bizarre photograph and blots it out with a puff of smoke. But Arcángelo can see Isabel multiplying on the infinity of kiosks and the processions of the morning; here she comes, smiling atop the minibuses, stretching on the banners borne by the Union Youth of Berazátegui, her hand raised high in welcome from the Red Cross ambulances. Isabelita now belongs to everybody, but there is a secret tendril of her that Arcángelo alone knows: not the prayers they both shared at the Basilio Scientific School nor the effluvium of love she must have sensed that last afternoon during the zarzuela at the Teatro Avenida. No. The Isabel that belongs to Arcángelo has never been outside his dreams; he has possessed her there, smelled her, watched her secretly, turned her off and on with all the tumult of his blood. But not anymore, Arcángelo Gobbi. She is on her way to reality, now. She will remain as incomplete inside you as the twenty-five-foot portrait still being assembled on the General's left. The same elbow, hair ribbon, and shoulder of the dress they are beginning to put on her will now be missing from inside you.

And at this point Arcángelo brings down the curtain because the orders given him by José López Rega must be carried out on this very platform starting from the very moment—right now—that day breaks.

3

PHOTOGRAPHS
OF THE WITNESSES

What am I after? Principally, to know who Perón is. That's what the editor of the magazine *Horizonte* wanted. What is a man of such dimensions like? Zamora, the reporter, was thrown by the assignment: There's no way of finding that out in a month.

The editor ignored him. That's how long we have—one month. Perón will be back any time now. Our readers are drooling. What are we supposed to feed them, rehashes of speeches, glossy photospreads? The official Perón is pumped dry. Another one has got to be found. Tell about the character's early years, Zamora. Nobody's really done it. Sure, there's been no end of glorifications, myths, collected papers, but the truth, never. Who was the General? Decipher him once and for all, Zamora. Reconstruct the words he never dared say. Describe the impulses he must have repressed. Read between the lines . . . The truth is what was hidden, right? Look up the witnesses from his youth. Some of them are still alive, I'm sure. That's the ticket! That's where you begin. The Perón the Argentines know was born in 1945 at age fifty. Preposterous, right? A man has time to be lots of things before he's fifty.

Zamora solved the problem in the most expeditious manner. He interwove the statements of some seventy persons into chronological order. He stroked the boat frenetically twelve, fifteen hours a day, oblivious to life going on. What could life have done for him?

Other reporters envied him his success, the superb finales of his articles, the vividness with which he captured a character in a line or two. But Zamora was convinced he was a failure. The romance of his marriage had become unbearable routine. The poems he daily promised himself to write never went beyond a second verse. The vomitous assignments he accepted for money—to buy the freedom to be able one day to release, unhurried, the novel he was carrying inside him—had misguided his youth forever. A healthy twenty-year-old piece of ass in a motel and a couple of foreign assignments a year kept him contented. But he was now up to his nostrils in the swamp and it was too late to crawl out.

Lifting Perón's veils one by one had been exciting while it lasted, no denying it. He'd taken unexpected pride in his work. But now the editor of the magazine wasn't satisfied: Something's missing, he had said. Haven't you been reading what the others are doing? Two special correspondents in Puerta de Hierro, day and night; two more on Cámpora's tail. Look at this, Zamora, outstanding photos of the exile, year by year. How can this scrawny story compete . . . without something more? We're going to lose, like the war. How about full-page ads in *La Nación* and *Clarín?* The General as never seen before . . . the naked truth. How does that sound to you, Zamora?

Like a crock of shit, boss. The truth is unattainable, it's in all the lies, like God.

That's how the idea came up of exhibiting history. Exhibiting— that was the verb that seduced the editor—but in the flesh! *Horizonte* will mount an opera at Ezeiza, *il risorgimiento*, a resurrection of the past. We'll bring in all the witnesses who can still walk, Zamora. We'll make them the welcoming committee. It has to be arranged fast. How about we proclaim them "Yesterday's Heroes," something like that, anyway, in a special edition two weeks before? Just think of it. Schoolmates, cousins, in-laws all irrefutably linked to our magazine's logo, kissing the native soil together with Perón.

On the eve of June 20, the editor of *Horizonte* got López Rega's authorization to assemble his guests in the lobby of the international hotel at Ezeiza. Osinde, the head of the organizing committee for the return, would under no circumstances allow access to the runway. He also disapproved of certain names. What was Julio Perón, the General's first cousin, doing on the list—a man who said in public that he was ashamed to be his relative? And María Tizón, his first wife's older sister—why exhume such ancient history? He agreed to their being served breakfast. Taking pictures . . . no problem. But he preferred—to be frank—that they keep their distance from the General. Let them be brought up to the airport terrace and participate in the arrival from there. I have room for ten, and that's that. Putting up a sign with the name of your magazine . . . no problem. But it will cost money. Isn't that enough for you?

It will be nauseating, Zamora complained: the apotheosis of Argentine cesspool journalism.

The editor was annoyed. Focus on the present, on our changing nation. Why all these old-fogey sermons?

Julio, for his part, had also hesitated for days before accepting the invitation. He was already upset enough that they had wheedled an interview out of him. And, even though he had measured his every word, his tone of voice and certain involuntary sighs gave him away. He had twice turned down this peculiar encounter with his Cousin Juan: because we haven't spoken to each other since we were twenty years old. How about that! And because you never chose to answer my letters. What can we expect from one another, Juan Domingo? Tell me, what do we mean to each other, anymore?

The one who finally convinced him was his sister María Amelia, Frene's widow. She was willing. She had been given a solemn promise that there would be nothing offensive to the memory of their father, Tomás Hilario Perón, whose suicide in the pharmacy on Calle Cerrito was still the subject of occasional gossip. They're going to give us the photos they've discovered, Julio, and the police reports. If that's the price I must pay for my peace of mind, I'll go.

Then so will I. I'll shake hands with Juan if he offers, but I will not talk to him. I've shut myself up on Calle Yerbal for thirty-five years on his account, denying my own name. I am that silence, and who does he think he is to break it for me?

When Cousin Julio walks into the hotel lobby on June 20 at 8 a.m., he notices that the other breakfast guests are also ill at ease. They talk sitting on the edge of their chairs. The farmer Alberto J. Robert and Perón were boyhood friends in Camarones. A wad of chewing tobacco bulges out his cheek and when he looks at anything, his blue eyes, clouded by cataracts, turn to glass.

"I remember Perón's father so well . . . Don Mario," he is saying. "He was very good at working alligator skins. The two of us together used to make reins, muzzles, halters. And we went hunting, too. Yes sir! Stalking the guanaco for days and days . . ."

Are we supposed to be telling stories? Cousin Julio is alarmed. He already did that once. Nothing doing! No stories!

Zamora comes over to reassure him: The guests are just talking among themselves, catching up on the past with one another. Have you met Don José Artemio Toledo yet? He's a first cousin, too. And his wife, Doña Benita? They haven't seen the General in forty years.

José Artemio wears a beret, which he touches with his fingertips as a form of greeting. Benita has not taken off her fox coat and her face is flushed with the heat.

"Is that so? Cousins on which side?" asks María Amelia, pulling her chair up to Julio's.

"Through the Toledos," Benita replies. "José Artemio's mother and the General's mother were sisters . . . The question has often come up as to how that could be: sisters of the same father and mother with different family names? We don't know. Entanglements of the folks from around those parts . . . Lobos, Roque Pérez, Cañuelas, 25 de Mayo. It's all one small world out there."

The waiters have finally set up the breakfast tables. Zamora installs Captain Santiago Trafelatti and Señorita María Tizón at either end. She is wearing a pink suit. She has heard—she laughs as she tells it—that in the evening Perón will fly over Buenos Aires in a balloon and that he will pass along greeting the people avenue by avenue. Maybe when he sees us he'll invite us along. We could ask him. Captain Trafelatti, a former comrade-in-arms, doubts it is true. Perón would never do such a thing. He has vertigo.

Horizonte has left a folder containing documents and photos at each place setting. The guests become excited when they discover them. Not Cousin Julio. He has no intention of revealing anything and doesn't move a muscle.

He comes from a family brought up to dissemble. A year and a half after his father died, his mother, still in deep mourning, remarried, leaving the children in the charge of Aunt Vicenta Martirena. The aunt would tell them fables at bedtime, all of which had the same moral: "There is always a feeling / for every occasion. / Choose the one that fits the best / and you will surely pass the test." And so, they grew up learning to ingratiate themselves and to say what the grownups wanted to hear.

Señorita María Tizón hands around an enlargement of a snapshot of her sister Potota and Juan Domingo standing next to a Packard. ". . . in the summer of 1930, on their honeymoon."

". . . of 1929," corrects Benita Escudero de Toledo. "I know exactly. They were married on the fifth of January, 1929, at seven-thirty p.m., not in the church, but in an improvised chapel at the bride's house, because of Juan's deep mourning. His father, Don Mario Tomás, had died shortly before. Here are the wedding invitations to prove it."

Tenderly, María Amelia also examines the photographs in her folder. "I can't believe it," she whispers in Julio's ear. Then, in a loud voice: "Thank you, Señor Zamora. Now, I feel that it has all been worth the trouble."

The pictures they have received are, indeed, such a living breath of the past that they seem more like phantoms than photographs. In one, María Amelia, lovingly embraced by Aunt Vicenta, is standing, reading from a primer. In another, she and Julio are playing dominoes, seated on velvet-covered stools against an ornate background of flowers, Greek columns, and curtains with gilded fringes.

"They were taken a short time before Juan Domingo came to live with us at Aunt Vicenta's school. Isn't that right, Julio?" asks María Amelia, eager to volunteer information.

"No," her brother says, reprovingly. "They were taken in 1900, on the last day of the century. Look at the name of the photography studio: Resta and Tascale, at Calle Corrientes and Rodríguez Peña. The date must be in back on the wax seal."

Although he has relieved himself before sitting down at the table, Julio gets up to go to the toilet again. For the last few days he has been bedeviled by leaky sphincters. He feels as though the parts of his body no longer belong to him. He has seen his double chin in the mirror tremble of its own accord and then stop when he stopped watching it. Also, his left shoulder rises up unexpectedly, of its own volition. The same sort of thing is happening to him with his urinating. He has a constant sensation that a drop is leaking out, but it is not. When he touches the place, it is dry. Now, he has wet himself, with no idea when it happened. And, even though the fireplace in the hotel lobby is blazing and there is an electric heater at his feet, the dampness has seeped through his trousers, giving him chills.

When he stood up from the table he reached for his folder as though absent-mindedly. Selecting the farthest stall in the men's room, he closes and bolts the door and, after voiding the paltry stream of urine that is left, he sits on the toilet seat.

There are three photographs. He arranges them on his lap in a pile so that he can pick them up one at a time. For an instant, he again senses the same flash that went off at the time they were taken. And he sees the photographer emptying magnesium powder into the tray and then poking his head under a black cloth, and then the sooty explosion again, moist perhaps, which would account for the sepia blot on the plate. That's why Grandmother Dominga isn't visible in the background. And the images are now gradually developing inside him just as they did in their now remote acid solution. Juan and Julio, their hair cropped close to their skulls, except for short bangs. The two (with María Amelia and two schoolmates behind, sitting in wicker hammocks) wearing white overalls. Although Juan Domingo has a browbeaten expression, he looks husky and tough, hardened by the icy Patagonia winds your father tanned you with. I told you to smile, Juan, and you answered that you still hadn't gotten over feeling shy; you hadn't been in Grandmother's house even a week. I wonder if the sadness that shows through in that round face of yours was because they had practically abandoned you and you couldn't get over it. I, on the other hand, show no feeling whatsoever; the magnesium flash washed out my expression.

The same happened in this group picture of the classmates of the third and fourth grades at the Colegio Politécnico in the 2300 block of Cangallo. I have the same far-away look, my eyes already glassy with the premonition of misfortune in store for me. And you, although you're scowling, you're awfully fat, Juan Domingo, with a part in your hair and wearing an Eton collar and big bow. The monitor, Enriqueta Douce, whom you can see in the center of the photograph, with steel-rimmed glasses, used to say that you were my vampire, that I was shrinking so you could get bigger.

Ah, yes, Enriqueta! She telephoned me at the end of '48, surprised that you should have stated in one of your biographies that we went to the Internacional de Olivos School, which was attended (you said) by only the "sons of wealthy families" and not to our modest building between Azcuénaga and Ombú where even the plant collections and maps were middle-class. I wonder if you even remember Enriqueta, the niece of Don Raimundo Douce, who owned and ran the school. She insisted on correcting you that summer of '48, and sent a letter of clarification to the office of the President of the Republic, politely referring to your memory lapse as a *lapsus linguae*, even though I warned her not to; that the past meant nothing to you but betrayal. I told you, Enriqueta, that Juan is like that about everything. He talks not of his father's farm but of his hacienda, and, besides that, he tried to tell me that his mother was the great-granddaughter of conquistadors when everybody in the family knows she was the daughter of a conquered Indian. Some pen-pusher in the presidency answered Enriqueta in your name, Juan, promising to correct the *lapsus* at the first opportunity that presented itself and that you would be inviting her very soon to the presidential residence to reminisce together about "the good old days." What difference does it make anymore that you stood her up and never gave her the chance to wear the new dress the poor thing bought specially for the occasion. She's suddenly gotten so old that she doesn't even know what the past is. On the other hand, I find it disgusting, Juan, that you keep claiming you went to the Internacional de Olivos, not the Politécnico on Cangallo. The error has now spread into all your biographies and you gave yourself the double satisfaction of rearranging your own life and at the same time disturbing that of others.

Isn't that what you've always done—shifted your history from some drab place to another more impressive one, and dragged all the characters in it along with you? Aren't we, by any chance, your classmates, former students of a school we never attended? And when I think about it, would Don Julio Perón be sitting here on a hotel toilet sneaking a look at these old photographs, if not for one of those theological disturbances caused by Juan Domingo in the histories of others? Seven old people have upset their daily routines to give you this welcome. They will be making fools of themselves embracing you as they hold the special number of *Horizonte*, which they haven't even looked at yet: the true story Zamora wrote based on what they told him.

Although Julio hadn't opened up and his interviews didn't total more than a couple of hours, Zamora had pestered the others like a horsefly. And some miracles had resulted. For example, José Artemio Toledo and Benita Escudero continued to preserve intact the nuptial bedroom of Cousin Juan and his dearly beloved Potota, including her bridal gown and, fading among the jars on the vanity, their bows never untied, the packets of letters they had written each other during Juan Domingo's long absences. And what of Señorita María? After having so steadfastly resisted Zamora's blandishments, did she not end up by offering him her diary, at a moment when the other Tizón sisters had wandered off for a moment from spying on her through the curtains.

Only Cousin Julio finally drove the reporter away by boring him with more and more listless monosyllables. But here he is now, against his will, completing the Cabala of the seven witnesses. Seven for the number of sounds (Zamora said), virtues, and sins. And because the lines of the triangle over the square, which reflect the lines of heaven over earth, also total seven.

The last of the pictures on his lap doesn't belong in this excremental place. A profanation, an outrage! It is a masterpiece by the photographer E. Della Croce that brings back to life a jug-eared young man with close-set eyes, upon whose forehead the first fierce portents of death are visible. With a shock, Cousin Julio notices that the photograph was taken two days before this same young man, Tomás Hilario, his father, killed himself with cyanide behind the counter of a pharmacy. And he feels a wild animal tearing at his entrails, hears it snapping in a final attack on his courage. But since nobody has ever taught him to suffer, Cousin Julio doesn't know what to do about the clawing, how to extinguish it, what pain will wipe away this tear. He is gripped by a ravening fear. Of what, he cannot be sure. The thunder, the storms that are raging? Are they the past? Or are they the questions the past can no longer answer for him?

4

BEGINNING
OF THE MEMOIRS

"I've belonged to others all my life, Cámpora," the General is saying. "How can you possibly suggest that now, at seventy-seven years of age, I don't have a right to belong to myself?"

Outside, in Madrid, the night of Saturday, June 16, is cracking open. The heat and dryness are scandalous.

For at least fifteen minutes President Cámpora has been standing, listening with deepest respect to the General's reprimands. Cámpora is wearing a new ceremonial jacket that he hadn't wanted to put on even on the day he took office. A large Peronist shield is pinned below the pocket next to the blue-and-white sash draped across his chest. Perón, in contrast, sprawled in the easy chair at his desk, has decked himself out in the loudest combination his wardrobe affords: a red guayabera shirt, two-tone shoes, and shiny ice-cream trousers. He keeps his peaked cap on. Periodically, a repertory company of poodles jump into his lap. The General's thoughts then drift away entirely from Cámpora and wander like crickets through the poodles' curls.

"You've come to Madrid just to go to parties," Perón reproaches him. "While I, to set an example, have turned down all invitations. Imagine, on your account I even invented a fistula that's bothering me! You've come to hear and make a string of speeches—flatulence of the spirit, Cámpora, to my way of thinking. Consider the poor country you've just come away from . . . for the privilege, as you put it, of visiting me. All I hear from Argentina is about factories being occupied and guerrilla attacks. You'd have done your duty better by staying and cleaning up those messes . . . by governing. I gave you the power. Use it. What do I need you here for, Cámpora? I'm amortized. I can return to our country absolutely on my own. I was saving this week to devote to myself, to think, to be tranquil. But you had to take it into your head to go traveling with a bunch of loafers who are asking me for personal audiences, to receive them lined up in single file. Hundreds of them! And they call at all hours. The neighbors are complaining that the telephone lines of the whole sector are jammed up. They don't leave me alone. It's as though you were doing it on purpose, Cámpora. That you turned the pack of them loose on me to dishearten me, so I won't want to go back."

The President lowers his head disconsolately. "You misunderstand me, General. It wasn't that I wanted to visit you in Madrid. It was our country that sent me . . ."

There is a knock at the door. The dog in the General's lap jumps down and skitters around the furniture, barking.

"Come in, come in!" Perón calls. A newspaperman from the Efe agency, whom the secretary has taken by the arm, steps into the scene. Cámpora is taken aback. Hasn't the General forbidden the presence of witnesses? But no: "Sit down, please. May I offer anyone coffee?"

Annoyed, the President consults his watch. "Excuse me," he says, "I was about to leave. Generalissimo Franco will be arriving at Moncloa momentarily. I am at least fifteen minutes behind schedule. I came in the hope that you would be able to accompany me, General, but I must resign myself to what cannot be . . ."

Perón throws wide his arms. Once again—his expression explains—Cámpora has failed to understand him.

"Now you can see that it wasn't our country that came to visit me. Our country wouldn't be in such a hurry to get to the banquet at Moncloa." And, removing his cap, the General turns to the newspaperman. "As a matter of fact, that's what I was just telling Cámpora, that with all the disintegration and chaos in Argentina, we can't indulge ourselves in junketing around the world guzzling champagne. That's why I have to return to my poor country, to keep them in line."

The President is midway into a bow that will signal his withdrawal when the General's last statement restores to his spirit the dignity that has been so undermined by this trip to Madrid. "How right you are, sir," he replies, his chin quivering. "You are the one who should be in command in Argentina." Stepping back a pace, he removes his presidential sash, and standing on tiptoe he tries to drape it across Perón's chest. "This doesn't belong to me. I accepted it only to serve you. Since you are the rightful owner, I return it to you."

The General is not thrown. Paternally, he disencumbers himself of Cámpora, saying, "Hold on, man! What an idea to try to hang a sacred symbol like this over a guayabera!"

And, suddenly, with no transition at all, he is overpowered by an urge to be alone, irresistible as a cough. That's what happens in old age, he'd been told: moods change unexpectedly. Sadness is summer, vexation is spring.

He wants to be left to himself. Perhaps I won't tomorrow, but right now, I want to be by myself.

He instructs López Rega to see Cámpora to the gate of the October 17 villa, where a cortège of limousines and motorcycles, their headlights on, is waiting. And, taking leave of the Efe correspondent, he says, "The heat and the bustle of moving have lowered my blood pressure to ground level, young fellow. We'll have a chance another time for a long, leisurely talk . . . in Buenos Aires, no doubt."

He notices that the President, walking through the garden between the pigeon lofts, has turned to wave good-bye. The General then throws out a disquieting invitation, which, years later, biographers will not know whether to attribute to guilt or sarcasm.

40

"Come to communion with me tomorrow, Cámpora! And don't stay out too late tonight, mass is at seven."

He should have been in bed, himself, by now. Puigvert and Flores Tazcón, his personal physicians, have both recommended that he always retire before ten o'clock. How to obey though when work remains unfinished and he feels time running out? For months the General has denied himself the slightest distraction. Sometimes, Isabelita tempts him to watch *Captain Blood* with Errol Flynn or "Call Unicorn," the most violent episode in the *Cannon* series. No, señora. He had to concentrate on his rereading of Lord Chesterfield's letters to his son Philip Stanhope in which the General discovered rules of etiquette he wished he could instill in his undisciplined Argentina.

"Time is at an end," he says to himself when his attention wanders from the book. The millennium, the flood, the trumpet calls of the angel of the apocalypse? "Your time is at an end, Juan," his mother told him in his South Pole dreams: the vertigo into which all horizons will sink, the forsakenness into which all your ages will melt.

And for that reason, he must keep himself from sleeping, as has been happening for the last two weeks. He is correcting his Memoirs. Or, rather, he has been introducing himself into the Memoirs López has written for him. The General has been watching him for months at the arduous task of transcribing cassettes and doctoring documents.

Not until now does he realize, perhaps too late, that the Memoirs were the cross that was missing from the Peronist church. More than the tabernacles of his master classes in political leadership, or the collections of his speeches, the Memoirs would serve to indoctrinate the masses with his example. He made a mistake when he remarked to his seeing-eye dog, Américo Barrios, in Santo Domingo, "No memoirs! I'm allergic to memoirs. If I write them, I'll feel like I'm no longer living. Let somebody else do them." López, then.

Indoctrinate, instruct . . . the idea obsesses him. The masses must become impregnated with his virtues, see themselves in Perón's past. He had already said that, in a way, in 1951: "The masses do not think, the masses feel and react more or less intuitively and systematically. But who originates such reactions? The leader. The masses correspond to the muscles. I have always said that muscle doesn't count without a brain center to set it in mo-

41

tion." It was clear that his past would cause virtue to flow naturally from future generations.

Evita had already intuited that when she published *My Mission in Life*. The public needs fable and emotion, not the colorless pap of the doctrines with which, much to his regret, he has had to nourish them.

Behind him, in the library and beside the maté gourds and sippers he had collected in exile, are the binders with the clean copies of the Memoirs. He does not recognize himself anymore in some of the anecdotes, but the documents are there and don't lie. López is right, old age has wiped out many things. The real name of Potota, his first wife, has eluded his tongue so many times! Wasn't it something like . . . something like . . . Amelia, María Antonia, Aurelia, Amalia, Ofelia Tizón? Memory had always been one of his most trustworthy gifts and he was losing it.

Sometimes in his efforts to resuscitate it, López would show him photographs stained with oxides and sepia blots. He would point to one of the figures and challenge him: "Who was this, General? See if you can remember." And he would shake his head, "I don't know, I don't know. This one looks familiar, but that one . . . I never saw that one before . . ." The secretary would then uncover the other half of the photograph and say, "Look here, General . . . Don't you recognize yourself anymore? That's you in 1904, 1908, and 1911 . . . Here, on the other side, is your first cousin, María Amelia Perón. You lived in the same house with her for almost three years . . ." "In Camarones?" The General was intrigued. "No, not Camarones; in the school directed by your aunt, Vicenta Martirena." "Is it true what you're saying? That this María Amelia is a first cousin of mine? And what about that boy, López? Tell me, who's this with such a scowl?"

Now he wants to be alone with his memories. He puts on his glasses, brings the pages up close to the light, and rereads the first paragraph of the Memoirs, which hasn't yet satisfied him.

> *My father was the son of Tomás Liberato Perón, a physician and doctor of chemistry . . .*

Why not take a step back and pull his Sardinian great-grandfather, who disembarked on Rio de la Plata around 1830, out of the shadow of the Mazorca,* and his Scottish great-grandmother from whom his father inherited his blue-flecked eyes. I am a crucible of races, Argentina is a crucible of races. That is the first indication of the analogy between my country and me. Let's point it up. The General digs around among the documents Lopéz has labeled "Ancestors" and, extracting notes from here and there, proceeds to rewrite.

> *As far as I have been able to learn, the first Perón to set foot in Argentina was Mario Tomás, a Sardinian merchant. He held a passport issued by the King of Sardinia and such credentials quickly secured for him the help of other Sardinians. He opened a shoe business, which was an immediate success. Some say he grew rich by selling boots to the Mazorca but I rather suspect that my great-grandfather, as a good businessman, must have lit candles at all altars without stopping to look at the faces of the saints. Years ago, we had a portrait of him in our house in which he was wearing a black suit and a lace collar. His face was that of an honest man, something about which I never make a mistake.*
>
> *He had been living in Buenos Aires for only three years when on September 12, 1833, he married Anna Hughes Mackenzie, a Scotswoman with blue eyes. Both spoke broken Spanish and so had to communicate in the universal language of gesture.*

That's more like it. They wrote him from San Juan that the name Pedro Perón appears on a passenger list for 1823. Another Perón, a certain Domingo—could that be his great-grandfather?—landed at the port of Buenos Aires in 1848, coming from Montevideo. The General decides to skip these details so as not to blur the sharp outlines of the story. Nor will he dwell on the clouds of bankruptcy that in 1851 menaced the family business, which was mortgaged to several Unitarian usurers. Rather, he concentrates on cutting out the excesses with which López had adorned the following paragraph.

> *Of the seven children the Perón Hughes gave their adopted country, most outstanding was the eldest son, Tomás Liberato,*

* The name by which the police were called in Buenos Aires at that time.

43

born on August 17, 1839. The life of this [distinguished] *ancestor is replete with honors. He was a follower of General Bartolomé Mitre and a national senator for the province of Buenos Aires; Chairman of the National Health Council, which was the equivalent of a ministry; and a major in the army who saw* [heroic] *active service during the war with Paraguay. He carried out various missions abroad, particularly in France, where he lived for some time. He also* [spilled his blood] *took part in the Battle of Pavón. In 1867, shortly before taking the final examinations for his medical degree, he married* [a lady of high position, Doña] *Dominga Dutey. That grandmother of mine was Uruguayan, from Paysandú, the daughter of* [noble] *French Basques of Bayonne.*

More than one historian wanted to correct these data when their publication in the magazine *Panorama* was authorized by the General. They claimed that his grandfather was not a senator but a provincial deputy; that the Sarmiento administration granted him a scholarship for only six months in Paris in recognition of his devoted service in the medical corps during the yellow fever epidemic. But he did not take part in the war; that has been refuted. He was not even able to leave the blood clinic that was set up in Buenos Aires for the wounded. Although a distinguished person, he was not a celebrity. Why has the General insisted on adding false luster to his grandfather's name when the actual honors were sufficient? Attacks of megalomania, as an anonymous reproach put it. Don't you remember that you yourself had a biography written of Sr. Perón when you were lord and master of the Republic, which, although laudatory, did show respect for the truth?

Of course, I remember all that. But what does it matter? I see no difference between my grandfather's portrait that—I admit—López Rega touched up a bit in the Memoirs, and the flesh and blood of reality. Dammit, are they or are they not substantially the same person? The passion people have for the truth has never made sense to me. I have the facts on this side of the river. Very well, I copy them as I see them. But who can guarantee that I am seeing them as they really are? Somebody or other once wrote that I should study the documents more closely. Aha! Here are the documents . . . all I want. And if they aren't there, López invents them. All he has to do is hold his hands out over a paper to make it turn yellow. So he has told me. He has me so confused that when I look at a childhood photograph, I don't know if I am really in it or López put me there.

But what I feel about the facts is on the other side of the river. And, as far as I'm concerned, that's all that matters. Nobody will ever know what the Mona Lisa or her smile looked like because that face and that smile are not her own but the ones Leonardo painted. Eva said the same thing: "One has to put the mountains where one wants them, Juan. Because where you put them is where they remain. That's history."

I never knew my grandfather Tomás Liberato. I know that he had insomnia and that in his last years, when he was barely able to stand up, he would spend his nights shut in with retorts and Bunsen burners, trying to isolate the virus of insomnia. He got the idea that the virus traveled back and forth on the legs of locusts and so he boiled and distilled the insects to analyze the water. This left such a penetrating smell in that house that after the first years of mourning were over, my grandmother had to move out because even new clothing continued to stink of grasshoppers. I have no way of knowing whether those stories really happened that way or not, but my grandfather felt that that's the way they were and passed them on in those words. If there are other truths, it doesn't matter anymore. What I am telling is what will go down in History as the truth.

All right, General, now you can go ahead without any scruples until the time you entered military school. Forget any uncomfortable details. Leave them out. Blow them out of these official Memoirs so that not even a speck of dust is left. Every man has a right to decide his future. Why shouldn't you have the privilege of choosing your past? Be your own evangelist, General. Separate the good from the bad. And if you forget or confuse something, who will dare make corrections? Then, let's reread the Memoirs as they stand in López's final draft.

Toledo and Sosa were the family names of my maternal grandparents. As far as my information goes, all my ancestors on that side were Argentines. Some say that they established the fortress of Lobos in the days of the conquest. I won't vouch for it. All I know is that my mother was born in that town among the poor working people of the countryside.

My father, Mario Tomás Perón, was destined to lead a more cosmopolitan life, but chance turned him into a man of the pampas, too. He was born on November 9, 1867.

(What about your mother? López insisted. What was her date of birth? If we put in the one, it wouldn't look good to leave out the other. The thing is, the General responded, I don't remember. We celebrated her birthday in the beginning of November. But the year, the year? . . . Leave it this way:)

There are many versions of what led my father to work the land. I know that he began studying medicine because my grandfather insisted, and that at one point he dropped out. I read somewhere that his studies were interrupted by typhoid fever, but he never told me anything like that. He said that he simply got tired of it. In 1890, a year after his father's death, he occupied land he inherited in Lobos and stayed on farming there. I, Juan Domingo, was born in Lobos on October 8, 1895. My older brother, Mario Avelino, was a few weeks short of his fourth birthday at the time.

Around 1900, my father sold the house and the hacienda because he said that it was no longer country but a suburb of Buenos Aires. He went into partnership with the firm of Maupas Brothers, which owned a large tract of land near the Gallegos River, in the region of Patagonia. And he began all over again.

He left everything behind when he moved except his people and his horses. He organized a cattle drive to travel 1,200 miles overland. He kept his best peons on and put them in the charge of a foreman by the name of Francisco Villafañe— Pancho, to us. This wonderful retainer with the capacities of a superman did not even ask what he was supposed to do. He drove the cattle south and after several months set up camp at Cabo Raso, the first stopover set by my father. When we arrived with my mother, everything was all ready for us at "La Maciega," which was the name of the ranch.

(There is an ominous sign here, López Rega told him. Your father went into business with the Maupas brothers to work a tract at Rio Gallegos. Why did he stop at Cabo Raso, then, which is over

600 miles to the north? How should I know that? the General answered. Those stories go so far back they sound to me like somebody else's. The secretary shook his head. Try. I don't recall that the story is the same as you tell it, General. Perón was intrigued. How do you know? he asked. I know, López responded. Every time you let a thought drop, I pick it up like a handkerchief. And I keep them all right here, inside these borders, within the invisible pencil line I draw around my body.)

My father was strict in all matters that had to do with our upbringing. He would make use of anything to teach us a lesson. But we didn't feel that he loved us any the less for that. We used to go out hunting rheas and guanacos. We often got pretty badly banged up because riding the Patagonian pampas can have a lot of surprises. We had eight greyhounds that did the hunting, but one had to gallop to keep up with them, and gallop hard.

My mother, now there was a horsewoman! She was an Amazon. And in the kitchen nobody could match her. There wasn't anything she didn't do well. My mother was our doctor, adviser, and friend. She was the confidante and the shoulder to cry on. When we were learning to smoke we did it in her presence.

Her generosity was legendary. She made up for my father's strictness. One time, a Turkish peddler came to Cabo Raso. His name was Amado. He had ridden sixty miles to find my mother. He threw himself down at her feet, and said, "My leddy, I die. If you not cure me, I finished." He had a disease called tetter, a nervous infection of the skin. My mother prescribed for him immediately. She surrounded the area of tetter with a wide ink line. The Turk was fat and we had to use up one of the large bottles on him. After a week he was better and stayed around a few days more thanking her. When he finally left, he would not hear of my mother not accepting his wagonful of goods. "Poor Turk healthy, get new wagon and new fortune."

(Did I interpret correctly what you asked, General? That I highlight the virile features of your father's portrait and the feminine ones of your mother's? No half-tones, so the readers won't be confused, just exemplary lives. Is that what you want? López asked as they walked down the attic stairs, at the pace of convalescents, after he had completed the first binder of the rough draft. It's fine this way, replied Perón. Just as I wanted it.)

They closeted themselves to read shortly before midnight. Isabel was asleep and the dogs, quieted down now, were in their kennels. At the outset—had a year already gone by?—they used to meet at the desk where the General is now going over each page. A breeze out of a furnace was blowing then, just like now on this night of June 16. Outside, on the other side of the fence, the watchmen of the Guardia Civil were slapping at the air with their flashlights. "This is not the place for confessions," the General had said. And López had answered, "You're right. Listen to that light . . . the guards are photographing us."

They vacillated for several days, moving papers and cassette recorders from the dining room table to a little chamber hidden under the stairs, until finally they ventured into the only retreat in the house, a room López called the sanctum. It was on the second floor and had been used in the past to store cleaning utensils. A little winding staircase connected it with a garret where the General kept his war atlases, mounds of correspondence, and copies of newspapers from his years of glory. But, everything was changed in the house since the memorable afternoon in 1971 when his mortal enemy Alejandro Lanusse gave orders to return to Perón the body of the General's second wife, hidden for over fifteen years under another name in a cemetery in Milan. Evita was there. Her presence could be felt.

Isabel engaged an architect to enlarge the attic and put in a window, and she had it carpeted and furnished with two couches, a prie-dieu, and a retable with the classical portraits of the deceased. Upstairs in the garret, now whitewashed, spotless, equipped with air filters, she lay in her coffin below the perpetual flame of six red lamps shaped like torches. Isabel had insisted that the body be lighted with real tapers but the embalmer explained that the dead tissues were being preserved from any blemish of decay thanks to certain flammable substances. And he recommended that even the lights in the attic be protected against the danger of short circuits or sparks. Few visitors, only those closest, came to the sanctum, and almost no one to her sepulcher other than Evita's sisters when they were in Madrid, and Isabel, to leave her flowers on Sundays. The doors of the sanctum had been covered in velvet so that no noise could be heard. That was where López took down the General's reminiscences, and both would read, lost in thought.

During the first months of this task, Perón would shut his eyes and let himself be carried away, whispering story after story, and it was as if the room filled with feathers. Sometimes, on coming back to himself, he would not find his secretary there. Immediately, his body became drenched with an odor of flowers and benzine. "She!" he would say. "It's Eva and she wants to come down from the attic." And he would shake with terror. "López!" he would go down the stairs, calling out. It always surprised him to find the secretary at his desk, busy transcribing the cassettes. Although haggard from lack of sleep, he was swept along by the excitement of writing. Not only did he lace the Memoirs with thoughts of his own, but he incorporated stories overlooked by the General, which he, however, remembered perfectly. "Read this page. Why did we leave out that summer?" he would say, excitedly. "Think, General. Go back. January, 1906. They dressed us in mourning and, if that were not enough, a black ribbon was pinned to our sleeves. Aunts Vicenta and Baldomera took us, in that getup, to General Bartolomé Mitre's funeral chapel to pray; you and I, walking ahead, Cousin María Amelia and Cousin Julio following, holding hands, faces very serious. Baldomera was brave enough to kiss the great man's forehead. The rest of us went to sign the mourners' register. Remember?" And the General would reply, "Now that you mention it, I remember . . . like in a mist. But I can see only my cousins. I was in front by myself making my way through weeping crowds. Buenos Aires was like a cemetery. We were streaming sweat and the heat of all those flowers was suffocating us. But you, López, what were you doing there? How old were you?" The secretary would never answer.

Perón was amused by such fancies, but in the mornings when he heard López's voice reciting sections from the tapes that had already been corrected—"My father, Mario Tomás . . ." or "My best friends were the dogs . . ."—he felt as though another body were trying to dislodge him from his own body, and he would clutch the banisters on the stairway in an effort to keep hold of his sense of identity. "That's how I am best able to take care of you, General," López soothed him. "That's the way I attract into my own organism the ills that are going through yours."

Now, rereading the pages of the earliest days, Perón recognizes how painstakingly the secretary has corrected his slips. He has presented the true story, the one that must have taken place, and the one that will undoubtedly prevail. He can proceed, then, his mind at rest, to go over the Memoirs that follow:

Everything changed when we went south. Although our new ranch—named "Chankaike"—was built to withstand the cold, life was hard. In winter the thermometer could drop to 28 below zero. The struggle against nature was our daily fare but life was always full of adventure. We grew up in absolute freedom, subject only to the supervision and guidance of an old teacher who gave us our elementary schooling.

He was a city person, a friend of my father's who was having a hard time surviving in the country. My real mentor was Sixto Magallanes, whom we nicknamed "Chinaman." He had been one of the best bronco busters in Lobos. I learned to ride before I could walk and took my first ride with him on a half-broken bay.

Some of the peons Pancho Villafañe brought from Lobos stayed with us for years. They were considered family, and I treated them like uncles. We never thought of them as peons in the pejorative sense of the word as used by the Argentines for so long.

Our customary haunts in Chankaike were two huge plains. The Trade Winds which blow at 60 miles an hour dampened our enthusiasm for being outdoors. When the temperature fell below 20 degrees, we stayed indoors. One time I was caught in such terrible cold that my toes were frozen. When I started to warm them, the nails fell off. But the Lord knows what he is doing. Better nails grew in than the ones I had before.

My best friends were the dogs that abound in the South because of the herds of sheep. One dog can be more valuable on a ranch than several peons. Those animals left me a permanent souvenir, a calcified hydatid cyst in my liver.

After the terrible 1904 winter, my father bought six or so miles of land in the center of Chubut, at the foot of the famous basalt plateau. The only springs of that enormous region are there. We remained in Cabo Raso for a time waiting for our house on the new ranch to be finished, and at the end of 1905 we moved.

Although from then on, I saw very little of my father, the impression he left with me is very vivid. He was one of the old guard, one of the last of his kind. He became sheriff and honorary justice of the peace in every place we lived. Those posts went to the settlers with the greatest prestige. You can imagine, then, that my house was a public office as much as a home. He presided over his patriarchate from there, enjoying everybody's respect and friendship.

He was an unusual man, especially in his absolute uprightness. And he had such character! One day, a very poor Indian came to see him. My father spoke to him in the Tehuelche tongue, which immediately placed them on a footing of confidence. His name was Nikol-Man, Flying Condor, and I was struck by the fact that, despite his humble status, my father treated him with great deference. I asked him why. "Note the Indian's dignity," he answered. "Dignity is the only inheritance his elders left him. Some people called them thieves, but they forgot that we ourselves are the thieves, having taken away all they had."

In March, 1904, I was sent to Buenos Aires to continue my education . . .

(An obbligato of gargles suddenly descending from the upstairs bathroom desecrates his reading. The General recognizes the uproar with which López Rega accompanies his ablutions at the stroke of midnight. Each gargle is followed by a rending expulsion of phlegm and a drum roll of farts almost immediately after, to relieve pressure in the secretary's stomach.

(*Your* stomach, General, López has corrected him. I have nothing to do with it. It's the air that goes into your mouth and later uses my body to escape. How is that possible? Perón asks. My digestion has always been excellent. But the secretary insists: The gargles are mine. The other noises you transfer to me.

(March, 1904? The General ponders. Something is off there. I was at school in Buenos Aires that year, but I also recall the famous winter that depopulated Patagonia in those same months. Those are two recollections that can't be together; one of them must have felt out of place and changed position, López reassures him. In these matters, General, it is not a question of lapses of memory but of inaccuracies of reality.

51

(Was it in 1904, then? Or the following summer? He can still picture himself arriving at the big house on Calle San Martín, his hands stained blue with berry juice. He carried a knapsack over his shoulder, and hanging from his belt a jar on the base of which his mother had painted *coirón* flowers so that the child would never forget where he came from. His grandmother received him with indifference, turning her cheek to be kissed without bothering to stop swinging in her hammock, while his two aunts, of imposing carriage, hands on hips, sent him to the back to wash himself in the sink. Was it really in 1904? The General struck out the last sentence and wrote an amplified version in the margin:)

But the lessons my father and the old teacher gave me did not measure up to the family's expectations for me. I had to go to Buenos Aires, where my grandmother on my father's side would take charge of completing my education. I passed the examinations for the first grades of elementary school as an unmatriculated student and quickly caught up.

(That's better. Now, the thread can be picked up again.)

The change was enormous. The hard and weathered little gaucho was being transformed into a city boy. At ten years old my thinking was almost like a man's. I went around Buenos Aires on my own, and my mother's or grandmother's skirts held none of the attractions they did for other kids of my age. I considered myself a grownup and acted as such.

My grandmother was already quite an old lady then. I, therefore, took her place as head of the family. This influenced my life profoundly because it made me begin to feel independent, to think, and to make decisions for myself. I was not very studious or diligent. Sports, yes. There was nothing I liked better.

Years later, when I entered the Olivos International School, I spent a good deal of time on the soccer field. It was one of those institutions for the sons of the rich, which offered many advantages. I went through three years at Olivos carrying a program that was quite unusual in the freedom and responsibility it allowed us. It was there that I became a soccer player.

52

Those were the days of the famous alumni team whose members were heroes to us.

Like any typical boy, I learned by rote what was of no interest to me, and for the rest I used my judgment. Ordinary teaching concentrates on memorization. And toward the end of life . . .

(Here the General stops. The thought that follows has gone round and round in his head frequently. But, was it something he had said? Is it really his phrase or his secretary's, who, reading his mind, has let it light on the page?)

. . . man knows as much as he remembers. Man knows as much as he remembers.

Yet it is not the exact memory of things that counts but what one makes of it, the coloration given it.

By the time I finished my second year of high school, I had to decide about my future. I considered following my father's advice and taking up medicine. That was the profession that predominated in the Perón family. They say that my great-great-grandfather was a surgeon in Alghero, a small port town in western Sardinia. My grandfather was also famous and honored as a physician. My mind was almost made up, and in the third year I began to concentrate on anatomy, which was the most difficult subject to pass on the medical school entrance examination. But some schoolmates were visiting me around that time who had just entered the Colegio Militar.

They were very enthusiastic about life there and the interest the teachers took in building the character of the boys. "That's for me," I said. And so I discovered the soldier in me I have never given up being. I took the entrance exam in 1910. At last, at the start of the following year, I enrolled as a cadet.

(All was in order, then. López had been able to clean up the smudge of cousins and aunts that was blurring the Memoirs. Forgetting about Vicenta and Baldomera Martirena, in whose house the General grew up, made it unnecessary to mention Grandmother Dominga's first husband. A widow who remarries is neither martyr nor paragon. The shades of Cousins Julio and María Amelia had also been whisked off the stage, with what justification, López? To sidestep Uncle Alberto's embarrassing suicide and so expunge any debilities in the Perón blood? Or to underscore the point that he, Juan Domingo, had been free and responsible from the time he was a boy, a real paterfamilias as you so aptly put it?)

"López!" he calls. Behind the screens, to the right of the desk, the secretary is waiting for him on the landing of the staircase. He is wearing an iridescent dressing gown and smells, at a distance, of Lancaster toilet water. "This first chapter is very good, López," says the General, getting to his feet. "Keep it up that way. How are you feeling for tonight? My talk with Cámpora undid a lot of knots inside me. He wanted to drape the presidential sash across my chest. Can you imagine! As though the country could be set back on track with a gesture! I want to dig more thoroughly into these Memoirs, López. Now that the mustiness of the past has been dried out, I feel like talking."

"That's what I'm here for, General, so that you can remember it all," he says, holding out his arm in the murkiness of the stairway. Perón leans on it. "Walk slowly here. Clear your spirit. Good. Now, step forward. Little by little. That's it. Next step. Hold onto the banister with that hand, so I can guide you. One, two, one. Concentrate on me. Up! Don't be afraid of the night. I'm above, in the sanctum. Do you feel me?"

5

THE COUNTERMEMOIRS

With a din like that going on outside, such silence inside the house wakened Noon Antezana. Whenever he walked into silence, his body felt the imminence of disaster.

Yet what is there to be afraid of? Diana is beside him, asleep, and Operation June 20 is planned down to the last detail. Ox Iriarte has rechecked the motor and tires of the Leyland bus for the umpteenth time. Pepe Juárez has cleaned and oiled the arsenal, Vicki Pertini and a battalion of volunteer seamstresses have slaved to finish the letters on the banners: PERÓN OR DEATH, REVOLUTIONARY ARMED FORCES, WELCOME GENERAL, MONTONEROS WITH YOU. Noon himself has visited encampments of the delegations from Berisso,

Florencio Varela, and Cañuelas before turning in for the night. In the afternoon of this June 20, having marched from the Llavallol rotunda, the columns of militants will arrive to bring up the rear at the platform on the Ezeiza freeway. Noon will then give the order to open ranks in a pincer movement and so take over the first thousand feet of the demonstration in front of which the General will terminate his eighteen-year exile, proclaiming the birth of the socialist fatherland.

How could inside be so different from outside? Here in the house all that can be heard is breathing, as though something were expiring. By this time, everything—fear, family, health, pride—has been jettisoned along the way. Everything forgone just to see the coming of this day, to embrace this bit of history. But outside, outside, what can history be weaving in this moment?

Noon sits up and lights a cigarette. He senses—impossible not to, no matter how far away—Diana's imperious body. This odyssey and Diana date back to the same time. At the end of March, Noon had pledged to Perón that he would see that the special squads were disarmed and prepare them for a time of peace. "We have to start setting up schools for preachers," the Old Man insisted. And Congressman Diego Muniz Barreto, on his way through Puerta de Hierro, had suggested Diana Bronstein as his assistant. "She's first-class, Noon. A born mobilizer. She's being wasted as a union file clerk in Almagro."

Muniz himself introduced them in his office on Calle Florida, after they returned to Buenos Aires. The moment he laid eyes on her, her body half-hidden behind the tanks of tropical fish the congressman collected, Noon felt his whole being sink into total bewilderment. He stood helpless before the mass of red hair that undulated with piraña-like sensuality, submitting to intense eyes out of key with her freckled face, and lost his sense of equilibrium as his gaze fell between Diana's breasts whose upturned nipples scented the heavens.

She was the daughter of a Rumanian tailor who had married, by correspondence, an insipid little Polish woman. At home only Yiddish was spoken. As soon as she entered college, she strove to cut herself off from that language, to wipe out all family memory, to be born again an Argentine. A professor of logic initiated her into sex and the permanent revolution. After two years he wanted to marry her. For Diana, a disillusionment.

56

From that time on, she permitted no man to choose her. She did the choosing from among the workers she indoctrinated at the textile mills and candy factories she infiltrated. Naked in bed, she patiently read to them from Che's diaries and the handbooks by Marta Harnecker, tenderly bent their heads over biographies of Trotsky and Rosa Luxemburg, and then helped them discover the nuances of pleasure with a wisdom that always took her by surprise. "There's no reason why a revolution of the body should conflict with a revolution of the people. The poor are denied so much already; why should we also be denied pleasure?" she would say in justification of the wildness of her orgasms.

In 1972, a candy packer called Big Angelo weaned her away from her Trotskyist passion. "The Fourth International," he told her, "was the last link in an anachronistic form of socialism, and a defeated one at that. In Argentina all revolutionary roads lead through Perón." Diana was outraged, declaring this an insult to the intelligence. In the name of what ideology are they talking? Perón was a classic example of opportunism, an underdeveloped imitation of Mussolini. The working class still trusted him, it was true, but the task of the revolution was precisely to unmask such an imposter for what he was, to oust the union bureaucrats who grew fat in his service. Big Angelo held her in thrall and with unforeseen authority ordered her to read John William Cooke: His letters to Perón from Havana will clear up your doubts. It's now or never, Diana, my love. History will be brushing right by us and I won't let you go without your having touched it.

Diana hesitated for several weeks, until the slaughter of a guerrilla group in Telew—which she considered an unmistakable sign of state terrorism—and the tumultuous wakes at the Peronist headquarters, finally convinced her. She agreed to be a Peronist soldier as long as they permitted her to hold her own opinions. No personality cult, no blind verticalism. She went to work with a union leader in Almagro, the very afternoon of the guerrillas' funeral. The meeting with Noon converted her into a full-time militant.

In no way did she grant Noon the privilege of seducing her. It was she who telephoned him without warning after resisting weeks of siege to invite him to a hotel for the sheer pleasure of matching her strength against that presumptuous body. Their room smelled of sex, but it was impossible that anyone could ever have made the mistake of being in love there. The bed had a canopy decorated with plaster angels on the verge of falling off. The humiliating plastic mattress cover showed through the patches in the sheet. Outside the windows, masked by ancient velvet hangings, one could make out the monuments of Recoleta cemetery. Immediately upon entering, Diana wanted the lights out. It was a revelation. Their bodies meshed with no need for explanations, entering together into the same spasms and emerging to the same remembrances.

Diana began to live with a sense of constant danger. She was terrified of falling in love. Fear kept her away from Noon, mercy brought her back. She felt him so solid and, at the same time, such an orphan, so eager for power, and ignorant of love and pity, that when he told (always reluctantly) some scraps of his life story, it made her feel like enveloping him in the foliage of her hair and putting him to sleep on her lap . . . my poor Noon, poor dearest!

True, Noon had grown up on his own, in the care of nursemaids who stuffed him with ice cream so he would leave them alone. His parents, who separated before he learned to walk, settled the argument over custody by dividing it in half, six months for each, with neither, finally, ever having a full year. Suddenly, after endless periods of forgetfulness, they would go through epidemic outbreaks of guilt and quarrel over who would take him on a boat trip to the Tigre or for a weekend in Punta del Este. But, once they had possession of Noon, their enthusiasm lasted little more than an hour. One of the few things they agreed on was to register him as a cadet in the Liceo Militar. Noon was ready for any misery except that of dogmatism and discipline. He was slow in resigning himself to the torture of being awakened before daybreak, shocked conscious in a cold shower, and forced to undergo weeks of close-order drill, cross-country runs, and situps. Gradually, he learned that to exact obedience, one had to keep oneself always at the extremes, obeying like a slave and commanding like a god. He began to tame his body. Though he hated sports he stayed at school on Sundays, pole vaulting and lifting weights. On one occasion, a sergeant punished the entire class by making them stand at attention in the horses' watering troughs filled with blocks of ice. Noon was the only one to last the entire hour without fainting, out of pride and contempt for the weakness of others. However, he swore that as soon as he became an officer, he would find that sergeant and repay him.

His correct name was Abelardo Antezana. His face was round and lively with an incongruously jutting chin that had a dimple so deep it looked like a bullet hole. In English class during his first year, the teacher sent him to the blackboard to write a list of irregular verbs. Strands of sunlight entering the window lit up his hair. The teacher stood observing him. "Lift your head, cadet." Embarrassed, Noon obeyed. The teacher went on in English. "It's wonderful. You have a noon-face." "What?" The class laughed. "You have a noon-face," he repeated and switching to Spanish: *"Su cara parece un mediodía."*

The nickname stuck. When he played soccer, the cadets on the opposing team knew that calling him "noon-face" would throw him and that when he was running down the field with control of the ball, they could make him miss the goal by yelling, "Stop hogging the ball, Noon."

In the spring of 1969, when he was to receive his second-lieutenant's sword—fourth in his class but best artilleryman—a chance circumstance changed his life. He met Juan García Elorrio at a cousin's wedding. Juan was fiery, brilliant, an indomitable debater. He walked with a slouch and had a broad, balding forehead. He ran a left-wing magazine, *Cristianismo y revolución.* Although he preached heroism and saintliness, he could conceive of no way other than martyrdom for attaining those states.

His forefinger aimed at Noon's unbreakable jaw, García Elorrio catechized him deftly from the first encounter. San Martín's army was being reborn in an invisible tide of new liberators, he said. These were the young Peronists, Christians, ready to give up their lives in a struggle against the oppressors of the poor, condemned to slow death by starvation, illiteracy, and disease. "Just who is the enemy?" Noon wanted to know. Juan had no doubts: the illegal usurpers of the country, the invaders from within, the gang of generals and admirals who had sold out the country to imperialism.

One memorable lecture by García Elorrio finally convinced him. "The duty of every revolutionary is to make revolution," Juan explained, predictably but fervently. "And the honest man's duty is not to close his eyes to the frightful violence from above, and not to fold his arms. How is it possible to remain unmoved by the example of the new martyrs Camilo Torres and Ernesto Guevara, our brothers in justice, our teachers in charity? They will live forever in the rifles of the nameless guerrillas who fight throughout Latin America, in the rebellious machetes of the peasants and the avenging dynamite of the miners. In Argentina, those martyrs bear the names of John William Cooke and Eva Perón for whom the only salvation lay—as it does for us today—in the revolutionary consciousness of the Peronist people . . ."

Enlightened and exalted as well by a heroic ideal that would lead him straight to rebellion against the values of his parents, Noon requested his discharge from the Colegio Militar and went over to the ranks of the enemy. This decision was made with such firmness that no one dared deter him. In December, he learned from the newspapers of the parades and patriotic vows of his former comrades. He, meanwhile, had already organized his own youth militia, and he had spoken with Perón.

He saw Perón innumerable times in the next three years. He went to the villa in Madrid as spokesman for the extreme radical groups and outlined, as usual, audacious projects to harass the military dictatorship. Even the plans that seemed unfeasible were always approved by the General. "If you've got the right people, do it, Antezana. The regime must not mistake us for sheep."

And Noon charged ahead. He organized an assault on the sentry boxes of the presidential guard in Olivos, the blowing up of thirty-eight Fiat oil tanks, and the launching of balloons to float into prisons bearing slogans that would raise the morale of jailed militants: FALLEN MARTYRS ARE NEVER FORGOTTEN and SPILLED BLOOD IS NOT NEGOTIABLE.

In April, 1973, a few weeks after the Peronist victory in the elections, Noon returned from Madrid with forebodings. He had found the General too eager to recoup power. Anybody who posed a threat to that final glory touched off his rage. As for revolution, forget it. He wanted to come back to his country as a man of peace. "I will blow out all the fires with one breath and be pitiless to anyone who relights them." Noon had bet on Lenin and the grand prize turned out to be Kerensky. "The alternative is simple," Perón had told him. "We must choose between time and blood. If we want to move fast, we'll need rivers of blood. I would rather we travel on rivers of time."

He hoped to regain the army's trust, that they would respect his experience as a leader. He therefore intended to begin by instituting only mild reforms, changes by eye dropper. "Take a good look at me, Antezana. Do I seem like a bomb thrower? No sir! I'm going to show the Argentines that institutions are more important than revolutions. I have said on more than one occasion: 'I'm a beast without teeth, an old vegetarian lion.' I'm not fooling anybody, but there are a lot of people interested in fooling themselves with me.''

Still, Noon left Madrid convinced that if the masses were to rise up demanding revolution, the General would not hesitate—as in 1945—to raise that banner. Whoever won control of the streets would have Perón in the palm of his hand, Noon reflected. He would have to be shown that the 1973 Peronists were not the unconditional Peronists of 1955 and that the Peronist doctrine of *justicialismo* had to be brought into step with the times.

At a meeting with his comrades in late May, Noon decided to rent a villa on the Camino de Cintura less than a mile from the Ezeiza freeway. From there he would direct the march of the 20,000 veteran militants who were to cut off the demonstration from the flanks and engulf the Old Man in their slogans of insurrection.

On June 3, a Sunday, he and Diana moved into a big old gloomy house surrounded by misty woods in whose depths was a stinking pond swollen with mud and rotting leaves. A week later, Vicki Pertini and Ox Iriarte installed themselves with maps and Peuser guidebooks with which to make a detailed study of the field of operations. Noon, however, preferred the rehearsal to be done on a sand table, as in the Colegio Militar, with little blue flags for the loyal troops and black ones to pinpoint the enemy's anticipated responses.

When the great moment was finally at hand, Noon called a meeting in the dining room of the old mansion and explained that it wasn't going to be easy for them to advance head-on, but that there was no alternative. The platform was surrounded by fascist forces: to the right, on Route 205, a police battalion of elite sharpshooters who would screen the passing revolutionary columns. On the flanks, ahead of the security cordons, there would be first-aid posts and ambulances protected by the secretary López Rega's strong-arm squad. To the north, the lineup of water-cannon trucks with radio communication to the command center directed by Lieutenant Colonel Osinde from the hotel at Ezeiza; and standing guard on the platform itself, the right's most accomplished assassins, the bodyguards of union bigwigs and of Isabel the usurper. The patriots of the socialist fatherland would have to shoot their way through the hosts of the reactionary fatherland.

Squatting on the floor, Diana checked out every detail in her own notebook. When, lost in thought, she lifted the cascade of her red hair with both hands, the blood vessels seethed in Noon's belly, deranging his faculties. Vicki Pertini, whose senses were a logarithmic table—she never allowed herself to be distracted—used the pause to switch the position of the little flags in the sandbox on the table, while Pepe Juárez explained in his hoarse voice that their stores of ammunition were more than sufficient for any defensive measures.

Diana then reported on the strategy of taunting she had set up with her group. Between nine and ten in the morning, a gang from Lanús called Golden Throat would stand near the platform, just below the music stands of the orchestra, and would spread out in groups of seven to ten, keeping within the thousand-foot perimeter. Toward noon, after they had mingled with the neighboring gangs, they would open fire with an innocuous little rhyme: "Let's go to Ezeiza, let's go, *compañeros* / Let's welcome home an old Montonero," putting the stress—innocently, of course—on the last word. And right after that, before the heat cools down, a shantytown chorus from Berazategui, the Blue Sewer, will chime in with the Throat, raising the volume a notch with: "We want the country Peronist / but Montonero, too, and socialist," and keep it going nonstop till Perón is over Argentine territory. At this point, after being alerted by transistor radio, the Throat boys will then rub it into the Isabelistas where it hurts the most: "There's one Evita, and that's all. / So why not stop bustin' your balls?" Meanwhile Blue Sewer brings out the whole repertoire of threats beginning with: "The union bureaucrats have gotta, gotta go." At that moment, we come on with our banners flying; the General leaves Ezeiza for the platform in a helicopter and as soon as we see him arriving, we join in from all sides with the marching song that can never go wrong, the highpoint of the occasion: "All United We Will Triumph." The Throat and the Blue Sewer, bursting their lungs in unison, will stick in a revolutionary stanza—what do you think of it?—"Before it was the resistance, / now it's Montoneros and the FAR / off to fight with Perón / to fight the people's war." Meanwhile thousands of pigeons will be set free and the girls of the Evita Group will send up balloons. The Old Man will throw open his arms up there on the platform and start to cry, because it's all going to be like a dream, for him, too.

The cigarette Noon had just smoked leaves an aftertaste of moss and beetles in his mouth. Smelling Diana, watching her half-open lips chapped by winter (by life, according to her), Noon wishes it were all over already and that there were nothing ahead for them to anticipate but their mingled ardors, their enjoyment of one another, learning and unlearning one another to find each other all over again. He still cannot believe that they are there together; it must be a freak of nature, a lucky stroke of history never to be repeated.

Noon's skin is still smarting from the heat of the bonfires he had visited in Cañuelas, Florencio Varela, and Berisso before retiring for the night. He had observed the number of comrades multiply on the outskirts of the Llavallol as if they were walking on mirrors. At a kiosk in Temperly he had bought the final editions of *Crónica*, *La Razón*, and a special edition of *Horizonte* devoted to the General: "Perón: His Entire Life / Documents and Photos of 100 Witnesses," with a plastic cover and a giant poster of the man himself smiling, looking like a fierce eagle.

Back at the house, he had drawn Ox and Vicki into the hall to show them the commercial crap he had bought, but now, feeling the slow sting of sleeplessness spreading through his body, he bends over the pages of *Horizonte* and reads, scornfully at first, then alarmed at the holes that the 100 witnesses have gouged in the patriarch's biographical corpus. He's been tattooed by somebody with these stories: folded up in time like a sheet, reduced to his human dimensions.

Sensing that Perón is, at last, about to happen to him, that Perón will let himself fall into his consciousness, Noon leans over these unexpected pages as toward an abyss.

1. PROFILES OF THE ANCESTORS

Mario Tomás Perón would never forget the spring of 1886, when he arrived in Lobos. The railroad station was still so new that the inhabitants celebrated the arrivals of trains decked out as for a christening. Young men settled themselves on the platform well before the scheduled time, sleek and expectant, backs to the wind, which kept trying to muss up the ends of their mustaches. Girls strolled arm in arm with their cousins, anticipating compliments. In those days, most courtships owed a debt to the railroad.

Mario Tomás Perón, then nineteen, was tall, husky, bronzed, and not much given to conversation. His pride was the beautiful penmanship he had developed at the Colegio Nacional; his passion was horses, which he rode and cared for with the skill of a cowboy. He had come to Lobos with its healthful air to recuperate from typhus.

Hoping to develop the young man's taste for the study of medicine, his father had made a horseman of him. Once a month, Mario would saddle a team of bays and accompany him on calls to patients at Roque Pérez, Cañuelas, and Navarro. Since the sight of blood made him faint, he preferred to pass the time in the open fields with the peons. Those trips were responsible for his later infatuation with botany and archaeology. When he came to Lobos, his baggage contained a collection of herbs of the pampas and a treatise by Cuvier on mammalian fossils.

He was the oldest child of Tomás Liberato Perón and Dominga Dutey, an easterner from Paysandú whose family had emigrated from Chambery, in Savoy. She had been married at twenty-two in February, 1867. She was a widow, and her daughters Baldomera and Vicenta Martirena by her first husband were to have a greater influence on the life of the Peróns than any of the blood relations.

Tomás Liberato was descended from a Sardinian, Tomás Mario, and a Scotswoman, Anna Hughes, who came from the neighborhood of Dumbarton. Going back more than four generations, all Peróns bore the same given names so that mothers would always have a Mario or a Tomás to remind them of their husbands, and because lineage—as Anna Hughes said —is transmitted not only through the surname but by the baptismal oils, as well.

Thus, Mario Tomás's younger brothers, born in 1871 and 1872, were named Tomás Hilario and Alberto Mario and were earmarked by paternal will to be chemists or biologists.

Alberto Mario was a maverick. Attracted to the military, he refused to enter medical school. In 1905, when he had risen to the rank of captain, he began to suffer from the same agonizing insomnia that had plagued his father. One November morning, after three days without sleep, he fell from his horse, fractured his spine and died on the spot.

Grandmother Dominga, having suffered so through Don Tomás Liberato's insomnia, had Alberto Mario's bedroom, including the hallway through which he had passed in the torment of his last three nights, disinfected with acrolein to prevent contagion of the rest of the family by the virus of his sleeplessness.

Perón homes, for one reason or another, always smelled of disinfectants and eucalyptus vapor, if not of animal vaccines and pharmaceutical acids. The males were brought up amongst bottles, by women as hypochondriacal as they were industrious.

Mario Tomás was born on November 9, 1867, at the time of a cholera epidemic in Buenos Aires. His father, busy inspecting sanitary conditions in the meat-salting plants, was unable even to be present at the delivery. In the years to come, he would see his sons only when they accompanied him on visits to distant patients, riding behind him bearing saddle bags filled with provisions and cupping glasses.

When Mario Tomás came to Lobos, Don Tomás Liberato was already suffering from melancholia. He would remain shut up in his laboratory for weeks on end studying the habits of the locust. He was not even aware that his oldest son had left home.

The mason Juan Irineo Sosa and his wife, Mercedes Toledo, had lived a mile or so from the town square of Lobos on the main road since 1870, in a mud-and-wattle hut he had built with the help of neighbors. It had a dirt floor. At first, they put in a pair of facing doors to let the air circulate, but since one of them opened on an alleyway of ill repute . . .

All shores of reality brim over simultaneously. Diana stretches and reaches her fingers, swift as a spider, toward Noon's back. He hears without seeing the ardent flight of that creature summoning him with all the voices of the animal world. And at that very moment, Vicki Pertini knocks on the door discreetly but urgently.

"Can you come out a moment, *che?* They're already blasting the shit out of each other at the overpass! The Huns have the platform surrounded."

Noon puts aside the copy of *Horizonte:* "Are you listening, Diana?"

She has heard so clearly that her mind has already pictured the situation, though her voice is still heavy with sleep: "Not yet six a.m. and the battle for the thousand feet is joined."

But, as usual, Vicki Pertini has alarmed them needlessly. His cigarette-blackened mood lightened by a bitter maté, Noon Antezana puts in order the reports that keep coming from the supposed battle front. All is well. The incident at the overpass was nothing more than a brush between two unaffiliated groups. True, there were shots and one man was wounded. Sympathizer or outsider? They don't know his name. He's been taken to the Ezeiza hospital with a bullet in his intestine. They must be operating by now. Aside from that, Vicki's alarm did have some foundation: a thousand of López Rega's henchmen and Union Youth have formed an iron ring around the platform. They've occupied a school a hundred yards to the south on Route 205. And they're blocking the approaches. Wasn't that expected? Yes, Pepe Juárez sighs, but we had hopes of a miracle, a mass attack of diarrhea maybe, or Perón disavowing them. There's nothing to be done. We're just unlucky with our disasters.

Ox returns from a tour of inspection. All's well, he announces cheerfully. Operation June 20 is at full sail. He saw over 3,000 comrades with supplies of powdered milk and bags of bread coming down Route 205. They were bundled up with ski masks and ponchos, as if the celebration were going to last a month. He stopped off at an encampment of cowboys from the pampas, near La Salada, two miles to the north, where he stayed to listen to them improvise songs in honor of Perón. I came away from there scared, he reports. Time has stood still for those people. They were talking like Perón had never left. And I came back here asking myself what we were going to do with them all, what country we were going to put them in?

Finally, they feel daybreak. Dayfall. The sun is bursting out from somewhere. Noon is unable to contend with the light and orders that it be made to leave, that the windows be closed momentarily. He convenes his general staff in the hall at the sand table and decides to begin the long march at once. Ox and Vicki will drive the Leyland bus to the Llavallol rotunda; Pepe Juárez and the shantytown volunteers will follow them on foot, along the railway tracks to the freeway. Diana and he, Noon, will lead the Monte Grande and Cañuelas contingents toward Route 205. At twelve, all

66

will gather at the water tower on Calle Almafuerte, three-quarters of a mile behind the platform.

Before leaving, they glance at the photographs of the ghosts in *Horizonte*, shrug their shoulders when they see a document reproduced that they cannot explain, ignore the voices of the witnesses. And the magazine remains there when they leave, expiring in the shadows among the mock cities of the sand table.

The mason Juan Irineo Sosa and his wife, Mercedes Toledo, had lived a mile or so from the town square of Lobos since 1870 in a mud-and-wattle hut. At first they put in a pair of facing doors to let the air circulate, but since one of them opened on an alleyway of ill repute, Juan Irineo had to block it up. They owned two large beds, a pair of iron pots, a wash basin with pitchers, and several chromos of saints pasted on cardboard backings.

Juan Irineo kept his riding gear at one end of the room and, at the other end, there was a small mirror at which the daughters combed their hair and a strand of horsetail to hold the family combs. Juana, born on November 9, 1875, was the eldest. Her childhood had been carefree, a life on horseback. Afternoons were spent sipping maté with neighbors at the hut next door or hanging around the guitar sessions at the general store.

Neither parent had any idea of their family histories and supposed them to be vague and involved. There were so many Toledo Sosas, Sosa Toledos, and just Toledos in the family, the kinship among whom would have been so exaggeratedly incestuous, that it could hardly have been the case. Sometimes there arrived in town blond mestizos whom Juana called cousins. They were put up with no questions asked, not for fear that they might try to claim some false kinship, but rather that they might reveal some intolerable truth.

A family biographer assumes, without any supporting documents, that Juan Irineo's parents came from Castilla la Vieja. Juana was to tell a different story to the people in Cabo Raso: "They were brought up near Guasayán, in Santiago del Estero and, as far as I know, were of pure Indian blood."

When Mario Tomás met Juana in 1890 they were both in mourning for the death of parents. Don Tomás Liberato was done in by sleep. One fine day, after months of insomnia, drowsiness suddenly overtook him out in the open country. He lay down on his saddle bags beside a stream, and when he awoke, drenched, he was seized with such a violent attack of chills and fever that death did not even give him time to change his clothes.

Juan Irineo's fatal illness also came as a surprise. One afternoon on his way back from the fields, he told his wife to wrap up enough clothing and food for a long trip. "Where are we going?" she asked. "I'm going by myself," he answered, and at that very moment, standing beside his bed, he vomited up a black fluid. "So that's what it's like to die," he groaned, as he pitched forward, his eyes glazed over.

The daughters were left in such straits that they had to go to work as servants in the homes of foreigners. That's where Mario Tomás met them. He was enchanted by Juana at first sight. When she waited on table at the Cornfoots' residence, she treated the guests with even more disdain than she did the ladies of the house. She had a round Indian face. Under her glowing little eyes jutted imperious cheekbones. Her broad, blunt nose blended well with her large mouth, always primed to smile.

Among the old settlers of Lobos are vague recollections— hearsay, really—of secret trysts between her and Mario in Las Garzas ravine. Many years later, one of Juana's cousins would compare their romance with Hugo Wast stories she had seen at the movies, although there was a happy end in this case, since the well-born seducer did not abandon the orphan country girl.

Early in the fall of 1891, Juana discovered that she was pregnant. Francisca Toledo, another cousin, related that she was so dismayed by her bodily disturbances that she took the signs of pregnancy for liver disease.

Mario Tomás was also stunned by the news. "If I get married," he wrote his brother Tomás Hilario, "it will be a terrible shock to my poor mother. They advise me around here to give the girl a little money and forget the whole thing." But he did nothing, just let time go by.

A boy was born on November 30, 1891, with Aunt Honoria and Cousin Francisca in attendance. Thirteen months later, he was christened Mario Avelino Sosa on Christmas Eve in the parish church. Euphoric, Mario Tomás asked his brother Tomás Hilario to make the trip from Buenos Aires to be godfather.

Lobos went through years of such abysmal torpor that even the dust, when stirred up by the feather duster, hung over the furniture always in the same pattern. In 1896, the first streets were paved with cobblestones, and curbstones were installed. Rumors of impending war with Chile reached there very late, after the peace agreement was signed. To celebrate this lag in the arrival of the news, the Lobos Athletic Club organized a field day of sack races, cockfights, and jumping contests, attended by 3,000 inhabitants of the region.

The name of the town's main thoroughfare was Buenos Aires. The Moore family had a house there, with balconies flanking the portal, green slatted shutters, and a fig tree and jasmine bush in the yard. At the end of 1891, Mario Tomás asked to be accepted as a lodger. He was given the room on the right, facing the street, which he occupied almost until he left Lobos.

He worked as a court officer for several months between 1893 and 1894. His closest friend, Juan Torres, kept urging him to give up his job, which he disliked intensely, and to join Juana once and for all somewhere far away, to spare her the humiliation and insults of the young men whose clothing she washed.

Vacillating by nature, Mario Tomás, although he did not relish creating a scandal, was at the same time unwilling to leave Juana. She became pregnant again early in 1895.

The respectable families of Lobos were displeased by this news. Don Eulogio del Mármol, whom Dr. Perón had asked to keep an eye on his son, removed Mario Tomás from the scene by placing him in charge of Los Varones, one of his farms. The good women of the town proved less indulgent. They ordered their daughters to cross to the other side of the street whenever Mario came into view and forbade his name to be mentioned at any social gathering. As Señora del Mármol said, "There is nothing as contagious as a bad reputation."

Mario meanwhile enjoyed his isolation. He was out in the

69

open country before daybreak, bringing the horses to the stable, cultivating the crops, clearing the brush. He believed that he was destined for a rustic life and vowed never to change.

On October 8, 1895, while driving a herd of broncos to Roque Pérez, he was overtaken by the news that his second son had been born. He returned at a gallop.

2. THE EARLY YEARS

On the cot in which she had slept since infancy, attended only by her cousin Francisca, Juana had a far easier delivery this time than she had with Mario Avelino. The Toledos had made preparations for a girl. Even the diapers stitched by Grandmother Mercedes had little pink ribbons. And Aunt Honoria, who had decided to give the infant her silver earrings, prayed to God miraculously to change its mistaken sex.

The first baby picture taken at the age of five months already showed a close resemblance to his mother. He had the same thick black hair, Indian face, and eyes immune to surprise even at that age. His baptism was delayed for two years because his father wanted him named Tomás Alberto and his mother, Juan Tomás. Since it was impossible for them to come to an agreement, Honoria proposed naming him Juan to satisfy the Toledos, and Domingo for the paternal grandmother. On January 14, 1898, he was taken to the ruin of the old parish church. Cousin Francisca and Juan B. Torres were the godparents.*

From the time Juan Domingo was able to sit up by himself, his father settled him in the saddle and rode him around the pampas teaching him the language of the animals, the crops, and the rain. Don Eulogio del Mármol gave him a dapple-gray pony and put him in the care of Sisto Magallanes, one of his

---

* In 1971, José López Rega revealed that the birth year of 1895 actually corresponded to Juan Domingo Perón's fifth incarnation. In the previous ones he had been Per-O, an Egyptian queen whose name means "The Big House" and who governed the villages of the Upper Nile around 3,500 B.C.; Rompe, the fish whose beak is an electric sword, and who inhabits the ocean depths east of the Isle of Disenchantment; Norpe, a bulldog that bit Marco Polo in Cathay and was punished by poisoning with ground glass; and the Jesuit priest Dominique de Saints-Péres, Descartes's teacher at La Flèche school, who was killed by a bolt of lightning in the domains of Perron, where he was the guest of his pupil. In 1970, Perón admitted that he had written some of his articles under the pen name Descartes, "because the philosopher used my name (Perron) and I wished to reciprocate."

peons, who taught the little boy to ride at a gallop. Sisto the Chinaman was a simple rustic creature who had to be locked up on nights with full moons because he would climb to the top of the windmills and try to fly. However, he had a remarkable gift as a teacher and in his deep, drawling voice would explain the reason for droughts and why worms were curious, as if those were the most obvious things in the world.

Mario Tomás soon grew tired of sedentary life. At the end of 1898, he sold off his gear and saddles, concluded his association with Don Eulogio on good terms, and set out with Juana and the children for the Juan Atucha tract near Roque Pérez, where he rented a farm and some grazing land. They were unhappy with the house they found there and the isolation of the region. Three months later, they moved to the hacienda of a certain Dr. Viale who gave them a few hectares of land.

In February or perhaps March 1899, Juana and her cousin Francisca were washing clothes beside the cistern. Juana was seven months pregnant and the oppressiveness of the heat made her gasp for breath. Nearby, Juan Domingo was hunting frogs, which he tried to tame using a willow rod. It was midday. The women had just wrung out the sheets and were hanging them on the lines in the patio. "If I take one more step," Juana said, "the baby will jump out of my throat."

Her cousin, fearing a premature birth, helped her to bed. She was about to apply compresses on her when she heard Juan Domingo shout. She ran out and spying the willow rod at the edge of the cistern realized the child must have fallen in. She thought she was able to see him under the water through the reflection on the surface and called to him, in vain. Then she threw in the bucket, hoping to hook it over his body. She succeeded on the second attempt and managed to pull him out. He had fainted, but except for a few scratches was unhurt. "If not for me, Perón wouldn't be going down in history," Francisca would say when her nephew was President.

Dismal months passed. Mario Tomás spent nights sitting up in bed, unable to sleep. He had no desire to tend fields that did not belong to him. Juana, aware of what insomnia signified in the Perón family, was afraid that Mario, too, would be consumed by unhappiness. When she heard him wake up, she would light a candle, undo her braids, and begin sewing the children's clothing in the most matter-of-fact way. And so, talking about cooking, illnesses, and the like, she kept him distracted until his anxiety passed.

Juana's third child had the good luck to be born dead. He was greenish in color, not fully formed, and instead of eyes, had two black eggs, without lids. Juana was told that she had delivered a tape worm, and Aunt Honoria never would reveal where that noxious fetus was buried. "All we knew," Francisca was to say half a century later, "is that she left it under a tree and the roots became contaminated." The night of the birth, Mario Tomás had a presentiment that somebody was casting an evil spell on them. "We can't stay here any longer," he decided. "I'm going to get the cattle together and drive them south."

Doña Dominga's house was small, white, surrounded by hedges. Mario met the Maupas family there, distant relatives of the Martirenas, who were interested in improving the management of their haciendas in Chubut. An agreement was promptly reached. Mario was to run La Maciega, a tract in Cabo Raso 125 miles south of Puerto Madryn, where he would be able to raise his own sheep and share the profits.

In the spring of 1900, Mario Tomás set out on a foolhardy trip driving a herd of five hundred head of cattle to the southern wilderness. Before his departure, he entrusted Juana to the care of his mother.

During the year of enforced loneliness that followed, Juana took to spending long periods at the Ramos Mejía farm, until Doña Dominga finally gave in to her siege. Juan Domingo contracted chicken pox there, which his grandmother relieved with warm baths and talcum-powder compresses. No sooner did he recover than he came down with whooping cough. Baldomera treated it with an empirical remedy that consisted of pushing him in a swing in the park before daybreak when the trees give out oxygen and the air turns blue.

In September, 1901, Mario Tomás returned to Buenos Aires. And, as he had promised, on the 25th of that month he married Juana with neither ceremony nor celebration. She signed the marriage certificate in a childish, sprawling hand that remained unchanged until her old age; he signed with his double-ellipse flourish. The last paragraph stated: "The couple recognizes Avelino Mario [sic] and Juan Domingo, born in Lobos, as their offspring."

Two weeks later they were on their way to Patagonia on the ship *Santa Cruz*. No sooner had Juana set eyes on the desolate coast of Chubut and heard the savage howling of the wind than she had a premonition that now the family would not be leaving that place. In a letter to her sister María Luisa she related that, on seeing the beach pebbles gleaming in the icy October sun, under the flocks of seagulls, Juan Domingo had asked whether those birds laid hot coals instead of eggs.

The Peróns landed in Puerto Madryn next to the railroad pier and waited for the train until the next morning. There was a bronze plaque on the wall of the station with an ominous warning in six languages: 51 MILES WITHOUT WATER FROM HERE TO CHUBUT. As the train plunged between the sandy hills it seemed to them as if the horizon were covered by a vast, rusty sheet of pebbles and scrubby plants.

And that's how it looked into infinity. They obtained a large old wagon in Rawson and pushed forward for a week between the sand dunes. Halfway there, they were overtaken by a vicious gale that threw up sand, pebbles, and dry dung, forcing them to make a detour to avoid bogs and sudden drops. Juan was disturbed to see that in this wasteland where all creatures lived in constant alert, the sheep kept on grazing, oblivious to everything—roaring winds, fury of man, and threats from the sky—their muzzles buried in the shrubbery. From that time on, sheep rated last in the hierarchy of his love for animals, well behind bats, snakes, and rats.

Mario Tomás cleared the land and filled in the swamps, transforming La Maciega into a flourishing hacienda. There were close to fifty miles of land, between nine and ten thousand head of sheep, and the best house in the region, built of wood, with a peaked roof, wood stoves, and a bathroom with a tub. Even the furniture, scarred by the boots of the peons, wore a coat of polish.

When the Peróns came to Cabo Raso, a Frenchman by the name of Robert, a widower, was settling in Camarones, thirty-five miles to the east. A horseman, he had come from Luján the year before with his motherless son riding behind, and a drove of five hundred sheep. The rigors of the trip were so extreme that when he arrived he had only a hundred sheep and the emaciated horse he rode.

Alberto, the son, described the depths of loneliness in which they lived. "We learned to talk to ourselves so as to at least have the company of one's own voice. We gradually lost human traits and took on those of the animals of the region. We learned to withstand thirst, keep our heads turned to one side to avoid the sting of the dust, and to anticipate cracks in the ground before taking a step."

In defense against such isolation, the Peróns and Roberts became inseparable. The village of Camarones, at the edge of the sea, consisted of ten houses, one store, and the post office. A hotel was being built in those years, but to no purpose, since the only potential guests who arrived would not venture off their ships.

Family visits lasted many days. Nobody could afford the luxury of traveling twenty miles of a morning only to exchange a few words and make the trek back the same afternoon. Alberto Robert has recounted how the Peróns would arrive at his house in a wagon drawn by three horses, the cowboy Pancho Villafañe galloping out ahead, blowing a trumpet like a postilion as they entered the yard. Juana immediately took over the kitchen. After an inventory of available provisions she would launch into the mysterious confection of various stews of dried meat that stretched exactly until the end of the visit. Having been trained by the Toledos, she was such an accomplished midwife that pregnant women came from as far away as Bustamante Bay and even Los Mártires Valley, a two-week trip, just to have Juana bring a breech-baby out head first, untangle umbilical cords, and make sure, after the placenta had been expelled, that a twin had not been left inside.

At seven, Juan Domingo had already completed his apprenticeship as a horseman. He could lasso, gallop through a gully, and cleanse wounds. Guanaco hunting was his passion. He would post himself on top of the water towers of La Maciega to watch the movements of the distant guanacos and plan a daybreak attack.

As he was to say later, those were his dress rehearsals for war. The guanacos grazed in the ravines and on the slopes of the hills, their bodies blending into the ocher shrubbery. Camouflage and fleetness were their only defenses. When a

horseman was sighted, the lookout neighed to warn the females and young, and then enthusiastically entered into a
duel of wits with the hunter.

Juan Domingo enjoyed nothing so much as confusing the
animals with false signs, rolling stones down the ravine or
raising dust a long distance from where he was hidden with
devices made of ropes and blinds of branches. He would
creep into gullies and spring out onto the plain, attacking by
surprise from the rear, or he would rush them on the flanks
where the lookout guanaco was less vigilant.

In the spring of 1903, Mario Tomás foresaw a new rash of bad
luck. A letter from the Maupas brothers, delayed by blizzards, notified him that La Maciega no longer belonged to
them. They had sold it between April and May to the Mittau
and Grether Company, which would appoint another manager. He was authorized to stay on as a helper, with the right
to graze his sheep on the hacienda but no longer to share in
the profits.

He was stunned by the news. He tore up various reproach-
ful letters to the Maupases and finally, at Juana's behest,
started a lengthy correspondence with the army and ranchers
of the zone, inquiring about public lands still available for
settlement.

He felt that his wanderlust had now ebbed. Even in that
period of blackest despair he refused to leave Patagonia. A
newly arrived justice of the peace recommended him to a
friend, Luis Linck, who had bought up a wild tract sixty miles
west of the Gallegos River in the territory of Santa Cruz.

The Peróns accepted the misfortune of reclaiming scrub
land. They boarded ship one day in October, 1903, and
reached their destination on All Saints Day, a Sunday. From
that point on, the trail is clear because Mario Tomás began
writing his impressions in a *Cooper Almanac*. Sparing of
words in the expression of his feelings, he noted down only
such matters as changes in weather, episodes of ill health,
and diseases suffered by the sheep. Vague and unenthusiastic
references were also made to various courtesy calls paid at
Los Vascos, the neighboring settlement. The only intimate
entry graces the page corresponding to December 25, 1904:

"It is now four years since Tomás Hilario died. May God grant him peace. May God forgive him for taking destiny into his own hands. Such is the lot of men whose wives repay them with infidelity. As for me, what would I do? Me? Me?" This was the only time in his life that Mario Tomás's penmanship looked askew.

The lands to which they were coming had been purchased by Luis Linck toward the end of 1896. Seven years later, the caretaker's house—the only shelter in the neighborhood—was collapsing. The snow had melted and frozen repeatedly on the kitchen table, and even the floorboards had been smashed by the axes of marauding woodsmen. The landscape was the one splendid feature. The house was nearly encircled by an arc of hills, and further in the distance there were nests of ice crystals and crowns of cones on the araucaria pines between the hollows and ravines.

Juan and Mario Avelino had left Chankaike between April and May of the previous year. They could barely sign their names, and nobody had taught them to read. Mario Tomás decided to entrust the education of the two boys to his half-sister Vicenta. She was the principal of a school for girls on Calle San Martín in the center of Buenos Aires and lived on the top floor of the same building with Baldomera, Grand-mother Dominga, and Tomás Hilario's orphaned children.

An entry in the *Cooper Almanac* indicates that nobody was there to meet them when they landed in the port of Buenos Aires. With the family bringing up the rear, the father walked across the docks and up into the city along Calle Corrientes. Each carried a knapsack on his shoulder, a cardboard valise, and clay jars and canteens of water hanging from his belt because the Peróns no longer conceived of worlds without dust storms or people who did not live at the mercy of thirst.

When they were a few steps from the corner of Calle San Martín, Juan Domingo tried to scale a wall to pick berries, fell and scraped his nose. A slender gentleman dressed in a black frock coat and derby hat hurried over to help him up and cleaned off his scratches with an immaculate white handkerchief.

Mario Tomás walked back to thank him and announced his name: "Perón." "A relative of the doctor's?" the gentleman inquired. "His son," Mario replied, "but it is hard to tell, now that I am a farmer." "I am a farmer, myself," the man admitted, removing his hat before Juana, "and you have no idea how much I regret that one can no longer tell by looking at me." Then in the most natural way he picked clusters of berries for the children, handed his card to Mario, and said, as he left, "If I can ever be of any service, call on me."

Juan Domingo, his lips purple with berry juice, entered Aunt Vicenta's house looking like a person with a heart condition, and was not given permission to kiss his grandmother until he had taken a bath and scrubbed himself with a brush. Before going to bed, he told María Amelia the story of the gentleman and asked his father to show her the calling card.

The girl kept the card among her schoolbooks. Years later, she saw the gentleman in the frock coat from a balcony on Avenida de Mayo. He was alone in a carriage and the crowd was cheering him. María Amelia threw sweet peas down to him and joined excitedly in the chorus: "Long live the President!" But she did not remember the calling card, not even when cousin Juan Domingo joined a plot in 1930 to overthrow the gentleman, nor even less when the gentleman died in July, 1933, and she insisted on following the casket to Recoleta cemetery among black-shawled washerwomen weeping incessantly.

In the jewel box she inherited from Doña Dominga, under her departed husband's wedding ring and a medal found in her father Tomás Hilario's suit the night of the suicide, María Amelia still preserves the gentleman's calling card, now faded and limp:

HIPÓLITO YRIGOYEN

LOS MÉDANOS HACIENDA

---

3. THE TERRIBLE REVELATION

When Juan Domingo awoke on the second morning after arriving in Buenos Aires and found that his parents had gone without saying good-bye and left him in the care of those stern ladies, practically strangers, he was seized by a fit of uncontrollable despair. Since the boy would not stop crying and beating the floor with his fists, Aunt Baldomera brought holy water from the church of Our Lady of Mercy to purify his thoughts. María Amelia, forsaking her dolls, tried to be sweet to him. That was worse. Juan Domingo was shaken by paroxysms of trembling, like one possessed. When he went to bed he became tangled up in the sheets and ended up tearing them to shreds. He had to be locked up until the fit subsided. And should the frenzy recur, Vicenta and Baldomera hurried to cover the pride of the house: the pendulum clock with bronze figures of tillers of the soil on the face.

For two days and two nights Juan Domingo's wailing tore at his cousin's heart. At one point, she awoke and knocked on his door: "Would you like some water, Juancito?"

"What I'd like is for you to die, that's what. I want you all to die."

Time dissipated that grief, too. In the afternoons, Cousin Julio took Juan with him to catechism class at Our Lady of Mercy parish house, and the two served as altar boys on Sundays at seven o'clock mass. In the mornings, they went to the school on the ground floor, at 548 Calle San Martín, officially known as "Girls Upper School, Section 7" even though nine of the thirty pupils were boys.

"Since he was several years older than the rest of the class, Juan Domingo took charge of their games. He thought up speed contests in multiplication and invented memory tests using paragraphs from their reader. He was taller, stronger, fatter, rougher, and—taking advantage of Mario Avelino's passivity and Julio's premature attacks of melancholia—he harassed them by making them walk on stilts while he followed whacking them across the calves with a stick.

In 1905, Juan surprised María Amelia with his contradictory behavior. Suddenly, he decided to spend all his savings on a doll for her. As he presented it, he warned her, "Every time you play with it, you must remember that I was the one who gave it to you. Understand? Me!" And the very same day, or the next, he would spatter ink all over his cousin's impeccable copybooks. Aunt Vicenta overlooked his pranks on the theory that he would outgrow them. Baldomera, however, confided her apprehensions to Doña Dominga. "What do you imagine could be going on inside that child, mother? Is it that he was abandoned . . . what he felt when they left him behind? Or is it in his nature, the Ladino-Indian temperament he inherited from Juana? Sometimes, when I observe him closely, it seems to me that he has no blood in his body, as if he had been emptied of feelings. But no sooner does that boy realize that I am looking at him, than he puts on a feeling as if it were clothing, petting me, looking for affection, crying, laughing out loud. I have never seen a child like him, so dark within, so full of light without."

Men are doomed to be remembered for their excesses not their banalities, but the opposite was true of Juan Perón: the most notorious episode of his childhood is irrelevant. The story that changed his life has been kept in the dark.

With respect to the former, suffice it to say that Doña Dominga's husband had left her the skull of Juan Moreira, a legendary gaucho shot down by the police in the courtyard of La Estrella whorehouse on the outskirts of Lobos. At dusk, before their aunts set out the kerosene lamps in the Buenos Aires house, Juan Domingo and Cousin Julio terrified the serving maids by lighting up the skull from inside with candles.

The second event took place between February and March, 1909. Fifteen months before, fleeing the cold of Santa Cruz and because of certain misunderstandings with the owner of Chankaike, Don Luis Linck, Mario Tomás Perón had taken to the road again, heading north until he settled on some public lands that covered two square miles some ten miles from Camarones and two or three from the sea. The only possession left him was a flock of a hundred sheep, almost all with mange, which survived thanks to Doña Juana's creosote baths.

Mario Avelino, sent back to Patagonia because of a stubborn case of bronchitis, was the one who came up with a name for the new ranch. "Are we there, Papa? Then, is this what you said was the future?" he asked as they lowered the furniture from the wagon, fighting the wind.

Mario Tomás built The Future so reluctantly and with such uncertainty that the family lived in it only at bedtime. It was an adobe hut with a low door at which they had to stoop to enter. On the west side was a window about a foot and a half high, with rickety wooden shutters. The parents' bed was to the right, next to the entrance, separated from the children's cot by a cretonne curtain. Saddles and implements were kept at the other end of the hut. For food or shelter from the cold, the Peróns preferred the peons' quarters where the stoves were always kept burning.

Once a week Don Mario visited the justice of the peace in Camarones, and after a lengthy discussion about diseases of sheep or lurking pumas, he would proffer his beautiful penmanship for inscribing in the official records deeds, births, and sales of horses.

"I am learning this job of justice of the peace," reads Mario Tomás's penultimate entry in the *Cooper Almanac* on December 6, 1908. "Romero has promised to leave me the post when he goes. I must practice my penmanship more." And, the last entry, two days later: "The frigate *Quintana* is expected to pass here tomorrow, a mile or so out to sea. Juan will surely be arriving for his vacation."

Every year when school was over, Juan Domingo would busy himself with complicated preparations for his trip south. He made the rounds of the Buenos Aires docks for several days checking on fishing boats that might be venturing as far as the Gulf of Saint George until he found one that would take him aboard. Or, he would try to get passage on a freighter bound for Chile across the Straits of Magellan.

The crossings were always stormy. No captain would risk his vessel by approaching the coast beyond the Valdés Peninsula. Passengers, then, had to land wherever they could. Juan had the good fortune to be picked up by a tugboat from Camarones whose pilot was familiar with the currents and knew how to avoid the treacherous tides. Nor did the danger end on reaching shore. Travelers would slip as they stepped onto the pebbly beach and were often tossed head over heels by an unexpected wave.

Juan arrived on December 9, as his father had assumed. His friend Alberto Robert was waiting for him near the dock with two saddled percherons to accompany him to The Future. Alberto listened insatiably to his friend's descriptions of Buenos Aires, where the trains ran like moles in the depths of the earth and carriages traveled under their own power.

Juan Domingo was three years older and patronized him. Alberto admired Juan for his eagle eye, formidable strength, and scornful attitude. Sometimes, when they would be riding along at a leisurely pace, Juan would suddenly dismount, yelling, "Last one to touch the ground is a dirty louse." Or teaching Alberto vowels, he would have him write, "Mamma is a pata, mamma is a peta, mamma is a pita," which led to "puta" (whore).

Although Juan was a very good guanaco hunter, he had to admit that Alberto was better. The boy knew when the ground had been undermined by rodents—where a horse could easily sink in. He was able to guess the routes taken by guanaco troops when they scattered, and where females sought refuge to hide their young. "You've got a dog's instinct," Juan would say, praising him.

On a morning in February or, perhaps, March, 1909, Juan Domingo accompanied his father on one of his visits to Justice Romero. A fearful heat drifted down from the mesetas as they rode in the sulky with their mouths shut to keep from eating dust. Alberto followed behind on an Arabian mare. They had advanced a little more than three miles when Alberto suddenly sensed a troop of guanacos nearby.

Juan Domingo went out of his mind. Never had he been that close to so many animals at once. And what most excited him this time was his unusually favorable position, hidden in the gully. He was spoiling to move, to surprise the guanacos and bring one down with his whip. He could imagine them, their senses all keyed up, moving about on the plain, confused, searching for the dark point at which death might explode.

Alberto was not as confident. He made signs indicating the disadvantages. Juan would have to jump out of the sulky onto the rump of his horse, crouching and silent, while Don Mario

Tomás continued on his way without changing pace. Even supposing the guanacos suspected nothing, once they took off, no horse could catch up with them.

Nevertheless, they went through with it. Juan passed to the mare and his father headed the sulky to Camarones. The boys remained rigid for a moment, holding their breaths. The wind favored them, carrying the rusty smell of the guanacos to their nostrils. Suddenly, they heard the neigh of a female above them.

"Now!" yelled Juan, spurring the mare. And they dashed out on the plain. A *chulengo*, the soft, defenseless young of the guanaco, crossed their path. Alberto broke its neck. There was no time to raise the whip again. In that instantaneous flash of the kill, the troop fanned out and disappeared behind sand dunes. One of the animals galloping last hung back. Alberto figured it was the mother of the *chulengo* and that she would be coming back for it in a little while. "Let's hide and wait here for her," he said. But Juan disagreed. He was sure he had injured a second animal and insisted that they follow the trail into open country.

They advanced two miles under a sun so murderous it seemed to be inside their heads. Finally, from the top of a hillock, they made out the troop. On dismounting, shotgun in hand, Juan fell flat. The sharp edge of a stone bit into his left arm, tearing out a wide chunk of flesh. Blood spurted into his face. He scarcely breathed, but the gun slipped from his hand, and the infinitesimal noise it made, muffled by the sand, was enough to frighten the troop.

Juan Domingo was not disturbed by the pain of the wound but by the amount of blood he was losing. He tore his shirt sleeve with his teeth and with Alberto's help tied a tourniquet around his arm. But the bleeding did not stop. The sound of their own voices was frightening. To make matters worse, the wind was lashing them with swirls of burning hot sand. They were unable to gallop. The mare retraced the path homeward, walking the league and a half to The Future.

When they arrived, there was an unusual, heavy silence. They saw the sheep grazing at a distance. Several peons, sipping maté in the shade of a scraggly tree, were guarding them. Alberto tied up the mare and went around to the kitchen for help. No one was there.

Juan called out anxiously, "Mamma." The sound was erased by the silence almost before the words left his lips. "What's with my mother? Where could she be?"

They looked for her at the peons' quarters. She wasn't there. Then they ran back to the house. The door was closed but unbarred. Respectfully, Alberto pushed it open. What he saw was unforgettable, the image a parasite that was to gall his memory for years after.

To the left of the door, stuck in the horse tail for the combs was a white, heavy-toothed one made of horn that did not belong to the family. To the right, on the parents' bed, he saw the naked bucking forms of a man and woman. The cretonne curtain had fallen in the fury of their encounter.

"Mamma," Juan called out again.

Alberto turned and caught beneath the bloody smears on his friend's face a grimace of inhuman suffering. He heard him repeat, "Mamma." He did not want to look at him. He felt Juan leave the house and go to hide in the sheep pens. Shortly afterward he heard a tormented wail of fury.

Doña Juana came running out into the open, her hair undone. She had thrown a man's poncho over her apron. Behind her in the dimness of the room, Alberto saw Benjamín Gómez, a drover, putting on his boots.

His mother wanted to clean Juan Domingo's wound, but the boy would not let her touch him. He washed the blood off himself, with Alberto changing the water in the basin for him. One of the cowboys came to bandage his arm.

"I have the grippe," Doña Juana explained. "I began to get heavy chills, so Benjamín offered to put the cups on and give me a rubdown."

Juan Domingo nodded his head, "Uh-huh, uh-huh." That was all he said. Nervously, the mother sought Alberto's understanding. "Now, I don't want you boys carrying stories to Mario Tomás. Don't be upsetting him about me. Mario Avelino, either. If a man talks about a woman's ailments, his balls rot and his ding-dong falls off."

The following day, his wound swollen, Juan Domingo put his whip and shotgun away in the winter chest, packed his knapsack, and without saying good-bye to his mother, rode to Camarones. He wandered around town for a week, tightlipped. He ate the food Alberto brought without tasting it and spent the nights on one of police officer Manuel Verdeal's cots.

That long penitence ended when a freighter, *Primero de Mayo*, anchored in sight of port on a calm and transparent sea, waiting for bales of wool to carry to Buenos Aires.

It was the first time Juan Domingo did not turn around to wave good-bye after having stepped onto the boarding launch.

6
FIESTA AT THE VILLA

"I'm not me anymore," says President Cámpora early on Sunday, June 17, when the General's return to Ezeiza is still three, nearly four, days off. "I'm somebody Perón made." His face is haggard, furrowed by grim portents and failures. The circles under his eyes that recede in moments of joyfulness are now sunken and black, as though holding some hidden shame. He is wearing a dressing gown and pajamas rumpled by his body's restlessness. Sitting through the night with him in the armchairs of the bedroom Franco has provided him next to the Moncloa gardens are a few confidential advisers. All are exhausted. They arrived in Madrid on the morning of Friday the 15th after traveling thirteen hours, but Spanish protocol gave no quarter. Only the night before, they had sat through two hours of speeches at the welcoming banquet offered by Franco. They retired at 2 a.m. At 4:30 Cámpora is on the telephone to one adviser after another seeking counsel. The story he tells is murky, fouled with ciphers that have no keys.

Why has General Perón abandoned us like this? Why does he humiliate us, snub us? I called him up two hours before leaving Buenos Aires and asked if he would be meeting us at the airport, if he was planning to attend the banquets, and if he intended to give the response to Franco's eulogies or whether I should. Don't worry about it, he answered. Relax. And then he doesn't show up anywhere. What a spot to be in! Franco was annoyed. Will the General be coming? he wanted to know. I tried to smooth it over. He promised to be here. Let's wait a little longer. But nothing doing. And later on, when I wanted to know the reason for his disregard, do you know what the General did? He burst out laughing. What do you want me to say, man? he answered, patting me on the shoulder. I'm sick, can't you see? And I said, Fortunately, I can see that you aren't, General. I find you looking quite healthy, thank the Lord. Then, he stopped laughing. I have [this is how he put it] one of those terrible memory migraines. The promises you made me and didn't keep are aching, Cámpora. And these twelve years during which Franco treated me like a pariah, not even answering my letters, give me some awfully sharp pains in the memory. Have I disappointed you, sir? I asked him. I wonder how. Tell me in what way, so that I can immediately make up for it. He was noncommittal. Think, Cámpora, think . . . Who picked you to be the candidate? To whom do you owe the presidency? If it were just a question of my say-so, I wouldn't be throwing it up to you. But there are thousands of Peronists furious at you. They want to kick you out of the government, to liquidate your sons . . . Ah, that most of all. They want to blow their brains out with a pistol. And what am I supposed to advise them to do? he asked me. I couldn't believe my ears and just looked at him. I felt like an icy needle was going through my marrow. Advise them? What do you mean? I asked him. Order them to be merciful, General. Order them? I can't. What do I do afterwards if they disobey me? Better to try and persuade them. Take it easy, boys. Cámpora is a good man. Give him a little time to get his sons to resign from the government and to repent his nepotism. Hasn't he declared himself Perón's first liegeman? Don't they call him Uncle, the loyalest man of all? I do speak up for you, Cámpora. Nevertheless, in your place, I wouldn't rest easy. If there's just one Peronist who considers you a traitor, that's enough. Nobody can save you then. The General talked as though he didn't care what happened to us. I still can't make him out. I don't know what to do. I rack my brains asking myself in what way we failed him.

"We're guilty of delaying," one of his staff answers. "What I think is that we should all have resigned on the very same day we took over the government and offered Perón the presidency. He was expecting it, without delay."

Cámpora gets out of bed, ponderously. Scattered around the room in armchairs, the men he has been keeping awake smoke nervously. From time to time, to console the body, they order coffee which inevitably arrives cold.

"We didn't delay a bit." The President shakes his head. He tries to smooth down a few strands of his hair stiff with brilliantine that fall out of place as he leans forward to put on his slippers. "In fact, we spent the time urging him: Come back, General. Come, we need you. As long ago as March, I said to him here in Madrid: Sir, what would you think if I were to present my resignation at the beginning of my presidential acceptance speech and call for elections, then and there? What if I explain that I am no more than your delegate and that the people voted for me as such, but not a single one of those votes belongs to me? It would be premature, Cámpora, he answered me. You'd have a coup by the army the next day. There's no danger of that, I insisted. Nobody wants them. The army will have no consensus. But he stuck to his guns. Listen to me, Cámpora. I know my cattle. When the soldiers hit the streets howling for blood, all that those friends of yours will do is clench their assholes. Not even the dogs will have the guts to defend you. I asked him what I should do. Do I stay on a month, two months? You'll know, he told me. That's why I made you President."

They open the windows and the chill of approaching dawn filters in. They hear the insects awakening. But the night remains, draining them. Their throats are parched. "Time for a whiskey?" suggests one of the men. "No, let's not even think of it," Cámpora restrains him. "We—at least I—should take communion tomorrow."

A woman with glasses finally ventures to speak. "He wanted to put you to the test, Dr. Cámpora. Knowing Perón, that's all I can assume. He figured that as soon as you took over you would come looking for him. Without any publicity, on the quiet. Once the General was in Ezeiza, no military coup would be possible anymore. Nobody would rise up against him. That's what he was saying to you between the lines. But you stayed on the job, played pool in Flores, ordered the police to forget about cracking down on the people, sent a shipload of corn to Cuba, signed the pact between management and workers, raised wages and held down prices. You did the unpardonable. You became popular. Perón could take anything from you but that kind of rivalry. It gripes his guts. And you did disobey him in something, Dr. Cámpora. You let the guerrilleros out of jail. Twelve hours after assuming power, instead of going to Madrid, you pardoned the political prisoners. Didn't anyone tell you how outraged the General was? That he said, Cámpora is a jackass. Even drug dealers get away from him. Don't you remember?"

"Yes, but I don't understand. I was obedient, I was loyal. Last night, I told him: General, as history is my judge, I swear that if I erred, it was in carrying out your orders to the letter. And I showed him the newspaper with the statement he made in Lima on December 20, 1972. I remember it word for word: 'As its very first measure, a Peronist government would immediately throw open the jails, which are holding more than 1,500 persons . . .' And do you know what his answer was? That my worst fault was obedience. That I don't obey just this or that order, but all orders, blindly. Of the seven senses a man should have, you, Cámpora, lack a sense of timing. And he said more: that I don't grasp his hermeneutics."

"And you wanted to put the presidential sash on him and leave the staff of command at the villa," a press adviser points out.

"I wanted to give everything back to him, including my first year's pay as President. What other position was there to take? He told me that he was the one who gave the orders and I had to act accordingly."

All at once, the birds burst into loud chirping. The darkness disintegrates into a crowing of cocks and barking. They order coffee again, hot, freshly brewed.

"Too late to back out," muses the woman with the eyeglasses.

"I wonder how I should dress." Cámpora becomes uneasy. "The General is insisting that I take communion with him at seven o'clock mass and I don't even know what to wear. He'll make fun of me if I'm in sport clothes. He'll say, Is this the kind of respect you show for your office? And if I'm wearing a formal suit, he'll put on sport clothes, and say to me, Man, who else but you would think of putting on the dog at this hour of the morning? I don't know, he confuses me more and more all the time. Ask my wife, will you, how she has decided to dress. The General wants her to take communion, also. Ah, a suit. That would be best. Unobtrusive. With a hat? A mantilla?"

He drops into a chair, overwhelmed. Meticulously, he inserts a cigarette into the mother-of-pearl holder that is always with him. When he raises his lighter to it, he finds that his hands are shaking. He has smoked a great deal during these terrible days. The thin line of his mustache is stained yellow.

Never, in fact, did Cámpora seek out the lot that fell to him by sheer chance. In 1943, he was thirty-five years old and had resigned himself to a routine life practicing dentistry. His office was in San Andrés de Giles, to the west of Buenos Aires. He was a conservative, but there were those around who considered him radical. In view of those attributes, the military governor decided to appoint him town commissioner.

Cámpora filled the office impeccably. He organized the town's civic celebrations punctiliously, felt moved at every flag-raising, and administered honorably the meager funds entrusted to him. On October 12, 1944, he was raised (as he phrased it) "to heaven on earth"—he met his leader.

He had been invited to the inauguration of a hospital in Junín. The guest of honor was Perón. When they were introduced, Cámpora was effusive. "Colonel, you wouldn't believe how much I admire you." And he took advantage of the moment to invite Perón to honor with his presence the festival for the patron saint of San Andrés de Giles. Nothing was to part them from then on. Cámpora encouraged the colonel's clandestine affair with Evita and she in appreciation decided to adopt him. She called him "my duenno." In mid-1948, Eva imposed him as president of the Chamber of Deputies. He was uneasy. Isn't that too much, señora? Don't think, Cámpora, just obey. Submissive, Cámpora followed her everywhere.

Years later, when Evita lay dying of cancer, he sat with her all night long. At dawn, as he was placing a damp cloth on her fore-head, she took his hand tenderly. "Sit down," she said. And they looked long at one another. "I was able to be so many things in my life, Cámpora!" she said. (She was ice cold. Her eyes wandered.) "Housewife, farm girl, music-hall tramp . . . And look where it led. What do you think? Which way would Evita have been better off? In bed dying or happy getting fat in the ass with a kid in her arms?" (Cámpora became alarmed. He wanted to call the doctor.) "Was it worth it, do you think? I don't know what's going on any-more. I don't even know what day it is. Here in this bed, it's all the same to me . . . Who knows if it's afternoon or morning, or any-thing . . . ?" She tried to sit up but let herself fall back and, with a deep sigh, asked, "What time is it?" And he, in his stupefaction, answered, "Whatever time you say, señora. Any time you'd like."

When Perón was ousted in 1955, Cámpora was put in an Antarc-tic prison. Misfortune enhanced his submissiveness. John William Cooke, in the neighboring cell, wrote in a letter of April 11, 1957: "Cámpora has promised God that he will never get involved in politics again. He spends the day praying and in making it clear to us that he is no militant." Jorge Antonio was to round out the story some time later: "We escaped from prison into the hardship of the snow. Cámpora suffered so much that he nearly died. When he knew he was safe at last, he raised his hand, looked up at the sky, and said, 'Lord, I swear I will never go back into politics.' And the tears froze on his cheeks."

He was lulled by thirteen years of anonymity. He went back to filling cavities, molding false teeth, and raising new tomato hybrids in his garden at Giles. Toward 1965, he ventured, not without some trepidation, to write to Perón. The letter ended with a quotation from Dante: *"En la sua voluntade è nostra pace."* The General replied at once. "Drop the affectations, man, and get over here to Madrid the first chance you get. Your friend will be waiting for you . . ."

He went a couple of times. The two of them passed the days strolling under the trees of Puerta de Hierro, evoking past glories. Actually, Perón did the evoking and the other filled in missing memories.

From then on, Cámpora felt his life changing. He continued being the man he was before, but life got away from him, as with a horseman who watches his steed disappearing into the nothingness of the desert. He was acting in the interests of others all the time, pushed this way and that by hands strange to him but hands he trusted because they represented the General. One morning in November, 1971, López Rega called San Andrés de Giles and asked him to come to Madrid immediately. Perón had just dismissed his political representative and wanted to turn the post over to Cámpora. Once again he was tempted to ask, Isn't that too much?

So many things began happening to him that he failed to comprehend any of them. He bought a house in the city of Vicente López, just outside Buenos Aires, for the General to live in when he returned. He pleaded for the freedom of the widow of Juan García Elorrio, the editor of *Cristianismo y revolución*. (Juan had died in a mysterious automobile accident. His widow, Casiana, went on trial for publishing subversive literature.) He led demonstrations whenever one of his people who was a popular militant died under torture or machine-gun fire. He faced police sabers and tear gas. He became eloquent, condemning the military oppression more violently than anyone else. The young were always at his side, protecting him, drawing him into the infernos of their battles. Cámpora flew, in his dreams, on a magic carpet: Was it history? One night in June 1972, at the doors of the Gran Vía Hotel, he confided to Noon Antezana and two other friends: Sometimes, it's not so bad for a man to do what he doesn't want to.

In November of that year, Perón left exile for the first time. He was in Buenos Aires for four weeks. Convinced that the army would not let him run for president, he put Cámpora in his place. "I put him there because of his incorruptible loyalty," he told the press. "Cámpora in the government? Well, then, that means Perón is getting back into power."

Around that time, Zamora wrote a muddy article in *Horizonte* so elliptical in style that nobody paid any attention to it:

> Every human being, crude as he may be, no matter how conventional, will sometimes behave unpredictably; behavior which, while outraging the being, at the same time reveals it. We all believe we know who we are. None of us is capable of foreseeing what he will really do. For what we do, even when it goes against the apparent will of our conscience is, in the final analysis, who we really are. We are, then, what we do

more than what we think or say. And so, Cámpora is looking at his actions with astonishment, trying to see if he can recognize himself in them.

The error of philosophy lies in explaining man through what he thinks or perceives. Man is what he is: it is the tortuous and labyrinthine impulse that induces him to plot out a life that rarely resembles his life plan. Only in living do we know ourselves. Life betrays us.

"Give me my gray suit," Cámpora decides, on emerging from the shower. "For communion, I must be dressed appropriately."

On the way to Puerta de Hierro, exhaustion keeps him silent. His wife, María Georgina, strokes his hands, giving him courage. It is not yet seven in the morning and the air is already overheated. They pass through the gateway of the villa and continue on between the pigeon lofts; they see the General's silhouette in the distance, next to the brook, playing with the poodles under the ash tree. Fortunately, he too is wearing a suit and tie.

"Did you hear the radio this morning?" Perón walks toward them, his hand stretched out. "Pure nonsense. Comparing me with Don Quixote. They said that a President like you in Argentina is the same as Sancho on the island of Barataria. Somebody else on the national radio station makes me out to be the Count of Monte Cristo: I will return to my country only to get even for the foul deed committed against me. And they interviewed an Argentine correspondent. I wish I could remember who it was. That man went so far as to advise me (imagine this, Cámpora) to have your head. That stuff shouldn't be paid the slightest attention. Those people talk just for the sake of talking . . ." And carrying the dogs in his arms, he turns toward the chapel. "Come on, let's go in. We'll make our peace with God."

A little before nine o'clock, when mass is over, a swarm of visitors descends on the villa. In the General's office, playing with the ceramic horses that infest the desk, waits Giancarlo Elia Valori, *gentiluomo di Sua Santitá*, adviser to Greek colonels, whom Perón assumes to be an intimate of Paul VI. Lurking around Valori, as always, is Don Licio Gelli, aloof, dipping into the histories of Bartolomé Mitre that adorn the library. Everyone in that house owes Mitre a favor, Valori often says.

Scattered between the anteroom and dining room is a parish of Goyaesque figures: former boxing champions, tango singers, the usual union leaders, and a couple of ambassadors wearing gangster suits. In the kitchen, Doña Pilar—Generalissimo Franco's sister— is busy next to Isabel frying crullers. Briny mists rise from the cellars. Perón will be serving his guests *puchero*, an Argentine-style stew.

Cámpora wanders about the dining room again feeling alienated from everything. He recognizes López Rega behind the screens studying a sheaf of telexes he has received from Buenos Aires. From time to time, a message disturbs him. He picks up the phone and issues orders. The President has no idea where or to whom. Nobody says anything to him.

He wonders what he is doing there and how he might escape from it all. He busies himself looking at the photographs in the dining room, soon—the following day—to be taken down and packed: the General on the balcony of the Pink House, his arms lifted in greeting to the distant crowd; the General riding in a parade on his horse Mancha; Evita in her finery at the Teatro Colón. He sees himself in two of the photos, always smiling. Everything was a lot clearer in those days; everybody wanted to be exactly what he was.

All at once, María Georgina, who is holding onto his arm, shudders. She senses a dark weight of malaise bearing down upon the house: something, she doesn't know what, a blade cutting into the happiness of those people. Were the conversations not so boisterous, were there not such a welter of arms, guffaws, loud greetings, María Georgina would say that cavernous moans were descending like a miasma from the moldings of the ceiling. She? The President's wife opens her mouth. And, immediately, she seals off her astonishment with her two hands.

"Tell me. Isn't she in the house, upstairs?"

Cámpora looks at her, discomfited. "The deceased?"

"Her body." María Georgina nods. "I bet you Evita's still here, up in the attic."

Cámpora is alarmed. "Be quiet, woman! Nobody mentions that here. They don't let anybody see her. I don't know what they intend to do with her. Just forget about it."

Shortly after noon, the General, who had retired to rest, comes down to the garden in a bad mood. He has had nightmares. When

Isabel went to wake him with a cup of tea, she found him groaning, drenched with perspiration. A man who suffers so much in his dreams should never go to sleep, she will commiserate with him at lunch.

Doña Pilar, Valori, and Licio Gelli are at the General's table, López Rega and his gunmen at Cámpora's. Since the first day he was elected President, Cámpora has felt the secretary's hostility. War will break out between the two at any moment and he takes it for granted that the General, obliged to make a choice, will protect Cámpora's enemy.

A Spanish newspaperman, Emilio Romero, has planted terrible suspicions in him: López intends to put Isabel in the government, and Cámpora (he says) would be the only obstacle. If that is true, then I don't matter much, the President retorts. Perón is the real obstacle. Romero insists. She, Isabel, assumes death will soon take Perón. He is an old man, almost seventy-eight; it won't take much. What I am going to tell you, Cámpora, took place in 1970. And I was there. It was autumn. Isabel served tea, as usual. A fat fellow from San Nicolás, I think, indiscreetly alluded to Perón's age. He said that he was looking younger. That at this rate he would never die. We all turned pale. As you know, Cámpora, the General is not to be reminded of those things. López broke the ice. He said that, unfortunately, all men are mortal. The leader wasn't concerned about that. What he did want, however, was for his doctrine to be immortal. What he needs is a relay. Not a successor but a relay capable of keeping the doctrine just as it is, pure, unchanged in any way. The steelworkers thought that López was aiming to take Perón's place and became alarmed. They asked if he had considered who that person might be? The secretary very coolly said that he had already considered that: Señora Isabel. Nobody can uphold a man's doctrine better than another person of the same blood. At that point, Perón cut in: Did you say Chabela? López, don't be such a damn fool! There's no consanguinity between Isabel and me, thank God. The secretary then fell back on his occult authorities: That is the law today, General, but according to Paracelsus and other ancient sages, the spirits of a husband and wife impregnate one another. Their bloodstreams mix like anilines. Perón was left thoughtful. A year later, the army returned Eva's body. The political game became complicated. And they called you in, Cámpora. The subject did not come up again.

That's very unlikely, Romero. I don't believe it. (The President flatly rejected the suspicions.) I am positive that Isabel is in good faith. If López Rega tries to use her, she will refuse. I have heard her say a million and one times that she is not interested in power.

Romero disagrees. The wife (he believes) is tormented by ambition. She is a hypocritical woman and, therefore, unpredictable. Until now, we all thought López is using her. It's the other way around. López, rather, is an instrument of hers. When he is of no use to her, she'll sacrifice him, too. That hysterical little rat is implacable. She has destroyed all her adversaries. She's gobbled up even the loyalest. She's primed with elephant meat.

Cámpora has been trying for some time to ingratiate himself with both López and her. On the last occasion, no more than two days before, he softly implored them to trust in his loyalty as in that of a brother.

"Has the General ever given you his opinion of loyalty?" the wife asked.

"Many times," Cámpora replied. "I have heard him say that after so many deceptions, he can now distinguish between the loyal man and the traitor at a glance."

"That's correct," López agreed. "But he has also said that it was not enough. That the best way to assure a man's loyalty is to put others at his side to keep watch over him."

"Is that so? And in my case, who would that be?" Cámpora asked, in an effort at jocularity.

"We two," Isabel answered, very seriously. "Daniel and I are the others for you all."

Right now, the spider web of that infinite surveillance takes shape before the President's eyes. López, eating, eyeglasses on the end of his nose, receives messages incessantly: telexes, maps with markings on them, statistical tables containing codes. The latest reports mention a conspiracy. It is all still vague, barely shadows of rumors. One or two columns of Montoneros—he has been informed—plan to occupy the platform when the General arrives at Ezeiza. They will seize the microphones, demand several heads (his, in particular; they call him the "witch doctor"), embarrass Isabel by chanting that there was only one Evita and that she is irreplaceable. But, more than anything else, they will call for Peronism to be turned into a revolution *moto perpetuo*, the socialist fatherland. Are they really Montoneros? One of the reports assumes that they are not, but rather August 22nd Marxists of the Fourth International.

If it is true about the plot, those flames will have to be extinguished with blood. In such cases, the General cannot be counted on (López knows that). He will repeat: "I do what the people want," without recognizing that his people have changed. The General has to be forced to see reality; he must be presented (as the señora has insisted) with *faits accomplis*.

The secretary is convinced that Cámpora is party to the intrigue. The youth have had him in their pocket since a long way back and they manipulate him. They are incubuses. Hasn't he even quoted Che Guevara several times in his speeches? Various people have told the General that Cámpora is deeply impressed by the Cuban model. That he would like to found a Castro-Peronism.

Even when he is face to face with his enemy, the secretary acts as though he were alone. He gives an order that a call be put through to a certain lieutenant colonel in Buenos Aires, so he can order him over the phone to locate officer so-and-so, an expert in antisubversive control. All the dogs must be turned loose, he decides, against the suspicious columns. The names of the leaders must be ferreted out, their lairs raked over with a fine-tooth comb.

The most recent telex reports that a local customer in a bar in Monte Grande was overheard saying that a sniper with a telescopic sight was going to shoot the General during the confusion of the arrival as he walked toward the bullet-proof box on the platform. But the message ends disappointingly. The police arrested the regular and gave him the full treatment: manicure, permanent, and "butterfish." They pulled out his nails, drove him out of his mind with an electric prod, and ducked him in a tub filled with shit. And got nothing. It turned out to be only gossip, the irresponsible fantasy of a barfly, a reflection of the mass paranoia.

Don't let that discourage you, López tells them. A close watch is being kept on Rodolfo Galimberti, who holds a grudge against the General and is capable of anything. Robi Santucho who hates our guts is under surveillance. A dragnet is out for Firmenich, Quieto, Osatinsky; the first careless move we make, those characters will rip our eyes out. And most important of all, find out what Noon Antezana is up to. He's the worst megalomaniac of all. The others think they're good enough to take Perón's place. Not Noon. He thinks he's better. Get going! (López works feverishly.) Any disaster is possible in the next three days.

The gunmen disappear from the table. And he, disregarding Cámpora, rereads the telexes, his cheeks bulging with sweet potatoes and tripe. In the distance, under the ash tree, a blind harpist is plucking out the waltz "From the Soul."

After so much moving about from table to table, the General's smile is coming unstuck. All that remains of it is a somber smudge along the edges of the lips. A Uruguayan bard with a pitch-black mane insists on improvising an ode to him with guitar accompaniment. "Later this evening," the General fends him off. The people are high on wine. Out on the porch, the boxers are whirling around, stamping out a tarantella. At Raul Lastiri's request, Doña Pilar Franco attempts a few flamenco steps. Shortly before six, the *puchero* sticking in his throat, President Cámpora finally returns to Moncloa Palace. López Rega's daughter, Norma, says good-bye to him with a devastating comment: "Poor Don Héctor! They used to like you so much, and now they say such nasty things about you."

The sun is going down. When the General tries to get out of his chair, he can't. His muscles don't listen. He licks at his thoughts to ease his body. It relieves him. Furtively, he manages to make his way to the house. He climbs the stairs to the sanctum, the anteroom of the sepulcher where Evita lies. The hurly-burly of the garden has hurt his lungs. But up in that refuge, no sound can be heard. He picks up the binder of Memoirs the reading of which was interrupted the night before, and riffles through the pages. All at once, he pricks up his ears. What's that, what's that? Ah, it's the silence entering. It's coming from the attic where she is resting, safe from this world. Eva, the *ave:* her muteness is the bird he now feels flying.

There is a tiny shower of dust. Is that she scattering this dust over things, pollen of nothingness, a flurry of no meaning? What else could Evita be shedding but the oblivion that enwraps her, the many years without thought, the dankness of the non-places in which she has slept: closets, cellars, coal bins, ship holds. What is the wake she leaves behind? Is it this silence, this blankness? Even under such conditions the General envies that eternity, the now-recovered glory, requiring nothing of anybody. Truly, though, is that what he wants? In other times, Perón used to believe that if he could imagine the past with enough force he would be able to return to it again, smeared with berry juice, a knapsack over his shoulder, correcting the inappropriate gestures of long ago and giving the answers that had then escaped his lips; he used to think that if yesterday's good health could be breathed again even for a moment there might perhaps be no illness tomorrow. How difficult that is! the General has written. How is a person supposed to know which is the proper feeling that will enable one to understand what a feeling is, what it is that we give this vague name to?

The only feeling he has experienced unblurred to any extent is fear, which he would like to efface from his memory: to assert that fear does not exist now, and that, therefore, it might (must) never have existed. It wasn't the trivial fear of death but something worse —fear of history. He has suffered at the thought that history will tell in its own way what he suppressed. That others will come along and invent a life for him. He has been afraid that history lies about what it says of Perón, or that it will find out that Perón's life has lied to history. He has said so many times that a man is no more than what he remembers. He should say, rather, that a man is no more than what is remembered of him.

He also had a remote feeling, even realer, perhaps the only feeling he ever experienced that he could smell and touch: the suffocation that gripped his chest when he crossed the threshold of the Colegio Militar in 1911, the palpitations of the esophagus, the tremors of the tongue. The entrance was muddy. A passing car spattered one of his trouser legs and he tried to clean it. His hands were left smelling of horse manure.

How did I tell that? I wrote: *This is what I want. And I found in myself the soldier that I never left off being. I applied for admission in 1910. The following year, I entered as a cadet.* (The first two sentences are his, the other two López's. They had been taping thoughts that afternoon. What afternoon was it? They were trying to understand the country from a distance, drawing flowers on a piece of paper. Bubble ideas, General. And one day, López cut them out. His poor birds of thought—they flew away. He should have been firmer. He should have ordered López to write the following instead:)

98

[In 1910, wilderness still embraced Argentina. It invaded its entrails. That's where I come from, the depths of the wilderness. From the Argentina that did not exist; we were wind, dust clouds, in those times. They made us study Alberdi's Bases for admission to the Colegio Militar. I learned from that book that the best law to apply to the wilderness is to get rid of it. To govern is to populate, I read. We can conquer the wilderness by making it disappear. I was just a kid, and I thought, What a strange statement! It's like saying that the best thing to do about nothing is to abolish it. That the best way to have nobody is to decree that nobody exists. Just the silly ramblings of an adolescent.

[I took the examination on December 1, having recently fulfilled the third-year high school requirements, and on March 1, 1911, I entered the old mansion in an almost empty part of the town of San Martín. The street car depot was nearby and there was a general store across the street. I was to spend three years there. I was only fifteen; still a child, you might say. That was when my parents delivered me to the fatherland. And under the fatherland's protection I grew and became a man.

[I feel the past. I can see myself in those days. I feel the past inside me like a film that jumps in the projector. I see myself saying good-bye to Grandma Dominga. Did I cry? If so, it was when I was alone, at night, in the Colegio dormitory. If I did, it was in silence, so that nobody would know. I thought of my parents, lost too, in the solitude of Chubut. With them, I was somebody. Now, suddenly, I was nobody.

[Many years afterwards, while watching a TV series in which inhabitants from another planet lose themselves among crowds of this world, I realized that what I had been since that time was a transplant, a tree whose roots had forever been cut by fate. A nearly homeless being, with families that kept being snuffed out like candles, one who learned only to command and obey. But not to feel. I was inculcated from childhood on with the idea that feeling was weakness, something feminine, a quality of the spirit that must be nipped in the bud.

[I see myself sitting in the schoolyard, a soldier-barber clipping my hair savagely down the skull, leaving barely a paltry tuft; putting on my fatigues; the days graphed according to this regulation, that order. No one could allow himself a polite word, a smile, a tear.

[The cadets were quartered with the soldiers in a big shed we called "the stable," which had a sheet-metal roof on which the raindrops rattled. Reveille was at 5 a.m., summer and winter. We had three minutes in which to wash our faces, and five to be in formation in the yard, fully dressed. We drank a cup of hot maté with milk and after that went out on the soccer field for a pitiless session of close-order drill. I found out then that a man does not realize how far he is capable of driving his body, what the limits are of its almost infinite power. The thing is that we rarely try to carry it to the point beyond which it can go no further. One does not really feel that he exists until his body begs for mercy. At other times, one never stops to think: This is me, here I am, here is a tiny spot that I call my place in the world. Some time later, I heard that there was a Jewish philosopher who had the same ideas as mine, but no one knew when he had written them. I don't know, either, whether he had felt them as I did in his own flesh.

[Life was very hard in the Colegio but I was ready to make any effort, any sacrifice. The icy mornings of San Martín were nothing compared to Patagonia, and a soldier's daily tasks ended up being fun for me.

[We had leave once a month, beginning on Saturday after morning formation, and were required to be back on Sunday before 10 p.m. Serious infractions were punished by denial of this only time off. The more unruly elements were made to sit in the punishment hall, hands on their knees, from reveille to retreat without getting up except to go to the latrine and the mess hall.

[Academic classes were held in the afternoon. We studied history, natural sciences, geography . . . The program was similar to that of fourth-year high school. Compulsory military service had recently been instituted as a device for inculcating Argentine spirit in the millions of semiliterate immigrants who came to populate our soil. I recall that Don Manuel Carlés, who later established the fascist militia of the Argentine Patriotic League, was one of my most enlightened teachers. His subject was literature but his classes were veritable harangues in which he treated us as though we were already officers in command of troops. "The nation," Carlés would say, "expects you to know how to redeem the uncouth, ignorant, depraved conscript." His purpose was to put us on our guard against anarchists who were already infiltrating everywhere and disrupting our political life. Most of them were foreigners. They were going into the factories, agitating the workers with their bitter preachments, and Troy was burning there. Nearly 300 strikes broke out in 1910.

[My father used to say that no Argentine is completely an Argentine until he has founded a town or planted a field. When I was about seven or eight years old, he sat my brother and me down next to the fire. "Roca took this country's best land away from the Indians and gave it to his friends," he told us. "The fat cats who couldn't get any that way bought it up at ridiculous prices with the army's connivance. Mario Avelino and I will take care of the little bit of land we have. Juan Domingo must become a soldier so as to keep them from taking it away from us."

[Both my father and grandfather wanted me to study medicine, but I will never forget those words, spoken perhaps during a fit of depression or impatience. Sometimes it seems to me that my future was decided the moment I heard them. I took up a military career not to appropriate land for myself—since I have none—nor to build towns—which I would have liked more—but to learn to build men: to lead them.

[I had no interest in money nor material appetites of any sort. How could I have had if a second lieutenant earned the same miserable 200 pesos a month as a teacher? I couldn't even rent a passably decent apartment in Buenos Aires for that amount.

[We received our instruction in the art of leadership from German officers. At the time I entered the Colegio Militar, the Argentine Army was still operating under the old tactics of General Alberto Capdevila, based on French manuals and regulations. But we were already being equipped with Prussian rifles and cannon. We knew Mausers and Krupps. The traditional kepi we began our studies with was soon replaced by the German helmet topped by a large cone and an Argentine shield just below it.

[We acclimated quickly to the new system. We marched in cadence, and commands were given Prussian-style. There was never any question of thinking, only of obeying. Sometimes, *our tempers got the better of us, but we kept right on going. The names of von Clausewitz, Schlieffen, von der Gorz were as legendary to my teachers as, let us say, Napoleon. In 1914, General José Felix Uriburu returned from Berlin, where he had served as a member of the Kaiser's personal guard. He came back such an obsessive germanophile that the cadets all called him "von Pepe." The same happened with many others.*

[One of my happiest remembrances of the Colegio is of the comradeship, the cultivation of enduring friendships. Almost all 112 of us who received our second-lieutenant's sabers together are dead now. Most of them were descendants of immigrants, mainly Italians. I was one of the few with at least three generations of Argentine descent. Since we lived apart from civilians, we ended up constituting a family. It has been said that I never had any other family, that my only real feelings were for the army. And what's the problem with that? I didn't distinguish between the fatherland and the army. In 1955, a camarilla of traitors wanted to leave me without one or the other. It forced me into exile and decided by decree that I was no longer a general. That didn't bother me. In the final analysis, I went on being Perón. But to be left without an army was very painful. It was like being abandoned by one's family. And I immediately thought: I'm like Argentina; I, too, have a wilderness's fate. Their intention was to condemn me to nonexistence, to oblivion, to the empty plains. To have no name, no past, to live without roots. The dictatorship of usurpers of '55 decided that from then on I was a cipher. I began to ponder that: let's see where to put that zero, to the left where it doesn't count, or on the other side. And so, they obliged me to fight. They did me a big favor . . .

[On December 13, I graduated and received my second-lieutenant's commission . . .]

He should have put his foot down and ordered López to write in that same intimate way . . . the family, the wilderness, as he felt them. But the secretary was thinking of history: Be more historic, General. Do you know what I mean? Try to make the image look a little more like marble. Don't give yourself away. Don't let them know you. Greatness is made up of silences. Did you ever hear of a great man leaving the bathroom, pulling the chain, going around in his underdrawers in front of people? Family? What do they amount to? Relegate them to oblivion. You didn't act this way before. You never used to ask questions, General. Then, stop doing it now. Great men should only give answers.

He has something there. López can be very sensible when he wants to.

There's no reason why history should know that I, Juan Domingo Perón, have a right to vacillate, to weakness and inability. That at seventy-seven years of age I can come up with no better answer than a good question.

All right—the secretary said to him—question yourself. Spill your guts. Take the plunge. What happened to you the night of the hazing when you came to the Colegio Militar? Pull that painful thorn out of your side, once and for all.

But he couldn't. There are prisons for memories that are impregnable. They are best off left as they are, expiring. How did López cover up? Under what kind of cloak did he hide those shadows? Let's see. What page was it?

I took my entrance examination in 1910 and entered as a cadet at the beginning of the following year. It was the custom to haze the new boys. The hazing consisted of inhuman beatings that knocked the last remnants of civilian arrogance out of us and, incidentally, served to toughen our spirit. Before I entered, one group of cadets had gone through the humiliating experience of having to run naked, on all fours, over the frost-covered yards. Others were turned out of bed in the middle of the night and forced into troughs of ice-cold water. One boy landed in the infirmary with a broken rib because of the beating he took.

I was prepared for any hardship. I obeyed the second-year cadets without a word of complaint and, when I was in second year, did the same with the third-year cadets. I figured that to command, you first had to learn to obey. But hazing seemed like out-and-out brutality to me. In June, 1911, three months after I entered, we found out that the second-year boys were planning one hell of a hiding for us. They were going to ruin our first parade on the day we were to pledge allegiance to the flag by leaving us so battered and aching that we wouldn't be able to march properly. The cold was intense, the temperature

having dropped below zero almost every night. I got my class-
mates together and said to them: We have to prevent this out-
rage. Let's get the third-year cadets to back us up. And that's
what happened. We appointed a committee and took the first
steps. We've got to put an end to hazing once and for all, I
insisted, so that nobody will ever have to carry away unhappy
memories from this school. Everybody was in favor. It was my
first political victory. We appeared before Lieutenant Colonel
Agustín P. Justo, the assistant director, and he was on our
side. Those savage practices were abolished from then on.

(A man should not be what he remembers but what he forgets.
Like the history he has just read. It is not the history he still carries
with him, branded in his thoughts with fire. The words moulted on
the way from mind to lips. Somebody tampered with them. López?
Or Perón, himself, in his will to forget?

(The secretary has also challenged him to tell about the maneuvers they went through near Concordia in the summer of 1913. But
the General was against the idea: I have nothing to examine there,
in that past, he said. Nothing to answer.

(Nevertheless . . . Ah, the maneuvers! López recalls. Some of
us were predestined to die that year. Do you remember December
3, General? We broke camp in Ayuí at daybreak. We planned to
march a few miles along the bank of the Yuquén River and continue on in trucks to Jubileo station. But Colonel Agustín P. Justo
vetoed the idea. He said that the resistance of the human body can
always be pushed a little further, and that the further we set our
body's goal, the further we would go. He ordered us to advance on
foot along a sandy road several leagues from the river bank where
the trucks were waiting for us. Justo had the sense of humor of a
hyena, I recall. He had forbidden hazing because of its cruelty,
and now, he was submitting us to torture, that frozen smile on his
face.

(Two cadets fainted at the very beginning of the march. The sun
had uncorked 122 degrees. You, General, had a sprained ankle.
Every once in a while, I unlaced your boot and massaged the swelling. There wasn't a tree, a water hole, even a trace of greenery to
be seen in that immensity of sand and crevices. There was a moment when it rained birds. You saw them, López Rega? Were you
there, too, in that horror? I marched and I marched, the secretary
replied. Don't you remember? I was one of you Juan Peróns. I saw

how the sun was sticking to the birds' wings and I said to myself,
They are going to fall. I saw how the sun pierced the birds' necks
and sent them tumbling into the sand fields. It's raining, you said.
And I said, It's the only rain of birds we will ever see in our
lifetime. We were carrying sixty-five-pound knapsacks and some
of our comrades collapsed under that fiery dome. Walk, Juan, walk
—you and I kept repeating. I'm an infantryman, walking is my
trade. We were among the first to arrive at Jubileo station. The
train had been waiting many hours for us. The General shook his
head: Maneuvers? Birds? Let's tie all that up into a big bundle of
memory blanks. Let's be kind to memory, López. Let's not scare
it.)

*I graduated as a second lieutenant on December 13, 1913.
For a long time I kept in my wallet clippings that gave a very
good description of the ceremony: the drum rolls at daybreak,
the arrival of the Minister of War, General Gregorio Vélez, our
military formation in the yard, the speech by the director of
the school, and the infantry exercises on the field in back of
the building. Twenty years later, when I looked for the clippings to show the Tizóns, my in-laws, all that came out of my
wallet was a yellow powder. They had turned to dust.*

*That summer, as usual, I went to Patagonia on my vacation.
My father had given me a present of three books and asked
that I keep them always at hand. They were* Letters to My
Son, *by Philip Stanhope, Lord Chesterfield;* Plutarch's Lives;
and Martín Fierro, *by José Hernández. My father wrote an apt
dedication in each volume. In the Lord Chesterfield: "So that
you may learn to make your way among people." In the Plutarch: "So that you may be inspired by these great men." And
in the José Hernández: "So that you will never forget that,
above all, you are a* criollo."

*I used Plutarch's magnum opus many times when I was
teaching military history at the War School. Its biography of
Pericles taught me the gift of patience. That great leader's
slogan was "All things in due measure, well-balanced." I
quote it often to the ambitious and impulsive when they ask
my advice.*

As for Martín Fierro, *I know it by heart. There's scarcely a
speech of mine in which I didn't find some pretext for quoting
from its splendid verses. At the time my father gave it to me, it*

*was considered reading for peasants, and didn't enjoy the rec-
ognition it later received. More impressive to me than the figure of Fierro, an army deserter, a bandit, and a bit of a savage
—he even went to live with the Indians—was the common
sense of old Vizcacha, who offered profound lessons on survival to the forsaken, uneducated little gauchos of those days:
("Every piglet to his teat, / that's the way to eat.")*

*Fate intended me always to work with men. In order to keep
faith with my good luck, I made sure that those who worked
with me should take away with them only the best of remembrances. My enemies say that remembrances are inventions.
That memory dances to the tune of power. That when I was on
top, my mistakes were cleared up with propaganda and when
I was at the bottom, the worst in me came out. My answer to
that has been that forgetfulness and ingratitude are also inventions.*

*I had just turned eighteen when I was assigned to the
Twelfth Infantry of the line in Paraná. I was in command of
the first company, a unit made up of eighty privates and ten
noncommissioned officers. The barracks, located near the
river, was a rickety building consisting of huge sheds without
windows. It had been built to house Jewish and Italian colo-
nists. When I arrived, it was known as "Immigration."*

*For the first time, I discovered the depths of our country's
poverty. The children of peons were raised out in the open like
animals; they were illiterate. And the parents died in the
prime of life, their lungs eaten away. I saw youngsters at the
port carrying 150-pound sacks through nine-hour shifts. I
learned that the women contracted tuberculosis from carding
wool and from the sweepings of the cigarette factories. What
impressed me most was that they looked on the future with
disdain. Rather, they didn't look. They were blind to time.
The past was always so dreadful that it was instantaneously
wiped from their memories. And so, the good and the bad that
befell them were attributed to fate. Or, more accurately, the
good to Providence and the bad to the government.*

Absorbed in reading, the General has forgotten that below in the
garden of the villa the fiesta is still going on. The sound of voices
on the stairway reminds him. He hears them rise, muffled, ob-
scene. What are they saying? The man, drunk, is looking for a bed.

The woman is struggling. If they've gotten this far, that means the house is already taken over, its skin infested, fouled with scabies. Will nobody stop them? The General becomes terrified. He can sense the pawing just outside the door. They are trying to enter, groping for the doorknob. Would they have the audacity to violate the sanctum? Don't they know that, up above, Eva, *ave*, the bird might awaken?

"Come down from there, damn you!" López's distant shout of deliverance reaches the cavern of the sanctum. "Come down and get out!"

(It would have to be he, protecting the little bird, snatching her out of the way of profanation.)

The General breathes a sigh of relief and relaxes. Standing next to the door, he hears the couple go. He recognizes the voice of a bodyguard. And the woman's, too—a poor slut. López chases the hangers-on from the dining room, clears the bedrooms of stragglers: "Get moving, now! Leave the house!"

Is that music? Once again, nothing can be heard. How much night is there left outside? And how much of Madrid is left him to live?

Pensive, the General returns to the Memoirs. A white moth of a plaster flake has lit on the page. (Are you coming, now, so soon, to read me the past? She and I never discussed that. It was painful to us both. This material is very old, *ave*. You weren't even born then:)

> *It was the winter of 1914. I founded* The Boxing Club *in Paraná on the same day that we learned of the assassination of Archduke Francis Ferdinand in Sarajevo. I was always crazy about boxing but in those days we just slugged, no science. We didn't even know about bandaging our hands. I broke my knuckles with a bad punch. You can still see the lumps on the back of my hand.*
>
> *I would spend hours by myself looking at the river and passing the time studying the motionless map of the stars. It was then that my first, shall we say, metaphysical searchings arose. I asked myself, as in El Moreno's poetic joust with Martín Fierro, what is the stuff of eternity, where does time go, at what point of the infinite universe do things begin, and at what other point are we able to see the end?*
>
> *I discovered some of the answers unexpectedly. It was on an*

afternoon in December of that same year of 1914. The sky was so clear and blue that not even the birds dared blemish it. I was sitting on a bench on Avenida Costanera. Suddenly, a maw of darkness opened on the horizon and I could feel the crackling of a black flame. It became night in a second. The air was swollen with a venomous stench. It was as though the entrails of the earth were rotting. A vast whirlwind of locusts fell on the city and destroyed all its greenery. I thought of my grandfather who blamed his insomnia on them and boiled their legs in retorts trying to find the virus that kept him from sleeping. Ignoring the foul odor and the turbulence, I stood at the edge of the river and watched the locusts lay their eggs. I picked up a female, pulled her wings off so that she couldn't escape, and observed close up: the hard shell of the eyes, feverish antennae, imposing mandibles. And I asked myself: If God is everywhere, as the Gospels say, he must also be in the heart of a locust. Digging with my tie pin, I tried to find the female's heart. I searched and searched. There was nothing there. I dropped the insect on the ground and left. That afternoon I learned that God can be found only where there is good and that He cannot coexist with evil. That answer has remained with me forever.

I was promoted to first lieutenant at the end of 1915. A few weeks later, Regiment No. 12 moved its headquarters to Santa Fe, on the other side of the river. Part of the troops were quartered at the old Sociedad Rural, which was called "The Fair" in those days. The rest, I among them, moved into an orphan asylum.

I had the extraordinary good luck at that time to be serving under Bartolomé Descalzo, one of the finest officers our army ever had, who was then a captain. On one occasion, I asked him if the events of our life and the date of our death are already recorded in our destinies. "Only death is recorded," he answered, "because no one is ever known to have died on the eve. But life is something else again: a real man never lets fate make the decisions he should make." I have repeated those concepts many times. So many times that people think they are mine. They aren't. They are Bartolomé Descalzo's.

Years of turmoil began. On April 2, 1916, democratic elections were held in Argentina for the first time. I preferred

Lisandro de la Torre, whose supporters were concentrated in Santa Fe, but voted for Hipólito Yrigoyen who had the interests of the working classes at heart. The army was concerned about anarchist agitation. On July 9 of the same year, at the end of the parade in celebration of the Independence centennial, somebody pushed through the crowd, and to the cry of "Long live anarchy!" fired a shot at Dr. Victoriano de la Plaza's head just as he was handing over the Presidency of the Republic. Fortunately his aim was bad, and the bullet bounced off a balcony of the Pink House.

That should have been a warning to Yrigoyen, who took office three months later. But it wasn't. His administration was met with strikes and social conflict like fireworks. It was to be expected. Yrigoyen had aroused too many expectations among the workers and peasants and was taking too long in fulfilling them. He, personally, received delegations of railroad and textile workers—something no other president had done—and delivered speeches against the owners. But then he sat back and didn't push the reform laws we were all expecting. The masses lost patience and rose up. Yrigoyen had personally suffered brutality at the hands of his predecessors and would not use repression. But neither did he know how to take control of the situation. He was facing unbridled anarchism, inspired by such dangerous ideologists as Malatesta and Georges Sorel, and imagined that the police could stop people like that. Naturally, they always overwhelmed the police. So, he called out the army. We officers were disappointed at the ineptness of this President who, on the one hand refused to lose popularity by cracking down as he should have and, on the other, involved the army in unpopular actions.

(As he reads these sentences, the General clearly recalls the stress he placed on each as he was dictating them, his unexpected hoarseness during the final ones, the fury with which he pronounced the names Malatesta and Sorel and thought of Cohn-Bendit and Alain Krivine, Buenos Aires of 1917 becoming transfigured in his mind into Paris of May, 1968. Wasn't this havoc wrought by the idealists? By those assholes of the intellect, dogs of the spirit. They used disturbances to undermine Yrigoyen's greatness, General Charles de Gaulle's glory.

(What he had dictated with rage, he now reads with sadness. And he asks himself if this afterwards from which it is being told has not already destroyed forever the yesterday in which the events took place.)

Captain Descalzo had an unfailing instinct for controlling an uprising before it got out of hand. In 1917, he led us to Rosario to occupy the yards where streetcars were parked, to forestall anarchist sabotage. In 1918, when I was transferred to the Esteban de Luca arsenal, he said to me before I left, "We are moving into the darkness, Lieutenant Perón. The most terrible of storms is beating at our door, and the President cannot or does not want to hear it. The war in Europe has ended with the defeat of the best army in the world, and now the anarchists are looking our way." I was moved by his words. "I would like to ask a personal favor of you," I said to him. "When the time comes to face up to the enemy, call me. I want to fight at your side, Captain."

I had a heavy work load in Buenos Aires. My passion for sports, which I never lost, absorbed my thoughts. I practiced high jump and pole vault, played basketball and soccer. But my main concentration was on fencing. I won the gold medal for épée at the 1918 military championships. I had a very elastic technique, as though I were fencing with a foil, and my opponents couldn't stop me.

It snowed in Buenos Aires on June 22. The people poured gaily into the streets. I was uneasy, however. I watched the designs formed by the snowflakes on the windows and reflected that I would soon be twenty-three years old. I felt the emptiness of time. I knew that I would soon have to be getting married. Although I enjoyed my life alone, I needed a serious-minded wife alongside me. An officer with a home is looked on more favorably.

In those days, we rarely went to parties and the idea of making love to a girl from a respectable family never even crossed our minds. We went to dance halls where the women were for hire. Whenever one of us wanted to empty his body, he would go to one of those women and that was that. Later, the whorehouses were closed down, and, as a result, instead of paying professionals to take care of their needs, young men seduced the daughters of decent families. The men of my generation did not fool around in those matters: we were respectful in the home. Outside, however, we danced and enjoyed ourselves to our heart's content, but only in cabarets with the professionals.

Many years later, I wrote a short article in which I told of a very rigid General who never removed his saber or kepi even in dance halls. A little French girl once asked him how he made love. His answer was, "I don't make love. I buy it ready made." And that was my thinking. I wanted nothing to put me off course in my military career, and so for a few pesos I took care of my virile needs.

Captain Descalzo's prophecy came true before anybody expected. The anarchists had their sights fixed on us. The year 1918 ended with a few strike skirmishes in Pedro Vasena's steel works. Stirred up by the anarchists, some of the workers demanded higher wages and better working conditions. Many wouldn't go along, and so the movement failed, but the seeds of discontent were sown.

The blowup came on January 3, 1919. Vasena had a plant on Cochamba Street, near the Constitución section. The warehouses were in Pompeya, a few blocks from Riachuelo. There was a constant stream of trucks running between the two places with an escort of mounted police. On the morning of the 3rd, the strikers broke out of a vacant lot in a surprise attack, shooting at the trucks. A woman bystander was killed. Someone else was killed on the 5th, and on the 7th, things took a turn for the worse. The anarchists charged again, and the police attacked with guns and swords. Five workers were killed and twenty wounded. Yrigoyen wanted the problem settled and ordered the Minister of the Interior to try to get Vasena and the strikers to come to an understanding. Under government pressure, the company backed down, making an offer of a 12 percent raise and promising not to take reprisals.

Nevertheless, the January 7th dead served the anarchists as a pretext for putting the country on a rebellious footing. Many anarchists who became famous in later years cut their eyeteeth in those skirmishes. It was part of a well-organized international conspiracy. This was obviously the case because Spartacist rebellions broke out in Berlin in 1919 the same week.

The battle there was settled in a few days with the death of
Rosa Luxemburg and her comrade, Karl Liebknecht. This de-
capitated the movement and order was reestablished. But,
here, Yrigoyen continued trusting in Providence.

It was a terrible summer. Buenos Aires was on fire. The only
breeze in the arsenal yard was made by passing flies. Even the
horses neighed out of nervous tension. The dead were to be
buried January 8. The anarchists called a general strike for
that day. We all dreaded a catastrophe. The police were
poorly trained, and it was going to be easy to overwhelm them.
The army would have to intervene.

My duties at the arsenal consisted of guaranteeing a supply
of ammunition for the troops. I had an enormous amount of
work inasmuch as between eight and ten regiments were quartered in Buenos Aires alone. As expected, the funeral degen-
erated into street fighting. More than 600 died. On the 11th,
General Luis J. Dellepiane called in Sebastián Marotta, one
of the anarchist leaders, and things calmed down.

The workers at the Vasena plant won some benefits from the
tragedy. The company cut the work day to eight hours and
raised wages by 30 percent.

But deep wounds do not heal from one day to the next; they
must be tended. My former professor Manuel Carlés, supported by Vice Admiral Domecq García, founded the Argentine
Patriotic League, which was joined by a large number of
Catholic and nationalistic youth. They formed shock
troops whose main mission was to bring foreign agitators
into line. Their methods were sometimes violent, but they
were well-intentioned.

According to the census of 1914 our population was eight
million inhabitants, with one third born outside Argentina.
Much of the country's basic industry was in foreign hands. In
Patagonia, the newly arrived adventurers from Europe quickly
fleeced the gullible criollos. The British in northern Santa Fe
had an empire almost as large as their native land. It was
called La Forestal. Their business consisted of cutting down
the vast red quebracho forests from which they extracted tannin. The concession, which stretched from San Cristóbal to the

*borders of the Chaco, covered over five million acres and con-
tained seven or eight towns where, I believe, some 10,000 men
worked.*

*Everything under those skies belonged to the English: the
stores, the water, the jungles, the security forces, and the
women. Fortunately, they paid little attention to the women;
they lived in big houses surrounded by golf courses and formal
gardens and gave parties with entertainment provided by famous musicians who were brought in direct to that wilderness
from the Teatro Colón. I heard that they hired Toscanini's
entire orchestra in 1903 and that in 1915—shortly before the
tragedies that brought me to those parts—they arranged a
recital by Caruso. Our little* criolla *women gave them indiges-
tion. They preferred the love of their insipid blondes.*

*In July, 1919, the towns rose up demanding higher wages
and hygienic housing. La Forestal organized its own repres-
sive army. They released the most hardened criminals from
prison, put them in uniform, and gave them guns. Torture and
murder began. The company shut off the strikers' water and
electricity. The army stepped in once again.*

*One Saturday that same July, when my shift at the arsenal
seemed more interminable than usual, I was handed a wire
from Captain Descalzo. They were sending him to La Forestal
to restore order, and he wanted me to go with him. He had
already arranged my transfer and the appointment of a replacement. Lieutenant Perón could not refuse.*

*Descalzo put me in command of a detachment of twenty
soldiers and assigned me to the village of Tartagal, where
some 400 families lived. I have never forgotten those jungles.
One rode through their denseness and saw swarms of birds like
cobwebs in flight. Swamps stretched on both sides of the road
and there were gleaming little towers that looked like bonfires.
They were anthills. The* quebrachos *were in the distance, trees
50 to 100 feet tall, with twisted, knotty branches. Brick-colored
dust hung in the atmosphere, drying everything it touched
because of the tannin. No man survived in that environment
more than twenty-five years. The English did tours of duty of
eight to ten months. The* criollo *peons had no choice but to
endure that hell until they died. The highest wage paid was
100 pesos a month, and the workers were obliged to spend their*

113

earnings in the company stores of La Forestal, where a package of maté cost 2.50 pesos.

I reached the vicinity of Tartagal on a freight train. The engineer pointed out a path in the jungle and told me that the village was almost four miles away. My men and I started off on foot. We were more than halfway there when I noted suspicious movements among the trees and gave the order to hit the ground. We began to advance in zigzag. I preferred to remain standing, motionless, concentrating on the silence. All at once, I heard the safety on a Winchester being released behind me. I kept cool. Descalzo had asked me to avoid a massacre at all costs. What to do? I took the only possible course. I raised my arms and shouted, "Halt! Halt! Show yourselves whoever you are. Don't be afraid, nobody will harm you. I am an officer of the Argentine Army, and we are here to help you, not to fight you."

Some ragged peons with several days' growth of beard came out of the underbrush and approached me apprehensively. They told me that the water had been cut off and that they had no food for their children because the company had shut the only store in the village.

I advised them to lay down their guns, that they would get nowhere here by force. That, after all, the Forestal Englishmen were people, not monsters, and must have some feelings. Let me talk to them, I said.

I took them back to Tartagal, escorted by the detachment. I looked up the person in charge of the store and ordered him to open up and start selling. He was a young fellow by the name of Sosa who tried to brazen it out with me. He lay back on his bed, yawned, and began wiping the rheum out of his eyes. He told me that the store belonged to La Forestal and couldn't be opened without written permission from the owners. I had to shout at him: Obey my orders! I assume the responsibility in the name of the Argentine Army. The kid started to turn his back on me, saying, No army means anything around here. The only authority in this territory is La Forestal Land, Timber, and Railways Company.

That made my hackles rise. I drew my revolver and said, Open this store at once, or you won't live to tell the story! And I made him get up and go out just as he was, in his underwear. It was eight in the morning. The sky was red.

I left three soldiers to guard the fellow as he waited on the people and went off with the rest of the detachment to look for the Englishmen. There were two couples. One of the men had had the tip of his nose rebuilt. I suspected he was a boxer and brought up the names of Jorge Newbery, González Acha, and other great fighters of the day. He had never heard of them. His world was strictly British, and he lived in those Godforsaken quebracho forests as though they were a suburb of London. Some men can't adjust to their time, others can't to place, and this Englishman was one of them.

I invited him to go a few rounds with me, and he accepted with pleasure. He had a recreation room behind his house equipped with billiard tables, exercise bars, and weights. We got right to work stringing up ropes to make an improvised ring. The Englishman lent me a pair of gloves and helped me bandage my hands. I asked one of my soldiers to act as timekeeper and gave him a whistle: one short blast to begin a round and a long one after three minutes.

We began. The man was a professional. He feinted a few tricky jabs, maneuvered me into a corner, and then nearly knocked my ear off with a left hook. My knees buckled, and I hit the floor. I could see the worried faces of my soldiers and hung on as best I could until the end of the round.

Between rounds, one of my men said to me, Please don't let us down, Lieutenant! That really hit me. An officer of the Argentine Army cannot allow himself to be beaten before his subordinates. Especially in a fight with a civilian, and a foreigner, to boot. I was blind mad but controlled myself. At such moments, only a cool head and guile can save matters. In the next round, I kept away from the Englishman, took a couple of kidney punches, and began to stagger as though I were dazed. My opponent became overconfident and moved in for the kill with his guard down. I found my opening and landed him a tremendous roundhouse to the temple. He dropped to the boards, out cold. We counted more than thirty seconds, and when he didn't come up, we emptied a bucket of water over him. His wife began to cry because we were messing up her floor. The whole thing was forgotten right away and we became friends.

They invited me to dinner. The meat was tender, but cold and flavorless. When we reached the dessert, I said to them,

Now, what's your problem with improving conditions for the workers?

They called in one of the managers to explain the situation. Several of the demands were easily resolved. Peons earned an average day's pay of three pesos and were demanding a fifty-centavo raise. It was granted. They worked between twelve and fifteen hours a day and wanted a maximum week of seventy hours. Granted. They wanted extra pay for Sundays. Impossible. A week's vacation. Also, no. If he were to give in on all points, they would be back with new demands next year, the manager said.

One of the Englishmen hinted that the company might prove to be more generous if there weren't so many anarchist infiltrators among the peons. I asked them if they had any proof of what they were saying. They showed me some file cards prepared by the provincial police.

I offered them a deal. If they granted all the workers' demands that seemed reasonable to me, the army would take care of the anarchists. They embraced me warmly and gave their word of honor that the bargain would be kept, at least in Tartagal.

I walked back to the store where half the town had gathered. I got up on a platform and announced what I had arranged. The women cheered and the men wanted to carry me on their shoulders. Seeing that everybody was satisfied, I asked them to look out for their own future from now on and to report immediately the anarchists who were stirring them up. Both parties signed an agreement, which I witnessed.

That night the peons organized a dance. They invited me and I accepted on condition that no alcohol be permitted; my men were going to have to walk the four miles to the railroad tracks to wait for the train that passed at 7 a.m.

I appeared in the evening with the two English couples. No La Forestal representative had ever mixed with peons before. Everybody felt a little uncomfortable at the outset, but I invited one of the gringas to dance, and that eased the tension. Unfortunately, a boob of a bugler of the kind that never seems lacking had brought in liquor and was passing it around under the table. One of my soldiers had too much, got high, and began making passes at a foreman's wife. The husband pulled

116

a knife, ready to kill. I saw the move coming and held his arm back. No woman is worth a decent man's time in jail, I told him. I ordered the soldier to be locked up, begged the gringos' pardon, and left.

Several months later, the anarchists returned and began agitating all over again. La Forestal broke the agreement that had taken so much effort for me to arrange and cut off the people's water once more. I heard that a smallpox epidemic had decimated the towns and that a jumpy worker had killed a conscript in Villa Guillermina. The Twelfth Infantry was sent in with machine guns to clamp down. There was a massacre, but I had no part in it.

I was promoted to first lieutenant on January 16, 1920, and assigned to the Noncommissioned Officers School. I remember those days as clearly as if it were now. I was happy but didn't realize it, since happiness always seems to be something that we've left behind. I walked around Buenos Aires in a state of absolute euphoria. I had lived such a full life already that I felt like I was on my second time around. It was hard to imagine that I was barely starting my voyage.

The General leaves the sanctum, crossing to the other side of the border. Fortunately, he never has the occasion at home to be himself. The self clutching the banister, weaving its way over the carpet, is not the General but a representation of him, a body that gradually assumes the gestures he has fashioned for the role. On reaching the first-floor bedrooms, the smoke of the grilled meat and the commotion of the guests holds him back.

What if he were to take his shoes off, turn on the TV, and, finally, perch himself upon his own oblivion. They were showing a tear-jerker on the second network, *People Will Talk,* with Cary Grant, an incredible story of a certain Pretorius who is dominated by his sinister servant. The first network has "The Adventures of Nick Carter," which he has enjoyed many times. He is about to give in to temptation. But no. There are only a few bits of Madrid left for him and who knows how much life? Resigned, the General walks toward the garden. He takes a deep breath. And then steps out, the Perón smile in place.

7

THE LETTERS TELL
THE TALE

"All men are born with two densities," Don José Cresto declared before his students at the Basilio Scientific School on his return from Madrid. "One is the density of what we are. The other is the density of what we might have been. The second one was just snatched from me by my namesake López Rega." Attendance at the temple on Calle Tinogasta had thinned down during that winter of 1967 to ragamuffin little servant girls without boyfriends and arthritic widows hoping to converse with the spirit of their departed husbands. The collection plate yielded a few miserable pesos, not even enough to buy his cigarettes. In addition, he himself was going downhill. So many years had been hung on his body that he walked bent over and trembly as a sheet of flypaper. His tongue continued at odds with words; those that didn't come out twisted were chopped off in the middle. Yet he lived tranquilly, slept peacefully. Change terrified him.

The real misfortune began, as is always the case, with a piece of good news. Shortly after the New Year of 1964, his goddaughter Isabelita sent him a postcard asking him to consider coming to live with her in Madrid.

> *You are very lonely, godfather, and, to tell you the truth, I miss you. Every morning I brag about you to Perón. I tell him of the times when you used to read letters without opening the envelopes and how you were able to cure people with an invocation or two. Perón says to bring you here, for you to come whenever you like . . .*

To entice Cresto, Isabelita sent him an open ticket from Buenos Aires to Madrid and a tender telegram: "Godfather, you send us the date. We send you our hearts."

"We" meant the General too was summoning him. That finally convinced Don José. Here, he would have to face the ruination of his scientific school, the mass evictions by the government, soup kitchens, unfair competition from the courses in Christianity. There, History awaited him. Would a great man like Perón agree to fusing the Basilio doctrine and the twenty *justicialista* truths into one? Was it possible for the two ideas, entwined in a marriage of the intellect, to interpenetrate and succeed in attracting all of humanity? Outside of John XXIII, Negrita Skruchoff, Mousy Dung, and Young Fitscher Kenedy? The future would then be in the hands of Cresto and Perón.

The point of his pencil well-oiled with saliva, Don José laboriously composed a telegram that at last announced the transferral of his destiny: "SAT COME. MEET ARIPROT. JOSECRISTO."

Isabelita deciphered it, to her husband's surprise, as meaning that they should meet her godfather on Saturday at Barajas Airport.

Perón was dismayed at the sight of this scruffy character whose long nails wore new moons of mourning. Nevertheless, he tried to be polite on the drive from the Barajas Airport to Puerta de Hierro. "Chabela has told me that you know how to cure with the word. I am quite familiar with the subject, myself, because my mother was

accustomed to doing it in Patagonia where there are so many un-
derprivileged. How did you learn, Cresto?"

"Before my feet stalled. After that, no more."

"His false teeth. After he got them, he seemed to lose the gift,"
Isabel translated.

When they crossed the Paseo de la Castellana and turned down
Calle General Sanjurjo, Perón remarked dolefully, "Here's Madrid
for you, Cresto. I wish you the best of luck."

"I, too. And I hope to bump into my wife's pneuma that'll be
looking for me in these Yuropes."

"She'll be here, godfather, she'll be here," Isabelita assured
him, pressing his hands.

Appalled at his guest's ignorance, the General deposited him in
the house like a piece of furniture and from that day on took no
notice of him. Cresto, however, insisted on following him about
everywhere, though always at a respectful distance.

As for Isabelita, he brightened her days. She took advantage of
any pretext to throw herself into her godfather's arms, calling him
papa, and spent long intervals sitting on his lap. After supper,
when the General had retired and the lights were out, the two
walked up and down the stairs with large lighted candelabras,
searching for Doña Isabel's soul. Then, they would close themselves up in one of the first-floor bedrooms where they invoked
deceased friends who were submitted to interrogations that sometimes lasted until morning.

Soon, inexplicably strange things began happening at the villa.
Sounds were heard from nowhere and there were silences when
everyone was talking. On one occasion, the General opened the
sideboard, and a cough was heard to crackle inside. Another time,
in mid-afternoon, he felt the treads of the stairway groan as he
stepped on them. One Sunday in the summertime, around ten at
night, noises disturbed their supper. The General, José Manuel
Algarbe (his private secretary at the time), Isabelita, and her godfather were at the table. A strong wind slipped in like a snake
under the tablecloth and chilled the soup. Other airy shapes began
chasing one another through the house. Algarbe, whose levelhead-
edness was beyond question, feared an attempt on the General's
life and got up to call the Guardia Civil. When he picked up the
telephone, a noise nipped at his hand and drew a drop of blood.
He then ran to the garden to summon the guard at the gate. The

two of them checked the house from cellar to attic and found nothing.

That same night Isabelita's mood suddenly changed. She became melancholy and spent hours locked in her bedroom weeping at the slightest provocation. She ensconced a hand-colored photo of Doña Isabel Zoila on her bedside table and changed the flowers before it daily. When autumn came, she resumed the custom of walking with lighted candles behind Don José, and of invoking spirits. It was inevitable, after all that effort, that Doña Isabel Zoila should appear.

She materialized as a puff of blue smoke, warning them not to question her about the future because the dead are not permitted to draw aside those veils. She did promise, however, to throw open the doors of the past for them. Isabelita wanted to know what it was like in Paradise. "Gives me the vapors!" the deceased replied. "There's a star-spangled bed where the souls pass the time hugging and kissing." "And what have you got to do with all that astrogoly?" Don José demanded to know. But the blue puff of smoke elongated itself, turned away from them, and disappeared.

When the godfather looked for the General to report the story, he found him very upset, his mind elsewhere. "Perón doesn't want to be disturbed," Isabelita explained. "He is having bad forebodings."

Visitors followed on one another's heels at the villa, going off into corners in small groups, whispering among themselves, so that Cresto would not hear them. He soon found out the reason for so much secrecy. The General had promised to be back in Argentina before the end of 1964, and with December approaching, he felt obliged to keep his word. Cresto noted certain suspicious signs in one of the visitors. This was a man with a sad face, hair slicked down, and a crooked smile. His name was Augusto Vandor. "Keep an eye on him, General, because they are going to turn that pancake over," Don José predicted. Isabelita had to take him aside and beg him to be more circumspect.

On December 1, 1964, Perón left for the Barajas Airport hidden in the trunk of a Mercedes Benz. The plane in which he was traveling landed a little before ten the next morning in Rio de Janeiro. He was not permitted to go any further, and that same night, at the request of the Brazilian government—prompted by the Argentine chancellery—he was obliged to return to Madrid.

After this failure, the time had come, in Cresto's opinion, for the General to move his queen. Oracles of the Arab Al-Mu'tamid, which he was wont to consult in times of confusion, revealed to him that:

> *We are a game of chess in your hands,*
> *If the knight checks, the queen saves the king.*

Isabelita considered that nothing fit in better with the General's preoccupations than this cryptic message. Perón felt that as a consequence of his exile the reins of the movement were slipping from his fingers. Vandor swore loyalty from afar but hinted prophetically, especially to his contacts in the military, that the General was already lost among the clouds of Olympus. Peronism needed a new leader; himself, of course.

"What's your recommendation, then, Cresto?"

The godfather gave forth: "If they won't let the captain spread the sword, then he must spread the pox."

Perón decided to lose no time in unsheathing his name. On May 10, 1965, Isabelita traveled to Paraguay. She bore a letter to General Stroessner from her husband and had instructions not to set foot on Argentine soil no matter what guarantees or enticements were offered her. She acted with utmost discretion. When her presence was discovered by one of the news agencies, she begged pardon for her Spanish accent. In the street, somebody asked her if it was true that she practiced spiritism. "That is an outrageous question," she answered, stamping her foot. "I am a militant Catholic."

When she returned to Madrid, a month later, Perón embraced her with tears in his eyes and told her that this would not be her last trip. "Your next one, Chabela," he said, "will be to Buenos Aires." In the middle of August, word reached the villa that Vandor was meeting every week with army officers, plotting a coup. A slogan, perfect in its duplicity, emerged from those meetings, and was already current among the steelworkers: "To save Perón, you must be against Perón."

The time had come. For a month, the General instructed Isabelita in the art of leadership, giving her several phrases to learn by heart each day. He urged her to introduce herself to everyone as "the General's other self" and always to speak in his name. At the beginning of October, when he felt she was ready, he accompanied her to the airport and told her, "Be careful, my girl. If I lose you, I will have no one left."

He had Cresto. No sooner was he alone with the General than Cresto wouldn't let him out of his sight for an instant. At eight in the morning, when the master of the house took refuge at his desk to tape secret orders to his tactical groups and to work on his correspondence, which now as never before demanded the subtlest nuances in his repertoire, Cresto's silhouette could be seen posted in an armchair at the other end of the shutters, making its presence known from time to time by hawking up phlegm.

Whenever Perón came into the dining room for dinner, whether there were guests or not, Don José was already at the table, fork in one fist, knife in the other, a spattered napkin hanging from his neck. Since Algarbe had left Puerta de Hierro ten months before, the godfather had become overfamiliar and rude. There being no one to take him to task for his behavior, his uncouthness had free rein. He disliked bathing and wherever he passed, a pungent stench of sour urine was left hanging in the air.

One night in December, he went too far. The General had been invited to dine with the newspaperman Emilio Romero. They wanted to compare notes on alarming reports coming out of Buenos Aires and needed to talk privately. Perón had prepared two statements attacking Vandor and was interested in discussing them with the newspaperman.

> *Those boobs think I am dying and have already begun to quarrel over my clothes. What they don't realize is that the corpse will rise up against them when they least expect it . . .*

The first ended like that and the other began, as follows:

> *There is no longer any reason for half measures. I will be very clear: the personal enemy is Vandor and his clique. They must be hit with all we've got and stopped dead in their tracks. In politics, to wound isn't enough. You must kill.*

The dinner with Romero was a disaster. To throw Cresto off the trail, the General announced at 8:30 in the evening as he went up to his bedroom that he had an upset stomach. He then sneaked into his coat and tiptoed through the garden as far as the gateway where a limousine was waiting. When the chauffeur opened the door, the jolt of a poisonous odor, like a sick rat, struck his nostrils. It emanated from the tiny body of José Cresto propped in the back seat. There was no choice but to take him along.

Cresto wolfed his food with such noise and broke into the conversation so indiscreetly that Romero preferred to leave any confidential discussion with the General for another occasion. When Don José finished one course, he celebrated with a loud belch and prepared for the next by hawking up various gobs into his maw and spitting them into a vase on the mantelpiece behind him.

Although winter descended in all its bitterness just before Christmas and wasn't to let up until well into February, Cresto did not want to deprive Perón of his company on afternoon strolls. Cresto would emerge, a toothpick jutting from his lips, and, trotting behind the General, would try to describe the scenery of the other world and to teach him control of the passions. Between the exertion of the exercise and the pirouettes of the toothpick, almost all the instructions came out garbled. Perón paid no attention. He considered the old man about as smart as a donkey's rear end.

The fact of the matter is that Cresto operated at a different level of intelligence. When Isabelita had to go to Buenos Aires, he left her with just one admonition: under no circumcision should she have contact with her family; her life depended on it. Soon after she arrived, her mother fell ill with cancer and begged Isabelita to come see her at the hospital. Desperate, she telephoned her godfather for advice. Don José repeated: "You know you mustn't, under no circumcision." Months later, when Isabel was traveling in the Chaco, she was notified that Doña María Josefa Cartas had died hoping that her daughter would at least attend her funeral. Again, Isabel was forbidden.

Somewhere between March and April, 1966, Cresto sent his disciples at Calle Tinogasta a strange letter, which seems to allude to the creation of a golem. To this day, nobody has been able to decipher it:

> *My deer true beleevers: I have had ocasion to enfuse Life into Something too big, mitebee superior to Me, I dont know. But is so great that mitebee it will ambrase me totaly and evin grow al around me like the fatt that cuvers the flesh. I have finish the Work and any moment I expeck the Work to turn agens me. It figure. Doin anythin so grate make me week. As I put al I have in it. An sHe dont wantto axcep that I am a doer.*

She donteven dare look me in myeye for which reazins my bronckials hurts me sum. I am treeting miself with avoidation of esternal clenlines wich duzint agree with internal clenlines. Well aDios. Reed this jus for yurselfs then bernit. Sined: JoseCristo.

Meanwhile, Isabel made headway in the undeclared war against Vandorism by flourishing the name she bore. "I am a mother coming to reclaim her children who have strayed from the fold," she would say. And when she was advised to go back to Madrid to avoid an attempt on her life, she replied, stubbornly, "Only my dead body will leave here."

In March, 1966, Vandor tried to impose a caudillo supporter as governor of Mendoza. Perón ordered Isabel to go to Mendoza and launch an opposition candidate. For almost a week she traveled the provinces in rattletrap cars, kissing babies and receiving letters for the General. Vandor's man lost.

Three months later, her mission accomplished, Isabel returned to Madrid accompanied by a bodyguard/factotum who had offered his humble services without remuneration. That was José López Rega.

He had been introduced to her as a faithful dog, of absolute trustworthiness, by Bernardo Alberte, a major who had been Perón's aide-de-camp. He had used López Rega's print shop to turn out underground publications and leaflets for the resistance movement. Whenever Alberte was late in paying or asked for a discount, López would pat him on the shoulder reassuringly and say, "I'll be paid back, Major Alberte. I'll be paid up. One day. It's all for the cause."

That day came at the end of February, 1966. On orders from the General, Alberte organized the security escort that was to travel to the province of Cuyo with Isabelita. Recalling that López had been a corporal in the police force, he included him in the group. At a secret meeting, Alberte introduced him to the señora for her approval. It took place in Alberte's house at seven o'clock in the evening. López had exhumed the blue suit he saved for neighborhood weddings and wore a rosette in his buttonhole. When the señora entered, laden with packages and complaining of fatigue, López leaned towards her, looked hypnotically into her eyes and said to her, "I am a messenger from Our Lord."

Witnesses heard no more than that. Transfigured, Isabelita

asked to talk to him in private and half an hour later emerged from Alberte's office, a radiant smile on her face, looking as rested as though she had just awakened from years of sleep. From that moment on, she let no one divert the miraculous envoy from her side. And instead of Lopecito, she began to call him Daniel.

When the time came to return to Madrid, López asked the señora's permission to write to the General. It was important to inform him of who he was and his purpose in going.

"It isn't necessary," Isabelita told him. "I have recommended you highly enough already."

"It is necessary. As in all Annunciations, we need an angel. Inform the General that Norma Beatriz, my daughter, will come to him this Sunday bearing a letter."

Perón was quite surprised at the length of the missive brought to him by a timid little girl in short skirts whose features were half-hidden by very coarse, dark, bobbed hair, stiffened with spray. His eyes lingered over a few of the paragraphs:

> *I belong to a LODGE that fights for the advent of THE THIRD WORLD,   exhaustively. THE THIRD WORLD will be consolidated through three magnetic vertices: in ASIA (Beijing), in AFRICA   (or Libya, in its absence), and the slanting L of AMERICA LATINA. The work of ANAEL, the lodge you recognized when you welcomed our predecessor by that name, the so-called WIZARD OF ATLANTA, 15 years ago, will be completed when the TRIPLE A goes into operation, which is obtained by drawing a straight line from Lima to BUENOS AIRES and from there to San Pablo   I was one of the first   BASIC UNITS   I filled a humble confidential post at your side, my General,   presidential custodianship. Now you can see how the LORD maintained "royal capitals" close by yours! All through my life I have studied the soul of human beings   particularly among all the high occult hierarchies.   THE LODGE is composed of honest people   But everything is under vigilance.   I am personally taking care of your wife's security   proven efficiency and disinterest. I am determined to movementize when the SEÑORA's political matters*

126

are more   organizedly on their way   ISABEL
PERON's objective which, apparently, has been forgotten by
the Peronist leaders in their zeal to occupy positions not yet
ripened enough for them
             with respectful regards.

When Cresto embraced Isabelita in the Barajas Airport and tenderly stroked her hair, calling her "dear daughter" over and over again, he noted a certain coolness not quite at the point of outright rejection. His intuition told him that the influence of this stocky man with the sinister blue look who was traveling with her had undermined his guardianship. Don José was surprised that his goddaughter, so retiring by nature, should enjoy giving orders and accepting such tireless adulation: May I relieve you of your handbag, señora? Shall I start getting the reporters off your neck, señora? Cresto recognized at once that this rival's adroitness was posing a serious danger to him. He would have to get him out of the way as soon as possible.

Before leaving with the General, Isabelita asked her godfather to find a clean, cheap pension for López Rega, to wait while he washed up, and to take him to the villa for a talk with Perón. Have the bill sent to me, she told him. We owe this man many favors and he must start being repaid in some way.

Cresto recalled a smelly pension on Calle de la Salud where guests were not admitted until after ten at night. He sang its praises to López in the taxi. "The owners are umbligating with the telophone, and they change the sheets daily, with much putrefraction." In passing, he tried to pump him.

"Will you be bringing over your family?"

"I gave up my job and family for the cause. And I will serve it with my fullest devotion."

Don José recognized that it was not going to be easy to do battle with this man. They arrived at the pension after climbing three murky flights. Cresto happily inspected the room in which strips of the wallpaper hung damply off the walls. The bedspread smelled of stubbed-out Tuscans. Taking his leave, the godfather lied, saying that Perón had "foreboded" all visitors for a week so he could be alone with Isabel. Then, after that, since it was summer—he said—they would be going on vancations to the Guamarrama mountain. They would be back in September.

"Then, I'll call the señora to give her my regrets," López countered.

"You can if you want, but the General won't like such importanance at all. Can't you see it's nine months he hasn't seen my goddaughter?"

"This undividual is so pleculyer," he explained to Isabel, "that right from the airoprot he phoned some cousins. Then he asked me to taxi him to Atocha stanchion and I dropped him there. He will let you know when he gets back, dear daughter. That's what he told me."

Isabelita was upset at this sudden erratic behavior. López (or, rather, Daniel) had told her in the airport that the only relatives he had in the world were his wife and daughter whom he was abandoning for devotion to the Peronist cause.

"I don't know anything," said Don José, shrugging his shoulders. "I only repeat what I see."

Left to his own devices, López was unable to control his anxiety. When he tried to push it aside, taking long walks through the arcades of the Plaza Mayor or seeking distraction in the taverns of Calle Echegaray, it would catch in his throat like a fish bone and make him gasp. He had never known uncertainty before, and now he was engulfed by it. He often thought of the Gobbis. They had mentioned to him that Don José kept Isabelita's guilt feelings constantly alive and in that way held her under his thumb. Guilt for never finishing anything, for being nobody, neither a dancing teacher nor a piano teacher, half an Argentine and half a Spaniard, political spokeswoman one day, housewife the next. She could never be a whole person without Cresto's help. For the time being, she was only "a wife of." *Isabelita de Somebody.* The antidote López Rega applied for giving her self-confidence appeared to have been effective: You can do it, Isabel. I'll make you a person in your own right. I'll prepare you for the moment when Perón is out of the picture. Little by little, and you'll do it.

From the moment he met the General, López began to make up for lost time. How many tapes in support of the dock workers' strike do you want sent to the tactical command? You'll have them tomorrow. Are you behind in your correspondence? Outline what you want to say, and I'll make rough drafts for you. Is the señora going shopping? I'll accompany her. You haven't received *La Razón* or *Clarín* for the last couple of weeks? I'll go down to Aerolíneas and see what the trouble is. He seemed tireless. He knew the General's books by heart and sometimes surprised him by reciting sentences not yet written down but still to come. They will come because you have thought them many times.

He was at work in the villa before 7 a.m. and never left until he was certain there was nothing more he could do. He strove to be always discreet and silent. He did not charge one centavo for his efforts. He was the opposite of Cresto. Problems seemed to evaporate in his path.

In October, 1966, he set up an import-export business on the Gran Vía. In partnership with an employment agency based in Bonn and Cologne, he sent servants and workers to the two cities and received 3 percent of their wages for one year. It required little effort on his part to recruit more than eighty peasants and, in this way, he soon amassed a small fortune. Convinced as he was that good luck can be kept on one's side only by paying its tithes, he always set apart a portion of the money for printing post cards with portraits of Perón and Isabelita, which he mailed throughout the world.

By the beginning of November, López Rega began to breathe with his full baritone lung capacity. He left the pension on Calle de la Salud and moved into an apartment in the Salamanca section, where he secretly instructed Isabelita in spiritual-transfusion exercises.

Not everything turned out favorably for him, however. Sometimes after a good session, when his disciple was ready to leave, having mastered the strategy of perfumes and the capriciousness of colors, López—Daniel, by then—peeping down at the street through the shutters to assure the discretion of the visit, would spot José Cresto's disheveled profile as he sat at the cafe opposite his building, watching the door out of the corner of his eye. Without looking up, Cresto would greet him with a nod or a movement of his hand, as though he were there expressly to be noticed.

One afternoon, in the garden of the villa, Isabelita decided to put his concern to rest.

"You guess everything, Godfather. You must have seen then that my studies with Daniel are innocent. Completely innocuous."

"Nocent, maybe, daughter, but nocuous." The old man wagged

129

his head. "If that man isn't after you for flesh, he wants you for lambition."

Nonetheless, he persisted in his surveillance.

Madrid was ill-tempered that November. It was hot even at night. López's senses were so aflame that as a means of giving them respite, he wrote down thoughts under which he placed corresponding musical notations:

> *Of Two We Shall Make One Indivisible and Eternal*
> *Si—Do—Fa—Re—Mi—Sol / Mi—Ti—Sol—Ti—Do*

And he composed a frenetic series of letters announcing the imminence of the volcanoes of the last judgment, the waters of the flood; that we have now reached exactly the midpoint of eternity, where Time is simultaneously remembered and forgotten. Most of the letters were for his comrades at the Rosa de Libres print shop. However, they also went frequently to the great masters of the Quimbanda Orders in Paris and Porto Alegre, requesting them to be witnesses to his clairvoyance.

(I am usually frightened by what I feel in me. I hear this wind that has just passed through me and I whistle to it: You will no longer be able to endure this greatness, wind. Prepare yourself. You will not endure it. I sometimes stay in my room and bleed, to relieve myself. Is this life? Is life the blood I sweat in the soles of my feet? Hear me, Villone, Arcángelo, Prieto, Piramidami, Cacho, Nilda! I am one reality on the exterior, but there is another reality inside me that I cannot yet reveal to you: a cloverleaf where the realities of you all cross. You may think that my being on the heights will change my course. No. I am a breath. They tell me in my ear that I am the Good. And, as for the Evil, they order me: You, Daniel, exterminate it. Do not let it come to pass.) Toward midnight on November 16, 1966, he wrote to his friends at the print shop:

> *I have succeeded in having the General brought back to life. He is strong as a lad. Young. On several occasions I touched his innermost depths and felt the building shake.*
>
> *My ant's task begins, slow, decisive.*
>
> *I have been late in preparing the General. This week I at last felt I could speak to him openly. Among other things, I*

130

told him that my trip was not for the purpose of accompanying ISABEL nor to rest in his mansion. That I have come here in search of a final definition of WORLD CONTROL and I will not leave without it. The General has asked of me that his life be prolonged to permit him to finish institutionalizing his movement and retire as America's patriarch and philosopher.

I amazed him. He immediately realized that now nothing is hidden from the eyes of the LORD. That all is attainable. But I did not want to frighten him and stopped at that. I went no further.

You will understand from this how difficult it is for me to keep on being little López instead of DANIEL. How it strains my patience to keep from exterminating worthless figures, once and for all. Jorge Antonio? Will die. Onganía? Will fall and once fallen, won't be worth a rap. Cooke and Américo Barrios dead and have only to realize it. Vandor is condemned. The LORD's finger has painted a bloody cross on Aramburu's forehead. Admiral Rojas? An unburied corpse.

I must rescue ISABELITA and bring her over fully to our side. I can't sleep trying to decide the best way to make clear that It was I Who rescued her. I am still not sure if I should transfer the power of WANDERING DEATH to her or to leave her immaculate in the purity of her spirit. When the time comes, the LORD will show me which way is best.

José Cresto, whom she introduces as her godfather, interferes with my work. You must help me frighten him away from her. Instruct Valori before he leaves to denounce Cresto as an anarchist infiltrator. A way must be found to link him to Vandor or some even more terrible enemy. I have never asked anything of you. But now your turn to act has come.

May the LORD be with you and enlighten you.

Even before the first letters for help arrived, López had already enlisted Isabel in his war against Don José. On New Year's night, shortly after the toasts, he solemnly swore to give her powers that not even Evita could have dreamed of: to make her the Supreme Queen, the Daughter of the Lord Savior of the World.

She lowered her eyes and blushed as she said, "May Our Lord give me the strength to deserve it."

Straining his wits, General Onganía discovered at that time that

Argentina's organization chart was identical with that for a stable. He took a seat in the topmost box and set about governing. Perón, who a few months earlier had declared solidarity with Onganía's coup and the good boys supporting him, turned his back on them almost at once. Hundreds of factories shut down. Strikes broke out daily. In Tucumán, half the population filled the soup kitchens. The number of pilgrims to Puerta de Hierro seeking counsel swelled. The General greeted them all with the same remark: "What might have been a hope has turned into a disappointment."

Don José tried so hard to ingratiate himself with Isabel that his bronchi improved miraculously. He would take a sitz bath twice a week and then come down to the foyer in pajamas and slippers, and perfumed so that his hygienic exploit would not go unnoticed. But he knew in his heart that there was nothing to be done. Even the General spoke to him gruffly, something out of the ordinary in one so evenhanded in his courtesy.

One morning, shortly before lunch, Don José came out to take the sun in the rear of the garden. A stagnant heat descended as though wrapped in veils. Distantly, the General's voice could be heard dictating letters. Every once in a while, the cooks would break out in a song from a zarzuela. Suddenly Don José felt a twinge in his legs. He went to sit under the ash tree and got a whiff of dampness that reminded him of Buenos Aires. For the first time, he realized that he was isolated, alone, many leagues away. The poodles scampering around under the pigeon lofts ran over and licked his hand. He pressed them to his chest to feel their warmth and petted the curls on the top of their heads.

"Let them alone, you useless old fool!" the General shouted in a hoarse, furious voice, as he stamped down the porch steps and confronted Cresto. "You useless old fool, leave that dog alone!"

"I only wanted . . ." The godfather could not find the words to excuse himself. He heard the General panting with rage, saw his bloodshot eyes, and was frightened. Unconsciously, he lapsed into a rustic accent. "But did you see, now, how they licked away at me?"

Perón turned white. His gaze wandered. Wheezing, shocked by the memory of a dead language aroused in him after so many years, he exclaimed, "Get out of here! Leave my mother in peace!"

"His mother?" pondered Cresto. "What did his mother have to do with anything?" He soon found out. The person Perón had hated most in his life was a man by the name of Marcelino Canosa. He was from the same region as Cresto. Doña Juana had begun to live with him a few months after she was widowed, despite being in deep mourning. He was the same age as Perón, and Doña Juana called him "son." Juan Domingo felt bitter because such a mother could not be invited to the officers' club.

No sooner did López find out that the General was haunted by that memory than he obtained some photographs in which Canosa, an old man now, stood next to a large picture of Doña Juana. López had them so skillfully retouched that Canosa's crooked smile, fox-like face, and hooded eyes mimicked Cresto's features. This lethal weapon in hand, López waited for the right moment to drop it in Perón's lap, giving him to understand (as one horrified at his own suspicion) that Don José had taken possession of Canosa's spirit in order to bring it out into the open at the first opportunity.

They got rid of Cresto through trickery, a sign that they still feared him.

Although born on April 7, Cresto insisted on celebrating his birthday on February 3, at the same time as Isabel's. The afternoon before, he went to the Plaza Mayor, where he bought a rag doll dressed as a flamenco dancer to which he attached an amulet of Jujuy mica like the ones Isabel's deceased godmother used to make. That night, he wrapped the present in cellophane, and stepped proudly down the stairs. Isabelita, hiding in the curtains, slipped out behind him and covered his eyes, with the kind of sweet blandishment Don José had almost forgotten.

"Guess who!"

"Dear daughter!" The old man disengaged himself and turned to embrace her.

Isabelita held him off. "Tomorrow is our day, remember? I would like you to come down to have breakfast with me and Daniel. How about eight o'clock? I have a little surprise for you."

"And I, dear daughter, have one for you!"

Don José Cresto went to sleep, humming. At five in the morning he took a bath in eucalyptus water and perfumed himself from head to foot. Through the window, he watched the birds disporting in the puddles of cold water and felt an unfamiliar sensation as the sun began to rise, yellower than usual, over the rim of the mesetas.

At breakfast, he competed with his namesake in the art of prophecy. Scowling, López announced that he had descried Isabelita risen above the crowds in the Plaza de Mayo, wrapped in a mantle of mourning, the presidential sash across her breast. Cresto considered the vision incomplete.

"The goddaughter's scension will have to be over Evita's orpse."

"Oh, Godfather, Lord knows where the military have stuck poor Evita away," Isabel said, pouring herself more coffee.

"Where they've got her now, I don't know. But I do know where they're going to push her off on you. Right here, little daughter, at the top of this house."

Cresto gulped down the huge chunk of bread he had dunked in his coffee with milk and when he felt it plop into his stomach welcomed it with a belch. He then undid his napkin, fitted a toothpick between his teeth, and started to get to his feet.

Isabelita held him back. "Not yet, Godfather. Look under the tablecloth. Your birthday present is there."

It was an Aerolíneas Argentinas ticket to Buenos Aires on a flight leaving that night.

"You need a breath of the fatherland, Don José," López said, smiling at him. "They're complaining at the Basilio that you've abandoned them."

Although he suspected a stab in the back, the old man could not determine where it might come from. "Thank you, little daughter, thank you," he stammered, feeling the envelope from the travel agency without opening it. He concentrated his five senses in his fingertips and, at last, it came to him. "But this is only a one-way ticket. How will I get back?"

López reassured him. "What am I here for, Don José? Am I not the person who takes care of such matters? Inside of two weeks, an envelope will be waiting there for you. So don't be impatient. And, who knows, maybe the señora will even go personally to bring you back."

But Isabel's attitude had changed. She did not even thank him for the doll and the amulet, and scarcely moved her cheek toward him for the good-bye, not returning the traveler's resounding kiss and ignoring his tears. And just before takeoff, as she suffered the last embrace, she made a comment that chilled his trip with gloomy presentiments.

"How," she asked, "could Godmother's death have changed so many things? When we were living in Buenos Aires we were different people, you more of the spirit, I more of the flesh. Little by little, life has now changed us around."

134

As soon as Cresto had left, the tension at the villa was relieved as with a sneeze. The General was rejuvenated to the point where he went back to having coffee at the California pastry shop and to strolling the Gran Vía, chest thrust out. From pure lightheartedness, he would occasionally turn to glance at the legs—the feet and, particularly, the toes—of the Spanish girls. Isabel was possessed by an urge to purchase clothes, and when spring came she made two trips to Paris with Daniel. López Rega's pretensions also rose. He sent out letters to Lyndon Johnson and Leonid Brezhnev proposing their participation in a Conference on Cosmic Harmony to be presided over by General Perón and inspired by Perón's famous speech on "The Organized Community." Receipt of the messages was never acknowledged.

Arcángelo Gobbi, at least, answered. He printed each letter separately, leaving the a's and o's half-formed, as though moths had eaten away their bellies. But the few lines contained such spectacular revelations that only the Lord Himself could have dictated them:

> I must confess that I felt resentful toward you for a while because you left, dear Daniel, without a word of warning. But now I understand the secret. And I am impressed at the heights to which you have risen.
>
> In accordance with your wishes, Villone has asked Valori to start the campaign against José Cresto. Valori was about to take off on a plane and promised to write to the General from Rome giving him proofs against Cresto. And, if necessary, steps will be taken at the Holy See to obtain his excommunication.
>
> One doubt still perturbs my spirit, Daniel. I believe I told you that when my father and I arrived in Buenos Aires, we began to attend a temple of the Basilio Scientific School on Calle Tinogasta. The spiritual director was named José Cresto. I wonder if he is the same person. A very warm-hearted girl, Isabelita Martínez, also attended . . .

So much had happened in such a few years that López Rega was surprised to find Arcángelo Gobbi missing from his memory. Could he have been that boy with all the pimples who walked stooped

135

over and dreamed of the Virgin? Of course, that was Arcángelo! He could still picture him suffering over the death of the star Betelgeuse.

López Rega had learned some time before that the will to power was based not so much on what one does as on what one is ready to do. That all power resides in the knowledge of (he was going to say, sensitivity to) where the weaknesses of another lie: in his sexuality, his mind, his past. Now that Providence had given him such infallible access to Isabel's past, why not pursue it?

That same afternoon, he wrote Arcángelo, invoking the "supreme spirits that unite us" and "the noble cause to which we have both devoted ourselves":

> I call upon you to inform me in full detail of everything you ever knew about the SEÑORA. Omit nothing, no matter how trivial it may seem. Describe for me the changes of odor you noted in her defecations, the duration of her menstruations, the teaching she received from Doña Isabel Zoila, what colors and perfumes she liked, the type of clothing she wore, what they thought of HER in the neighborhood. Everything. If you have any document, letter, or diary in which she is mentioned, directly or indirectly, send it to me immediately. Find out for me who she kept company with and what she liked to buy at the shops. What she talked about to the baker. I repeat: I want to know all. The better you carry this out, the greater the blessings and thanks you will receive from our LORD.

The news Arcángelo sent him far surpassed López Rega's expectations. He was, at last, able to reconstruct Isabel's itinerary from Montevideo to Medellín and to imagine what happened to her between Cartagena de Indias and Panama when she became the protégée of Joe Herald, the theatrical manager, whom she and Perón wished to erase from history.

To stimulate Arcángelo's loyal devotion, López entrusted him with increasingly secret and dangerous missions. He sent him as a courier between the labor unions and the Archbishop of La Plata, to infiltrate the cells of the National Revolutionary Army (which was at the time plotting to kill Vandor), and to convince the Last Lap mystics that Perón was not the Messiah.

Late in the winter of 1972, he decided that Arcángelo was seasoned enough to join the Order of the Elect. Of what use could this boy be to us? the police inspector David Almirón asked him one morning in Madrid. Is he a sharpshooter? Does he know how to make a bomb? López answered: He doesn't fit into that category. He gets nervous, his palms sweat, his eyes go glassy in front of a woman. But he's pitiless. And useful. There are plenty of men who are good with their hands. We need more who are pitiless. That same afternoon walking through the arcade of the Royal Palace, he reflected, I want him cruel, and with no mind of his own. Understand, Almirón? I want him unconditional. And, now, I have the right man to train him. Coba. Lito Coba is the one.

The moment he was alone in his room at the top of the villa, López Rega wrote:

> *Arcángelo: You must begin preparing your body's resources. The General will be returning for the first time to the fatherland in the middle of November and we will have to defend his mission of peace with our lives. The left wants to involve him in their Jewish-Marxist project and then to finish off ISABEL, the only obstacle in their path to wiping out the Christian family in Argentina. Although we have already taken the measurements of them all for their wooden kimonos, we must keep our eyes open even in our sleep.*
>
> *On Friday, October 6, Lito Coba will come to the print shop. You must ask for 45 days vacation. Lito will tell you what is expected of you. Obey and trust him as you would ME.*

Arcángelo was to go through desperate attacks of jealousy and fits of hopeless depression before he admitted that if Lito was above him in Daniel's hierarchy, it was because he had been better trained. His features were angular, his hair thick and brown, his expression vacant but alert. He had a network of important friends whom he had taken on pilgrimages to Puerta de Hierro: bankers, big landowners, managers of financial organizations, surrogate presidents of international corporations. The General would receive them all with the same remark: "What reason could you have for being against me if you never had it as good as under my administration? The poor were not as poor then and the rich were richer."

What impressed Daniel most about Lito was not his connections

137

but his wizardry in the science of alchemy, the precision with which he was able to reel off the numerical keys of Notarikon and interpret Nostradamus's prophecies.

In addition, Lito handled his body with the grace of an athlete. At the high school Olympics, he had excelled in the pole vault and back stroke. However, his eyesight was poor, and his marksmanship disastrous. Daniel had taught him the science of aiming by ear. Lito practiced for months shooting blindfolded at moving targets, missing and trying, over and over again, until finally he learned to sense the movement of what was invisible to him, to detect the scraping of a caterpillar's body along the bark of a tree. Shortly before Arcángelo became a member of the Order of the Elect, Lito gave a final demonstration of what he had learned at the little Cañuelas camp they used as a hideaway. He took up a position in a dark cabin, a Beretta in his hand. Fifty yards away, Inspector Almirón let a pigeon loose and shouted, "Go!" Lito kicked open the door of the cabin, listened for the beating of the bird's wings, and hit it in the beak with a single shot.

There was no doubt in Arcángelo's mind from the first moment Lito brought him to the camp that he would have to undergo the same unrelenting discipline. And with no complaints.

The big old house at the Cañuelas camp where he was going to live could be seen from a distance at the end of a road lined with poplar trees. It was pink with a tile roof and had convent-like galleries. There was a cobblestone courtyard at the entrance.

"Stay here and don't move till I come back," Lito ordered him.

He waited for half an hour. There wasn't a breath of air and the sky was the color of the sun. Half a dozen bruisers wearing dark glasses suddenly appeared from the depths of a gully and filed slowly over to Arcángelo. They all felt his flabby muscles. One of them listened to his heart.

"Strip!" they ordered him.

Arcángelo obeyed without hesitation. A blast of pain exploded in his testicles. He dropped to his knees. They kneed him in the pit of the stomach, gave him a karate chop in the back of the neck, ducked him in a tub of shit until he lost his breath. He regained consciousness on what seemed to be the bottom of a septic tank. The air that reached him was stifling and putrid. There wasn't enough space to sit down or even to squat. He was burning with thirst.

138

Hours, centuries, later, after he was pulled out of the tank, worse still awaited him. They taught him to climb straight walls that had no cracks, made him work out on the flying rings, bars, trapeze. Each time he felt his muscles giving way, they changed the site of the pain with an electric prod applied to his gums, groin, nipples. They wanted him to recognize in his own body the language he would later hear in his victims' bodies. During the siesta, he practiced with Itakas and Beretta carbines destroying straw figures and toy birds on the rifle range.

On November 15, Lito informed him that Perón was already in Rome and would be flying to Buenos Aires the following day on an Alitalia plane. A holy war could be started this very night, boys. The Lanusse dictatorship won't dare kill the General here on his own ground. Daniel has alerted us. Daniel thinks they will try to hit Perón before the trip, in Rome. We are the Elect, the vanguard, the holy troop. Only one of us has not yet gone through the initiation ceremony.

"Arcángelo!" he called. Soft, icy voice. "Strip!"

His eyes empty pools, Arca removed his shoes, jacket, and blue jeans, and remained standing in his socks. Lito patted his balls with auto grease moving up, little by little, to his asshole. Open your legs, slowly, Arca. A burst of quicklime tore into Arcángelo's guts, abolishing all recall at one stroke, opening in him sores, mollusk beds, wasps' nests, sewers. He felt one more thrust, and another. He heard Lito bellow between gasps, "Now ya know what a macho feels like, son of a bitch? Now ya know what a macho is?"

For an instant, he thought they were teaching him out of hatred for the General. But almost immediately he recognized that it wasn't so: that Daniel was there speaking to him of heroism and martyrdom.

Finally, Lito told him, "Get dressed, now."

He felt the scourge of humiliation. He looked at the faces of the torturers, one after the other, and spat a gob of bile and blood into Lito's eyes.

"Viva Perón!" shouted one of the Elect.

"Viva Perón!" answered Arcángelo with his remaining strength.

Perón arrived in Buenos Aires on November 7, 1972, and returned to Madrid almost a month later, after having passed through Asunción and Lima. Now, as June 20 dawned, Arcángelo was waiting for him to stay for good.

He awoke under Isabel's enormous portrait. He did not expect her to recognize him when she saw him again. In a matter of a few months, Daniel had transformed him, from afar, into something else: hero, personage? Day was breaking. The black glow of the dawn descended. At one edge of the sky, Arcángelo saw (was always seeing) specters of nature: foam of comets, breasts of Virgins, angels that tore out their beating hearts to offer the Lord.

And he also felt that he was entering history. That all this was the Annunciation or the Epiphany of a new time. And that Arcángelo Gobbi would one day read his name in the pages of that time.

8

MILES IN AETERNUM

The pendulum clock of the international hotel at Ezeiza Airport has not yet struck nine. God knows if it ever will, thinks Cousin Julio, sitting down at the breakfast table, his trousers wet, the photograph of his father, Tomás Hilario Perón, in his jacket pocket. God knows if at this very instant of eternity—June 20, 1973—time might choose not to advance any further and we would all stay here forever, living this present with Juan Domingo traveling endlessly from Madrid, and I, without memories but, also, without death.

Isn't the hotel pendulum clock the same one that was already in existence in the past? The figures of the tillers forged in bronze on the face of the clock inside the corona of Roman numbers are the same ones we saw in Grandmother Dominga's house. And there is a statuette of a woman on the mantelpiece next to the clock. It looks like the one Juan Domingo and I used to admire in Our Lady of Mercy Church when we were altar boys with Brother Benito.

What did it look like, Amelia? You wouldn't remember. Your thoughts have tripped over the opera that Radio Nacional is going to broadcast right away, and once they've tumbled down they can't get up again. I, on the other hand, still see it. The faint light that came in through the transom of the sacristy is—more or less—the darkness over the pages of the magazine *Horizonte* here next to me on this hotel table. I am the adolescent Julio Perón and I am the old cousin: the light hasn't wanted to move in all those years.

You must remember, Juan Domingo. You were fat. The two of us had haircuts, nearly baldies, with bangs. Playing innocent, you asked, "Brother Benito, would you happen to know in what way Our Lady is different from other women? I mean," you said, pointing to the statuette in the sacristy, "if Our Lady has muscles, bones, and a belly like an ordinary mortal? If she goes to the toilet?" I can't imagine what must have gone through Brother Benito's head. He stood there looking at you very hard as though you were a thread that was too thick which he was going to have to put through the eye of a needle. I was nearly thirteen, you were older.

In silence, the priest picked up a handful of pieces of chalk and drew two figures on the blackboard of the sacristy. The one on the left side was of the body of a woman in cross-section. It showed her intestines, the spongy tissue of her breasts, and the cavities of the genital system. The figure on the right was of an almost shapeless woman (like the statuette) whose breasts and abdomen were covered over with blue shading.

You are big boys, now, and it's better that a priest should be the one to teach you those things, said Brother Benito. Let's see, Juan Domingo, what is this called? Guts, you answered. The small intestine of the female, the priest corrected. Mortal women have a small intestine from twenty to twenty-three feet long. See that? And another one measuring more than five feet. Both are filled with excrement and foul-smelling matter. What I have sketched here is called—he hesitated a moment—the vagina. It has two heavy lips, with hair, where urine stays stuck. Under the lips is a prong that's called the clitoris. Our Lady, however, is immaculate and has none of the blemishes associated with original sin. She was born with a womb of mist instead of flesh and never had to defecate or urinate. Her breasts appeared after her holy, and only, birth, but they disappeared when the Child Jesus was weaned.

Brother Benito's drawings disquieted the cousins, who went around for months trying to find new revelations on female anatomy. At one of the shops in the waterfront district an Armenian offered them a book for fifty pesos that contained vaginal marvels. It clearly showed (he told them) that Japanese women's lips down there were slanted to match their eyelids. Since the boys could not pay any such price he wouldn't let them see even one illustration. They did spend thirty centavos, however, to look through a stereopticon at a peep show of a woman undressing to a waltz played on a pianola. The one Juan Domingo got to see was an Indian with enormous breasts; Cousin Julio's was an odalisque who covered her nudity with her long tresses.

But when the odalisque finally smiled, something tipped into Julio's memory, a stone from another time rippling the smooth surface of the water.

That was it. The opera María Amelia is listening to is interrupted. There is a long silence, a tremor within the silence like that of planes when they cross the equator. And immediately on the radio a hollow beep announcing that it is nine in the morning. God knows if it will ever strike again. It is striking. The pendulum clock is ringing out the hour. Time is moving again: there it is. At the table in the Ezeiza hotel, Señorita María Tizón is busy writing a description in a notebook of the conjugal bliss her sister Potota afforded Juan Domingo. She intends to give her impressions to the reporters later on in the afternoon after the General has left the platform. Absently, Captain Santiago Trafelatti leafs through the special number of *Horizonte*—Perón: His Entire Life / Documents and Photos of 100 Witnesses. Zamora had brought a generous supply of copies only a moment ago. There is now a swarm around the table. The Captain looks at the photographs and, from time to time, on seeing his name in a paragraph, he stops to read: "Santiago Trafelatti."

On the radio, the announcer reports that the Aerolíneas Argentinas plane *Betelgeuse* with the illustrious General aboard is flying over the Atlantic at cruising speed. It is two minutes after nine, Buenos Aires time.

The opera again enfolds María Amelia's heart. Isn't it incredible that on this morning of June 20 the radio should have broadcast the very same opera that she and Juan Domingo heard fifty-six years ago in the Teatro Colón? Isn't it miraculous that I can feel it, still intact, in the cellophane of such a distant remembrance? It was winter, like now, July, 1917. The cousin returns, step by step, to that night of her youth. She listens.

I, María Amelia Perón, hear once again the starch of full dress in the theater, see myself stepping over the puddles between the many carriages, the horses snorting vapor and froth, and in the gilt mirrors of the lobby I meet my full-length image once more in that green taffeta dress and Grandmother Dominga's fox cape.

It's all there again. The orchestra tuning up in the intermissions, the elderly women coughing in the shadows of the boxes, the theater's maternal chandelier that has set out its wet lights in the dome to dry. I see the tracery of the title on the cover of the program: *Manon.* And below it the signature of the composer: Jules Massenet. I would say that the voices have the same tremolos as before. The tenor is the only one I miss. The Chevalier des Grieux here on the radio is not Caruso now; not the one from that night.

You went to the theater under protest, Juan Domingo. You had come in from Santa Fe with papers from your regiment and Aunt Baldomera begged you to escort us. You had to put on your dress uniform. You looked very much like Manon's cousin, Aunt said. But the opera bored you. You were yawning, remember? At the climax, María Barrientos, the soprano, sang the aria the other woman is singing right now on the radio: *"Adieu, notre petite table."*

Aunt and I choked up. You covered your mouth with your glove. Then, Caruso came on in his priest's habit. He was suffering. He bit his hands. He wanted to reach out to God but he didn't know how to get Manon out of his mind.

I could scarcely bear it. You, Juan Domingo, began to slap your saber against your boot. Manon arrived, threw herself into Caruso's arms, and cried out: *"Je t'aime."* The lights came on. You stood up impatiently and said you would wait for us outside. And that the lies of the theater infuriated you, and worse still those of a woman like Manon Lescaut who deceived men so basely. You missed two acts, the best ones. Will you be missing them again, tonight, and when you get off the plane will you be slapping your sword against your boot? *"Ah, mon cousin, excusez-moi! C'est mon premier voyage!"*

It is still early but they keep breaking into the broadcast of the opera. A gap of silence yawns again. Then, suddenly everything is roaring; it's as if one's ears were over a pit full of dying animals. "We are transmitting on a national hookup from the platform at Ezeiza. Here the entire country is waiting for General Perón. Stay tuned, *compañeros!*"

Now the radio says: "This is Eduardo Suárez. I am talking to you from the platform. I bring you the slogan for this great day: 'Peace and Order.' Try to save your energy. There are still many hours to go before the General is with us. We must receive him with all our strength and all the power of our voices."

Another voice chimes in: "Let's liven up the party with some of our own native music. No more speeches." The station broadcasts sambas by Los Chalchaleros. And the bass drums booming in the distance. And the shouts of the vendors. "Get your soda pop, soda pop! Sangwidges, sangwidges! Here's your return pennants! Get your Perón-return pennant! Buy *Horizonte*, the *Horizonte* special number! Get a Perón cap, your T-shirt with The Macho's decal, a flag, the Peronist shicld!"

María Amelia glances at the pages Captain Trafelatti is skimming and sees in passing an adolescent photograph of herself leaning against a rock, a somber, melancholy image bereft of future.

She picks up another copy of *Horizonte* from among the leftovers on the table. She searches and finds herself again, smiling at who knows whom: at the purgatories ahead. And, almost without wanting to, biting her lips, now, she dips into those ancient relics of life. She reads there:

4. HANDBOOK OF OBEDIENCE

> "For a soldier there can be nothing better than another soldier."
> *Juan Perón,*
> *Charter of Grupo de Oficiales Unidos*
> *(an unofficial organization of army*
> *officers to which Perón belonged),*
> Bases, *March, 1943*

The year 1909 was the worst in Juan's life. Between May and June, Don Raimundo Douce, principal of the Colegio Internacional on Cangallo and Ombú, decided that fifth-grade students should study a preparatory course to skip sixth and pass directly into high school.

Juan and Julio, who were the oldest, by far, in the classroom, could not refuse. Since they were too big to sleep in their grandmother's house among all those women, they were allowed to become boarding students and ate and slept at the school. Many of their Sundays were spent alone in the big, empty schoolyards because their grandmother, involved in the household chores, forgot to send for them. They passed the time playing marbles and handball. When night fell, they wandered about the classrooms carrying a kerosene lamp, exciting their imaginations with the huge charts of invertebrates and dicotyledonous plants hanging alongside the blackboards.

Sometimes, Enriqueta, Don Raimundo's niece, took pity on the boys and visited them at the school on Sunday mornings to heat up their soup. Or, after prayers, she would go to the dormitory with them and, sitting next to the door—always on the outside—she read to them Jules Verne's accounts of undersea voyages and expeditions to the Pole, until the boys fell asleep.

Just before Christmas, a painful incident occurred. When vacation began, Juan Domingo said good-bye to his grandmother and aunts, telling them that, as usual, he was going to look for a boat to take him to Patagonia. Two weeks later, a police patrol found him asleep in a shed at the docks. When the sergeant shook him awake, Juan said to him in a piteous tone, "Mamma, mamma! Where has my mother gone?"

They took him back to his grandmother's house on Calle San Martín. He explained that he had missed all the boats and was intending to stay on the docks until March helping the stevedores and sleeping in the shelters for vagrants. His parents sent him a couple of letters from The Future. Juan Domingo did not reply.

Giving in to Aunt Vicenta's supplications, he agreed to go back just for the summer to the bedroom he had had as a child. He washed with creosote and permitted his lice-infested hair to be shaved off. His aunt made the bed with linen sheets. And that first night, seeing him lying half asleep, she felt such a surge of tenderness toward him that she went over to the bed to give him a kiss. Juan pulled away from her, bristling like a hedgehog, slapping at her to drive her away. "No woman is going to kiss me!" he shouted, weeping. "I'll never let a woman touch me!"

Toward the end of January, Grandmother Dominga, after sending Mario Tomás and Juana a reassuring telegram, considered that such a rebellious grandson could be tamed only by strict discipline. She had read a news item in *La Nación* reporting that scholarships for military studies had been in little demand that year and that the army was preparing to recruit reserve officers to fill the vacancies. She found out that a middle-class boy, reared in love of his country, had an excellent chance of winning a scholarship if he had graduated from primary school and could pass a very elementary examination on language, mathematics, and Argentine history. Nothing else would be needed—she was told—except a little pull.

She therefore sought help from those congressmen in the public health field who used to frequent their house at Ramos Mejía, reminding them of her husband Tomás Liberato's services to his country. Somebody promised to intercede for Juan with Julio Cobos Daract, the history professor at the Colegio Militar. One April morning, Doña Dominga walked to Dr. Cobos's office, muddying her skirts along the open trenches of the subway construction, her grandson in tow. They had a long wait. Cobos received her standing up, with indifference, and told her that if this "strapping lad" got good marks on the entrance examination, he could consider the scholarship his.

Juan Domingo came in fifth. In consideration of a contract that obligated him to serve as an officer for a minimum of five years, he would receive tuition and meals gratis plus a stipend of 200 pesos when he graduated as a second lieutenant.

On March 1, 1911, when he entered—knapsack over his shoulder—the rundown building that was used as a barracks, Juan was aware that he was being branded with fire, but with nobody's brand; that he existed not as a person any longer, but as obedience, that his thoughts pulsated in unison with the others. I am no longer just Perón, I am Perón minus something. I will have what others reject; I will convert myself into what others want me to be. I will learn the trade of obedience and of being nobody, so I can practice it on the rest.

Martín López, the official freshman instructor, explained to him that until the end of the year they must consider themselves "featherless bipeds," the lowest form of life in a complex chain. They had to obey the noncommissioned officers, the second-year cadets, and accept all orders, regardless of how improper or cruel. "There can be no discipline without blind obedience," he said. "And without discipline, nobody can succeed."

The following day, when their uniforms were issued, Juan Domingo felt in his flesh the strict truth of those warnings. After reveille and breakfast, while they were waiting in the yard for the instructor, cadets of the upper classes began to lurk about. One of them approached Santiago Trafelatti and ordered him to remove his shoes. "Stand on one leg, like a chicken. Now let's see that heel of yours." Trafelatti felt a vicious stab in the arch of his foot and was unable to hold back a yell. The assailant displayed a bloodied knitting needle. "This mare's hooves are still soft," he said, doubling over with laughter. His companions guffawed. "This mare is going to need a lot of breaking-in to harden those hooves."

They were lined up in the supply room and given their uniforms. Juan Domingo was trying on his cap when one of the second-year cadets came over to him and snatched it away, handing him his own worn-out one in return. Another cadet took his Garibaldi blouse. A third appropriated his trousers and ordered him to put on a pair of threadbare britches redolent of horse manure.

Saúl Pardo, the youngest of the new students, tried to protest. The sergeant who was distributing the uniforms ordered him to step forward and stand at attention, naked. "Don't you like it, featherless biped?"

"No, sergeant," the boy answered.

"Six hours in the coop, then, for being a sissy and a creep. And when you come out, you'd better like it. Understand, chicken?"

An officer standing in the doorway of the supply room looked on approvingly and said, "Mark that lesson down in your memory books. Obedience is obedience. To obey strengthens character and squelches arrogance. Those who enter here are worms. When they leave . . . if they leave . . . they will be men." And he ordered them to line up in the dirt yard within five minutes.

The only way to the yard was through a passage some forty feet long. The second-year cadets had taken up positions there, straps, whips, ropes, and spurs in hand, awaiting the featherless bipeds. Juan decided to cross the line of fire in the first wave. He thought of how the guanacos run zigzagging, stretching, and ducking, to avoid being struck. But no matter which way he went, he got clipped. He felt the end of a horse-whip crack into his kidneys, the teeth of a spur rip the back of his neck, the edge of a strap open a gash in his back. He reached the other end, battered, burning with rage, and with the terrible misgiving that this was to be repeated on a daily basis. A minuscule consolation helped him sleep that night without aches or muscle cramps: he had discovered that while feigning to be only protecting himself from the blows he was able to hit back, stick his fingers into an eye, knock out a tooth with a well-placed head butt.

Eighty bunk beds were jammed into the stable. Juan's was next to one of the doors. Trafelatti slept in the upper. Shortly before retreat, a week after arrival, a group of ten of the featherless had managed to remain hidden in the dormitory while the others underwent ritual punishment outside in the corridor. Trafelatti, who was crouching behind some boxes, saw Juan enter suddenly, pale and panting. He heard a shrill whistling sound that came not from the boy's lungs but from some deeper cavern, and recognized it as the gasping of fear. In the darkness, without abandoning his hiding place, Trafe-latti ventured to ask what had happened. "I knocked out two of Pascal's teeth with my head," gasped Juan, "and he ordered me to come out tonight to fight him."

Pascal was the school's star athlete, a six-foot-six, 250-pound bear whom nobody had been able to stand up to in the gymnasium ring for more than half a minute. His specialty was a left-hand uppercut, "the death blow."

The fight started at midnight under candlelight. A third-year cadet acted as referee. Twenty featherless bipeds stationed around the ring held up the candlesticks. Juan

Domingo was gritting his teeth. Pascal, his lips swollen and numb from the impact of Perón's head, danced in his corner, warming up his imposing musculature.

"Time!" barked the referee.

The giant cocked his right. He moved sluggishly, as though his strength had been left somewhere else. "Don't let him trick you, Perón!" cautioned Trafelatti. Juan Domingo covered his face with his fists and tried to keep out of Pascal's reach but the athlete's infinitely long arms were everywhere, his bulk overflowed the immensity of the ring.

Suddenly, Pascal advanced. He barely grazed his adversary's shoulder but made it look as though he had smashed it. Then he went to work on Juan's face, jabbing first at one temple and then the other, the forehead, the side of the mouth, without straining, at half-power, to the middle, the back, the left, leaving not a rib unpunished. Juan Domingo felt his gums being skinned, a tooth knocked out, as Pascal plowed a furrow in his lips and closed an eye. His temples throbbed like a bird's craw. "Stop the slaughter!" shouted Trafelatti. But Pascal shook his head, still not enough.

He backed into his corner and stayed motionless until he saw that Juan Domingo had caught his breath and was coming toward him, blindly, looking for a clear spot through which to punch. Pascal waited. He danced around Juan, dropping his guard with an animal-like rhythm that flowed not from his feet but his neck. Perón gathered his strength, set himself, and let loose a brutal blow to the solar plexus. He felt his knuckles crunch as though they had hit a stone wall. The giant was pitiless. With infinite contempt, Pascal slowly raised his left. Trafelatti watched the explosion of that Cyclopean fist with horror. Juan Domingo's time stopped. He felt the earth quake and everything go black. Pascal's death blow hit him between the eyes and the world turned over.

Trafelatti washed Perón's wounds and put his battered bones to bed. A medic diagnosed a cracked knuckle and notified him that he was missing three teeth. They bandaged his hands. Not a complaint was heard out of him. On March 12, 1911, at around 3 a.m., Trafelatti sensed cautious movements in the cot below. He looked down and saw Juan Domingo, still weak, disfigured, packing his civilian clothes into his knapsack.

He was leaving. Deserting. Abandoning his scholarship, forfeiting his fate. He was giving up being nobody to become nothing.

"You leaving, Perón?" Trafelatti managed to ask.

At that moment, they heard the footsteps of the patrol nearing the door. It was their last round before reveille.

"Lie down, Perón," whispered Trafelatti. "Get under the covers. If they see you like this, I'll get arrested, too."

Juan Domingo hesitated momentarily and dived into bed with his leggings on.

A man is not what he thinks, but what he does. A country is sometimes what a man left undone. Who would say that afterwards, in the old age of that night of 1911? Trafelatti? Perón? Neither of them remembers it any longer. They confuse words: fate and state, Perón and *nación*. To them, memory, history are tangled into a knot.

After his fight with Cadet Pascal, Juan Domingo devoted himself to fusing his identity with the army's, to ignoring the command of his own desires and obeying the most irrational desires of his superiors. The real universe died. The Milky Way, Grandmother's pendulum clock, the streetcar bell, the memory of the sad Sundays of the boarding school at 2300 Cangullo. Those accidents of reality now became absolutely meaningless to him. Only the army existed. And his persona, watered down with regulations, stood on the shore of the army. To be obeyed, you had to learn to obey. *Yes, lieutenant, yessir, yes, captain, I will obey your abecedesire.*

He cultivated Trafelatti's friendship. On weekdays, they went running together along trails of loose sand or stones to strengthen their legs and competed with one another on the flying rings and horizontal bar to harden their biceps.

Regular visits were paid to the school by Teutonic gentlemen, officers of the German Imperial Staff, who observed the teaching and suggested pedagogical variants. It was rumored that one of those lieutenant colonels earned as much as the Argentine Minister of War merely because he was a Berliner or a Prussian. Juan Domingo was very impressed on seeing, at a distance, the imposing gleam of their pointed steel helmets. He noted a certain scent of aristocracy in their monosyllabic, guttural orders. If authority had a body, the Germans were the mirror that reflected it. In a few weeks the discipline became as rigid as a post. A ritual of behavior was followed even for crossing one's legs. The old French manuals of tactics were replaced by the works of von Clausewitz, von Moltke, and von Schlieffen. When he put on his dress uniform, Juan Domingo's thoughts flowed in another direction. He strutted. He was not just Perón, but Cadet Perón.

Dress, shower, eat, parade, reveille, retreat, mess. Everything preordained. Even hazing came to be a necessary horror. Beat me to harden my body. I am not who I am. Impossible not to be proud of such a difference.

On Saturday afternoons when they were off duty, Juan Domingo and Trafelatti busily pressed their uniforms, powdered their crotches and armpits, and contemplated their reflections in the clubhouse mirror before going out. They took pride in the clothing that molded their figures so elegantly: the hussar jacket with frogs and shoulder braid, red piping along the trouser seams, the French kepi.

They rode a streetcar through dank slums that smelled of manure. Near the San Martín depot, outside a bar with red lanterns and *papier-mâché* flowers, monumental women were always stationed, gulping beer and dishes of polenta. They exposed chalky-white flesh and laughed screechily, toothless, like birds. Corporals and sergeants spoke highly of the skill with which those ladies could detail, in their foreign tongues, for only fifty centavos, the possible requisitions of love. They were off limits to cadets because just being touched by them could produce an incurable disease that only permanganate baths and red-hot needles in the urethra might palliate. Pascal, being invulnerable, had dared to assuage himself with them numerous times and they had even shown him photographs of themselves from the days when they had all their teeth.

Juan Domingo and Trafelatti sought less truculent recreation. They would go to the circus in the neighboring towns, Santos Lugares, Tropezón, and Munro. No sooner did the manager see uniforms than he would offer an impromptu reception. The orchestra of trombones rendered out of tune the overture of the San Lorenzo March. The clowns presented a skit about a French sergeant mocked by the cadets in German: "Pooshopsh nitcht, vee not vondat! Ach, rowss!" The lights went out. The aerialists came on and took a bow. The drums rolled. After a few rheumatic turns on the trapeze, the lights dimmed, and a spotlight picked out the manager. "Ladies and gentlemen, honored cadets, the storm will now be suspended because of the show." The trombones launched into a piece that did its best to suggest a rural air. Two gauchos, knives on high, leaped from the stands into the ring. The spotlight turned red. One of the gauchos insulted the other for no apparent reason. The offended party begged the public's indulgence—the affront to his honor called for revenge. The duel began. The offender dropped his knife. The other gaucho magnanimously permitted him to retrieve it. The action was then repeated the other way around. This time, the bad gaucho slit his rival's throat to the accompaniment of cold-blooded cackles. He then fled, running in place at top speed. Now, the lights suddenly came up. Army detachments appeared on the scene: hundreds of soldiers holding back a pair of spavined old nags. Imagine the gunpowder and the flags, ladies and gentlemen! Imagine the cowardice of this treacherous gaucho, caught by the nation's heroic troops! Look how he begs to be pardoned. Shall we pardon him? Nooooo! To jail, then! The circus is Circe.

Proud of his insignias, his cape, the cockade that crowned his kepi, Juan Domingo applauded. *I am Perón, the cadet. I am the army*. And the show came to an end amidst clouds of blue and white smoke. A wonderful night!

On Sundays, Santiago and he got up late. Dripping brilliantine, they went to show off in the atrium of the church of San Martín. They pretended to be admiring the girls' hats so that they, in turn, could feel free to admire their uniforms. After mass, they strolled around the square and stopped at the pergola where the firemen's band played popular waltzes. They listened, their faces transfixed with expressions of deepest gravity, and then retired, stiffly, one hand resting on the sword hilt, the other clutching the gloves.

In May, 1911, a merciless cold wave struck Buenos Aires. The mornings found the fields white with frost. Stoves had to be installed in the dormitories of the new cadets. All of them had chilblains. Trafelatti's ears blistered. In addition, they were nervous, tense. They were scheduled to parade on July

9 before the strict German inspectors and they were still having trouble with the goose step and change of position with Mauser while marching.

In June, the temperature dropped even lower and the unceasing wind made practice on the rifle range impossible. It was around that time that the second-year cadets thought up a hazing so diabolical that it effaced all memory of former sufferings and left rooted forever the dogma of obedience.

It was Pascal's idea. Until that time, hazing had been a game the routines of which were familiar to the victims. The element of surprise was lacking. From then on it would be a ritual. Violence could be refined to any desired degree. Officers would look the other way. They themselves spoke of hazing as a Darwinian process of natural selection that would keep the army purged of the slothful and the weak. "Thus is *esprit de corps* forged," said the Minister of War at one time, giving to understand that this was also the way the *corps d'esprit* was forged.

As the cold grew more intense, the second-year cadets let the freshmen relax and forget the hazings. Every once in a while, before retreat, they would be ordered to carry boxes of stones around the yard or undress and dress in one minute. But that was all. Life became monotonous. Without fear of the hazings, the rehearsals for the parade lost their edge. On June 28, the temperature hovered at zero all day and the local prophets forecast that it would drop even further by morning. Pascal decided that the moment was ripe for the ritual.

The freshmen had supper at eight o'clock, played cards, and retired at ten. Juan Domingo and Trafelatti went to look for the noncommissioned officer from Ramallo who taught them boxing. Inexplicably, he was not there. Around two o'clock in the morning, the second-year cadets, wearing fatigues and spurs, burst into the freshmen's stable. Everything happened at once. They turned on the lights, ripped off the blankets, and ordered them to line up naked beside their cots.

"Cadets fall out to the yard, out to the yard," Pascal shouted. "We will now give you fifteen minutes of horsemanship."

Stunned, Trafelatti reached for a blanket with which to cover himself before going out into the cold. He was caught. One of the older cadets who had stayed back considered the small, frail body, and took pity on him. "Put on your under-shirt and shorts. Get going, hurry!"

Outside, the cold split the air. The freshmen tried to evade the freezing pavingstones, which was like stepping on hot coals, by standing in the shadow of the passageway. A few had managed to throw blankets over their shoulders, others wore woolen underdrawers. They were all shivering, helpless, their noses dripping.

A spokesman asked for a truce. "Why not wait until after the pledge of allegiance? We're going to catch a pneumonia, sir. Might be, we could even have a disaster. We're not arguing about the order. We will obey it. But we would like it put off for another time . . ."

Pascal let out a guffaw. "The cadet's scared, is he? Are you feeling chilly, poor little fellow? Jump, soldier, jump and learn what courage is."

A fat lummox with a split eyebrow, whose toadying of Pascal knew no bounds, announced that the featherless bipeds would be graduated that night to quadrupeds.

"I want you in formation, as for parade. On four feet. A superior will then mount each one. You will walk, trot, and gallop. Nobody better lay down on the job or try any tricks. Anybody who collapses, fall out in the passageway. I give you one minute to rest and then you start all over at zero. Have you got it?"

Juan Domingo was a little over fifteen years old at the time and weighed less than 125 pounds. He managed to furtively kick a blanket into the passageway, and although he was finally able to cover himself with it, his testicles were icy and aching. Hidden behind a pillar, he tried to make himself invisible. He sensed that Pascal was watching him. He could see him adjust his spurs, button his overcoat collar, and tighten the belt. He felt him approach, voluminous, like a bear.

"Take off the blanket, Perón. I want to ride you bareback."

Trafelatti also heard Pascal's order. He saw Juan Domingo obey unresisting and incredulous, like everybody else. He was secretly grateful that the man's bulk had stopped at Perón before reaching him. He's going to break his spine, he said to himself, knowing that he would never forget having had the thought.

They sent the freshmen to form separate lines ten feet

apart. The cadets who were going to ride fell in behind each line.

"Reins!" shouted the fat boy.

Pascal forced an iron bit with a braided rope at either end between Juan Domingo's teeth.

"Featherless bipeds on all fours . . . hutt!" The crust of ice that covered the yard splintered. "Cadets, mount! Forward at a walk . . . hutt!"

Juan Domingo closed his eyes. The mass of the torturer on his back was incredible. He felt the weight of the entire planet bending him in two. The palms of his hands passed over a knife-edge of ice, the cold anesthetizing the bloody cut almost immediately. Pascal's spurs jammed into his kidneys. There was a smell of hay and horses. He moved forward.

"I must obey, I must obey!" he repeated. "I'm a man. I can do more than I can do."

Pascal urged him on with a quirt. "Colt, let's trot!" And Perón, forcing himself to crawl on, kept saying to himself, "I'm a man. Here I go." He lost his breath for a moment. Next to him, the other bipeds, in a pack, were swirling around him, gasping. That gave him heart. "I won't give up! You won't make me desert, you son of a whore! Give an order. I'll obey. Am I a horse? Yessir, I'm a horse. Whatever you want me to be." A strap slashed at his legs, the insatiable spurs dug into his buttocks. "I'm going ahead. Here I come!"

He never knew when the torturer let up on him. Shouts and whistle blasts could be heard. Somebody was crying. The boots of the guards echoed in the passageway. The last that Juan Domingo saw were bloodied sheets of ice, in which his body gradually fell asleep.

The freshmen did not appear at reveille the next day. Their knees were raw flesh. Juan Domingo's elbows were infected. Foul-looking sores appeared on his hips. He fell ill with fever. One day went by, and another. Santiago Trafelatti resumed rehearsals for the pledge of allegiance but he, Perón, could not. His convalescence lasted longer than anybody else's.

Colonel Gutiérrez, the director of the Colegio, ordered an immediate investigation but since the freshmen refused to break the code of silence, the vicious cavalcade of June 29 went unpunished and, hence, unremembered. Like the rest, Cadet Pascal had to take his turn at guard duty in the infirmary. He walked the corridors, indifferently, taking no notice of anybody. All were now equal in his eyes, all bore his cattle brand.

The more Juan Domingo became nothingness of nothing, the more the Argentine Army became his universe, his reality, the capsule of his ego. It was the future, the only possible future; it was his body, now tattooed by obedience, now inconceivable out of uniform; and since he had to suppress his past, the army completely took up the place of the past.

The freshmen pledged allegiance to the flag on July 9, and paraded, somewhat battered but nonetheless proudly, before the German inspectors. Months of routine followed. Required to choose a service, Juan Domingo and Trafelatti decided on the infantry, to become barracks soldiers, teachers of the rank and file. They figured that the battles of the future would be fought not on horseback but hand-to-hand, after interminably long marches.

They were subjected to forty-day campaigns in the environs of Córdoba and to the north of Concordia, Entre Ríos. They were convinced that the fatherland lay within them alone. The miracle of *esprit de corps* was being consummated. For a soldier there was nothing better than another soldier.

During those months, Perón began practicing his new soldier's signature. He wrote simply Juan Perón, slanting the J to the left and the P to the right, like two trees blown by contrary winds.

Finally, on December 19, 1913, he received his first-lieutenant's saber. Of the 110 cadets who were graduated, Juan Domingo came out in the middle sector, *uomo qualunque*, in 43rd place, the number of the year in which everything would begin for him. He was assigned to the Twenty-second Infantry Regiment, in Paraná. Trafelatti, who wound up left back, found his desired destiny in Tucumán.

That final afternoon was unbearably hot. Juan Domingo, sweating in his dress uniform, returned to Grandmother Dominga's house on the train that ran though the sun-scorched suburbs. One of his comrades, Saúl S. Pardo, had unexpectedly given him an album of photographs and newspaper clippings. Juan Domingo discovered his own boyish face of 1911 there, saw Pascal raising the flag, and Pardo's quizzical expression. He paused at the last of the clippings:

LA ACCIÓN, PARANÁ, DECEMBER 10, 1913

Disastrous End to Maneuvers

Cadets of the Colegio Militar, who bivouacked for a month on the fields of Sr. Soler to the north of Concordia, returned yesterday to Buenos Aires in a physical condition that provoked the disapproval of their parents. In July of 1911, various complaints were brought to the attention of the authorities regarding mistreatment of this same class of cadets at the hands of upperclassmen. Those responsible for the illtreatment now appear to have been high-ranking officers.

Letters to this newspaper, whose signatures were requested withheld, assure that immediately following war games between blue and red forces, all of which were successfully concluded on the 3rd of this month, the infantry section broke camp in Ayuí and prepared to bivouac on the coast of Yuquén Chico, after which they would continue on to Jubileo station. The assistant director of the Colegio, Colonel Agustín P. Justo, ordered that the route be covered on foot, despite the fact that the day promised to be intensely hot and oppressive. The infantrymen marched over sandy terrain and many of them, unable to withstand the ordeal, fell along the way with sunstroke as a result of which trucks and cars of the Army Sanitary Corps had to come to their rescue . . .

A bottle of sparkling cider was uncorked at the grandmother's house, and Aunt Vicenta delivered an impromptu speech praying to God to bless the fortunes of the brand-new officer. The following morning, cousin María Amelia supplemented the album with another clipping:

LA RAZÓN, BUENOS AIRES, DECEMBER 18, 1913

Annual Celebration of the Colegio de San Martín

Equal or, perhaps, even greater luster was attained (etc.) . . . After the drum roll and a brief pause, Señorita Mercedes Pujato Crespo, President of the Asociación Pro Patria, spoke in highly laudatory terms of the Argentine Army, immediately following which she pinned the coveted gold medal on the breast of the outstanding student of the year, Sergeant Eduardo Pascal Malmierca . . .

A telegram from Don Mario Tomás urging him to come at once to Camarones dampened Juan Domingo's celebration. In 1910, his father had inherited the post of justice of the peace. For a number of months, he made the daily trip between The Future and Camarones. Then, tired out, he left the farm in the care of Doña Juana and Benjamín Gómez, and installed himself in the little sheet-metal cabin used by the people's magistrates as a courtroom.

In October, 1912, with no explanation, he gave up The Future, the joys of calligraphy, everything. He decided to look for another tract of land in the Patagonian wasteland and settle it alone, if possible. He dreamed of a city with minarets, empty streets, and only one inhabitant. He then called upon Juan Domingo to come and give his approval to the dream.

Mario Tomás waited for his son near the docks with a saddled percheron. Sadness engulfed them as they embraced, as if the echo of some misfortune had brought a lump to their throats that would remain there always. As they rode toward The Future, the father scarcely spoke. He held his body erect in the saddle, but let his head hang. He made a vague reference to sleep. It seemed to Juan Domingo that rather than seeking a new life, his father was inventing a city in which all his past lives would be lost.

He found the farm neglected, as though awaiting abandonment. The sheep were going through another mange epidemic and his mother had delayed the shearing in the vain hope of curing them. The rusting corrugated walls of the house went unrepaired. Even Mario Avelino, who used to perfume himself with jasmine toilet water in anticipation of his brother's visits, greeted him absently, at a distance. His mother said that her first-born had spent so much time among the guanacos that he had changed into an animal of the wild.

Juan Domingo advised them to sell The Future before the buildings collapsed. He had heard (he told them) of a high stony plateau to the west of Camarones with springs belonging to no one. If the streams were channeled into irrigation canals, that soil might become fertile.

Somebody had named it Sierra Cuadrada, after a medieval utopia. Why not try their luck there?

"Sounds like a good place for a man alone," considered the father.

"He's taken it into his head to build a city for one man alone," the mother said.

"Maybe it would be better to found three cities, papa," Juan Domingo encouraged him. "Three cities for three people."

"The terrain should be explored first. I'll start out tomorrow," the father announced, taking off his boots and getting into bed with his clothes on.

At daybreak, he drank several matés, made a package of biscuits, and selected a spare horse. He wanted no one to go with him.

"Are you sure of what you're doing?" the younger son insisted.

"I was sure about only one thing in my life and I have lost that confidence. Let me go, now. I am commencing a pilgrimage of penitence."

Don Mario Tomás was lost for one hundred days. When he returned in April, he said that he had found the minarets of a sacred city in the midst of the wilderness, after crossing the Chico River and some salt hills. He wanted to leave his bones on those pampas. He sold The Future to a peon, loaded the wagons, sent Benjamín Gómez off with the herds, and waited for the rains to let up. He then set out to the coast for good, even poorer than when he had arrived.

Juan Domingo waited only a couple of weeks for him. Taking advantage of his officer's rank he boarded a navy freighter in Camarones and rounded Tierra del Fuego. He saw a few icebergs at a distance and heard the ice groaning in the straits. Listening to talk of the Amundsen and Scott expeditions to the South Pole, he too was enticed by the idea of such an adventure. He learned that the two men had set out at the same time from the Ross glaciers in the spring of 1911. Scott, the Englishman, depended on ponies, which didn't work out. Amundsen used dogs. However, they both reached the goal on foot. Scott, slowed down for more than a month by adverse winds, found on his arrival a sarcastic little message from the victor beside the hated Norwegian flag.

On the freighter, Perón saw some of the photographs taken by Herbert Ponting and Lieutenant Henry Bowers before misfortune finished them all. He saw the silhouette of the sailing ship *Terra Nova* on the rim of a frozen channel and the terrifying domes of ice in the twilight, discovered death, disoriented, too, by the whiteness of the empty sky, upon the faces of Scott and his four companions.

They made it on foot, Perón reflected. Pure will power allowed them to reach a limit of endurance never attained by an Argentine infantryman. Couldn't I be the first to unfurl the name of Perón there and save my father from his penitence?

Sailing through the frozen Antarctic seas, he dreamed of the Pole. He imagined it as a volcano rising behind a chain of glaciers. He saw himself forging across the mountains of snow, conquering the icy cordillera. He walked and walked, between stiffened froth, climbed down the cadavers of icebergs, was speared by stalactites. But he made headway. Finally, bloodied, invincible, he saw the gates of his goal, the volcano in the distance. But his mother was waiting there and would not let him pass. Every time the dream recurred, his mother planted herself in the same spot, her hair loose, a man's poncho over her house dress.

On February 12, 1914, Juan wrote to Pardo:

Lieutenant, I do not want to delay any longer in telling you that I took ship and wandered around our Fuegonian channels. You should see for yourself how sensational it is. Some fellows on the boat showed me photographs from the time when Scott came to those lands and died. They tell me that Amundsen, Scott's rival, was in Buenos Aires not long ago. It seems to me that we, as good Argentine infantrymen, ought to prepare such an expedition. What do you think, kid?

The family did fine in Camarones. We had an excellent shearing. My parents send you special regards. My best wishes to your family, with cordial regards, Juan Perón.

He mailed it from the Twelfth Regiment in Paraná, where he was instructor of troops. Soon, Archduke Francis Ferdinand was to die in Sarajevo. The Great War was preparing to smear history with blood. Juan Domingo was not aware of it, actually, until quite a bit later.

He allowed himself to become swaddled in years of nonthought. He was absorbed in outdoor sports, the body's demands, what he was to call "the contradictions of the musculature." He would feel his tendons pulling in all directions, grinding him up as if they were other bodies twisted in endless struggle, themselves giving commands and obeying them. Sometimes, he would sink into periods of indifference, of lassitude, of pure nothingness. Even at those times, he engaged in all types of sports, soccer, boxing, and blossomed as a fencer.

The inevitable happened. People saw him in Villa Guillermina and in Tucumán, 300 miles away, at the same hour. He became unable to locate a place to which he had to go. And, at the same time, places crossed his path along the way to which he would never have gone. Also, it took him a long time to find out the explanation for those changes. He was a little more than twenty years old and not overly concerned about the duplicity of fortune or of history. He did not know that a man whose spaces have been shifted around may lose his center of gravity at any moment.

9

THE HOUR OF THE SWORD

A leader of armies is not made by decree. A leader is born anointed with the oil of Samuel.

Alfred von Schlieffen,
quoted by Wilhelm Groener,
in The Testament of
Count von Schlieffen, *1926.*

Leaders are born, not made . . . and he who is born with enough of Samuel's oil, needs little more to become a leader.

Juan Perón,
Conducción Política, *1951.*

This cannot be the hand of chance. What bodily instincts have been triggered, what forebodings, to make all my illnesses come together just at this time, two days before my return to Buenos Aires, to wake me. They are trying to tell me something. Perhaps the approaching struggle worries them. I have been leading armies from afar for eighteen years. I don't even know what surprises the battle fronts may hold in store. Don't make my vacillations public, file them away so that my enemy may never know of them.

At 4:30 in the morning, I had cramps and shortness of breath. I woke up sweating. López brought me a tranquilizer. Deceits of the body, General. Pay them no mind. You look as strong as a stallion. Sleep them off, he told me.

But he couldn't. His heart was seething. I felt a stabbing pain. I wanted to go to the toilet. When I sat on the bed, my legs creaked. They'd turned to ice. López! I called, help me go piss. He carried me on his shoulders. See, how well you walk. Like a youngster! he kept reassuring me. In the toilet, all I could produce were a few miserable drops. My bladder was distended, my prostate was hurting, my body was full of urine. But nothing doing, just a few lousy drops.

And it's June 18, already. In a few hours, I'll be leaving all this. Dawn is breaking. At least, I have the consolation of knowing that what's been lived out here will remain here. Time cannot rot away memories. They can be taken along no matter where one goes, under foot, enfolded in the depths of the body. I wonder if the same could be done with places. What do you think, López? Imagine being able to look out of the window in Buenos Aires and have Madrid there, too, its cool, dry climate, the dove cotes, the dogs racing around under the ash trees. Ah, that would be another story! Just think of it! To be able to step out of the house I have on Vicente López into the shade of the Paseo del Prado, where I enjoy walking so much. If Madrid were there, what a different feeling I would have about leaving!

Now, hearing the sun breathe outdoors, the General feels his ailments retreating. All at once, he sees the huddled walnut trees spreading their plumage. Relieved, he goes out for a stroll in the garden, López at his side. Absently, he listens to the litany of gossip. Cámpora spent the night at a flamenco show and handed out carnations to the dancers. He had a barbecue breakfast at three in the morning at Tranquilino's. They must be getting him out of bed right now to attend that industrial exhibition. Enough, man! I don't want to hear anymore. Let's not waste our time on such tripe.

The sun, swelling in a fury of heat, suddenly bears down upon Perón, dazing him. Listen, López . . . the summer steam! Look at it swirl among the plants. And that noise! Like an army of ants. Let's go back to the restfulness of the house.

Since no visits were scheduled for this Monday and the servants were airing the rooms downstairs, the General suggested going right up to the sanctum and concentrating on the Memoirs this morning. How much further do we have to go, López? What period are we in now? I'd like to leave here without that hanging over me. And you're wearing me out, man. It's going very slowly.

They are startled at the foot of the stairs by the outburst of clocks striking eight. Isabel, still in her dressing gown, her hair in curlers, is busy between the bedrooms and the attic, a convoy of chambermaids trailing after her. She has already packed the blankets in the trunks but the dishes still remain to be done. My goodness, after that brawl yesterday, it's been impossible to catch up with things. The last one to leave was Pilarica Franco, and that must have been close to midnight. What a tumult! Daniel! Take it easy going up the stairs. Be careful with the General. Don't let him lose his breath. Where are you headed for, man? Up to the sanctum, again? What's so special about the dark? Why not stay down here! It's nice and cool in the bedrooms.

On the top landing, the General steps into eddies of wind that are always swirling around up there. They have been trying to discover for some time from where those currents are coming, whether from the cooling chamber that maintains the sepulcher at a constant temperature or from the being who lies above and who, when she sighs, and when she emits her pitiful non-sighs in the middle of the night, leaves trails like bubbles. Flies of the chill, the General calls them.

Those drafts. Do you feel them, López? the General asks. The house is getting unfriendly toward us, now. Just like dogs do, barking when the master leaves them.

Finally, they reach the sanctum. The secretary inserts pages from one binder into another, as though shuffling cards. If the story is moved from here to there, or if it doesn't go in at all, the effect won't be changed.

Let's see what you've done, López, the General says. He reaches for a lap robe and covers his legs. Spell me with the reading. I must rest my eyes and voice. Where were we?

Sir, at a question. Whether to take out your reflections on military life or to leave them in as they stand. They are lengthy. And technical. Some readers are apt to go to sleep on us along the way.

Is that what you're thinking, López? That I should leave out the very seedbed of my doctrine? Everything generates from that, from what I say about the art of war. How can you not see that? The rest isn't me. That's what Perón comes out of; he is the *troupier*, the pedagogue of leadership, the palace strategist. My wisdom is no more than that of the leader. And you intend that I shouldn't say so. That I should go jumping after the anecdotes like a monkey from branch to branch. Absolutely not! I don't give a damn about the readers. Let them fall asleep! Let them crawl into their hothouses and close their ears! I want that absolutely clear. I will not go one step further without explaining what kind of a soldier I have been. Do you understand?

I understand. López Rega reads:

> *Every soldier must realize that his trade is to handle men. To lead. Leadership is an art. As such it has theory which is the lifeless aspect of art. What is vital is the artist. Anybody can paint a picture or carve a statue, but a Pietà like Michelangelo's or a Supper like Leonardo's wouldn't exist without them. Anybody is capable of leading an army, but if you want battle masterpieces like Alexander the Great's or Napoleon's, you must look for a leader like them, anointed with the sacred oil of Samuel. A leader is not made by decree. He is born. Like the true artists.*

(Those are the same words we have already used many times, General. That's why I was in doubt. We wrote them here in that first book. Just let me see the exact title. Aha! "World War, 1914. Operations in East Prussia and Galicia, Tannenberg, Masurian Lakes, Lemberg. Strategic Studies." Not a comma changed. After that they appear in all your speeches and classes on leadership, in the identical form. And in your statements to the press. But somebody always tracked us down. One individual said that, in the beginning, when Perón quoted Napoleon and von Schlieffen, he would grant them their quotation marks, footnotes, and bibliographical entries. And that later on we skipped those niceties and just appropriated whatever famous sayings we had at hand. I think it's time we changed and found different words for the same idea. We should be more nationalistic. Sponsor our own. Drop Leonardo and talk about Quinquela.

The General is vehemently opposed: The Argentines don't know who Schlieffen is, López, and as time passes they'll forget what Napoleon said or didn't say. They'll ask, Such-and-such a phrase? Oh, that's the General's! And that'll be the end of it. Stop worrying, man! Nobody will dare to smear me, not even with accusations of plagiarism. My poor country doesn't have anything but Perón. I'm what they've got, and that's that. I'm Providence, the Eternal Father. Forget that nonsense, López. Keep going.)

In the gamut of my ambitions, priority has always gone to doing good, and as part of that, for the sake of those who need it most. I have never been able to conceive of love of country apart from that human concept, just as I cannot understand, either, how a country can be great with an unhappy population. I prefer a small country of happy people to a big country with miserable people. I can understand those who work for themselves. What is more, I can justify them. It seems fair to me that they should receive the material benefit of their efforts. But I can understand much better those who work for their fellow men without expecting anything in return.

(Perón and Jesus Christ, one and the same heart, López discovers. It seems enlightened to me. A perfect cellular resonance. Removing the lap robe, the General sighs, It's my Sermon on the Mount, López. My Beatitudes.)

It is necessary to build men first, good men, and then train them. The evil ones shouldn't be taught at all. Otherwise, only misfortunes will come about.

When I retrace the path my life has taken, I regret nothing. I have no reason to. I could always sleep peacefully. I have been calumniated, accused of the foulest offenses. They even wanted to kill me. None of it has disturbed me, nor do I care, because I answer only to my conscience and I am at peace with it.

On January 16, 1920, I was assigned to the Noncommissioned Officers' School. The first thing I did was to organize a gymnastics team and enter it in the town competitions. My boys got bored with winning all the time. I had graduated from the YMCA as a physical education teacher. I took a special course in education so I would be able to transmit my knowledge more effectively.

I also introduced basketball among the noncoms but I pride myself most on having inculcated in them the concept of saving. At the beginning of the month, I would deduct between five and ten pesos from their pay. And when they went on leave I limited the amount they could spend. Nobody spoke of pensions or social security at that time, but those ideas were already buzzing around in my head.

My only vice was cigarettes and I haven't been able to shake the habit to this day. I smoked Caftán, Condal, whatever. I even tried smoking Ombú. What they were made of, I don't know. But I can remember that whenever my lungs heard the word "Ombú" they tried to sneak off.

I can boast of having been a good company commander. Of the 110 men under me, I made a mayor of Buenos Aires out of one, and ministers and ambassadors of others. All were humble but loyal. They would have killed for me.

Those were chaotic times of profound ideological change. The floods of immigrants had abated but through their Span-italian and never-failing spaghetti-talk on Sundays, we began to absorb the foreign influence. Buenos Aires, however, was a mass of tenements. Shop clerks, seamstresses, and teachers earned barely enough for their food. Factories paid apprentices 20 pesos a month and a pair of cheap shoes cost 15.

Important visitors were, of course, shown a different city. Prince Humbert of Savoy, the Maharajah of Kapurtala, and the Prince of Wales, who arrived at almost the same time during the Alvear administration, saw nothing but luxurious mansions. Nobody took them to the auctions of women the Russians conducted in port brothels. I myself saw a fifteen-year-old Polish girl—who had been brought there on the false promise of marriage—sold for 200 pesos and a silver bracelet. Instead of being shown the slaughterhouses reeking of misery, the princes were taken to see the champion bulls of La Rural that shit 18-carat-gold turds.

One event is stamped in my mind forever: the speech given by Leopoldo Lugones in Lima at the centennial celebration of the Battle of Ayacucho. He touched off a tremendous row between the liberals and upper-class snobs who disapproved of his admiration for Mussolini, but he gave us young officers a lot to think about. We began to realize that the army should be the nation's compass.

The politicians were corrupt and, fortunately, had no contact with us. To shield us from corruption, General Augustín P. Justo, the Minister of War, requested President Alvear to issue a decree forbidding soldiers to belong to political parties. Our world was the army post, but the fatherland's symbols were inside it, and it was our duty to protect them.

*Leopoldo Lugones expressed those ideas wonderfully. In
Lima, he said:*

(It really made me sweat to dig up that speech, General. I had to
go looking for it at the Avenida Calvo Sotelo library. But here are
the lines you wanted:)

*"For the good of the world, the hour of the sword has struck
once more. Pacifism, collectivism, democracy are synonyms for
the same job held open by fate for the predestined chief, that
is to say, he who gives the orders because it is his right as the
foremost, with or without sanction of law, since he, as the
expression of power, merges with its will."*

(Read that again, López. It's worth it. That was the first time a
civilian dignitary ever stood up to say to us: Soldiers, take power.
It's yours, by your very nature. Others did, later on, in recent
years. But these are not illustrious forebears, or anything like it.
They are scoundrels, pawns of the foreign companies. There's
nothing left but shreds of the glorious army. Look at the generals.
They're scared. They all tremble when they hear my name. They
took away my rank, my uniform, and now they don't know what to
think up to keep me from taking revenge. They ask me, Would you
like to have your back pay, General? Would you like a statue in
Campo de Mayo? They're poor slobs afraid I'll leave them without
their teat. All they care about is their teat, the easy life, their
benefits. I know them all too well. I had to give a tranquilizer to
one who came around. Man, I told him, I won't do anything against
you. If your conscience is bothering you because you did something
wrong, that's not my problem.
(They've gotten into bad habits. All they care about is feathering
their nests. And to boot, they aren't even grateful. Look what they
did to poor Lugones. An honorable civilian, a true defender of the
people. He spent five years banging on the doors of the military.
Take power! he preached. Take power, now! And when we finally
did in 1930, what did they give him in return? A teacher's job. That
was a mockery. Lugones went into a decline. I tried to talk to him
at the Military Circle where we used to fence. I found him very
remote. He was in a state of anxiety for personal reasons I knew
nothing about. He was polite. We made an appointment, but the

next day he sent me a note postponing it. From then on, every time I ran into him, he would say, Later on, Perón, later on. I understood . . . he meant never. His troubles had made him unapproachable. Not long after, he committed suicide at an inn on the Tigre . . . Enough of that. Let's get back to the other part of the Lima speech.)

The nineteenth-century constitutional system is obsolete . . .

(Exactly. What I said in my message to Congress in '48: that the Argentine Constitution was a museum piece. Lugones was right. It was impossible to go on abiding by a law out of the horse-and-buggy era . . .)

> *The army is the last aristocracy, that is to say, the last possibility we have for hierarchical organization amidst demagogic dissolution. At this moment in history, military virtue alone expresses the higher life of beauty, hope, and strength.*
>
> *I was one of the few officers who appreciated Lugones's project in its full magnitude. But I was only a first lieutenant at the time. What could I do? The power was too far removed from me. All I looked forward to was a diploma from the War Academy and marrying a respectable girl acceptable to my superiors.*
>
> *In mid-1925, after I had spent a few months recruiting noncommissioned officer candidates in Santiago del Estero, I applied for assignment to the War Academy. Once again, I was following in the footsteps of my mentor, Major Descalzo, who had been given the chair of "Organization" there. I passed the examination with honors. When I was admitted, I felt that life was beginning all over again . . . that living only once is not to have lived at all. The only way to feel life is to start living it without waiting for it to end. Always starting afresh.*

(Calm down, López. Read without fidgeting so much. What are you looking for in those photographs, man? Why are you flipping all those pages? They are blank spaces, General. The Memoirs you condemned to purgatory. Look at this: Classroom notes, 1926. And this: a label from a pack of Combinados Mezcla cigarettes, the brand you actually smoked. And these blurred accounts: rent receipts for lodgings you took with six other officers. Look at the photographs: they're fogged with a dark shadow. You're smiling at the camera but yet you look like you're slipping away. It's fading, going more and more sepia. I've also cut reminiscences that were detrimental to you. Look here: in the summer of 1925. You arrived at the family farm in Sierra Cuadrada of Chubut. Your father was already looking gaunt and his only amusement was his pack of grandchildren. Mario Avelino had married Eufemia Jáuregui. They had four children. The second, Tomás Domingo, got the name that was rightfully mine. I could see that my father was suffering from a fatal disease. I finally managed to get him to Buenos Aires with me to see doctors. Have a look at this photograph, General. See the barren plateau where you lived, between dark stone pyramids. And here the maze of irrigation canals your mother was digging with the help of the peons. And here is the entrance with the sign "La Porteña." Can you see the memory? I see it all, Lopez, as if it were today.

(After the Buenos Aires doctors examined your father, they wouldn't let him return. He was being consumed by arteriosclerosis. The poor old man could hardly walk. We had to buy a small house on Calle Lobos near the corner of San Pedrito, south of the Flores section, where we moved in with Doña Juana. She returned to Chubut for the shearing, General. For only three weeks. And then, how devotedly she kept at my old father's bedside! We knew there was no hope. Don Mario Tomás's body, which we used to look upon as eternal, shrank and faded.

(That was when you met Potota. Do you remember how it came about? Of course not! It was so long ago. Probably at a family dance in Palermo. Let's see, now. It was, I think, at a party at the Army Club. I hear the music, a waltz. I danced with María Tizón, Potota's sister. And then with her. We talked about movies. I heard her play the guitar.

(Her name was Aurelia, General. She was the sixth daughter of Tomasa Erostarbe and Cipriano Tizón. He had a photography shop and belonged to the Radical Civic Union. She kept a close eye on her daughters. Potota was the shortest. She had a strange, low-pitched, but very musical, voice. Slightly husky, like Eva's . . . Stop laying out my remembrances for me, López. Shut up! You read my life story as if it were a department store inventory. I can't help it, General. It's because of the blanks you want left in the

Memoirs. Do you feel the blankness? Can you smell the silences? Aha, López. That's it. No more interruptions. Have Isabel notify us when she's serving lunch. Go on with the authentic Memoirs.

My body grew flabby because of the sedentary life my studies forced me into. I got fat, my weight going as high as 200 pounds. Well into 1927, General Alexis von Schwartz arrived at the War Academy. He was a brilliant professor of military fortifications who had served in the Imperial Russian Army. I used to stroll around Palermo with him after class discussing Moltke, Jomini, Clausewitz, and other military theoreticians. He would always say to me as we parted, "None is as great as Count Schlieffen."

It wasn't so easy to find books by Schlieffen in those days. Articles of his that piqued my curiosity appeared occasionally in the journal Revista Militar. *Schwartz lent me a work by him in Italian on the battle of Cannae. I devoured it in one night.*

At the outset, I was dismayed by the almost unending number of strategic plans Schlieffen devised in the course of his life. Then, I was intrigued by the fact that one plan often conflicted with another he had prepared for the same campaign. This can't be accidental, I thought. It was the product of an original concept of war. I began to recognize Schlieffen as a genius, that he was misunderstood even after his death.

Let's see. Year after year, even though circumstances remained the same, Schlieffen organized concentrations of forces at points he had previously left unprotected. He would lay out a strategy, defend it as impregnable, and almost immediately design a new one to demolish the first. At the same time, he required his officers to prepare a battle plan A, and a plan B as well that contradicted the first but was also perfect. Of what use to him were these apparent paradoxes? Ah, therein lay the secret of his greatness! Schlieffen proved to be disconcerting even in dogmas as irrefutable as that which called for defeat of one enemy before turning your forces against another. He counseled fighting simultaneously on all fronts. His first commandment was to take the offensive. To attack, always attack. Even when outnumbered.

Almost everything I now know I learned then. I applied it to politics. Clausewitz believed that war was an extension of pol-

itics by other means. I believe that things happen the other way around; that politics is an extension of war by other means, but using the same tactics. Years later if I was called to task for an irritating statement, I was able to reply, in surprise: How can that be? I said quite the contrary on such-and-such an occasion. Nobody can hold me responsible for a single idea that doesn't have its appropriate opposite. I have always maintained two attitudes, two or more plans, two or more theoretical lines with respect to the Church, the army, oil, land reform, urban guerrillas, freedom of the press. Because of my natural antipathy to sectarianism of any kind and because I am a leader. I cannot go about measuring things with the yardstick of a single dogma. That was Schlieffen's best lesson.

I have kept all interpretations of existing conditions in my files, those to be seen in positive and those in negative, because sooner or later either may be useful to me. Of course, this game of opposites must not be applied indiscriminately, but with consideration for very definite lines of thought from which the leader must never stray, under any conditions. Mine may be summed up in three apothegms: political sovereignty, economic independence, and social justice. That neither the rich nor the poor shall lack for anything. That there will be equal opportunity for all.

At the darkest moments of my life, when my adversaries were attacking me most viciously, trusting in the superiority of their forces, I responded with an attack. Attack, I said to myself. And I thought of Schlieffen. Attack, for strength still remains.

The War Academy wasn't all reading. They also sent us on long reconnaissance marches over rugged terrain and to do surveying on the border. Those trips to the Andes, between Mendoza and Neuquen, left my eyes hungry for nature. I was not Mohammed but the mountain came to me. The mountain was converging upon my destiny.

I was close to my thirty-third birthday, the age at which men look most deeply into themselves. Certain things were already clear. My country was my life, and the army the path by which I could serve it. The most enlightened of the officers were seeking to deliver Argentina from its agricultural destiny and demanded that President Alvear organize national indus-

tries administered by the armed forces, beginning with the steel industry.

Under Agustín P. Justo, the army had become a very important power factor. It was the army that pulled the chestnuts out of the fire every time there was an outbreak in the provinces, that put down the attacks on private property in the Santa Fe Chaco and on the wool ranches of Santa Cruz. And what did we get for our pains? Crumbs! It was only as a result of Justo's stubbornness that the military budget was raised somewhat. A lieutenant colonel was killed by anarchists and they took care of his widow with a telegram of condolence.

We were fed up with words. Those were times of violent change. Nobody but us was putting forward a plan for a new nation. And nobody but us could carry it out. I felt that the healthy forces of the country would come knocking at the doors of the military. And that we should be getting ready.

I recall the day Yrigoyen was elected President for his second term. It was an afternoon in April. The rainy season was beginning. I was at Lieutenant Descalzo's house looking down at the street from the balcony, at the people hurrying, the little cars, the yellow trees.

I sensed terrible sadness in the offing for the fatherland. I said to my mentor: "This country is not going to be the same after Doctor Alvear is gone. Politicians are a dying species. Yrigoyen is taking over the government, but we military will hold the power." Descalzo looked at me in surprise. "Do you want the power, Perón?" And I replied: "It's not a matter of wanting or not wanting. It's a matter of fate."

When the loneliness of my studies at the War Academy became too much for me, I began to look for a respectable girl of good family who was sensitive, with social graces. I found those qualities in Aurelia Tizón, who was called Potota, "precious" in baby talk. She was a normal-school teacher and an amateur painter and musician. She played the guitar and accordion very charmingly and recited poetry with remarkable expressiveness. I recognized immediately that her temperament and mine were very much in tune. She encouraged me in my studies and very tactfully always took a back seat. Her family had excellent connections with the Radical Party, and so, Potota combined expedience and attractiveness. I asked for

her hand in 1928. We planned to be married in October but my
father's arteriosclerosis worsened and we lost the poor old man
on November 10th. He faded away gradually and died quietly.

We postponed the wedding until January because of the
period of mourning. I never had a good memory for domestic
details, which actually serve as food for gossip rather than to
provide real understanding about people. And about Potota I
would like to recall only one thing: the unselfish love she
showed for me during nearly ten years of marriage.

(We haven't assigned the wife any age. López interrupts the
reading in the sanctum, breathing on his glasses to clear them but
succeeding only in clouding them up again. Adolescent? Preado-
lescent—a Lolita? I have a stack of contradictory dates here, General. Some people say she wasn't quite twenty when she married,
others say not seventeen. A Radical leader in Palermo, Julián Sancerni, lent me these photos. Take a look at them: 1912. This is of
your wife as a child. Sancerni is standing on the left, wearing
a badge. She is hidden in the middle row, sixth from the right, in a
gray dress with a white collar. Even at that age, she already had a
Mona Lisa smile and—do you realize—the reflection of the moon
in the last quarter was in her eyes, a sign of premature death. Both
Sancerni and she weren't more than nine years old at the time.
Let's figure that she was born in 1903. You must be right, López.
So be it, then. Look at the expression of that girl, so distant, somber, as though she wouldn't have known me. Is this she, then—
Potota? She never would use my first name, and never called me
anything but Perón. Even at moments of closest intimacy I was
always Perón.)

When we returned from our honeymoon in Bariloche, I re-
ceived my appointment to the General Staff. I also learned
that through the good offices of Lieutenant Colonel Descalzo I
was going to be asked to teach the course in military history at
the War Academy. I felt that the world was mine.

My thesis on the Battle of the Masurian Lakes appeared in
the Biblioteca del Oficial. *All the ideas I was to put forward*
throughout my life were already clearly set down there. I used
the argument of "the nation in arms," which is nothing more
than the subordination of the country's industries, services,

176

and energies to the objective of national defense. I also main-
tained, following Schlieffen, that any army, robust as it may
be, declines, ages, and dies with its leader.

(The General rouses himself from his torpor, pushes aside the
lap robe, and stands up. Take that sentence out of there, López
Rega. Put in its place: An already organized army will survive
intact even after the death of its leader. The secretary is upset.
Take out the sentence? That's not a sound thing to do, General.
Since it comes from Schlieffen, I wouldn't advise it. I suggest
completing the thought, rather. Saying—what do you think?—An
army can age and die with its leader if there is no replacement, no
heir, no incoming power that enters anointed by the outgoing
power. Period, new paragraph.

(Don't twist my orders around, López. Do what I tell you. Correct
that rubbish right away.)

> *. . . that an already organized army will survive intact even*
> *after the death of its leader. I have said over and over again*
> *that success cannot be improvised, it must be prepared. "The*
> *leader has to pursue victory to the ultimate, standing up like*
> *a man to the blows of destiny." I dedicated that book to the*
> *one who deserved it: "To Lieutenant Colonel Don Bartolomé*
> *Descalzo, as a small installment on my immense debt of grati-*
> *tude."*
>
> *Meanwhile, the country was lurching along. I shared in the*
> *general disappointment. My sympathies for Lisandro de la*
> *Torre waned in 1923 when he opposed the purchase of arms*
> *that Colonel Agustín P. Justo, then the Minister of War, was*
> *desperately demanding. After that, I was uneasy about*
> *Hipólito Yrigoyen's ambitions. He was looking for re-election*
> *at seventy-six years of age when he was obviously already*
> *suffering from senile incapacity.*

(Underline all this for me, López. I, at seventy-seven, return to
my country lucid and without ambitions. Let the difference be
clear.)

> *Although Yrigoyen ran away with 60 percent of the votes in*
> *the 1928 election, discontent in the army kept growing. It was*

177

common talk in the clubs that, pressed by the senior officers, General Agustín P. Justo was going to head a movement of national salvation. The rumors were so persistent that Justo had to publish a letter denying the allegation.

The army split into two sharply divided camps. One could be called "evolutionist." It maintained that the Argentines should kick out the Yrigoyen hordes and put an end to his personality cult, but that was all. This meant that if the army intervened in politics, it did so only to preserve the country's traditional structures and to call for elections as soon as possible. The other line, which had "reformist" overtones, stood for a complete reorganization of the government, based on the models of peace and order imposed by Mussolini and Primo de Rivera. Each group had its natural leader. The Evolutionists were headed by Justo and the Reformists by José Félix Uriburu, a pure and well-intentioned general, even when he was conspiring.

No officer with any sense could keep out of it. In all revolutions, what happens is that 20 percent are in favor, 20 percent against, and the rest are with nobody, waiting it out and then going along with the winners.

No sooner did Yrigoyen take over than bad luck struck. Meat and wheat prices dropped. The unemployed, vagrants, panhandlers roamed the cities. Prostitution and the rental of tenements, controlled by Jews, were the only businesses that flourished.

I was only a captain and, as such, somewhat on the fringe of those high-level dramas. On the fringe but not unaware. I recall the 1930 carnival, the parade on Avenida de Mayo, the people's feigned merriment. Before, the maskers used to squirt perfumed water at people, there were amorous adventures, strangers embraced one another. On that occasion, you would see people standing alone, detached, tossing confetti at the street musicians as though it were a duty. There was even a giant walking around done up as the King of Madness. But no one took any notice of him. Two other captains and I used to go to the movies together on days when there was a late matinee. There were always swarms of beggars around the entrances. They went about in clusters, broken out with pustules, coughing.

I foresaw the worst. Yet, I never imagined the enormity of the misfortune to come.

I was one of the first to join—on September 6, 1930—the movement that was to oust Yrigoyen. I went in ready to give my life to accomplish it. But I asked myself if Yrigoyen was worth all that. If Yrigoyen wasn't rather a man of dubious mettle who would bolt at the sound of the first shot.

I had my first meeting with General Uriburu in June of 1930 and committed myself to talk to Descalzo and bring him into the plot. My mentor was as worried as I about the spread of anarchism. The gangrene was advancing.

At the beginning of August, even the Minister of War was aware of the details of the military conspiracy. But nobody was concerned about stopping it. There were even those, in the midst of that chaos, who felt that Hipólito Yrigoyen himself wanted to be overthrown so he could go home and take it easy. When the possibility of revolution was mentioned, he would comment, "Nothing will happen. It's just political agitation which will pass." Pass, indeed! On September 6, 1930, one Argentina perished and another replaced it. History will decide which was the better. But that was like the line drawn on the sand by the conquistador Pizarro on his march to Peru. A line of no return. Now, we would never be as we were.

Even Vice President Enrique Martínez had his own plans for the coup. The poor fellow thought that we of the military were going to reward him with a promotion. But when he realized that he couldn't fool us, he was one of the speediest in vacating the Pink House.

Yrigoyen, bedridden for several days with pulmonary edema, at least had the strength of character to get up and look for help. It was a miracle that the revolution was victorious because most of the conspirators continued vacillating until the last moment. I was afraid it was going to blow up in our faces and that instead of a triumphal parade through the Plaza de Mayo, the party was going to wind up in Ushuaia penitentiary. Or shall we forget that the only ones with General Uriburu when he started the march on the capital that Saturday morning, September 6, were the Colegio Militar and the School of Communications? The bulk of the army were waiting for orders, it was not known from whom. The troops of

Campo de Mayo and Palermo went along with the coup when Yrigoyen was already toppled. A civilian—some poor upstart —took over the Ministry of War. And the army still hesitated. Divided, disorganized, confused, scared, it started out by anticipating defeat. A miracle saved it. What was it? Civic concern, hunger for change, the taste for new pleasures, which catches on so swiftly among Argentines. We were fed up with Yrigoyen. We wanted to see how we would make out with Uriburu. I remember the siren of the newspaper Crítica, *jubilantly announcing the revolution at around ten o'clock. At 5 p.m. the Pink House was evacuated. The people of Buenos Aires took to the streets and applauded the parading troops. Without that civic power behind us, we would have been lost. We went to take power, bodily, carried on the people's shoulders, as it were. When we entered Avenida Callao, Uriburu's car was showered with flowers.*

Yrigoyen was helpless. Mobs threatened his house. A few loyal followers took him to the Ministry of the Interior in La Plata, running the risk that he might not survive the trip. Dark circles under his eyes, gaunt, the President walked through the ice-cold salons. In that alien, invented, almost imaginary city, everything was unfamiliar. He must have been frightened. Somebody put a pen between his fingers and handed him a piece of paper with his resignation on it. Yrigoyen signed. It was a short note saying that he was leaving the government "absolutely," as though it were possible to leave it relatively. And the word was underlined. Even at the end, Yrigoyen seemed out of touch with reality.

I will always consider that resignation symbolic. For the Argentines, it was the first signal of civilian abdication. With that document, the future was now laid out for us.

It was not addressed to the Congress, as should have been the case, nor even to the victorious General José Félix Uriburu, but to the head of the military forces of the city of La Plata. It was as though the President had not foreseen the significance of that gesture. That, on yielding the government to any official whatsoever, he was surrendering not to an institution called the army but to brute force. Until that point, the military had been afraid to take power. With Yrigoyen's action we lost that fear forever. And it implanted the idea in civilians that the mere wearing of the uniform empowered a soldier to

> *do anything: take over a union, promulgate laws, direct a school, receive a president's resignation.*
>
> *This was so much the case, that even the Supreme Court was on our side. On September 10, four days after the coup, the judges solemnly declared that force was sufficient argument to guarantee order and the safety of the population.*

(Since your Memoirs for 'thirty end here—López said, his eyes glittering with excitement in the shadows of the sanctum—I have made some marginal notes. Everything can be amended as long as we have the time. Listen to this, General: the story you gave out for publication only three years ago. When you told Tomás Eloy Martínez that you went into the revolution of 'thirty like all the rest, blamelessly, obeying orders. Remember Martínez, the one from that magazine *Panorama?* Let me run the complete tape for you.

(From among the cassettes labeled "Memoirs for Eloy. Part II," López picks out the second. He adjusts the volume. The General's voice, sounding older and jerky, fills the room.

("Hipólito Yrigoyen's second term . . .")

(Lower that sound, López! The General becomes upset. Pointing to the ceiling, he whispers, Let's be respectful. You must never forget the deceased.

(The voice comes on again, not as loud.

("Hipólito Yrigoyen's second term did not turn out as well as the first. The man was quite old by then and his revolutionary fire had gone out. He was under the thumb of a court of pen-pushers and police agents. Whenever a minister wanted to see the President he was told that he was busy. And when Yrigoyen asked for the minister they would lie that he was on a trip to the interior. Bishops and admirals were made to sit hours in the waiting rooms (the famous 'holding pens'). Most of the time, they left without seeing him because the court let through the pensioners and panhandlers who took up his time.

("The army was not insensitive to these calamities and, of course, a tremendous reaction was set off. The chiefs expressed their concern. Descalzo got my support. I was just one of the many who committed themselves . . . I did so out of solidarity more than anything else. But it was the oligarchy that made hay of it. They realized they could take over the government by assault and that's just what they did."

(See what I mean, General? López switches off the tape recorder. So many twists and turns can lead to confusion. On the one hand, you say you were one of the first to join in the coup. On the other, it is unclear whether you were revolutionary by choice or by chance, whether President Yrigoyen deserved pity or respect. I also found out that Martínez threatened to publish a photo taken of you on September 6, 1930, standing on the running board of Uriburu's car, on the way to the Pink House with a victorious smile on your face. Martínez isn't the problem. We threw a good scare into him and that was that. Documents can be erased, destroyed. That doesn't worry me. What I want is for you to choose one version of the story. Just one, whichever.

(Now the General lets out a guffaw: Relax, man. Was that all? I'll explain it all to you. The reason I've been a leading figure in history time and time again, is precisely because I have contradicted myself. You've already heard about Schlieffen's strategy. You have to change plans several times a day, pull them out, one at a time, as needed. The socialist fatherland? I invented it. The conservative fatherland? I keep it alive. I have to blow in all directions, like the cock on the weathervane. And I never retract anything I say, but keep adding on. What may seem inappropriate to us today could be useful tomorrow. Dross and gold, dross and gold . . . You know very well that I'm not given to using strong language, but there's only one word for history . . . History is a whore, López. She always goes with the one who pays the most. And the more legends attached to my name, the richer I am and the more weapons I have to defend myself with. Leave everything the way it is. I'm not after a statue, but something bigger. To rule history. To fuck her in the ass.

(What sort of vulgarity do I hear? Isabel knocks on the door of the sanctum. Opening it, she stands at the threshold, hands on her hips, scolding. Just listen to the boys amusing themselves talking men's talk, while I'm down there going crazy. I can't handle that telephone anymore. Calls keep coming in from everywhere. Cámpora: should he come over? What do I tell him? El Pardo palace— I don't know how many times—if the General would like to say good-bye to the Caudillo in Moncloa or Barajas. One of Cámpora's ministers—I don't know which—asking for tomorrow's agenda. I haven't been able to sit down for a second to pick out the shoes I'm taking to Buenos Aires. Everybody's valises are packed, but mine are a disaster.

182

(Don't bother anymore, my girl. Poor thing! Let them leave us in peace. I'm way behind in all this work. What about the guards? What are they doing? Have one guard sit at the telephone and say, There's nobody here, the General has left. López, close the door. Put the blanket over me. The drafts from downstairs have chilled my legs. Pick up where you left off, man. Get going, on to the next year . . .)

All sorts of nonsense has been written about what I did on September 6th. That I accompanied Descalzo to the barracks of the Elite Guard, incited them to rebellion, and marched on the Pink House with them. Rubbish! The only true thing is that I spent two days without seeing my family, shaving with a dull razor to make myself presentable.

Descalzo, my mentor, had been appointed to the Infantry School. I didn't want him to go alone. Once again, he arranged my transfer. When he obtained it, we drank to the new army and the new fatherland. We were falling out of favor but were not yet aware of it.

Generals Uriburu and Justo were involved in a power struggle by the very first weeks of the revolution that turned all officers into suspicious elements. Loyalty was punished. Because Descalzo was close to Justo, they separated him from the Infantry School and sent him to a border post in Formosa. I was luckier. They put me on special status, pending assignment. To keep me from being idle, a job of geographical reconnaissance in the far North was created for me. Unwittingly, they did me a favor. Riding through the ravines of Salta and Jujuy, the country got under my skin as never before. All my senses glowed.

Terrible years began to unfold for the people. I was the only military man who didn't disappoint anybody. I claim no credit for myself other than having kept my eyes open and fought. What my eyes revealed to me my heart soon acted on.

There were thousands in the Chaco, Formosa, and Misiones who went about barefooted and were terrified at the sight of an automobile. In the port of Buenos Aires, shantytowns of tin cans and cardboard went up from one day to the next; tourists visited them as though they were a folklore show. In Avellaneda, Don Alberto Barceló's conservative clan handed out bags of potatoes and maté to the poor who crowded the doors of the committee. At the same time, they were running a network of gambling houses and brothels with an iron hand.

I took advantage of my temporary banishment to put together in a book the classes I had given at the War Academy. That was how my Notes on Military History *came into being. I continued turning to Clausewitz and Count Schlieffen for theoretical support but this time I formulated other ideas with greater clarity. For example, the doctrine of "the nation in arms." Also that of unified command for all forces, in peace and war. Both were later to be the keystone of Peronist organization.*

By 1934, I had published the two volumes of The Russo-Japanese War *in collaboration with Lieutenant Colonel Enrique Rottjer. One general had the gall to accuse us of plagiarism and brought us up before a rigged court, which, of course, found against us. We were obliged to apologize. Jealousy! They were all jealous.*

When Justo was elected President, I was already considered a figure to be reckoned with. General Manuel A. Rodríguez, one of the most upright leaders the army ever had, was appointed Minister of War. He sent for me immediately. "Perón," he said, "I have read your books closely. I believe our ideas are in accord. As of tomorrow, you will be my aide-de-camp."

On orders from the Minister, a commission under Colonel Fasola Castaño made a reconnaissance trip along the Andean border south of Neuquén, between Las Coloradas and Villa La Angostura. I was second in command. The beauty of the landscape made us gasp. When night fell, the atmosphere became phosphorescent. At dawn, we could hear the wild boars grunting among the poplars and birches. Amid all this magnificence, the Indians who inhabited those lonely reaches were dying at twenty of disease and neglect. I was afraid that they would be snuffed out like match flames and wanted to at least preserve what remained of their culture. I spent days questioning them through interpreters and, although I ignored the tribal legends, I did recover words, so they could be used by other soldiers when they came into the region. I put them together in a bilingual dictionary entitled Patagonian Place Names of Araucanian Origin.

Back in Buenos Aires, I found Minister Rodríguez looking very bad. He was the target of every political hate. Whenever he presented a plan for procurement of military equipment, the Socialists dug their claws into him. He was obliged to appear before the Congress at a time when his illness was at its worst. He delivered an unforgettable speech there. "Militarism does not always arise from the army," he said. "Militarism is usually an evil created by politicians when they utilize the army for purposes they shouldn't."

And a man like that had to die young! They say it was cancer that killed him. More likely, it was disgust. The country had been corrupted. Even the aristocrats turned lawbreakers. With utter shamelessness they became involved in scandalous deals involving meat, streetcars, electricity, railroads. President Justo was completely indifferent to all this. Ever since the last years of Yrigoyen's administration, the Pink House was an unlucky place, under a curse.

In October, 1935, Rodríguez, now terribly wasted, received me in his home. "General," I said to him, "I would like to go abroad. I have served three years. Thanks to you, I have broken out of my shell and I must try my strength in the world."

And this man who never smiled pursed his lips and looked at me paternally. "Very well. Go ahead," he ordered.

The new year began sadly. One day in February, they notified me that I was to be the new military attaché in Chile. General Rodríguez was dying. I hastened my preparations and got ready to cross the cordillera in a roadster.

(And right here, López interrupts, I reach for the utmost, the ne plus ultra. I captured you in words of flesh and blood.)

Fate has tempted me many times. Go this way, do that, said my destiny, offering me opportunities on a silver tray. I allowed those temptations to approach but never to become my masters. "I shall go where I wish to go," I told them. Every time fortune knocked at my door, it was my will that came out to greet her. I have been a ruminant of chance. I have munched and munched till it obeyed me. Some men let themselves be led by fate and by others. I have allowed only fate and myself to lead me:

(And, like an actor picking up a cue, Isabel waited for the end of the speech before calling from the turn in the stairway. General, lunch! Daniel, Cámpora is here! What shall I tell him? Perón sighs. Show him in, my girl, show him in. He removes the lap robe and shakes it out in case a memory might have dropped on it that could be picked up later by an outsider. He feels a body within the folds of his muscles that no longer has any relation to him, that moves as in a dream. He gets it to its feet and, turning to López, again voices the plaint of the morning. What drama now awaits? What misfortunes does the next chapter hold in store for me?)

10

THE FLY'S EYE

1.

I killed General Pedro Eugenio Aramburu.

Zamora has often recalled the proud face that spoke those words in the haze of the Gijón café in Madrid two years before. And, now, seeing it again, moving along the Camino de Cintura to the freeway, the flash of that unique face penetrates him like a laser (the deep dimple in the chin, the blond hair), and he can distinctly hear the scars each syllable left in his memory: I killed him and you can never write it. If you do, Zamora, that will be your finish. You'll have no more family. Your story will be ended. I executed the man. The reason is not hard to understand.

Things happen in two ways, either all at once or nothing happens. How to encompass it all to the last scattered entrails of reality without losing oneself? Emiliano Zamora, special-features editor on the weekly *Horizonte*, feels suddenly helpless, puny. His Renault 12 crawls ahead in contrary motion between webs of the advancing multitude. How to do it? Simply by narrating the times and places as they come through the densities of consciousness? How? With the sheep of reason or the fatality of the senses?

Who wouldn't be dizzied by the pressure of all those people? Even the muddy side roads of the highway are filled with thousands of bodies in pilgrimage to Perón's platform at Ezeiza. A battalion of bass drums crosses the federal shooting range in Santa Catalina. The war-shield kiosks near Monte Grande obstruct traffic. Zamora's Renault has been bearing constantly leftward, aiming toward downtown Buenos Aires. (Where had he read that by always turning left in a maze one inevitably reaches its center?) As he hunts for openings in the torrent, the car riding tilted over the culvert, almost scraping the ground, Zamora turns the radio on and off, incredulous at how the commentators abuse imagination in the way they return, between sambas, to that holy word: General.

A fly lights on the side mirror of the car. How come that insect is flying around in this cold? Its back is blue, wings smudged with soot, eyes greedy: compound eyes, of 4,000 facets each. The truth fragmented into 4,000 bits.

Let's see, now. I am Emiliano Zamora, tall, bald, scraggly teeth and scrawny frame, nicotine-stained fingers, chain-smoker of *Parisiennes*. I've gotten into a miserable situation. I am returning to Buenos Aires from Ezeiza, despondent.

The entire postcard of Peronism fits on the mirror underneath the fly: the headbands, bell-bottom jeans, T-shirts singing "Perón Comes Back and Conquers." Then, all of a sudden, the dimple in the chin: Noon Antezana.

I killed him, Zamora. I executed General Aramburu.

What an overpowering multitude! Noon, wearing dark glasses, carrying a staff that looks like a bishop's crozier, leads an endless Montonero column. A skinny, intense redhead shepherds the vanguard of the flock. I've seen that imperious face somewhere before, that gory outpouring of hair. In Córdoba, perhaps, in a house on Calle Artigas. I saw her in May, '69, capturing a police patrol and holding them for two hours. It consisted of an officer and five patrolmen: hostages—I heard her say—of the battle plan, of militant unionism, of people's power. The hostage patrol of the Córdoba coup. Ana . . . Diana? She was Jewish, I recall. And now she's gone over to the other band. She's no longer a Trotskyist. She's a Montonera. Following Noon Antezana. Or, perhaps, today, June 20, it will all be the same.

I thought the morning was going to slip by peacefully, that the product of my titanic parturition, "Perón: His Entire Life / Documents and Photos of 100 Witnesses," would bring a lull. In the lobby of the international hotel, still belching the breakfast shared with the General's cousins and ex–sister-in-law, I, Emiliano Zamora, fell asleep. I saw (imagined, rather) María Amelia listening, with an ecstatic expression, to the opera on the radio. I saw Captain Trafelatti circumspectly thumbing a copy of *Horizonte*. I vaguely understood that Señorita María Tizón would write her sister Potota's matrimonial history to be read that afternoon to the press. I shut my eyes. At that random moment, the editor of *Horizonte* telephoned me.

"Zamora? Do you know how long the plane from Madrid is delayed? Two or three hours. Don't plan to hang around there scratching your balls. Put the old geezers on a bus. Give them a tour. To where? You ought to know the answer to that. Around the runways, the woods, what difference does it make? Let them enjoy themselves. There's not many planes landing at Ezeiza today. Actually, only one. Get Osinde to arrange it. In my name. Let's see if he pays me back now for the favors he owes me. What do you mean, it's impossible? Relatives of Perón, childhood companions! *Che*, are you going soft? They're a bunch of dotty old fogies! You interviewed them, didn't you? So, what the hell do you care? Yessir, right now. You're going to have to expand this *risorgimiento* opera for me. I want the General's entire life, Part 2. I want you to put him in slippers, killing ants in the garden, watching a cowboy series on television. Decipher him, Zamora. And you want me to tell you how, besides? You'd be nothing without me. Go see Tomás Eloy Martínez, in my name. Call him at *La Opinión*. If he won't help, tell him to remember what I did for him when he didn't have a pot to piss in."

I obeyed. My servitude is now a reflex. Half an hour later, a boy with a vacant look, pimply face, lank hair arrived at the hotel. He walked bent over. A pistol bulged under his coat. A 9 mm Walther, I guessed. Osinde sent him. He was laconic. Outside, he said, there was a bus waiting for my witnesses. They would tour the lateral runways of the airport and visit the hangars. Three plainclothesmen would escort the vehicle.

I asked that they leave their guns behind. The passengers were all elderly people, I told him. They're relics, they belong to Perón's most distant past.

The man with the vacant stare puckered his lips, whether in scorn or surprise, I'll never know. He held out his hand. It felt damp, sticky.

"You can depend on me. My name is Arcángelo Gobbi."

I saw the witnesses of my story disappear into a bus crowned with fluttering Argentine flags. Ill with foreboding, I got into the Renault 12 and drove behind the hangars to Route 205.

Scrawled in chalk on a wall, I read endless anagrams of the five letters of Perón. I understood only one litany: OREN POR PERON, REO. PERON ROE PERO NO RONPE. PEOR. (Pray for Perón, prisoner. Perón gnaws but doesn't break. Worse.)

The fly then flew off because of the cold.

I looked through the window and the smoke cloud of the Gijón café in Madrid loomed before my eyes.

2.

Zamora plunged into the haze of the Gijón, not knowing whose voice it was that had awakened him in the hotel at 2 a.m.: "I'm going to tell you who killed General Aramburu. And where Evita's body is."

Somebody would be waiting for him between 10 and 11 p.m. at a table next to the window. Was somebody lying to him? No. He could recognize the smudge of a lie in people's voices. What, then?

He guessed the answer when Noon Antezana stepped forward to greet him. "I'm not going to ask you how you are because I know, Zamora. We saw you yesterday in Paris at six o'clock in the Bonaparte Café. And the week before we saw you in Gstaad with Nahum Goldman. Are you preparing another glorification of the Jews?"

"I'm just passing through Madrid, Antezana, and can't stay very long. Arrange a meeting for me with Perón."

Noon refused with a smile. "Perón has gone to the Guadarrama mountains. The goddam polyps are bothering him again. He can hardly piss. I'm offering you something better. You heard it. What I told you on the telephone."

"Too big a story, Noon. I don't want it. In any case, I don't believe it. If it's true, there's not money enough to pay for it. So, it's a lie."

Outside, the heat shriveled the gaunt trees. A gray-haired journalist, beard but no mustache, in a black cape, let out a sinister guffaw calculated to attract attention.

A woman applauded. They were all smoking.

Noon pulled out a sheaf of papers. He showed the title: "Report to General Perón on Operation Pindapoy / Juan José Valle Group." And he deciphered several signatures: Fernando Abal Medina, Carlos Gustavo Ramos, Abelardo Antezana.

"It's a story of justice," he said. "It should interest you."

"What's the price?"

The journalist in the black cape flourishing a curved cigarette holder challenged the café with another bellow. Noon's eyes narrowed.

"No price. That's the point. I'm here to keep the story from becoming a piece of merchandise. Your tragedy, Zamora, is that you know only a part of what happened. That makes you dangerous. You're not going to be satisfied till you know more."

The lights were turned out at the bar behind Noon. Faces were buried in shadow. Nothing but smoke could be seen.

"You're mistaken, Antezana. I know all I have to know." Zamora spoke tensely, with no hint of bravado. "I know where they hid Evita's body. I followed a trail I picked up by chance in Gstaad. It took me all the way to Bonn. I looked for the body where I was told it would be, in the coal cellar of the Argentine Embassy. It had no coal cellar but there was a garden. I assumed she would be there in the tulip bed, buried upright, as Rodolfo Walsh said. But she wasn't. I had occasion to check through some files. I knew that at one point in 1957, an oak chest containing old books and papers arrived in Bonn, and nobody bothered to open it. It was a rectangular box that had been dropped off and forgotten in the coal cellar behind the embassy where the garden now is. In the summer of 'fifty-eight, it was shipped out of Germany by truck. I learned that it crossed the border in the custody of three men, one of whom was an Argentine Army officer. That kind of attention seemed extremely unusual. Nobody dumps off some papers for such a long time and then, without having looked through them, sends them on so carefully. I had no doubt about it. It was the body."

"And now what will you do, Zamora? You've got hold of a hot coal. Will you publish the story? Douse yourself in glory?"

"See Perón. Offer him the story. Ask him how he would write it if he were in my place."

"That's why I called you, Zamora. So that you wouldn't waste your time. The General knows every last word of what you are going to tell him. That the body was entrusted to the Vatican. That it was buried in Lot No. 86 of the Campo Verano cemetery in Rome. It's a fake. We already looked there. There is no such lot."

Zamora slowly got to his feet. He expressed neither disappointment nor surprise. He just rose, until his head disappeared in the pall of smoke. "So, there's no more to be said. Why go on talking, then?"

The journalist with the beard and no mustache wrapped his cape around two women and walked them to the street. A swarm of insects flew into the café past the light bulbs. The waiters were dripping sweat.

"Sit down," Noon commanded. "Half of what you already know could cost your life. Now, you have to know the whole of it, if you want to go on living."

"I'm not an enemy," said Zamora.

"No," admitted Noon, "you're worse. You might be an informer."

The voices at the tables quieted down as if they were open drawers being shut by a lazy hand. Words stripped of all light, flavor, or form recognizable to the conventions of the senses began to reach his ears. What he heard was being tattooed onto his guts like a Siamese twin that he would have to carry with him everywhere. A body he would never be able to show anyone.

"I killed General Aramburu," said Noon. "I killed him and you must not write it. If you do, it will be the end of you. You will have no wife, father, or children. You will see them go one after the other, and you will beg to be allowed to go, too. The story of your life will end. And I will be able to do nothing to prevent it. Now, listen, because you're condemned to keep quiet . . ."

———

3.

The bus stopped for the second time outside a hangar. María Tizón, who has not moved in her seat, goes over the reminiscences she will be reading to the press in the afternoon.

> *My sister Potota was gifted with discretion beyond her years and was already equipped to be the companion and helpmeet of a man as studious and idealistic as Perón.*
>
> *She had a great vocation for culture and loved the arts. She was enamored of painting and music, particularly. She studied some piano and mastered the guitar.*
>
> *Among her incursions into the art of painting, her finest effort was the portrait she did of her husband.*

Arcángelo Gobbi stands next to the steering wheel, his lizard head snooping at her writing. Señorita Tizón feels an icy alarm signal along the nape of her neck. She is not afraid of the man, but his look, like a great empty lake over her remembrances, terrifies her. She spies Benita Escudero de Toledo through the window. She sees her walking out of kilter, her feet obviously hurting her. She raises the window and calls out, "Benita! Keep me company, Benita! Let's talk."

> *But this sister with her gaiety and contagious laughter was weak when it came to facing the loss of those she loved. She was broken to pieces by her mother's death. Potota survived her by only two years. Afterwards, foreseeing her own demise, she recovered her courage. At the end of the two months that her cruel illness lasted, strengthened by the Holy Communion she received daily and by the anticipation of a better life, she went with resignation. She died in Buenos Aires. Perón truly missed her. Some say she was his great love.*

The bus rolls through desolate pasture lands alongside the airport runways. Captain Trafelatti relates his adventures as a taxidermist. José Artemio tells of certain sedentary birds that nest and mate even in the winter. Helicopters fly by in tandem.

María Tizón would like to know how much Benita had come to learn of Potota's secret life. What confessions, what pangs? But she doesn't know how to begin, or where. She says: Don't you feel that knowing her was a gift from heaven? A gift from heaven, Benita replies.

They then remain silent. Cousin Julio drowses. On lowering her voice, María finally discovers the tone at which her memory and Benita's coincide. Whispering, they gradually grow confidential.

Don't tell me you foresaw that poor Potota would suffer as she did.

Yes, I foresaw it, Señorita María. I could see misfortune imprinted on her face from the very beginning. She would tell us everything. We were—please, forgive me—like sisters. One day, in a nostalgic mood, she said to me, Do you know where I met Juan, Benita? In the Capitol Theater on Calle Santa Fe. We were attending a benefit performance at which chance had sat us next to one another.

Of course! I remember that! They saw *Son of the Sheik*. Potota came home, trembling. Mother asked if she were sick and she answered, "It's nothing, nothing." It was pure emotion. During the night I touched her forehead. She had fever. Lovesick, that's what she was, Benita! The few compliments Perón had paid her threw her into a tizzy. How old could she have been? Let me see. She was born on March 18, 1908, so she must have been nineteen years old.

Was she blushing, Señorita Tizón?

Of course, Benita. She would blush at anything. When she played pieces by Albéniz on the guitar, they sounded so lovely that we would all come out of our bedrooms to give her a kiss. And do you know what she would do? Turn red as a carnation. Within a week's time, Perón was asking permission to visit her. He began by appearing at the house every Saturday. They would go for a stroll along the road and we would watch them from the balcony. What a lovely couple they were! He, strapping, with an athlete's physique. And she, so tiny and frail. One night, after they had decided to get married, Potota came into my room and hugged me. Oh, María, she said, I'm so afraid of being alone. I tried to soothe her. What do you mean "alone," little sister? Is it that you don't love Perón? Because if you do, then that love will fill your life. And she said to me: I love him very much. But his mind is far away from me. He is a soldier and can think only about his career. Mother came in and between the two of us we tried to console her. I stroked her hair, poor little thing, and Mother said to her: Such is woman's fate, Potota. To be left alone. Man to his work, woman to wait for him. Then, the Lord willing, children will come. And there will be no more waiting. My sister blushed. But, as you know, children never came.

I remember those months before the wedding so well, María . . . I remember a great deal about Don Mario Tomás's death and the mourning. The Peróns left the front door ajar and forbade any music. Potota sold her guitar. They would spend the day praying the rosary with Aunt Juana. What shall I do, Benita? she would ask me. I don't want to marry this way, in the midst of mourning.

She said the same thing to us, until Mother finally convinced her. You mustn't make men wait, she told her. They arranged a private ceremony in our house, without any celebration afterwards. And when they returned from their honeymoon, poor Potota's prophecy came true. She was left alone.

A greenish fly lit on the handbag in which María Tizón had hidden from Arcángelo's shameless prying the memorandum book with her notes and a couple of family photographs.

Look at that! A fly, in this cold!

The fly's avid eyes passed in a flash; eyes composed of 4,000 facets each. The truth divided into 4,000 bits.

4.

"There were thirteen of us," Noon continues at the Gijón café, "in the original Montonero cell. Ten took part in Aramburu's kidnapping. Six of us decided the death sentence. Those were not the figures Perón got when he returned to Buenos Aires. Twelve, not thirteen, founders were mentioned. And five judges. My name was omitted. I will be excluded from that justice forever. I appear only on the paper I showed you, Zamora. And now I must destroy it. That's how the General wanted it.

"Rodolfo Walsh has given a very clear explanation of the reasons that led us to the execution. Let me read you what he wrote: *Aramburu was executed on June 1, 1970, at seven a.m. His body appeared forty-five days later in the south of the province of Buenos Aires. Three extremely serious charges were brought against him: the massacre of twenty-seven Argentines without trial or justifying cause in June, 1956; the clandestine operation in which the body of*

Perón's wife Evita was snatched from him, desecrated, and taken out of the country; the pernicious initiation of economic violence. Aramburu's government laid the groundwork for the second infamous decade. The Argentine Republic, which remitted abroad barely one dollar per capita annually, began to negotiate loans benefitting nobody but the lender to pay off foreign capital using national savings, and to accumulate the indebtedness that now eats up 25 percent of our exports. One decree alone, No. 13.125, plundered the country of two billion dollars in nationalized bank deposits and placed them at the disposal of international banking, which will now be able to control credit and strangle small industry."

"Even so," Zamora says, "it wasn't necessary to kill him."

"Then, you don't understand." Noon was nonplussed.

"I never understand death."

"It was something beyond death. More important, and also more final."

Noon had arranged a neat row of papers on the café table. From a distance they looked like figures in an album. Zamora enveloped them in smoke. The heat didn't let up. It hung on, standing by the night like a sentry.

"We had to survive," says Noon. "It was therefore a necessity that an enemy should die. The more spectacular the sacrifice, the better for our existence. It's a Nietzschean concept. All new creation needs enemies more than friends. One substantial enemy rather than a hundred. We had him: Aramburu. There was no other candidate. In May, 1970, before kidnapping him, I wrote Perón, asking his advice. Once again, the General washed his hands. 'You'll know what has to be done, Antezana. You must have already weighed the consequences.' When it was all over, I came here to deliver this report: 'Operation Pindapoy/Juan José Valle Group.' The General laughed at the name, Pindapoy, a brand of oranges.

"You can imagine, Zamora, that I read over each of these pages more than once. What had become of Eva's body was an exasperating enigma to the General. Aramburu stubbornly refused to discuss it during the initial interrogations. He said that a question of honor prevented him. Finally, like pulling teeth, he confessed something. The body, which had been entrusted to the Vatican,

196

was in a cemetery in Rome. He gave us the lot number. As you already know, it was false.

"On June first, we withdrew at about four a.m. to deliberate. There were six of us and we wanted justice to be served even though the one concerned was Aramburu. Fernando Abal Medina read the charges. I conducted the defense, separating the moral considerations from the political. I argued that this man's crimes now dated far into the past and that it was possible for us to find some form of pardon. Shortly before the light came up, each of us wrote his sentence on a piece of paper. I read out 'death' six times.

"We remained outside for a while, smoking. We were on an isolated farm at Timote in the middle of the pampas. I found a phosphorescent bone among some rusty pans. Carlos Gustavo Ramus was saddling a horse alongside of me.

"I saw the red line of dawn on the horizon. I stood up and said, 'We'll execute him at seven o'clock. The prisoner must be notified to prepare himself.'

"When he saw me come in, Aramburu turned pale. 'What have you decided?' he asked.

"I spoke with solemn formality, 'General, the court has condemned you to death. You will be executed in half an hour.'

"Somebody—I don't remember which one of us—tied his hands behind his back. Forcing himself to keep calm, Aramburu asked that we shave him.

"'We have nothing to do it with, General,' I told him. And I touched my face. To my surprise, I found that whiskers had sprouted, too.

"We walked through an inside hall of the house and down into the cellar. I left a sentry near the door. In the yard, two of us went to work with carpentry tools to cover the sound of the shots.

"Aramburu stopped on the first step leading to the cellar and asked when his confessor was coming.

"'You'll have to confess before God, General,' I told him. "The highways are being watched and we can't bring anybody."

"He then continued down the rickety stairs. He turned his back on us and prayed for the salvation of his soul. Halfway through the prayer he stopped. 'What will happen to my family?' he wanted to know.

"Fernando replied. 'Nothing. Everything belonging to you will be turned over to your wife.'

"We stuffed a handkerchief into his mouth to muffle the death scream. We moved him close to the wall. I drew my nine-millimeter Walther and released the safety. I saw him shudder.

"Abal Medina called out, 'General, we shall now proceed.'

"He shut his eyes. At that instant, I fired. The bullet went straight to his heart.

"A month later, when I brought the report of the operation to Madrid, Perón noticed a peculiar error on Fernando's part with respect to the story, committed perhaps with the intention of enhancing the enemy's stature. Here's that version, Zamora. You may read it.

"*Abal Medina took upon himself the task of executing the prisoner. It is our policy that the major responsibility be assumed by the chief.*

" '*General,' says Fernando, 'We shall now proceed.'*

"*Aramburu spoke for the last time, 'Proceed.'*

" 'This word *proceed* is impossible,' Perón pointed out to me. 'Who ever heard of a man talking with a handkerchief in his mouth?' "

Two flamenco dancers noisily enter the café. Zamora wipes the perspiration from his face and, this time, it is he who smiles. "So, at death's door Aramburu flouted you. He kept his word of honor and didn't reveal where Eva is buried."

"That was the only thing he didn't tell us," Noon admits. "And I think that's why I, too, voted for the death sentence. There's just one more story. I had to stay in Madrid all that summer. I returned to Buenos Aires on September 8, 1970. A police patrol had killed Ramus and Abal Medina in a pizzeria on Calle William Morris the day before. I decided to leave Fernando's story as it was. I won't be the one to correct that last word he put in Aramburu's mouth. That 'proceed,' which never existed, will remain there forever."

"Now, it's my turn." Zamora rests a hand on Noon's shoulder. "I know who has Evita and where."

"I know you know," Noon answers. "If you weren't going to tell me, you wouldn't have come here."

5.

When Perón's seven childhood companions reach the tarred ditches surrounding the Ezeiza airport, an unending fiesta is revealed to them through the bus windows, scenes of which keep repeating as they proceed.

They see a web of pilgrims singing as they march through the eucalyptus woods. The women, wearing white kerchiefs on their heads, carry infants in their arms, the men hold up placards with a portrait of Evita in the full splendor of her beauty: in profile, lips parted, hair in a bun.

A line of trucks passes, moving slowly, loaded with families that have come from far away. Some of the trucks bear the names of distant cities: Aguilares, Monteros, Concepción, Choromoro. And on top of the cabins, Eva again, her smile a little smudged by the trip, but her hairdo intact.

Behind, a sound truck grinds out the music of "Captain Evita." And all at once, Evita comes on, her voice as it used to be, deep, hoarse, beating at the air: *Fanaticism is the wisdom of the spirit.* There is a pause. Then: *Dear comrades, fanaticism is the wisdom of the spirit.*

More women in kerchiefs follow, with infants in their arms. Some are laughing out loud. They are bathed in sunlight. A mild breeze is blowing.

"We must turn back to the hotel," Arcángelo, at the wheel of the bus, decides. "This road has been taken over by the lefties."

"Going back so soon?" Captain Trafelatti complains. "After all, we haven't seen anything yet . . ."

Arcángelo doesn't answer. He slowly shakes his lizard head as he estimates the multitudes moving along the horizon.

The bus has come several times to the ditches where the airport ends. The passengers have pointed in surprise at a swarm of flies over the bushes. Flies, in this cold? And they have seen lines of trucks bearing the names of prehistoric cities: Famaillá, Burruyacu, El Chañar, Atahona. "Could it be like in the opera," María Tizón muses, "where there's one background and they keep making it go round and round?"

Holding themselves aloof from the group's astonishing discoveries, María Tizón and Benita are the only ones who, in allowing themselves to be carried away by their memories, have managed to get anywhere. They have hardly emerged from the past. In lowering their voices, by entering together those houses of memories that both had shared separately with Potota, a hunger for confidences has brought them close.

Let us pick up the thread again. Benita has been saying:

They weren't married even a year when Perón decided that they should move to an apartment on Santa Fe and Canning. That was where Potota felt loneliest. One time I invited her to the movies but she refused. What an idea, Benita! she said. What if Perón should come home and not find me? She began to entertain herself by writing me letters.

MARÍA: She didn't even let me call her on the telephone. She was always afraid that any little noise might disturb Perón when he was studying.

BENITA: It all began with her anxiety about having a baby. When the business was late just one day, Potota wouldn't stop talking about it. What a fuss she'd make! Then, when it showed up there was an ocean of tears. What's the matter with me, Benita, what's the matter with me?

MARÍA: See what can happen! Without realizing it, mamma made it worse by keeping at her: Well, now, Pototita, when is the big day?

BENITA: I noticed in one of her first letters that she sounded very anguished. Look. Just read this. See how she bore the weight of her cross all alone, so as not to bother anybody.

> *Dear Benita,*
>
> *Before anything else, it will give me great pleasure to hear that you are sound in both health . . . and pocketbook. We are very well. Thank the Lord!*
>
> *All these last few days I have been on the verge of calling you but sometimes, on account of the rain, other times because of the cold, and still others because of parties we are having to celebrate the Revolution, the days have gone by without my paying you the much discussed and desired visit.*
>
> *Benita: I have also been wanting to see you and visit you to get those <u>needles</u> from you for picking up runs. I have several pairs of stockings I can't use since I don't want to ruin them by sewing them, so you can imagine how eager I am to go or for you to come and see me. Benita: Even though I am less busy than you, I would be delighted if you would come as Perón is always here in the afternoons and I have a feeling I can't explain about leaving him alone as, in spite of being closed in by himself, he occasionally asks me for something.*

200

Come to see me soon, just the same as if you <u>had lost the</u>
<u>needle.</u> You know very well it isn't out of <u>self-interest</u> as I have
always asked you to come, and Artemio, as well.

And what about your family? We have received a letter from
the family in Chubut. They are all very well and expecting us
for the summer. When you come, we will chat a little about
everything and particularly about <u>kiddies</u>, as I may even have
some news for you by then.

I am always the same: it seems like it's no use . . . Patience!
Maybe one of these days . . .

Benita: Telephone me when you receive this letter, as I want
to know when I can come to your house or you here.

Well, Benita I hope you are all well; regards to your family
and special ones from me to Artemio, and also from Juan.

> *With a hug from*
> *Potota*

Buenos Aires 10–9–31
The telephone number (in case you lost it) is 1053 Palermo (71)

MARÍA: My sister Dora and I visited her once in the summertime.
Potota's apartment seemed extremely gloomy to me. She had a
piano but never played it. We talked for a while. She squeezed my
hands! María, dear, she said, have you noticed how just about any
woman at all gets pregnant but I can't? We were worried when we
left. My sister Dora began calling her regularly on the phone to
cheer her up: Mother was asking about you, Potota. She says you
should come by and do embroidery for a while. The loveliest nove-
lette came out in *Home* magazine and she wants to lend it to you.
And things like that. Finally, Dora convinced her to go to a gynecologist with her. Potota's state of mind brightened at the hope of
some miracle.

BENITA: Perón had his troubles, too, María. When he was Minister of War, word got to him that Aunt Juana and a country boy by
the name of Marcelino Canosa were carrying on and had started
living together. It was terrible! But Potota convinced him to have
the relationship legalized before the army got wind of it. And that's
what was done. Perón took the trip to Chubut and got his mother
married.

MARÍA: Then, that was the time my sister Dora took advantage
of Perón's being away to take Potota to the gynecologist.

BENITA: That same week I received another letter. It was the last.

Dear Benita:

I wish that God is granting you and Artemio all the good health you deserve. I don't know what to tell you about myself. Benita, I have been suffering a lot, going through all kinds of analyses and palpations, hoping to be able to get pregnant. Today, I'll know the whole story. So far, the doctor assures me that he can find nothing. That is, I am normal. I hope to God! But at the same time I am having some very grave worries, Benita, if it's true that I have nothing wrong and am capable, I cannot understand why so much time has passed without my having some news.

Benita: It would be nice if you have time to bring me the little aprons you promised me. I am waiting for Perón to return any day now from Chubut, so please telephone me before coming.

Special regards to Artemio. A hug to you from,

Potota

Buenos Aires 10–3–1934.

MARÍA: What sad days those were! When she received the results of the tests, Potota no longer answered the phone nor did she want to see anybody. Imagine, Benita, how distressing that must have been. At home, we didn't know what to do. On top of everything else, my sister Dora was keeping quiet, too. She said that the diagnosis was not clear. One night, plucking up courage, I went to her room and confronted her. Do you want to drive us crazy, Dora? Potota shut up in that mausoleum of an apartment, and you here sitting on the whole thing! Come on, now, what is going on? She can't have children? All right, then, let her resign herself, period!

It's worse, Dora said. She can. Perón is the one who can't. And Potota will never tell him so.

BENITA: She did the right thing, María. I would have done the same. One should never wound a husband's pride.

MARÍA: The bad thing is that Potota was never the same again. As is always the case, one misfortune brings on another. Shortly after, Mother died. We all suffered very much, but Potota more than anybody. She crocheted little doilies and spent hours and hours scrubbing the apartment. In the afternoon, she would have

202

forgotten which of the wainscotings she had cleaned in the morning and would scrub them all again.

BENITA: They weren't doilies, María. They were booties.

How long after the bus came to a stop in front of the hotel did the two women remain aboard, whispering? When they get off, the changes they see surprise them. The passages are now filled with grim-looking, big-bellied men, armed to the teeth. They are wearing white armbands. Stray mules have wandered into the parking area and the men run them off, hitting them with chains.

Inside the hotel, huge portraits of Perón, Isabelita, and Eva hang from the ceiling over the reception desk. The halls smell of flowers.

It's really so unfair, complains María. Potota has simply been erased from all this. And taking Benita by the arms, she drops another confidence: How Perón changed after he married Eva! With my sister, he was a pleasant man, with good manners. Afterwards, he became uncouth, vulgar. Some say it was a pose to be more in tune with the people. I know that isn't true. He did it for Eva. So that she wouldn't seem so out of key.

Arcángelo, standing in the shadows of the lobby, has masked himself with dark glasses. He holds a grotesquely unwieldy weapon, much too large for his hands. He is listening with deepest respect to a brown-haired man with a vacant look.

"We can't lose any more time. The Lieutenant Colonel needs you. Go, right away, Arcángelo."

"Right away, Lito," he repeats, and immediately corrects himself, saying, "Yessir, I'm going."

6.

Now it's my turn. I know who has Evita, and where.

These words no longer interested anybody. When Zamora first dropped them to Noon Antezana in the Gijón café two years before, they could have knocked history off its track. Now, on June 20, 1973, no one would even stop to turn around if he heard them. By this time, everybody knows of the wanderings of Evita's body and who gave it rest. Let's think about tomorrow. Zamora wrote: In a short while, this country will have no past. The past is something unreal here, like a movie screen. Every instant a new (and worse) exploit of reality changes it. It can't even be oblivion.

It is past 11:30 when Zamora finally manages to get across Riachuelo and into Buenos Aires. He was supposed to be at an apartment on Calle Arenales at eleven o'clock to pick up a personal diary. Maybe the woman who promised it to him won't be there. Maybe she didn't wait for him.

The streets of Barracas are deserted. Flies and pieces of paper hover in the air. The sun is setting behind the buildings, cold as a medal. Near the Constitución section two boys are cleaning a barroom. The soapy water pours out, lapping at the venetian blinds, and spills a river of soggy cigarette butts onto the sidewalk.

Zamora hears the laughter of several flamenco dancers as they come into the haze of the Gijón café, puts his hand on Noon's shoulder again, and speaks: "I'll tell you what became of the body. As you know, I ran across some papers at the Argentine Embassy in Bonn describing the shipment of a rectangular oak box and I learned it was escorted across the border by three men. One of them was an officer of the Argentine Army. I didn't buy the idea that such precautions would be taken for a boxful of rubbish. There was no doubt in my mind that it was Eva's body. I assumed that the addressee held the key. It was a certain Giorgio di Magistris, Via Ceresio 86–41, Milan. I took the first plane out. It was the address of the Monumentale cemetery, near the Porta Garibaldi railroad station. Imagine the state of my nerves when I walked in. I was not expecting a grave with an inscription that read: *Eva Perón. Qui giace.* I was looking for just a mark, an indication of some kind."

Noon smiled. "So, it was in Milan, not Rome."

"The Via Ceresio, Milan. I spent an entire morning walking around the cemetery and, in the end, I had to come back the following day. A huge gateway, a ring of columns. I walked among the imposing graves. I went into the heroes' pantheon, the Famedio, where Manzoni is buried. When it was getting toward evening, I asked the guards. I mentioned Magistris and gave them the numbers on the paper from the embassy. *'Ottanta sei!'* one of them exclaimed. *'Ecco lo qua!'* And he accompanied me to a grim-looking building in the rear: *Tempio di Cremazione.* I felt dizzy,

204

sick to my stomach. It was a lost moment, like a dream. The number 86 was there because the price of admission was 86 liras."

Zamora saw Noon shudder. The flamenco dancers, glasses of sherry in hand, were waving at them from the bar.

"Those sons of bitches cremated her!" said Noon. "Why didn't you denounce them?"

"Because I wasn't sure. There wasn't a single bit of proof. If I had told the story, they'd still be laughing at me. A thousand fairy tales have been written about that body. I didn't want to add another."

The vast Avenida 9 de Julio stretches empty before Zamora. In the distance, beyond the obelisk, he sees a truck with flags flying go by. He feels the warmth of his own body in the Renault, safe from ridicule. Safe for how long? In Buenos Aires, ridicule awakes each day before the sun. Three months after that meeting with Noon, General Lanusse's ambassador delivered Evita's body to Perón in Madrid. And, all at once, the jigsaw puzzle fell into place. The telephone again woke him at two in the morning, but this time at his house in Buenos Aires. Noon was calling.

"Zamora? Did you see what horses' asses we were? It was my fault for not following through to the end."

"It's my fault," said Zamora, hanging up after he heard the story.

All of it had been in his hands: the numbers, the name, the places. Eva Perón had lain buried for years in Milan under the name María de Magistris. Her headstone bore an inscription that could not have been clearer: *Giorgio de Magistris a sua sposa carissima.* The location of the grave matched: Section 41, Lot 86. The name of the cemetery was different: Musocco, not Monumentale, on Via Garagnano, not Ceresio.

He feels demolished, useless, and unable to understand what has brought on a sudden attack of anxiety. He avidly smokes a cigarette to bolster himself and leaves the car in front of the building where the person may still be waiting for him. Señora Mercedes had promised, hadn't she, to let him read the diary she had kept in Santiago de Chile between January and April, 1938, when she and her husband were intimate—or close to it—with Potota and Perón? Hadn't she already told him over the phone, in confidence, all about the difficulties on the train trip over the cordillera, the arrival at the Ñuñoa houses, Potota's sudden decline before she was destroyed by cancer? Ring the bell and she'll be there to receive you, Zamora. Señora Mercedes, widow of the man who overthrew Perón in '55 . . . Mecha Villada Achával de Lonardi.

7.

Let's go, boys, let's go! Careful about not showing the banners, yet! If we give it away now, we're done for. Let's sing! What's the matter? Tonsils worn out, are they? Come on, everybody sing! *With Perón and Evita / Our country* socialista! *There's one Evita and that's all / so might as well not break your balls!* Look at that cloud of flies, Noon! Even the flies have come out of hibernation to listen to the Old Man. A glorious day, isn't it? Look at that sun! When I was a kid, an aunt of mine used to take me to Centenario park. They'd pull my braids and tease the hell out of me on account of this hair and these freckles of mine. But there was a boy on the merry-go-round who took a shine to me. Six-in-the-afternoon face, he'd call me. Or rusty face, or sunset face. But me, instead of taking it in fun, I'd feel miserable.

Come on, boys, let's go! What about that bass drum? *Che*, have you lost your voice? When I was a kid, I used to think: I want to be like Rosa Luxemburg, like La Pasionaria, like Isadora Duncan; I want to be Krupskaya reading a Jack London story to Lenin before he died. When I grew up I realized that I was dreaming of a love that was coming into being together with history: in action, with the masses. A love that can't be held in. Know what I mean? Like fire. Burning up in bed and in militancy. And, finally, I said to myself: Evita is all of that.

Watch out for that lineup at the school over there, boys! The ones with the green armbands. Don't let yourselves be provoked. Osinde and Witch Doctor López Rega have brought in goons from everywhere. But, *che*, let's not keep our mouths closed! Bust their eardrums! Let's go: *Perón, be brave / Put the Witch Doctor in his grave! If Evita was still about / She'd be a Montonera, without a doubt / If Evita was still about!*

Understand what I'm trying to say, Noon? I began asking myself: Diana, isn't love more deeply felt when one is in the heat of battle? Can't sex and history be fused? And I would answer myself: Very easy, Diana. You must live love as the norm within abnormality, let love be your breath of life, your dream within wakefulness. Dispense love like Evita does: meeting with the General from three to five in the morning, a marriage of secret lovers. Be—what shall I say?—the pharos of your phallus. You like that, don't you? Not fate but pharos. How about that! The pharos of your phallus. I'm crazy! I'm in love! I'm a woman. That word sounds better to me now than it ever did. I'm a woman!

Girls, one pace forward! Sing the march and put some feeling into it! Give it guts! That's the way. Louder! That's it, that's it! *With Peróoon, off to war / Off to the people's war!* . . .

Noon passes his hand over her shoulder, enclosing the indomitable thicket of red hair, and without thought, with the pure need of desire, senses the seething of that body. He remembers how on his return the night before from a tour of the Montonero bonfires in Cañuelas, Berisso, and Florencio Varela, on entering Diana's lips, parched by winter (by life, she says), he was wishing it were all already over, so that he could be there again, caressing her, never quenched. And he remembers that he looked at her fixedly, with that intentness only the darkness affords, and said to her, I don't want you ever to leave, Diana.

And she, laughing, began to expertly undo the knots still within Noon, freeing every tenderness hidden in his veins, salvaging the shipwrecks of his emotions. She fell to tracing his body with her fingers, a body that was of no use anymore to any but hers and, letting him enter into the tepidness of her sea, she answered with the hoarse, vehement words that had once been Eva's:

"I want to go only so that I can come back. I will come back and I will be millions."

Soon, he saw her fall asleep. He felt the fresh fires of insomnia coursing through his quiescent blood. He smoked and the ebbing smoke left a deposit of moss and beetles on his tongue. He smelled his arms so that the fragrance of sex might envelop him. And returning to the detestable pasquinade, "*Horizonte:* Perón: His Entire Life / Documents and Photos of 100 Witnesses," he plopped into the mud of another chapter.

"V. Now, we shall never be as we were. One Sunday in 1922 . . ."

———

8.

Looking through the side window of the plane at four in the afternoon, the General is able to make out the brown craters of the unpopulated wasteland. The sight stifles him. The spasm of a river opens green seams in the earth. Trees, bushes? What forsakenness! Is this the country I am returning to? the General asked himself later that night. To these endless plundered pampas, bled dry? I don't recognize them. They aren't mine. This is where I always wanted to die but now I don't know. Does any of this belong to me? As for me, to what do I belong?

López Rega distracts him with a cup of tea.

"The time is getting near," he says.

Isabel strokes Perón's hair.

"Really? Is the time getting near?"

Sitting next to the General on the arm of his seat, he unfolds another sheaf of papers covered with scrawled figures and endless strings of hieroglyphics.

"I instructed our colleague Norma Kennedy to read a press release in your name. Fifteen or twenty persons were immediately called together on the first floor of the international hotel. She has told them that in spite of the gunfire and imperialist plots, General Perón would be arriving on our soil today to stay for good. She has given out a report that the plane is an hour behind schedule. To discourage disturbances she has confirmed that you are to arrive at the platform on bridge number 12 and will address the crowd."

"Norma . . . a fine girl!" the General mumbles.

"But we won't be landing at Ezeiza," López clarifies.

"Where are they taking me, then?" the General inquires.

"To the army base at Morón, for security reasons. Vice President Solano Lima has agreed. We have requested that he and the commanders-in-chief of the three armed services proceed immediately to Morón."

They are interrupted by lightning flashes. The plane's lights go on and simultaneously they enter a bank of yellow clouds. The General suddenly becomes uneasy.

"What's going to happen now with all those poor people who have been waiting for me? Three million, they're saying. Two and a half million? Lord only knows what infernos they've gone through to come and see me. I don't like to be responsible for so much disappointment. What sort of grand gestures will I have to make now to reconcile them?"

"None," replies López. "It is an act of divine justice. What did they do during the eighteen years you were away? Nobody sacrificed himself. Nobody moved a finger. Everything was done by you alone."

"And Daniel." The señora smiles.

A fly lights on the General's inert, spotted hand. Its body is blue, wings transparent, eyes avid.

"A dipteron." The General shoos it away. "Flies here, so high up?"

They watch the insect ascend toward a ceiling light and come to rest there. It rubs its legs together.

"Oh, my goodness," the señora sighs.

"Look at it," the General says, pointing. "See those eyes. They take up almost the entire head. They are very strange eyes, each with four thousand facets. Those eyes see reality in four thousand different pieces. My Grandmother Dominga was very impressed by that. Juan, she would say to me, What does a fly see? Does it see four thousand truths or one truth divided up into four thousand pieces?"

11
TWISTS AND TURNS

. . . In addition to the aforesaid per-
sonal effects of Abelardo Antezana (a.k.a.) Noon and Diana Bronstein (a.k.a.) Skinny, (a.k.a.) The Redhead, (a.k.a.) Freckles,
clippings from the weekly magazine *Horizonte*, special edition
dated 6/20/73, of the article entitled Perón: His Entire Life / Documents and Photos of 100 Witnesses, with handwritten notations by
the aforesaid persons. All these effects were confiscated in the
search made at 1600 hours on the above date at the farm called
"Night Beach," located on Avenida Noria, Esteban Echeverría district, Buenos Aires Province . . .

One Sunday in 1922, when he came back to visit Grandmother Dominga, First Lieutenant Perón bought a certain
crudely made pamphlet at the newsstand in the Retiro station
that looked like one of the serialized romantic novels so popular at the time. There was a faded laurel wreath on the front
cover. It was Napoleon's 115 maxims on the art of war.

Juan Domingo pounced on those phrases with the voracity
of a love pent up too long. They unleashed an unfamiliar need
in him and he did not know for what.

*The great actions of a great general are not the outcome of
chance or fate. They are the outcome of planning and genius.*

Exactly. Perón wanted to plan the future, get a headstart
on it, foresee it.

The General San Martín Lodge was spoken of with caution
and respect at the officers' clubs of the time. It had apparently imposed Colonel Agustín P. Justo as Minister of War.
Many Yrigoyenist officers were on its blacklist. Perón wanted
at all costs to know what opinion was held of him in those
inaccessible circles and sought out the only one who could
tell him, his protector, Bartolomé Descalzo. He found him
annoyed: "I heard a Lieutenant Colonel complain about you,
Perón. They tell me he's a big wheel in the Lodge and that
man's unfavorable opinion can ruin your career. So, watch
your step, *che*."

"I do everything I am ordered to, Major. But how can I
protect myself against injustice?"

"If it were an injustice I wouldn't have mentioned it to you.
The lieutenant colonel was saying that you spend your time
involved in sports. And that he can't understand how it is
possible that a man practically thirty years old shouldn't be
concerned about settling down. The Lodge takes a dim view
of bachelor officers."

Perón felt the sting. He went around for several months
turning over the idea of marriage in his mind. In his adventures, the only women he had ever known were loud-
mouthed, unpresentable tarts, who flopped on couches with

their legs apart and spat on the floor. He begged Descalzo to help him locate a suitable prospect.

"Absolutely," said Descalzo. "My wife and I have our eyes on three or four good possibilities. We'll introduce you to them the first chance we get."

But the Perón family was overtaken by misfortune at that very moment. Juan Domingo had been expecting it. From the time he was a small boy, his mother had taught him that the course of destiny runs in cycles, and that fortune obeys a law of compensation: all happiness is sooner or later offset by misfortune. It never occurred to Perón, who had always been careful to keep his feelings lukewarm in order not to obligate himself, that success too had its price. He was the army fencing champion, a physical education professor, author of manuals on hygiene and morality for noncommissioned-officer candidates. A year after his promotion to captain, he was accepted into the War Academy. Too much good fortune in too short a time. He received a telegram from his mother toward the end of March, 1926: PAPA VERY ILL. PLEASE MEET US MONDAY TRAIN BAHIA BLANCA.

He scarcely recognized his father. Don Mario Tomás was suffering from tremors, he dragged along on practically his bare bones, and babbled thick sounds that only Doña Juana was able to interpret. He was suffering from arteriosclerosis and there was no medicine in isolated Chubut to help him.

He stayed at Grandmother Dominga's new house near the Flores station for a few days. Then, thanks to a subsidy Juan Domingo was granted by the army, they bought a big old house on Calle Lobos, where he had a room in which he was able to stow the maps and pennants he had accumulated over fifteen years of nomadic and barracks life.

Doña Juana busied herself raising chickens and making noodles. In the afternoons, she set chairs out on the sidewalk and deposited Don Mario Tomás in one while she gossiped with the neighbors. Juan appeared on weekends wearing a straw hat and a dark three-piece suit. When there was an open-air band concert, he could put on his dress uniform and, with his proud mother on his arm, take a stroll through the pergolas.

Shortly before the spring of 1926, he interrupted his drawing of a Napoleonic map to take a telephone call from Lieutenant Colonel Descalzo. "Be at the entrance to the Capitol Theater at ten in the morning," his mentor said, "and come prepared, Perón. My wife and I have what you are looking for."

He left home two hours ahead of time, dressed to kill. He wished to show himself for what he was—refined, charming, self-assured—and dazzle the candidate. But at no time did he wonder what she might be like. If Descalzo recommended her, why waste time? He had always eschewed the needless expenditure of energy ordinary men lavished on their sentiments instead of applying that same energy to concerns of power or work. He had to get married and Descalzo would introduce him to the proper person. Nothing could be simpler.

Through the window of an ice-cream parlor, Juan Domingo saw the lieutenant colonel's wife and a short, petite girl who talked without raising her eyes and kept her teeth covered when she laughed. He knew without the trace of a doubt before even meeting her that she would accept him as a suitor.

The theater was filled with young officers and their wives, who wore cloches and bows on their hips. Perón feigned interest in the involved conversation about puffed overskirts, pleated bodices, boyish bobs, and V-necks favored by Descalzo's wife. In the adjoining seat, the candidate expressed her admiration with obedient flutterings of the eyelashes. As soon as the lights went out and the pianist had reeled off an evidently oriental overture, Juan Domingo leaned toward her discreetly.

"Señorita Tizón, may I call you Aurelia?"

"Potota," the girl corrected, looking at him for the first time.

"Potota. I beg you to never lower your eyes again. You look at me so deeply that it gives me the chills."

"Chills? Forgive me, Captain. I'm very sorry."

"Ah, no. Not Captain. Call me Perón."

At the end of the film, when the sheik, infatuated with the dancer, lifts her onto his horse to rescue her from a devastating sandstorm, Juan Domingo whispered valiantly, "Thank you for coming. For a long time I've been wanting to find a young . . . friend . . . like you. May I call on you? I hope I am not too late to come into your life."

She didn't take her eyes from the screen. Many years later, she was to confide to Mecha de Lonardi that for a long moment, she was dismayed, unable to decide whether to squelch the Captain's ardor or discreetly to give it rein. An encouraging nudge from Señora Descalzo's elbow made up her mind for her.

"From my standpoint, whatever happens, there will be time enough. I'm eighteen years old."

Perón's smile, boyish but tinged with melancholy, in the darkness of the theater, dazzled her.

"I'll soon be thirty-one. That's not a pleasant surprise for you, is it?"

A tremolo from the piano electrified the audience. The sheik was panting lasciviously over the dancer's earlobe. Then, brazenly, he dared to lick her cheek. Scandalized coughs could be heard.

Two weeks later, at the same theater with the Tizón sisters, in the same seats, watching that audacious simulation of a kiss, Juan Domingo brushed Potota's gloved hands, for the first time, with the tips of his fingers.

During the exactly two years of engagement that convention demanded, she believed she was madly loved; that is, with respect, sedulous visits, and dutiful letters. But the final day of the honeymoon ushered her into a routine so dense that the signals of love became confused to her.

"Sometimes," she told Mercedes de Lonardi, "I would approach Perón looking for affection but he would keep me at a distance, not hurting me, but nonetheless with brutal firmness. 'You can never get over your childish ways, can you?' he would say. 'Don't you realize you're a married woman?' "

And even though she was left alone almost all day long, he would check on her everywhere she went, including even her most trivial errands. He didn't like her to talk to anybody, even her sisters. It was as if he feared they might implant whims and illusions in her that he would later have to root out. His possessiveness reached such an extreme that one afternoon, during a period in which he was most absorbed in editing notes on the military conspiracy of 1930, when she

214

had tiptoed out to the vegetable store, as she turned around suddenly to examine some tomatoes, she spotted Perón spying on her from behind a telephone pole.

The first demonstration of affection that Potota received from Perón came after six years of marriage. It happened by chance. Her mother, Doña Tomasa Erostarbe, had died of cancer. Major Perón, stealing time from his duties at the Ministry of War, accompanied the family during the night of the wake and also attended the ceremony at the cemetery, but disappeared immediately after. He was not present at the novenas or masses that followed. He came home to sleep and rose so early that Potota never was able to fix breakfast for him. To avoid upsetting him, she made no complaint.

On the rare occasions when Perón telephoned to say he was coming home for dinner, Potota would refresh her eyes with compresses and rouge her cheeks slightly—all that was permitted during mourning—in order that she should appear happy and unworried.

One morning, discovering that he had forgotten some maps at home, he hurried back to get them. The silence and darkness that met him when he opened the door alarmed him. He entered cautiously, unthinkable suspicions crossing his mind. All at once, he heard a doleful wail from the bedroom reminiscent of nuns at prayer or the sound that a cat makes on stretching. He threw open the door and snapped the light on. Potota was face down on the bed, weeping, a tear-stained photograph of Doña Tomasa in her hand. His heart was at last touched by this extreme of grief. He held out his handkerchief to her and gave her a kiss on the forehead. Waiting for the lump in her throat to dissolve, she choked back her sobs painfully, and when her eyes had recovered their habitual expression of humility, said, "Forgive me, Perón. I'm just a silly woman."

A smile flickered on the Major's lips. "That's all right. Eventually, those feminine pangs will pass. I must look for my maps now and get back to the office."

1926. Perón moves into a big old house at Calle Lobos 3529 (now Calle Gregorio de Laferrère) together with his parents and initiates his courtship of Aurelia Tizón, daughter of a prominent photographer in Palermo who was a member of the Radical Party.

1928. In November, Don Mario Tomás Perón dies after a protracted and excruciating illness. Our hero is obliged to postpone his wedding until January, 1929. On returning from their honeymoon, the couple takes up residence in the Tizón home at Calle Zapata 315.

1930. For the sake of privacy, they move to a spacious apartment at Avenida Santa Fe 3641, 3rd floor. The bedroom was furnished with a Louis XVI-style wardrobe, a bed with an extremely tall headboard, a dressing table, and a pair of facing mirrors six feet high that multiplied one's reflection to infinity. The main pieces in the dining room were a china closet, the top shelves of which had to be reached from a step ladder, a table with legs that rested on lions' heads, and a porcelain St.-Bernard-dog-and-Tyrolean-peasant-girl centerpiece. Drowsing in the living room, a piano that Potota was never to play.

1935. Doña Tomasa Erostarbe de Tizón dies. Our hero leaves at the end of the year for Santiago de Chile to take up his duties as military attaché. Shortly before their departure, José Artemio Toledo pays them a visit, admires the red roadster in which they are to cross the Andes, and praises Potota's courage for carrying a .22-caliber pistol in her purse for emergencies.

1936. Now living abroad, our hero receives the news that General Francisco Fasola Castaño, who had been his chief when he was on the army staff, has been retired from active service for issuing a statement against "exotic ideologies that seek to becloud and perhaps besmirch our own ideology." Aflame with patriotism, he sends him a declaration of support: "My dear General . . . I have faith in your destiny and in you as a man of courage and determination. No more than that is needed for victory."

Events took a new turn. Early in 1930, Captain Perón was more an armchair officer than one of action. He was now less interested in the blind system of promotion by seniority in the field services than in the one-eyed, sinuous pathways of the palace. He never went to sleep without first having read at least a page of Count Schlieffen and repeated aloud, as though praying, one of Napoleon's maxims. And a constantly recurring topic of his conversation was a book by the German general, Colman von der Goltz, *The Nation in Arms*, which had just been translated at the Officers' Library forty years after its publication.

He taught military history and the more he discussed his favorite authors in his classes, the more blindly he accepted all their concepts as dogma. "There is no worse crime against the spirit than that of failing to take advantage of an opportunity," he told his students. "When a strategist of genius commits a new offensive scheme to paper, what is his purpose in doing so? To enable other strategists to copy him! And if he is handing such an opportunity over to us on a silver platter, why not take advantage of it? In war as in politics, there is only one morality, the morality of utilitarianism. Holding something useful in his hands, only a fool will let it slip through his fingers."

He recited Napoleon as though it were the Creed. Schlieffen, however, was his Saint Thomas Aquinas: the translation of all supernatural enigmas in the light of the natural order. In invoking Napoleon, he recreated him. Taking a stock phrase as his point of departure he made permutations of it. *Man is everything; principle, nothing. / When principle is everything; man is nothing. / One man is everything; all men, nothing.* Schlieffen's ideas, however, so possessed him that rather than paraphrase them, he preferred to ignore the original author. At first, he put quotation marks around them; then, he underlined them; later, he intimated that they might have been from Xenophon, Plutarch, Titus Livius, beings who faded into the night of time and ended up recapitulated in Perón.

We beg the reader's indulgence for a final twist and turn. In the spring of 1971, nearly forty years after the events we are about to narrate, the poet César Fernández Moreno and the neophyte novelist Tomás Eloy Martínez questioned General Perón in Madrid about the coup that toppled Hipólito Yrigoyen's democratic government in Argentina and launched a succession of military protectorates.

You are all familiar with the setting: the Guardia Civil at the gateway to his villa, the poodles, the pigeon lofts, the elm tree. The General's hoarse voice inviting us in, López Rega setting up the tape recorders, Isabel offering the gentlemen coffee, all of which we will skip. Let us pick up only the bare bones of the dialogue, the voices intermingling, and reassemble the past (that past) just as it was.

The visitors had arrived well-armed with snippets of speeches, opinions that had streamed out of Perón over the years, and even a scholarly tome by a professor in the United States. The master of the house had no arms other than his memory in which, however, there was a ferment of long-ruminated sallies.

"We would like to point out, General, that even though you were still an obscure officer in the early 'thirties, you had nevertheless won the respect of your superiors. You had shown yourself to be discreet, helpful, trustworthy, you had a bone-crushing capacity for work, and at a time of unbridled lust for power, your political talents hadn't yet cut their eyeteeth. And so, you didn't seem dangerous. The years were beginning to weigh heavily on President Yrigoyen. He spoke little, listened less, and was surrounded by a hedge of sycophants who stood between him and reality to such a degree that he began to distrust even his sound reactions . . . he didn't believe what he saw. In 1930, the terrifying silence that emanated from the seat of power set certain army officers to thinking. Since nobody else is giving orders, why not we who know how to? A core of old colonels had scruples: toppling a legitimate government would involve spilling the blood of conscripts—civilian blood—and that would mean violating the regulations and codes they had sworn to uphold. The lieutenants and captains, however, were drooling. They were to share in the first dress rehearsal for *coups d'état* to come, to be allowed a glimpse of themselves, albeit just for a moment, in the mirror of power. You, Juan Domingo Perón, crossed their paths many times along the way: Ossorio Arana, Julio Lagos, Francisco Imaz, Bengoa, all lieutenants and cadets in 1930 who later turned on you. It was like maneuvers for a war against historical reason."

"Oh no, sir! I wanted no part of it. I was one of the last to know. On September fifth, the day before the coup, I had asked for a pass to Upsallata because I wanted nothing to do with those traitors to the Constitution."

"Then, how could you have written at that time in the notes you entrusted to Lieutenant Colonel Sarobe, that you were one of the first? That José Félix Uriburu, the leader of the coup, came to an agreement with you in June, 1930? According to what you yourself wrote, Uriburu announced that he intended to replace democracy with a corporatist state. Since he was a captain, you didn't dare contradict him. However, you offered to bring other prestigious figures with similar outlook and political orientation into the conspiracy."

218

"Organization was always one of my strong points. Things went well in 1943 because we were organized. But, in 1930 . . ."

"They brought you into the revolutionary General Staff in the Operations Section. You were given some minor assignments. That coup was absolute chaos, General, despite your efforts."

"Like the country, boys. All of Argentina went to pieces. Having such an old president hardened our arteries. We were poor, all right, but we weren't an object of pity, like now. Sure, Yrigoyen was popular, but he was very old by then. His revolutionary fire was all damped down. There wasn't anything left to do but turn him out. And who turned him out? The army? No! It was the oligarchy that had been ousted in 1916 and was waiting for the chance to claw its way back."

"Nevertheless, General, listen to what you said on April 8, 1953. Go back to your past for a moment and hear this: 'It wasn't the revolution that turned Yrigoyen out, but his own people. Those who are now going around making speeches. They are the ones who betrayed him . . .' "

"Don't you see? It was the oligarchy in cahoots with the Radicals who threw him out. Even Alvear himself, who was like a son to Yrigoyen, received the news of the ouster with a champagne toast. Human gratitude is like the bird that flies by: the only memory it leaves is the droppings."

"Then, did you admire him?"

"Yrigoyen? Certainly. He thought the same way I did."

"Then why did you join the coup?"

"Because I got taken. They deceived me, telling me that the government was stealing, that such-and-such a minister was keeping a woman on money from selling national railroad ties, and another one was doing business with pencils belonging to the schools. And the government, mum, didn't say a word. Me, just a captain, what could I do?"

"You described all the things you did. You told how in the evening of that September sixth, you forced your way through in an armored car, right behind the Elite Guard. You said that the people all around you were jumping with joy, throwing flowers from the balconies, shouting Long live Argentina! Down with Yrigoyen! You told how on reaching the Plaza de Mayo, you saw a tablecloth flying on the roof of the Pink House like a flag of truce."

"That's how it was, boys. And I heard Enrique Martínez, the

Vice President, asking Uriburu to kill him. Cornered there, the poor man got hysterical: I won't resign, General! You can kill me if you want to! Do you know how I happened to see that? Because I left the Elite Guard around five-thirty in the afternoon, walked as far as Calle Victoria where I caught up with General Uriburu's car. I climbed on the running board and entered the Pink House with him."

End of twists and turns. A new chapter now opens to a tango Discépolo would write five years later: "Cambalache" * . . .

. . . Following are the marginal notes made by the aforesaid Diana Bronstein in a confiscated copy of *Horizonte:*

> Note by the prosecutor: *The remarks reproduced below constitute good and sufficient proof of the extremist ideology of the accused leaders. Offered in evidence before the superior court.*
> *The Old Man had a Napoleonic nose for it.*
> *He had a big schnoz Oh schnoz!*
> *"We shall never be as we were." Lifted from* Wings of the Dove, *Henry James, last sentence.*
> *Twist and turn. Twist and turn.*
> *Fasola Castaño, (a.k.a.) Fa Sol La Tacaño, forefather of the national-fasolist fatherland.*
> *Pass me a faso, Noon, pass me an oliveyou.*

* Swap shop.

12
"CAMBALACHE"

Zamora had imagined her as
she no longer is. He had anticipated the same fragile, imperious
features of the 1955 photographs. He was not expecting to find that
time could be beautifying. When Mercedes Villada Achával
opened the door to him, Zamora wondered whether he had come
to the right place. Time had pressed the woman's beauty inward,
and it was as if she felt that to display it would be arrogant and that
she was now only the transparent chrysalis that served as its envelope. She has been a widow for over fifteen years. The men who
succeeded her husband in office had not been kind to her.
Strangely enough, unkindness became her: it cast a pale autumnal
light upon a bearing that must once have been overly proud. It is

obvious that she has not slept. There are violet-tinted hollows under her enormous dark eyes.

"Did you give up waiting for me?" Zamora asks, excusing himself.

Keeping in the shadow, she answers, defensively, "I never wait for anyone." Yet, when he enters she presses Zamora's hand warmly. "I am having gloomy forebodings. To be expected on a day like this. Sit down, man, sit down. Have a cup of tea?" She rises, her body tense. "Listen: that silence. These neighborhoods are deserted. A moment ago when I went out on the balcony and looked down at the street, I felt that tragedy was about to strike. You must have heard, Zamora, what people are saying: that the moment Perón sets foot in Buenos Aires the masses are going to burn down the north of the city. The family downstairs left yesterday for Mar del Plata. They took jewelry, paintings, their animals with them. They were terrified."

"You mustn't worry," Zamora reassures her, rising also. "Perón himself will prevent anything from happening . . . He has said that he is coming on a mission of peace and I don't believe he is lying. He can't last much longer and he wants to go down in history unblemished."

As his eyes adapt to the darkness, Zamora realizes that the apartment is in disorder and that, actually, Doña Mercedes Villada de Lonardi had been trying for hours to make up her mind whether or not to stay. Two small trunks stand open in a corner of the room. Behind her hangs an oil painting of General Eduardo Lonardi, with staff of command and presidential sash, gazing out on a horizon of slipcovered furniture. Steam rises from a silver samovar.

"History, history . . . ," she comments, shaking her head skeptically.

"You can't tell anything from here. There may be people in the Plaza de Mayo, but I don't know. The outskirts, however, señora, are a river. It took me one hour between Lanús and downtown. As I left Monte Grande, my car was caught in a mile-long bass-drum corps. The streets are cluttered with buses, trucks, jalopies turned every which way, blocking traffic. It's as if the whole country were under a hypnotic spell."

"The eve of the millennium . . . ," she suggests.

"Something like that. Argentina peering over the edge of the abyss of the end of the world. Have you been listening to the radio?"

222

"I prefer not to," she replies as she serves the tea. "The radio depresses me."

"It was announced on one of the news programs that Admiral Rojas has his house booby-trapped to protect it from attack by mobs. He is sitting in an armchair outside his front door holding a six-shooter. If the attackers break through the fence he will shoot the first five bullets and kill himself with the last. He has made some very pompous, very angry statements." Zamora consults a grubby notebook. "Just listen to this one. It's an exact quote: 'The tyrant due here this afternoon, to the country's misfortune, is playing out the farce of the prodigal son, dredging up new errors and worse schemes from the unfathomable depths of his perversity . . .' "

"Damn clown!" the invective from Doña Mercedes's lips apparently wakens her suddenly to another reality, and she fixes her eyes on Zamora. "What are you looking for? Tell me the truth. What do you intend to do with what I am able to tell you?"

He had been waiting for the question. "What will you tell me? Will you remain silent for fear of Perón's vengeance? I would like to ask you, 'Are you one of those who prefers history to write itself?' "

"I no longer mean anything. But General Lonardi is sacred. Let no one dare put a hand on him. So many newspapermen have told so many things that never happened, have patched together and ripped apart history in bad faith, that I don't know . . . I don't know . . . It's difficult to believe you will be any different."

"I have to be different, señora. I am not writing a biography like the others. I don't look for explanations. I judge nobody. Who am I to say whether a person acted well or badly. My problem is simpler. I'm interested in causes not ends; in the forces that are brought to bear on events. Just look at this special number of *Horizonte*. It has a huge gap in it. The title offers a complete life of Perón but it's not his complete life, only a part. The General remains suspended at the zenith of his glory, rising to Paradise with Evita. You won't get to see the defeated man, almost ten years later, puffy-eyed, waiting in terror on a Paraguayan gunboat for Lonardi's mercy. Would you like to know why I didn't get to the end? Because I was missing the beginning. Read these paragraphs from the magazine. There isn't a single line of the Greek tragedy your husband and Perón lived on April second, in Chile. That part is a blank."

"The enemy brothers . . ." Doña Mercedes sighs. Weary, she sits.

"That's the button I wanted to push," Zamora remarks. "Cain and Abel. Romulus murdered Remus so that the city (history) would carry his name. Red Ashvin and black Ashvin in the Veda, galloping side by side, one in the light, the other in the dark, as though their chariot would run forever along the edge of twilight . . ."

"Give me an idea of what you have written, Zamora. I want to understand what you're up to. What you intend to do with this."

Zamora hands her a copy of the magazine. He hesitates. Within, he feels a hazy uneasiness, outwardly he exudes calm.

"Would you mind if I looked at the television, señora? Just for a moment. Ezeiza must be boiling by now. And we'll be able to see a closeup of the platform . . ."

Doña Mercedes shrugs. "Watch if you wish. I won't. And, now, excuse me. I am going to turn my back to you."

She moves into the shadow near the desk, puts on her glasses, sits next to a lamp, and reads the following in *Horizonte*.

> After the 1930 coup, the army became fashionable. Society girls gave dances almost every Saturday in honor of the heroic cadets who had saved them from the rabble. An indicator of the degree to which the uniform had softened even the stoniest of conservative hearts was the marriage at that time of Mercedes Villada Achával, daughter of one of Córdoba's oldest families, and the lieutenant of artillery, Eduardo Lonardi, son of an Italian musician who played at village band concerts.
>
> Behind the scenes, however, the army was power hungry. To placate General Justo, President Uriburu appointed him Commander-in-Chief. For a couple of weeks the two pretended to be on a honeymoon. Justo placed his unconditional followers in positions of command and then handed in his resignation, biding his time. Captain Perón, who was still flirting with both sides, was appointed Minister of War. After having been assigned several important missions over a period of a few months, he fell out of favor. His mentor, Descalzo, had been pushed out of the picture into a post as chief of a remote military district in Formosa.

As Uriburu's prestige crumbled, Perón displayed his new-found sympathies for Justo more and more openly. In May, 1931, he was removed as Minister of War and sent to inspect the nation's borders. In other words, 'Go outside and see if it's raining.'

He walked from Formosa to Orán through bogs that swallowed up animals in the night and were fields of fetid flowers in the morning. He traveled by mule over chalky wastelands from La Quiaca to San Antonio de los Cobres where the inhabitants dressed in guanaco skins and spoke a language of gargling and phlegm.

One unbearably hot morning, he was notified that he had been promoted to major. This meant more than just a step up in the military hierarchy. From that moment on, he was a chief and would be commanding more than he obeyed . . .

Doña Mercedes jumped the hurdle of several pages studded with descriptions of the Patagonian landscape and rhetorical reflections on the "Siamese-twin tissue" that, according to Perón, joined the destinies of army and fatherland. She paused when she saw Chile mentioned. The reference consisted of a single item within a lengthy chronology:

1937. Our hero took Chile by storm. The military attachés of one hundred countries elected him to be their spokesman before President Arturo Alessandri at the celebration of Chilean Independence Day. His eloquent speech received an ovation. The President invited him to an intimate party he was to give two days later. Perón cemented a lifelong friendship with Alessandri on that occasion. After dinner, he sang, out of tune but with great feeling, the tango "Cambalache," which he characterized as a moral rhapsody of the Argentine soul. Luis Villalobos, a Chilean official who met our hero at the party, recalled that he confused the lyrics at the end of the tango and that Dr. Alessandri politely called it to his attention. Accompanied by Potota on the concertina, our hero had sung:

> *Siglo veinte, cambalache,*
> *Problemático y febril,*

El que no llora no mama,
*Y el que no mama es un gil!**

The President quoted the correct line to him: *El que no afana es un gil, / el que no afana.*†

The strong ties of friendship established in Santiago by Perón, now a lieutenant colonel, manifested themselves in March of the next year.

1938. Innumerable farewell parties were given in his honor before his return to Buenos Aires, where the Ministry of War had reserved an important mission for him . . .

"This isn't serious, Zamora." Doña Mercedes turns toward him, removing her glasses. "And you want to involve General Lonardi in this sort of gossip-column journalism!"

Zamora doesn't hear her. He had discreetly lowered the volume of the television to nothing but, nonetheless, muffled roars emerge from the set that might be the chanting of the crowd or the commentator's booming voice.

Aimlessly, the camera prowls the crowd, wanders over empty pastures, moves over fields of letters as though following swarms of ants, and holds on Isabelita's still incomplete photograph, which workers are hurrying to fill out. One shoulder, a piece of one ear, and the bow on her chignon are still lacking. Baskets full of pigeons are being unloaded from trucks at the edge of the platform. The symphony orchestra keeps going through the motions of tuning up.

"Zamora," Doña Mercedes repeats, and this time he looks at her, startled, as though emerging from forbidden waters. *"C'est fini?"* she asks, aggressively. *"Finie, la mascarade dégoûtante?"* And from the shadow cast by the lamp, she reaches out a sheaf of papers to him. "Take these, Zamora," she orders, shaking them. "Here you have the story of what Eduardo and I lived through in Chile with the Peróns thirty-five years ago. I was up the entire night copying it out of my notebooks. There is more here than you will have expected."

She rises and walks regally into the light. For an instant, age seems to have been shed from her body, as though the chrysalis of her beauty has opened and its former aureole now took wing.

---

* Freely translated: Twentieth century, swap shop, / Of panics and problems without hope, / If you don't squeal, you won't get your teat. / If you don't get your teat, you're a dope. /
† If you don't steal, you're a dope.

"I'll publish your story as it stands."

"Not so fast, Zamora. My children were advising me last night, until quite late, not to give you anything. 'Why this man? Why him, all of a sudden?' my eldest daughter Marta said to me. She is writing a book in tribute to her father. The fact is, I didn't know myself. Why you, Zamora? The revelation came to me now as I was reading this filthy magazine. It's because you know the other side of the story, Cain's side, and you're not leaving here without telling it. Because you wouldn't have called me unless you had a reason. God is just, remember? 'God is just': the slogan with which Eduardo overthrew Perón."

Her angry tone proceeds like a trained mastiff on a leash, serenely until menaced. She picks up her teacup and a drop falls on her immaculate skirt. At this point, Zamora and she feel the darkness of a thunderclap in San Martín Plaza two blocks away. The thought of a prophetic rain occurs to them both but neither says so: the red rain of the end of the world. Doña Mercedes, separating the slats of the blind, looks out of the window. The sun is shining. Thunder can be heard again, torpid as a dying animal. Now the thunder rolls in a monotonous humming, leaps like a grasshopper, and takes voice, grating out the unmistakable melody: "Perón, Perón, how great you are . . ."

Zamora is prepared for a tradeoff. He has brought a folder full of old clippings and he opens it for her to see.

"I won't tell you the other side, I'll show it to you. You'll be surprised. You won't often find this many conflicting passions in a single drama. Begin here. Read this report by the *Horizonte* correspondents:

ACT I. Perón reached Santiago in March, 1936. He moved into the Providencia. His working day began at 7 a.m. in a small office in the Matte Arcade that opened onto the private gardens of the Argentine ambassador. This arcade in which the drama will unfold that sealed the fates of Lonardi and Perón is worth describing. It is located in the main square. Its shops exude dampness. Handicrafts from the interior of the country are on display in their windows: copper pots, leather harnesses, clay ashtrays. The Argentine Embassy was on the fifth floor.

The building was surrounded by a depressed area with droves of beggars always obstructing the way. Roberto Arlt, who passed through Santiago in 1937, described it in a letter to his mother:

This is worse than Africa. The people have practically nothing to eat. For us Argentines with money in our pocket life is cheap, for the natives it is immensely dear. Statistics show that a Chilean eats a quarter of an ounce of meat a day. Two thirds of the capital is taken up by tenements dating back to colonial times. Tenements a block long with old roof tiles . . .

A routine aspect of the duties of the military attaché of that time, in Santiago as well as Buenos Aires, was procurement of the other country's maps, plans, statistics, reports of maneuvers, and strategic documents. They played at war, espionage, patriotism. President Alessandri, a man of the left, did not take this horse-trading in stride. The army and navy had been plaguing him since the beginning of 1935 with requests for funds to modernize their weapons. A pretext was needed: an imaginary enemy, a careless spy, a drummed-up war scare casting its shadow over a defenseless state. Perón, who foresaw such threats, spun his web in the shadows, backing off time and again when the moment came to act. Lonardi, in all innocence, seeking only to win approbation, swallowed the bait.

The story has three versions, all relentlessly unfavorable to Lonardi. The newspapers of the time do not mention Perón. They claim (the details must not be lost sight of) that, for at least a year, Chilean military intelligence had been on the trail of a former army officer, Carlos Leopoldo Haniez, who was thought to be peddling secret documents.

The head of intelligence, Colonel Francisco Japke, set up a series of traps. He ordered two of Haniez's former comrades to resume friendship with him and pose as accomplices. According to the weekly *Ercilla*, "superb wines, convivial dinners, never-ending toasts," were the order of the day.

The documents were to be sold through Guido Arzeno, an Argentine, the United Artists representative in Chile. Arzeno lived in apartment #311 of the Matte Arcade. Japke ordered a tap on his telephone and concealed microphones in the living room.

Emboldened by his comrades, Haniez's tongue loosened. The military attaché of a neighboring country, he told them, was interested in purchasing worthless documents at an exorbitant price. He was offering 75,000 pesos for the Chilean Army's mobilization plans and 35,000 more for the secret report on its latest maneuvers. A captain earned 200 pesos a month. The Argentines would be dropping a fortune in their laps, as though it were nothing.

Haniez's friends feigned pangs of conscience. Finally, they gave in. A meeting was arranged in Arzeno's apartment for eight o'clock, on Saturday, April 2.

A pause to recapitulate is in order here. Perón was the one who had inveigled Haniez. In the middle of March, Perón returned to Buenos Aires. At a final meeting with Haniez, he was to tell him, "Don't worry about a thing, man. My successor, Lonardi, has instructions to close the deal. He will deliver the suitcase with the money to whomever you bring the documents."

On the night of Friday, April 1, the traitorous officer was given a set of false maps and statistics prepared by Japke. The following day, a police squad burst into the apartment in the Matte Arcade. Lonardi was caught in the act of photographing the documents. Beside him on the floor was a valise filled with money. The detectives confiscated 67,000 pesos.

Three days later, the Argentine Government had the military attaché recalled and brought before a court martial. Arzeno and his wife were expelled from Chile. Haniez served two or three years in a military prison. He was seen in 1941 coming out of night clubs in Lima, dressed like a lord.

ACT II. Statement by Señora María Teresa Quintana, daughter of the Argentine ambassador at the time of the episode:

I was closely acquainted with Perón. My father, Federico Máximo Quintana, took an immediate liking to him and invited him to banquets and luncheons a couple of times a week. His image is still fresh and sharp in my mind. He had a sparkling personality, was very polished, and his observance of Catholic ritual was especially devout. When he was to leave, the farewell party given for him was a very special event, attended by the Chilean Foreign Minister himself.

The new military attaché, Major Lonardi, arrived around that time. He was not as brilliant as Perón and I don't remember his face very clearly. Out of gullibility or foolishness, he became involved almost immediately in an espionage affair that upset Father very much . . .

ACT III. Statement by Doña Enriqueta Ortíz de Rosas de Ezcurra, wife of the consul general in Chile from 1933 to 1942:

Perón? Of course! Certainly, I remember him. The day he was introduced to me, I remarked to my husband, Andrés, "Did you notice that character? He thinks he's got the world by the tail. That man has a highly exaggerated opinion of himself."

The embassy in those days was like a club of good friends. A week after he arrived, Perón had a horrible experience with Federico, the ambassador.

Federico had invited him to dinner. The women were all in formal gowns. Perón's wife, poor creature, turned out to be a fiasco. She was just a little thing . . . what can I say? . . . insignificant. Out of idle curiosity, I asked Perón what his impression was of our diplomatic corps. He answered like a lout. He said that our husbands were sent abroad more because of their names and connections than for their actual knowledge. "A lot of jackasses are running around loose, but I could get them in hand with a month of military training."

Imagine what that occasion turned into—an absolute frost! Federico, with an elegant gesture, intimated that we ignore the insult. I heard that his wife was annoyed enough to say that if he dared repeat the remark, she herself would order him from the table.

Perón must have felt the snubs because he appeared only occasionally at embassy receptions. I understood that he mixed with Chilean Army people and even tried to dupe one of them in some sort of mysterious espionage business . . .

ACT IV. Statement of Carlos Morales Salazar, author of *An Analytical Study of Justicialista Doctrine:*

The Chilean press ignored the case. We all know that military attachés have no function other than spying. When they come to a country, that is their only reason for being there. What other purpose could there be? To spy and to obtain arms. Perón passed the ball to Lonardi, who allowed himself to be caught. Was it Perón's fault? No! It was his own fault because of his stupidity. Naturally, Lonardi could never get over that terrible blunder and put the blame on the man who began being like a brother to him and ended up as his worst enemy.

Perón is very shrewd, very able. If he did anything wrong, nobody proved it. And Chilean history has given him a clean bill of health. The proof is that when he came on a visit as President, my country received him with all sorts of honors, and it never occurred to anybody to bring up the unfortunate incident of 1938.

"My God!" sighs Doña Mercedes bringing her hand up to her throat. "Is this the kind of drivel you newspapermen pass off as history?" She stands up. "Such obscenities?" Her glance is aged by the purple-tinged circles under her eyes. "I'm going to be the loser in this trade with you, Zamora. I should have foreseen it. I will be giving you the truth but in exchange I'll receive a bunch of lies. It's Perón's fault. Everything that ever passed through his hands came out polluted. The men, the army, this . . . poor country." She was going to say "shitty" but the word faded out in a hiss and does not pass her lips. "And now we are giving him another chance. Just imagine . . . !"

She turns sadly toward the television set. A flag is flying. A line of men in ponchos, wearing dark glasses, plods up the ramp to the platform at Ezeiza. The camera zooms slowly into a closeup of Perón's portrait, grim-faced, in civilian dress. A touch of cunning enlivens the expression.

"They finished Isabel's photograph in time," Zamora discovers. "They've set the elbow in. Look, now they're wrapping it in flags."

Doña Mercedes, her hand still at her throat, as though protecting herself against the darkness that now reaches her from infinite distances, isn't listening to him. "Nobody here has ever had a second chance. Not San Martín, nor Rosas, nor Lonardi. This is a cruel country. Irrational. Only the scoundrels get a second chance."

Physical discomfort emanates from the pages Zamora has been given, a hangover of the malaise that has lasted through the night and, finally exhausted, dissipates only now. They are pages that suffered deeply and were left convalescing from their feelings. They show it. On page 1 of Doña Mercedes's diary, the lines of a rough sketch cut across the writing—a woman's profile, a city seen from above?—and on the last two pages funereal souvenirs flake off each: a card with Potota's photograph attached to it announcing her death, and a clipping of the invitation to the funeral published in the newspaper *El Mundo*. As Zamora leafs through the papers, he is seized by the uncontrollable gluttony of all gossips. He has an urge to sink his teeth into all of them simultaneously.

"May I?" he asks, feeling upset immediately upon speaking. What am I doing in the middle of all this? None of it is mine. I'm an intruder in this story. He apologizes awkwardly, "I'm sorry."

"The light is poor here," Doña Mercedes observes, hands on her lap, covering the scarcely detectable tea stain on her skirt. "You'd better move closer to the window."

Zamora reads:

> *Santiago, Santiago. Cordillera, wasteland, mountain passes. My God, how far away! How terrifying if we must travel through those regions at night. Wastelands, mountain passes. I envy Eduardo, my husband. He is so sure of his destiny. I don't feel safe in these immensities, these cordilleras. May God help us! I can't feel safe.*

Bells toll in the distance.

"Bells at this hour . . . today? How strange! It's coming from the Church of Socorro . . ." Zamora hurries toward the television set. "I wonder if the plane is arriving. Is that possible, so early?"

From her chair in the shadow Doña Mercedes gives her consent. "If you are concerned, go ahead, listen to the news." She is facing away from the windows and the screen, but seems actually to be turning her back on everything.

Helicopters zoom over the crowd. An asthmatic exhortation can be heard coming through: "Let's have a rehearsal! Attention, comrades! Let's hear you now . . . ! How will we receive the General? Let's rehearse it. All right, let's go . . . one, two, three! 'The Peronist boooys . . .' " The voice goes hoarse.

Zamora understands. The bells were a mistake, too, a sudden discourtesy. They don't know how to handle the silence of the morning, so convulsive, cavernous. He switches the set off and goes back to reading Doña Mercedes's diary.

232

(Doodles: circles, arrows; a city or mountain?) The trip was extremely tiring. Something ridiculous but, at the same time, awful happened. My youngest daughter lost her pacifier. To spare the other passengers her crying, I crossed the cordillera closed with her in the washroom.

It was a relief to reach the Santiago station. As soon as our feet touched Chilean soil we forgot our troubles. My husband and I were brimming with anticipation. The post of military attaché meant a completely new way of life. We would enjoy a certain financial stability for a couple of years, a hiatus in the routine of counting pennies.

Eduardo—now a major—had been expecting to be sent abroad since the middle of 1937. At first, he was selected for a study trip to Germany. It was the usual stepping stone for those who were to become teachers at the War Academy. But strings were pulled against him and he was shifted to Chile.

Perón was waiting for us on the platform with his wife, Potota. I had not met them before. They made an excellent impression on me. They were extremely amiable and likable. They had found an apartment for us at the Lerner residential building in the Subercaseaux Arcade and moved there themselves, leaving their house in the Providencia section in order to keep us company so we would not feel lonely at the beginning of our stay. Elaborate preparations had been made for our arrival: the foyer filled with flowers, chilled fruit for the children.

Our husbands worked together. Potota and I were neighbors. In the afternoons, we would tour the city in the Peróns' automobile. They had just turned in their roadster for a Packard and were trying hard to convince us to take advantage of our diplomatic status to buy ourselves a car. "Take the plunge. It's a steal at the price," they kept saying to us. On Saturdays we went dancing. I would dance only with Eduardo. And so, it was natural that we should have a very warm friendship.

I could see from the beginning that the Peróns were an extremely close couple. Whenever Potota spoke of him, her pride overflowed. I recall one afternoon when we were walking together behind our husbands. They were both in uniform and very imposing-looking. Potota said to me, her eyes dancing, "What a fine figure they cut! They're such handsome fellows!

Don't neglect Eduardo. Chilean women are dangerous. Intelligent, attractive. And most important—amenable." Potota was tremendously jealous. Perón, too. They were both homebodies. She cooked and took care of the house; he spent his time with his papers.

Eduardo and I were seeing very few people at that time. Since we were new arrivals, we hardly knew anyone at the embassy. Naturally, our proximity to the Peróns and their kindness drew us to them more closely. We saw them daily.

I reread my notes for those days and am skipping over a raft of trivial anecdotes. Who would be interested? I see here a memorandum from February 7.

> Potota has been complaining of discomfort. Women's problems. "What do the doctors say?" I asked her. "Bah, they never find anything." We spoke of the Quintanas. According to her, they detest military attachés. She tells me, "Whenever they give a party, I come up with a headache. Their children throw shoes and papers down on us from the upstairs bedrooms. They've been taught to show ill will toward us." "It can't be as bad as you think, Potota," I reassured her.

Eduardo was quite surprised when Perón told him that he had received orders to remain in Santiago two months more. This was contrary to usual procedure. An officer was supposed to immediately relinquish his post to his replacement. It seemed an unimportant detail to us. Justo was to give way to the new President, Roberto M. Ortíz, in just a few weeks. I assumed it was a question of protocol.

That was not the case. Without being aware of it, Eduardo and I were heading straight into a terrible disaster.

One night we went out dancing. It was very warm. The men were confident of our discretion and spoke freely before us. Eduardo was disturbed by the ideological tight-rope walking of Alessandri, who flirted with both Conservatives and the Popular Front. Perón enjoyed scheming of this kind. He would draw arrows on the tablecloth to indicate the direction in which tactics were leading and where strategy was aimed. I don't know at what point the conversation shifted. "I've come upon something very serious," Perón said. "The Chilean Government is looking to provoke a border incident with Argen-

234

tina. *If this works, will the army be called up? Parliament here has rejected any new allocations for arms purchases. But in the face of a threat of war, it will have to give in. Somebody has offered to sell me all the documents for a song—the plan of the incident, the mobilization maneuvers. As you might expect, the Argentine General Staff has been advised of everything. We have already begun negotiations to buy them."*

He asked Eduardo what orders he had received from the Minister of War, General Basilio Pertiné.

"To cooperate with you in every way," my husband answered.

"I will put you in contact with a big Argentine gaucho by the name of Guido Arzeno," Perón said. *"We will conduct the operation through him."*

My husband and I stayed up talking until very late that night. Perón gave me the impression that he did not like being relieved of his post. He had become involved in a very delicate espionage operation and undoubtedly wanted to carry it through himself. Our arrival was an obstacle. Eduardo talked me out of that idea. He told me not to be ungrateful and to remember how attentive and affectionate they had been toward us. At the same time, though, he was suspicious of how easy it had been for his predecessor to get hold of the plans. *"I wonder if it isn't a trap,"* he said to me. He was uneasy about Perón having involved a civilian in such a confidential matter concerning national security.

On February 20, Roberto M. Ortíz became the new president. Pertiné was replaced as Minister of War by General Carlos Márquez. One afternoon, we went out for a walk in the square. We stopped at an ice-cream parlor.

"I've been ordered back to Buenos Aires," Perón suddenly announced. *"We'll be leaving in the Packard on March fifth or sixth."*

"What! How about the documents?" Eduardo was upset.

"It's all taken care of. The only thing you have to do is hold out your hand and they will fall into it like a big, ripe fig. The money is ready and Arzeno will give you the go-ahead. But, one thing I want to recommend is that you don't use the embassy for the operation. Go to Arzeno's house."

A person always has stirrings of conscience, a voice that tells him not to do this or that, premonitions, scruples. Eduardo had a heavy heart. He disliked intensely the idea of getting caught up in that web. But, at the same time, he didn't want to be considered a coward. On top of everything else, we found out around that time that Perón had been examining the contents of the waste baskets of all functionaries, on the pretext of checking embassy security.

It was a relief, in a way, when he left. A few farewell parties were given at which we all pretended cordiality but the old confidence was gone. It was not the same between the Peróns and us anymore. I felt very sorry for Potota, who was growing more and more emaciated. Shortly before leaving, she said to me, "I bleed all the time, Mecha. And no doctor can find anything wrong with me."

"When you get to Buenos Aires," I consoled her, "you'll see how fast they can cure you. It's only your depression that's doing it to you."

Everybody knows what happened after that. On April 2, at 8 p.m., Eduardo was arrested by Chilean intelligence officers while photographing plans offered Perón by a former lieutenant whose name was Haniez. Arzeno and his wife were also picked up. My house was searched. Fifteen thousand pesos that were to pay for the documents were removed from the safe. The next afternoon, Eduardo received a wire from Buenos Aires. We were to return at once. It was the end of the journey for us.

Never did a woman feel her plans as unjustly disrupted as I did. We had been in Chile for a little over two months. Eduardo's behavior had been tactful and honorable to the utmost. Would we have to leave, anyway, with our tails between our legs?

I am not one to accept defeat easily. I made up my mind to meet with the Quintanas myself and ask their help.

"My husband did his duty," I told them, "but the Chilean Government has overstepped the bounds. My house was searched. A diplomatic protest is in order."

Federico looked at me in astonishment, as though I were mad.

"Don't tell me that, Mecha! How could they have searched your house? Think it over carefully. I wonder if you didn't dream it. In times of crisis, people often lose touch with reality and imagine things . . ."

I left in despair. The following morning I found the answer in the newspaper El Mercurio. *The Chilean Foreign Ministry would not be sending a note of protest to Buenos Aires. The pact had been sealed at the cost of Eduardo's and my happiness.*

My husband was under house arrest for two weeks at the Savoy Hotel in Buenos Aires. My brother Clemente was told that he would be dismissed. Again, I decided to act. If this whole story began with Perón, it should end with him. God (I said to myself once more) is just.

It was pouring rain. The streets of Buenos Aires were flooded. I took a taxi and appeared at the Perón apartment. He opened the door for me with ill-concealed surprise. I'll never forget it. He was wearing a polka-dot dressing gown and brown-and-white slippers. My nerves were giving way and I was scarcely able to keep myself from bursting into tears.

"You are the only one who can save Eduardo," I told him. "Tell the General Staff the truth. Let them know that you and my husband were obeying Pertiné's orders. That you were behind the planning, spoke to Haniez, obtained the money, and made the contact with Arzenio. That you had left everything in place for Eduardo so that the documents would drop into his hand 'like a big, ripe fig.' Remember?"

"There's nothing I can do," he said, coldly. He was standing and so was I, soaking wet. "If your husband put his foot in it, I'm not to blame. It was very clear. I warned him not to photograph those documents anywhere but in the embassy."

Such shamelessness astonished me. "Perón! How can you say such a thing? I was right there myself when you advised Eduardo not to do it in the embassy. In the interest of national security, you said. There was no doubt about it from the way you spoke. You ordered it done that way."

"Don't twist things around, Mecha. I never said anything of the kind. And, now, for your own sake, leave. Women shouldn't be sticking their noses into affairs of state."

"You won't do anything, then?"

"Go," he repeated.

And on my way out, like a fool, I found the strength, from where I don't know, to ask, "How's Potota?"

That same afternoon, I saw Eduardo at the Savoy Hotel. He was very depressed. And the steps I had taken behind his back made him feel even worse. He chided me gently. Then, he became very upset wondering what Perón had meant by that threat: "For your own sake, leave!" My husband rarely loses control. But that afternoon, I watched rage gradually disfigure his face. It seemed to me as though his body were filling with ashes. It was he, but inside him there was nothing but ashes. It frightened me. It was raining incredibly hard. Eduardo raised his fist to the Buenos Aires sky. "God will make him swallow those words," he said, his teeth clenched. "God will make him pay for them, one by one."

A friend, Benjamin Rattenbach, interceded for Eduardo at the Ministry of War and salvaged his career. Our anger faded with time. In September, I saw Potota's obituary in the newspaper. I visited her grave alone, bringing flowers. I stayed a long while, praying and meditating. When I left, I was bathed in tears without realizing it.

Death notices, daisy pollen, yellowed newspaper clippings: remembrances copied by Doña Mercedes reached the last pages pell mell, exhausted. There are scribblings with lines bending like trees and, below, a river of words or doleful willows.

She remains with her back turned. Seeking refuge, she bends so as to be completely enveloped in shadow and only her hands move in and out of it at the mercy of the lamplight as she leafs through the photographs in *Horizonte*. Her body has disassociated itself from what her hands are touching, as if she feared that remembrances of others—of Perón—might jab like ticks into her blood.

Zamora jams the pages into the crumpled niches of the folder he had brought and turns toward the television set for the last time. What he now sees is disappointing: tedious welcome signs:

TO THE GREAT ARCHITECT OF NATIONAL RECONCILIATION

SUPE ACCLAIMS THE SYMBOL OF UNITY

THE KANGAROO POPULAR COOPERATIVE JOYOUSLY WELCOMES THE GENERAL OF ARGENTINA AND LATIN AMERICAN LIBERATION

FATHER AND MASTER OF OUR NATION, PATRIARCH BARD OF FATHERLAND, MAGICAL HERITAGE OF THE HEAVENLY SHIP /// NATIONAL /// GREETINGS FROM ROT-AR AUTOMOBILE WORKERS.

It is shortly before noon. Nothing is happening at Ezeiza.

238

13
CYCLES OF WANDERING

If the lieutenant colonel draws a red chalk mark on the blackboard and gives an order that the lefties mustn't cross it, they don't cross it and that's that. Why? Because the platform is there, is why. Eh? So's we'll put our blood on the line to protect it, I'd say. The lieutenant colonel is now going to ask us one by one to size up the situation: How do you thee it, Arcángelo? he lisps (I can't get used to that lisping of his). Looks easy to me, I'd say. I see it absolutely controllable.

I shouldn't have arrived late to the meeting, but at least I got here. How late I am, I don't know. The explanation of the operation is already going on. But the lieutenant colonel is repeating it for my benefit because he knows I'm solid. He trusts me all the way. I take a seat in the back next to the door. The room fills up with smoke right away because windows can't be opened. Top secret. There isn't a room in the hotel that isn't putrified forever with the stink of stubbed-out cigarette butts. It sticks to the curtains, carpets, everything. What a load of nicotine they must give out! The smoker's lung (I remember Daniel saying) is like a cockroach nest. The twelve of us they call the "Elect" are here. Lito, who came in after me, sits at the head of the table, on the lieutenant colonel's left, to preside. On his right is a woman comrade, biting her nails, no spring chicken anymore, a very nervous person but all guts. That's the only dame Lito Coba takes his hat off to. As she herself has told me, Norma's laid her life on the line in the resistance more than once. She's got balls.

Lito is the best and a real pal. When I look at him, I get a feeling like . . . I don't know . . . like my heart is breaking into a sweat. He was a little rough on me at first but with the experience I now have, I can understand how a tough initiation like that is necessary for a man. It hardens you up and makes you surer of yourself. He winked at me when he came in and then passed me a note that said: *That'th Etheitha.* I had to laugh. It seems the words the lieutenant colonel picks to repeat the most are always the ones that are the hardest for him to say.

There's an exact sketch of the platform on the blackboard showing the accesses and the weak points where the lefties could infiltrate, very clearly marked in red chalk. The platform is high enough off the ground so that a good check can be kept of the fan-shaped crowd. At three in the afternoon, the lieutenant colonel estimates that we already have two and a half million people. "Now," he says, "I want your clothetht attention." I copy down everything he says.

"Let'th plathe ourthelveth on the platform. Behind, there'th nothing. It'th a rethricted area of one kilometer and a half with three thecurity cordonth. Impathable. Now, let'th thtudy the right flank: Boarding Thchool No. One ith about two hundred yardth away . . ."

(A green circle: our territory.)

". . . which ith now a thentral thupply point. Food, firtht aid thtationth, armth conthentrationth, everything ith there. Now, notithe thith over here, nekth to the ramp . . ."

(More green circles and a heavy line.)

240

". . . ith an ambulanthe blocking the way. We have fifteen non-commissioned offitherth inthide, all heavyweight clath, ready to jump out at the thlightetht futh to thmash headth. That'th what we call the 'dithuasion forthe.' They don't carry gunth. Only pietheth of hothe filled with lead. Now look at the chalk line. It'th a cordon of militanth wearing green badgeth. Each one hathe a hardware thtore under hith poncho . . ."

(It's the same on the left side: a steel wall. We have an armored Dodge, a truck we can use as a battering ram, a squadron of guards with double-barreled shotguns. And, the danger zone—the famous thousand feet we have to defend with our lives—now has ropes and cables stretched across it where positions will be taken up by the Mechanics and Butchers Unions and sluggers from the Hotel Workers Union. The key point, the lieutenant colonel keeps insisting, is the platform. Everything is at stake there.)

". . . That'th Etheitha, boyth. It lookth like we have it under control when we thee it on the blackboard. But we don't. Gobbi will be in charge of the platform. Around two o'clock, a column of thirty-thouthand leftieth will try to push in on the two flankth and cut off the head of the demonthtration. We know their thignal: 'the thocialitht fatherland.' They will advanthe from behind the platform in a pintherth movement . . ."

(The lieutenant colonel draws several red arrows piercing the green defenses.)

Somebody asks, "How can they get through from the back if it's taken care of that they can't pass?"

"That'th Etheitha. By letting them in we will avoid premature bloodshed. We thurround them inthide our ring. We will uthe Hannibal'th thtrategy in the battle of Cannae . . . Any lefty able to get up to the platform will be a dead lefty. They mutht be pushed back with chainth, hotheth, clubth . . . Dithtract them by letting loothe the doveth and balloonth. Shoot only if nethethary. Any quethtionth . . . clarificationth . . . ?"

(Nobody speaks.)

"Gobbi?"

"I see everything clear. Looks easy, I'd say."

The old girl stands up. "Let's get going, then. Perón or death!"

That's the way to talk! Perón or death! That's all there is to it. I often wonder what it is the lefties are after. As far as I'm concerned, it's going back to '55 and *ciao*. The Peronist fatherland.

One people, one boss. With the General running the show, we'll be a power again in less than a year. That's what pisses me off about the lefties. What's all the drool over Fidel Castro and Salvador Allende? This socialism business goes down maybe with the starving in the underdeveloped countries but not with people like us who eat meat every day. I'd give them something besides doves and balloons. Lead! Clip their wings! An iron hand is the only thing that can straighten this country out. Hangings. A bonfire in the middle and burn out all the left crap. Clean it out! A purification! What was it the General said? The day the people turn out to hang, I'll be on the side of the ones doing the hanging. That's the way to talk! For our friends . . . everything; for our enemies . . . not even justice. Lito's told me: We ask you to show no pity, Arcángelo. When the time comes to put on the screws, have no pity for anybody. Not even for me, if it comes to that. Not for you, Lito? How can you say such a thing?

And my heart broke into a sweat again.

That night, no matter what, Evita's body was to remain emptied for all eternity. When the hour of Universal Resurrection strikes, she will be graced by another semblance, the Lord will know her by another name, the musical notes of her astrological sign will then have been changed. Her body will remain empty but her appearance will be unaltered. The same course of formaldehyde and potassium nitrate that keeps her body untainted will fill her veins, her heart will be awakened at the same point in her body each morning of history, nothing will becloud the divine serenity of her face. But her soul will have entered unfailingly this night into Isabel's soul.

Everything was now ready in the sepulcher. Before dawn, Taurus would be reposing in the house of Aquarius. The moon was propitious. Uranus and Mercury, the dominant planets, would be in consonance. The bodies would be oriented north-northeastward. The astrolabes indicated that the hour had to be midway between sunrise and sunset: eleven minutes to one o'clock on the morning of June 19, 1973. López knew four of the seven words he would have to pronounce: those in Bengali, Persian, Egyptian, and Aramaic. The ones in Chinese and Sumerian were still lacking. He knew that the seventh was formed by combining the sounds of Eva *ad infinitum:* Vea, Vae, Ave; all he had to do was establish the order in which to pick the letters.

The General's schedule must be changed, then. He would have to be made to forgo his siesta by immersing him in the reading of the Memoirs until night falls and then distracting him with visitors impossible for him to avoid. López would serve him tea at eleven o'clock, after the news, and put him to bed. He would need a deaf and dumb accomplice, a person who would ask no questions and would not blab. He already had such a person: Cámpora. Nobody could be better.

The secretary comes down the stairs from the sanctum with the agility of a bear, almost hanging from the banister, advancing faster than the torture of his plantar calluses. On his way through the kitchen, he orders lunch to be delayed (I'll snap my fingers when we're ready). When he reaches his desk, he finds Cámpora standing there, his hair plastered down with brilliantine. Effusively, he takes him by the arm:

How can we permit the General to leave without a little intimate reunion for him and his closest friends? He has been expecting one for days but doesn't like to ask for it. Why don't you organize a surprise for him, President . . . ?

(Cámpora arches his eyebrows: President? López, now in the cabinet as Minister of Social Welfare, has never before granted him this recognition.) . . . I'll take care of the household arrangements. You won't have to worry about that part. Call Doña Pilar Franco. Notify Ambassador Campano . . .

(On guard, Cámpora clenches his fists. No good can come of this, he senses. What's behind all this now after a week of icy relations and disdain for the authority of his office? The best thing to do is stall. He has an unassailable pretext.)

Not today, López, my boy. Let's leave it for tomorrow, the night before departure. Or, have you already forgotten that the General and I are scheduled to attend the reception at Moncloa at nine-thirty? We can't get out of that. It would be a monumental discourtesy.

President, we have already telephoned the Pardo* to beg off. We won't be attending. They understood. The chief of Spanish protocol spoke to me and said, We consider it quite understandable

* Franco's residence.

243

that General Perón should prefer not to go out. A sick leader is a sick state. May our Lord restore him to health quickly! Imagine that, Cámpora! The truth of the matter is that the General woke up again today with a fever of 99.3. He's almost eighty years old. We forget that. You have no choice but to attend the reception at Moncloa. And tell your sons to come, Cámpora. They haven't paid their respects to the General yet.

Now, the President is disarmed: Both of them?

Yes, of course, man. They're family, after all. And tell them to take the guests out somewhere at around ten o'clock. It would be a good idea to get the General to bed early. Tomorrow, when things have quieted down, I'll be able to attend a couple of ceremonies with you. In my capacity as minister, no? Just last night, the General was saying to me: López, why have you neglected Cámpora this way? Seeing that I'm ill, you go with him. Imagine, waiting until a day before we leave to give the order!

Moved, the President no longer harbors suspicions. Something has happened. The house's disposition toward him, so negative until yesterday, has suddenly turned in his favor. His eyes fill and, pressing the secretary's shoulder, he says: I know you've done a lot . . . I'm very grateful to you.

Once again, everything happens at once, as in a play. The secretary snaps his fingers. Isabelita bangs on the dining room door and calls out: Lunch! Lunch! You'll join us, won't you, Cámpora? And the General's voice filters down from the bedrooms: Where have you been, man? You've been lost for nearly a day. We missed you . . . Set another place, Chabela.

Oh, no, sir! I couldn't possibly stay. (The President's chin trembles.) I'd be happier here than anywhere else. But they have me running in circles, reneging on the treaties and letters of agreement signed by the military government before our victory. I came only for a moment on a little emergency consultation. How shall I conduct protocol in Barajas for our farewell? You hold the power, General, but you have no official rank or titles. When the Caudillo addresses you, in what form must he do so? I have sent a confidential note requesting that you be given the status of head of state. And as for me, whatever they wish. Everybody knows that I am a humble servant. But they are very fussy here. They have me so dizzy now with consultations that I have had, once more, to resort to Your Serenity, sir. What do I do?

244

At three in the afternoon, seated in the maw of his Memoirs and ledgers with notes, alone in the sanctum, the lap robe sheathing his stiffened legs (already somewhat varicose, and suddenly blue, as though the Buenos Aires cold had put in an advance appearance to nip them), the General sympathizes with this poor stand-in dropped into the center of the storm. You decide, Cámpora. Juggle your protocol any way you want. What do I have to do with these excrescences of power? I'm into other things. My age amortizes me. I've retired, now, even from exile. You go wrestle with Franco's acolytes and leave me out. It's enough that they're taking me to the plane. And that's too much. All I can expect from Buenos Aires is hard work and suffering.

He opens one of the binders of Memoirs at random and the shock of war comes into focus. He reads:

> *When I returned to Chile, tension could already be felt everywhere. It was evident that the planet was about to blow up any moment . . .*

(My fate was irrevocably linked to cycles of wandering. I emigrated, history receded. I was already accustomed to it. If I went to sleep a river, I prepared to awake a lagoon. Am I perhaps talking nonsense? Let's see what the preceding page says:)

> *. . . and in my last letters to Colonel Enrique I. Rottjer, I expressed a desire to circle the country on foot, to cover the wasteland from Lake Vilama to the Arizaro salt marshes, and from there to follow the line of the high peaks over the lakes and, on reaching Cape Virgins to cross the Strait of Magellan in one of our Navy's ships. Then I became a widower and the plan was put off.*

(I'm confused. What came after and what before? Now that I think of all the trips I made to the Milan cemeteries before Eva was buried there, time wavers in my guts. Why doesn't eternity happen complete in an instant? Why isn't everything that is to take place tomorrow decided now? Or is it that things happen like that, in bursts: that all things have already happened without one's even realizing it?

(I had been a widower for a month. It was October, 1938. The Minister of War ordered me to the Patagonian South on a tour of inspection. A Colonel Juan Sanguinetti was in charge. He had just returned from two years' service in Berlin. We disembarked at Comodoro Rivadivia and proceeded overland in rattletrap cars to the Argentine lake. Sanguinetti had been deeply impressed by Hitler. The man is a volcano, he said. He's going to sweep away everything. Hannibal? Napoleon? They were neophytes compared to him. He never had to study strategy, he was born knowing it. It's the Pentecost of politics: although he knows no language but German, a Japanese can understand him. We talked and talked along the mountain passes and glaciers. I imagined Hitler as a hero six and a half feet tall, a Colossus of Thebes. Sanguinetti said to me: His appearance is unfortunate. Hitler is a runt, but when he opens his mouth he grows.

(I wonder what made López Rega cut out those ominous frothings from that time? Let's see! Let's see what he was up to:)

> *Early in 1938, the Minister of War, General Carlos Márquez, one of the finest military minds I have known, called me into his office. He had full confidence in my discretion. When I was a cadet at the Colegio Militar, he was an instructor there and then my professor at the War Academy.*
>
> *"Look here, Perón," he said. "A world war is on top of us. No human power can stop it. We have made all the calculations but our information is very inadequate. The military attachés keep us more or less abreast of what's going on in their own sphere, but when hostilities break out, ninety-nine percent of what happens will be political phenomena, a matter of people more than armies. You are a professor of strategy, total war, and military history. Nobody is better equipped than you to send me the information I need. Pick where you want to go."*
>
> *Germany or Italy. There were no other options. I asked for twenty-four hours to think it over. We'll see, I said to myself. Hitler had transformed the Reich into a perfect clock. In less than ten years, public works and the armament industry were able to eliminate unemployment, increase foreign exchange*

reserves, and get a heavy industry into production. I had read Mein Kampf at least twice and was familiar with other good books on Hitler and his ideas. In Italy, after the occupation of Abyssinia, the Duce was getting ready to invade Albania. His popularity and charisma had caught the imagination of all Europe. Hitler himself admitted that Mussolini was his teacher.

What decided me in favor of Italy, however, was my command of the language. Since I would have to be in contact with people, there wasn't much I could do in Germany. I speak Italian as well as I do Spanish and, if I really exert myself, better.

The first place I landed was Merano, where in a matter of a few months I learned the secrets of Alpine warfare. I attended some courses in Turin on pure science and in Milan on applied science. Many concepts were clarified for me and many prejudices dispelled, particularly in political economy.

The revolution of the Soviets had a profound effect on Europe. The leaders who carried it out, Lenin and Trotsky, would have liked to see the fuse lit in Moscow catch immediately in Berlin and Madrid, but that didn't happen. Bolshevik ideas came up against an impenetrable wall on the borders of Western Europe. What did get through to the other side, however, was the socialism of Lassalle and Marx, but with the special characteristics of Italy, France, and Germany. That is where one must look for the real cause of World War II—in the accelerated development brought about by the ideological movements of the West. When the Munich Pact was signed, I could already see the storm clouds gathering. I said to myself: This is only a hiatus. The marathoners have just paused to catch their breath. The worst is yet to come. And that's how it was.

A few months after I arrived, the Duce invaded Albania and the Germans signed a nonaggression pact with the Soviets. War broke out almost immediately after. I took advantage of the situation to study the Eastern front. I took the train to Berlin. The German people worked well together and Hitler's enemies, of whom there were many at the time, were nowhere to be seen. The Wehrmacht officers were very nice to me. I communicated with them a little in French and a little in

Italian. Sometimes I gave out a few growls in German, a language only the devil and Germans can talk.

They took me to the Loebetzen Line in Eastern Prussia. The Russians held the Kovno-Grodno Line at the front. The chiefs of the two sides were friendly and I passed from one to the other with absolute freedom. I entered the Soviet Union in military vehicles quite a few times.

Back in Berlin, I read some malicious comments published by U.S. correspondents in their country. They described fascism and national socialism as tyrannical systems, which may have been true, but they did not stop to consider the magnitude of the social change being brought about by them.

In Italy, I set myself the task of picking the process apart in order to understand how the various pieces fitted together. I took note of a very interesting phenomenon. Until Mussolini came to power, the Italian nation had been going in one direction and the workers in another. They had no common ground. The Duce brought all the scattered forces together and moved them in the same direction. This was a resurgence of the guilds, but as true motors of the community, now. The people's sacrifice was not in vain. Each worked in an orderly way at the service of a perfectly organized state. And I thought to myself: This is what Marx and Engels were trying to approach but along the wrong roads. The utopias of Owen and Fourier appear here but in a more realistic, developed form. This is true popular democracy—the liberty, equality, fraternity of the Twenty-First Century.

I was unaware at the time of the concentration camps in which Hitler tamed the insubordinate minorities of the East, with a certain cruelty. In Italy, however, where they are all like us—sentimental and a little unruly—Teutonic stringency was unnecessary.

This golden experience lasted nearly two years. I saw Spain ravaged by the famines of the civil war. And I spent some time in Portugal, which was then a hotbed of espionage. But, I didn't want to leave Europe without having spoken to Mussolini.

On June 10, 1940, Italy entered the war full tilt. Several battalions of bersaglieri *moved into France. The Duce announced the news from the balcony of the Palazzo Venezia. I*

listened to him, as one of an immense crowd. I saw Calabrian
peasants, their eyes rapt on that great man, as if he were a
passing comet. I saw women of the people, weeping with enthu-
siasm as they embraced, all at the same time. I heard the
"Giovinezza" sung, voices raised, cheering the fatherland, the
empire, and the Duce. Carried away by the fever of jubilation,
I joined in, singing some of the refrains, "Eia, eia, alalà . . ."

The following day, I requested an audience with the Duce
through the Argentine Embassy. They couldn't give me one
before July 3, after his return from an inspection tour of the
Western front. I was shown directly into his office. It was
nearly dark. A single lamp entirely illuminated his imposing
shaven head. A moment passed before he raised his eyes. Then
he saw me and came forward to meet me, his hand out-
stretched. He inquired about the morale of the Alpine troops.
I told him the truth: that there was no army better prepared
for mountain combat. He smiled. "E vero, è vero. Sono bravis-
simi i miei Alpini." I felt like embracing him, but the solemnity
of the place held me back. I brought my heels together and, for
the only time in my life, instead of bowing, I saluted him
thrusting my right hand out, in the Fascist manner. The ges-
ture would not be looked upon with approval today. That ac-
tion of mine had no political implications and I could have
skipped it if I wanted to because there were no witnesses. What
mattered to me, was to pay him homage, military man to
militant, student to savant.

(López, what's bugging you? Why all the racket up there in the
sepulcher? I wanted to be left alone. What skullduggery are you
up to, now?

(None at all, General. Just straightening up before we leave. I'm
dusting, testing the fuses, checking the roof for leaks. Forgive me
if I'm making noise. No matter how easy one tries to walk, that
spiral staircase insists on creaking. And these flat feet of mine
never let up on me.

(You smell of grass, López. Cinnamon. And what are those
streamers you're carrying? Let me see. That other, the violet one.
What's this written on the edge in such tiny letters? Sounds like
some mumbo-jumbo: "Saravá Oxalá / Saravá Oxum Marê / Que
assim seja!" Moroccan, is it? Galician?

(I don't know, General. They are paper ribbons the maids drop while they're cleaning. They scatter them all over the place. How is your reading coming along? It's after three, already.

(Something's wrong with the Memoirs here, López. I don't know what. These reminiscences of the Second War aren't mine any longer. I read them and it seems to me that they go off on their own. For instance, look at this. Who am I here, saying this?:)

I had a number of secret meetings in 1941 to report the changes on the horizon to superior officers. The new Minister of War, Juan Tonazzi, understood me immediately but the other Neanderthal generals around him accused me of being a Communist.

They tried to take me out of circulation. Without realizing it, they were doing me a favor. I ended up at the Mountaineering Instruction Center in Mendoza. The country was suffering damp rot but shunting me aside kept my name clear.

Corrupt elements were wrecking the army. One group of nationalistic officers wanted to revolt but the conspiracy petered out, a victim of its own lassitude. The whole country seemed to be asleep, snoring away like beachcombers at siesta time. They wouldn't rouse themselves unless immorality or fraud was involved. The prestige of our sacred uniform had sunk to such a low ebb that a number of cadets from the Colegio Militar turned up in a dragnet of homosexuals. The scandal was very serious. It was hushed up to a certain degree, but the institution came out of it looking very bad.

My sermons began yielding fruit in the summer of '41. Ten or twelve young colonels who heard my last secret lecture, showed up in Mendoza and offered me their support.

"We haven't been sitting idly by," they told me. "We have already organized a solid block inside the army. If you want, we can take power in twenty-four hours." This was the initial nucleus of the GOU. In its idealism, purity, and impartiality, that group of men was capable of forging an Argentina that would be indestructible, just, and self-sufficient for a thousand years. We had an advantage that did not come up again: there were no civilian advisers or allies among us. That was the keystone of military power in the healthiest meaning of the words: Power is what put something in movement; military

comes from militaris, *that which concerns war. That's what we were looking for—to revive the idea of "the nation in arms."*

(López? That'll do, now, man! Come down out of the sepulcher! What's that caterwauling? What kind of music is that? Don't try my patience with your gargling now. It derails my train of reading. See what I mean. You've got me so I can't even talk straight with your disturbances. The señora is at peace. Let her rest. She's been hauled around too much already for the scant eternity she's enjoyed. La Eva . . . poor little thing! What is it you're praying to her? What does it mean?

(I'm coming, General. I'll finish in a moment and be right down.

> *Ogum chequelá undé*
> *chequelé*
> *chequelé undé*
> *Ogum bragada é a.*

(Look at your hand, López! You've hurt yourself. Look at all that blood!)

The people thought of her as a blue-eyed blonde, but when she came to Buenos Aires in 1935, Evita Duarte was no "Santa Lucia shopkeeper," to quote the popular song, and neither did she sing like a lark nor mirror the glory of the day. She was (they say) nothing, or less than nothing: a sidewalk sparrow, a bonbon bitten into, so skinny it was painful. Passion, memory, and death made her beautiful. She spun a chrysalis of beauty for herself and sloughed it off to emerge a queen, confounding reason.

Such a thing never even crossed my mind and she was very close to me (said the actress Pierina Dealessi, who took her into her company, taught her to walk properly, polished her diction). When I knew her she had black hair, pearly-white skin, and a pair of eyes so lively and filled with wonder that people didn't remember what they were like because they darted about so constantly and fixed so intently, one couldn't tell what color they were. As for the rest, Evita's face didn't say much: the nose prominent, quite bulky; rather buck-toothed; although a bit flat in the chest her figure stood up well, except for thick ankles about which she had a complex. A

251

pretty girl but nothing out of this world. Now that I stop and think of how high she flew, I ask myself: Where did a delicate little thing like that learn to handle power? How did she manage to acquire so much poise and speak with such command? From where did she get the force to reach the most doleful heart of the people? What was the dream that came amidst her dreams, what lamb's bleating stirred her blood, so as to convert her overnight into what she became: a queen?

That is the woman López Rega wants to introduce into Isabel's body, now, at eleven minutes before one o'clock on June 19. To make one soul engulf the other. It isn't that simple, however. They are unequal souls; how make an ocean fit into a river? What is more, not all of Evita's turbulences should be passed into Isabel. If that were done, López wouldn't be able to handle her. The deceased's golden tongue, her torrent of love would be of no use to him. It would be turning loose a hurricane, and a disobedient one.

López had been preparing himself all his life for this supreme challenge to the laws of providence. He had repeated on numerous occasions that he possessed more than the necessary knowledge and had lacked only the opportunity. Evita lay there now helpless in an oaken casket under the light of six red lamps carved like torches. No noise, no element that could vary the temperature, no possible threat from the dark of night could penetrate into the attic that Isabel had named "the sepulcher." The light is always at the same intensity, the seasons do not come or go, the air filtering through the purifiers is condemned to be air of nowhere. López had ordered a wooden crucifix with metal ribs identical with the one that had been in the Ministry of Labor twenty-one years ago to be placed at her head. The outer part of the copy is admirable, inside it is made of plastic.

Now that the moment is at hand to take the leap and taste victory, López hesitates: I wonder if the celestial forces have deceived me and I am where I'm not. Could it be that only my wishes have gone up to the sepulcher? And even if the make-believe alchemy of souls turns out to be real, what will happen to me if Evita's spirit rejects the transplant? There are so many incompatible substances in nature: olives and cucumbers, mangos and rice, oil and water! It might well be that the same could happen between these two beings that are so different, one that rose from nothing to become everything, the other with the chance to be everything ending up nothing. López pinches himself: I am here. Here. Nothing is hurting me. A dream, then?

He has confided his excitement to the killers who are protecting him. I'm going to have my golem, boys. Whatever Isabel says from this day on will be coming from my head. When you hear her speaking watch the way my lips move. I will be her ventriloquist. The killers nod. The most they were able to gather was that the boss, already very powerful, would now become invulnerable.

At the foot of the casket a hummingbird lies in a basin, its throat slit, sacrificed by López that afternoon while the General was reading his Memoirs. He has verified that sticking a pin into the craw of these tiny birds will produce a quick spurt of blood, like a match. But one must be very careful because no more than half a thimbleful can be collected. Another live hummingbird in a cage, feet tied, waits its turn. At midnight, López summons Isabel to the sepulcher. Drink a cup of tea, señora, and quiet your fears with a few drops of an opiate. Put on a silk robe, allow your thoughts to sink to your deepest self, then rise, and pray. You are well aware that the most disastrous setbacks are in store for us in Buenos Aires, that Perón will die there, and that when we are left widowed, the vultures will descend on us. Let us get ready. We need the help of a sacred soul to escape the dangers without harm. Stretch out on the cot beside the coffin of the deceased and try to sleep. Rest carefully. Dreams here are very fragile and the slightest disturbance can dash them to bits.

When he feels Isabel relaxed, he pierces the other hummingbird's craw and smears the sleeping woman's eyelids with the fresh blood. He then paints Evita's lips with a drop of blood and sits down to await the moment. He has left his own body in several places simultaneously. Through Isabel's bedroom window he deciphers the signs of the heavens, hears the throbbing of Sirius, Mars stretching, feels Betelgeuse's colossal throes. Everything presages death and resurrection, ark and ascent, flood and life. He stands at the foot of the General's bed holding vigil over his sleep. Fortunately, the visitors left early. And here in the sepulcher, you smell the odors of your anxiety, López Rega, and you blot up the dread of failure with your handkerchief. If you are only dreaming, if you are merely enclosing forms without substance in a fine wrapping, your game will be up, López. You'll become a laughingstock everywhere.

There's no time left. I must concentrate. In what order shall I cause the moira to pass from Evita to the other's body? How transfer the trees of soma, the joys of Kinvat to ignorant Isabel. Sink down, dream, fade away: learn to be, like death, the bridge between the General and the *descamisados*,* the standard bearer of verticalism.

At five minutes before one o'clock, López makes the first invocation: "BA," in ancient Egyptian, the long vowel held, the consonant given a half breath, so as not to fully separate the two. B A, that is, the power of the soul that returns to empty itself into a new vessel. B A, I am your body, Isabel, I fill you. The disciple, asleep, furrows her brow, exhales a yellow flatus: the pain from the needles that sew the soul.

López continues. Palm of the left hand on Eva's forehead, the right on Isabel's heart, a medium, a copper thread, a López of water recites in An-An Sumerian, Bajar Aramaic, Sāmsara Bengali, Doongo Chinese, Persian Fravassi: Angels of heaven and earth, sacred penises of the universe, see that this chosen one finds the end of her successive existences. Hear her, impregnate yourselves with the music of her muse. Tomorrow, the crowd will chant: *Isabel Evita, the fatherland is Peronist / Evita Isabel Perón, a single heart.*

At one o'clock sharp, the hummingbird's blood is now dry. López inhales the breath of the dead woman and exhales it upon the lips of the living one. Never has Evita's expression been so diaphanous. Isabel's face, on the contrary, is covered with quivering scratches and welts. The tenseness of her dreams is showing through. She is like a guitar.

Suddenly López's body contracts, his head sinking into his trunk leaving visible only the malevolent green of his little eyes, like a lizard's. He extends his neck again. And retracts it. He is silent for a moment. He rises. Stretching out his arms, he proceeds to slowly envelop the two women in the ritual prayers of Umanda, shrouding them in the hypnotized moths of a Camdomblé litany, *Salve Shangó, salve Oshalá.* The coating of blood on Isabel's eyelids is evaporating. *Salve a lei de quimbanda, salve os caboclos de maiorá, ogum maré ogum.* The traces of blood suddenly disappear from Evita's lips. *Que assim seja!*

* "The shirtless," Perón's proletarian followers.

The following afternoon, López slowly approaches Isabel in the first-floor bedroom. The poodles are barking outside. The sun is beating upon the windows. Withdrawn in some other world of the house, the General pursues his reading of the Memoirs. Isabel is busily rummaging in dresser drawers. Everything is helter-skelter, tissue paper everywhere, tangled veins of clothing, tubes of cosmetics.

Amidst the lethargy of that disorder, López releases the final invocation, still caught in his throat, the definitive one, the one that will prove for all eternity how much of Evita's immortal spirit has now passed into Isabel. She has only to respond with *Que assim seja!* and it will then be known at last if the two souls are one.

"Eva!" López calls to her. " '*Ave, vaé a e, aev a, la morte è vita, Evita.*' Eh?"

Isabel turns around. "What did you say, Daniel? Come over here a second. Help me, man! I can't find my pink slippers anywhere!"

14
FIRST PERSON

I've told this story many times,
Zamora, but never before in the first person. I have no idea what
obscure instinct of self-preservation prompts me to step back from
myself now to talk about myself as though I were somebody else.
The time has come for me to show my true colors, to bring my
weaknesses out into the open. Take a long look at these snapshots.
Perón and me, one spring day in Madrid, chatting. Read these
manuscripts corrected in the General's own hand. Glance through
this unctuous correspondence with Trujillo, Pérez Jiménez, and
Somoza that I managed to get hold of. Note the forms of address
he uses for that Holy Trinity: Illustrious Son of America, Bolivarian
Hero, Bountiful Sir. Listen to him here denouncing the interna-

tional Communist conspiracy, there to his adulation of Castro and Che Guevara. He is an unending contradiction of nature. Body of a bear with an owl's beak for a snoot. A wheat crop in the sea. He has no contours. He is a man of mercury. I think I know him well, yet I have spent more than seven years not knowing him.

(Zamora listens. It is a little past 1 p.m. It is peaceful as a mausoleum on the top floor of the building of the newspaper *La Opinión*. Thunder can be heard. Tomás Eloy Martínez stops talking. Is it about to rain? He recalls the cloudless sky, the crystal-clear atmosphere, winter insinuating itself meekly. Maybe it's drums. Any sound these days can be an omen. Today, June 20, 1973, in particular, noises issuing from their caves do so because they are portending something. Martínez feels vulnerable. I wish my friends were a little closer by, he says. I miss them. And I miss my children. They live far from here. Today, it would be nice to know they were waiting for me in the next room so I could go in and give each a kiss. Not one of them is here. I need them.)

I will continue telling it all to you in first person, Zamora, because the time has come for unmasking. The profession of journalism is fiendish. It's a living-through, a feeling-with, a writing-for. Like actors. Today you're being a turn-of-the-century tough and tomorrow you're Perón. Period, new paragraph. For once, I'm going to be the main character in my own life. I don't know just how. I want to tell the unwritten, purge myself of the untold, disarm myself of stories so that I can arm myself, finally, with the truth. See how it is, Zamora? I don't even know where to start.

In June, 1966, a magazine, now defunct, sent me to Spain to describe what it was like there thirty years after the civil war was over. I wandered about the dead villages of Andalucía, attended a bullfight in Toledo, spent nights drinking manzanilla by the liter with a poet from the Estremadura who had lost an arm in the battle of Guadalajara. I reached Madrid on June 28. Later that same day, Buenos Aires notified me that Arturo Illia, the constitutionally elected President, had been ousted by the army. My magazine wanted an interview with Perón.

I located him the next day. He received me at his friend Jorge Antonio's office near the Plaza de Castelar. I recall that there was a photograph of Che Guevara on the desk.

Did Perón have anything to say about Che? Zamora wanted to know.

Very little and, as far as I know, none of it true, I said. He told me that Che had broken the conscription law and was a deserter. If the police caught him he would be drafted into the navy for four years, or the army for two. Just as he was on the point of being arrested, he was tipped off by the boys of the Peronist resistance. So, he bought himself a motorcycle and took off for Chile.

That's strange, General, I said. This version doesn't coincide with the story at all. What story? he cut in. The story Che tells. What do you mean doesn't coincide? he replied. It must coincide.

We were alone together for over two hours. I was intimidated at the outset. I guess my hands were shaking. It was like stepping into a photograph outside the dimension of time. Everything was a surprise to me: his trousers with the high crotch to camouflage his paunch, the two-tone brown and white shoes, the Saratogas he lit with Ranchera wax matches. All at once, it was as though I were watching him on a movie screen and he had the same voice as Clark Gable or Gregory Peck. And inside of me I could hear one of María Elena Walsh's tangos:

> Do you remember, brother,
> In '45,
> When you-know-who
> Would come out on the balcony?

Those details may seem trivial to you, Zamora. They weren't to me. There I was smoking a Saratoga with you-know-who. For the first time in my life I could shake hands with a figure out of a drawing, could feel that a historical character wasn't just a written text. Now, don't take me to be all that naïve. By then, I had already met Martin Buber, Fellini, Gagarin. But the name of the one I was alone with now in a room in Madrid was Perón. He wasn't just a man. He was twenty years of Argentina, for better or worse. I could see the blotches on his face, the sly glint in those little eyes, hear his cracked voice. My whole country came through in that body. Borges's hatred of him, the Libertadora executions, the revolutionary trade unions, the labor bureaucracy, and, although I didn't realize it at the time, the Trelew dead, too, came through. I said to myself: This is the man to whom millions of Argentines pledged their lives in the Plaza de Mayo. Remember: "Perón or death"?; and the colonel Evita fell so madly in love with that she referred to

258

him as "My sun, my heaven, my reason for living"? I asked myself, How is it possible to stand up under a weight of that magnitude?

Then, I went up to him. I heard him saying exactly what I was expecting him to. I sensed that he always guessed how the other person saw him and immediately projected the anticipated image. He had already been the Leader, the General, the Deposed Dictator, the Macho, You-Know-Who, the Escaped Tyrant, the Boss of the GOU, the Nation's First Worker, Eva Perón's Widower, the Exile, the One Who Had a Piano in Caracas. God knows what other things he might be tomorrow. I saw so many of his semblances that I became disillusioned. He was no longer a myth. At last, I said to myself, he's nobody. He's hardly even Perón.

We drank tea and orange juice. He asked me to treat his declarations with discretion. He was an exile in Madrid and subject to very strict regulations. He was forbidden to discuss politics. I switched on the tape recorder.

What I sent off to Buenos Aires that night was not an article but his exact words. Imagine my discomfiture on receiving a telephone call around two o'clock in the morning at my hotel from a French newspaperman informing me that Perón had disavowed my interview. What would you have done, Zamora? Exhibit the tapes, right? Negate the negation. There was, in fact, no other course. A few hours later, the news agencies had heard my tapes and in Cable #20 reconstructed the facts reported in Cable #5 that were subsequently denied in Cable #10. I was choking on my sense of historical righteousness. My concept of truth was making a lump in my throat. I didn't catch my breath until I was at Atocha station sitting in a train headed I had no idea where.

In time, Zamora, I managed to piece it all together. On the day of the coup against Illia, the General needed a show of strength in the Buenos Aires press. He was relying on the rebels to call for immediate elections and then turn power over to the legitimate victor. I happened to be at hand so he used me as a loudspeaker. However, he couldn't break Spanish law on asylum. So, with no qualms, he repudiated me. He knew that professional pride would compel me to produce the tapes at once. His declarations would be read in Argentina. Political morality is always at the opposite pole from poetic morality. This is the abyss at which men part company; where the poet Trotsky is incomprehensible to the politician Stalin, Che to Fidel Castro, the Fascist Lugones to the Fascist Uriburu.

Had Eva not died when she did, she and Perón would also have come to a parting of the ways. They were birds of a different feather.

To return to my tale. Gradually, I learned how, on that night in June seven years ago, I had been a small instrument in a big operation; how, just as the General would say exactly what others expected him to, he could also manage to get them to carry out his wishes.

It wasn't done underhandedly. Perón himself put me on notice in all frankness on one occasion when we were discussing Evita: "I used her. Certainly, I did. Like everybody utilizable who is worth anything." In his mind, a leader was the ultimate incarnation of Providence. Don't laugh, Zamora. When I heard him saying that he could manipulate providence, I laughed, too. I thought he was joking. But I began experiencing some very strange mishaps and I stopped laughing.

In March, 1970, I telephoned the General from Paris to request an interview. To my surprise, he agreed. I didn't trust him and asked if I might bring a friend along. He said he had no objection.

The night before leaving, I took a stroll around the labyrinth of the Latin Quarter. As I neared the Cathedral of Nôtre-Dame, I heard shouting, saw a group of nuns running in terror, and was stopped at a cordon of agitated policemen. An old man had just thrown himself off one of the turrets and landed on top of a couple on their honeymoon, pulverizing them. This ill omen didn't let me sleep. I had nightmares. My back broke out in red welts, just like Perón's does.

I made the trip to Madrid by car with a wonderful friend of mine who possesses the gift of transmuting all he touches into poetry. Finding a haystack in a needle would not surprise him. It would make him crow with delight. We crossed the icy peaks of the Pyrenees without mishap. At one point, however, a wind entered the car and set up a buzzing inside. That's not the wind, it's flies, my friend said. It became very annoying. We opened the windows. Worse. We felt our necks being nipped and had to stop to wipe off the blood. Fed up, my friend recited an exorcism against the evil eye. The wind subsided at that very instant. When we got back on the highway, both our shirt fronts tore. Perón! said my friend.

We reached the villa on October 17, a Friday, at about 3 o'clock in the afternoon. The General was in the garden sprinkling ant

260

killer on the rose bushes. He rinsed off his hands and embraced us. As I was helping my friend off with his overcoat, Perón made the observation that man and his overcoat are locked in eternal struggle and that if nobody came to man's assistance, he was doomed to lose.

We laughed and my friend remarked, That could make a poem, a *haiku*. Did you just think of it, General?

Yes, he replied, I'm always coming up with parables and allegories.

Afterwards, we read that the same saying had appeared in an interview a year before, and seven years before that.

We sat down. Absent-mindedly, I mentioned the name of Vandor, a leader of the steelworkers and an enemy of his. Some months before, Vandor had been murdered inside his own union headquarters: two bullets in the chest and, as he fell, three more in the kidneys.

There you have food for thought, he told us. That poor fellow was bound to come to no good. He was intelligent, an able man, but very low key. When he tried to step out and take things over they tore him to pieces, like Simon the Sorcerer.

Another parable, commented my friend. Simon the Sorcerer who thought he was God. It's in the Acts of the Apostles and the gnostic texts of the Third Century.

That's where the metaphor came from, the Gnostics, the General said. Well, now. In 1968, Vandor asked to see me. I gave him an appointment in Irún, to the North, near the French border. He confessed his transgressions to me. He had sold out to Argentina's military government and to the U.S. Embassy. Be careful, Vandor, I warned him. Don't leave the fold. Not on my account. I forgive everybody. But you've gotten yourself in a fix. They're going to kill you. Your back is against the wall. They'll get you, no matter what. If you hang on to your U.S. connection, the Peronist movement will put you out of the way. If you change your mind and try to back out of it, the CIA will do you in. Vandor looked into my eyes and began to cry. What shall I do? General, save me! I told him not to be a damn fool, that he had gotten himself into such a mess that not even God Almighty himself could get him out. He returned to Buenos Aires and, sure enough, they let him have it almost immediately. I don't know which ones put the bullets in him, but I don't have to. I know who gave the order. Naturally, there was plenty of money in the middle and a lot of dirty dealing mixed up in the whole affair. It wasn't a question of ability. It was a question of decency. And Vandor wasn't decent.

Ah, Zamora! I felt as though I were in levitation within a story the implications of which my mind was unable to grasp. I had never heard anybody describe the death by violence of another human being so shamelessly, with such detachment. I played on my apparent obtuseness. I asked the General if he had regretted that death.

Soldiers look on death as a natural thing, he replied. Sooner or later, we all lose our lives that way.

I'll skip over the conversations that followed throughout Friday until dark and were continued on Saturday morning. There's no point, either, Zamora, in telling of the mishaps on the return trip: the deluge of birds in Soria and our accident as we drove into Paris. I became paranoid. I began to believe that my mishaps were being caused by Perón's design. It was a relief when I learned from a book by Américo Barrios that the General's culture in the area of Simon the Sorcerer stemmed not from the Gnostic texts but from a Jack Palance film.

I'd just like you to know what our last meeting was like, two years later. It was in the summertime. Night was falling. We were walking in the garden of the villa. The conversation was of dogs and trees. Suddenly, Perón stopped short and looked at me as if I were the last survivor on earth and he had at last found me just then.

Tomás! he said to me. Your name is the same as my grandfather's. I should have been named Tomás, too.

I was taken aback. I made some inconsequential remark. Then, for absolutely no reason at all, I explained that I was not a Peronist. He smiled. He asked me what I thought Peronism meant. What I remembered from that entire past.

All I can remember is what I didn't see, I replied. Something I will never have the opportunity to see. I remember you stretching out your arms in welcome to the crowds in the Plaza de Mayo. I see the banners fluttering, the throngs of workers singing *Perón, Perón* over and over again as you keep welcoming them, for the longest time. Nobody breathes. Thousands upon thousands of people in ecstasy raise their eyes to where you stand on the balcony of the Pink House. And the hollow of the immense silence fills with

262

your voice: *Cooompañeeros!* I hear you pronounce that one word and the cheering breaks out again . . . tumult. My recollections are from what I saw at the movies and heard on the radio. None of it is from my direct experience.

He smiled again. The images merged into a jumble in my mind and, at that instant, the General was fifty years old again.

Everything can be brought back, he said to me. Listen to the uproar in the Plaza!

I could feel it. I heard the multitude grow delirious, igniting the city like a torrent of lava. The glowing ashes rained down upon my memory.

Night closed in on the garden. The General stretched out his arms and exclaimed: *Cooompañeero!* His voice sounded youthful and husky, like it used to.

I grasped his hands. And then I went away from there like one bleeding to death.

15
FLIGHT

I never can get anywhere. The remark slips from Zamora like a button off a shirt. He has parked the Renault 12 at the door of the newspaper *La Opinión* so as not to repeat on his return to Ezeiza the agony of the trip out. He has taken a taxi at triple the fare to bring him "as close as it's possible to get," and discovers that where it's possible to get is right where he is, at the entrance to the freeway, six miles south of the platform. Trucks, stands, and caravans of bass drums clog the horizon. Light cannot even be seen in the distance, only a pit of human shadows.

Move ahead little by little, he suggests to the driver. Put this permit to circulate on your windshield. We'll get there sometime.

If we get there, the man says in resignation.

We have to, says Zamora. And he pushes back into the corner of the seat, smoking a cigarette. An ancient Zen poem suddenly sifts through his mind:

> *I wandered twenty years,*
> *Going East and going West.*
> *Finally, I returned to Seiken.*
> *I hadn't moved at all.*

Just like Perón: twenty years coming back to the same.

In the end, the trip to *La Opinión* was worth the trouble. After considerable shilly-shallying, Martínez entrusted him with some papers that reconstructed the General's years in Europe. They consisted of scorched maps, fragments of a monograph on winter warfare in the Alps, the wreckage of an unfinished article, and narrations by a Lieutenant Colonel Augusto Maidana who lived with Perón from 1939 to 1942.

Zamora glances over the material.

1. HIS PORTRAIT, ACCORDING TO MAIDANA

(Transcription. Check meaning of bunraku, in case the word happens to be spelled correctly.)

He doesn't seem human. Perón is a robot, a golem, what the Japanese call a bunraku. I caught him several times staring into space. Not many people have seen Perón stare into space. He was unmasked. He turned into a hollow figure, without a soul. No sooner did he come back to earth than he began to fill up with the feelings and desires of others, with necessities. Had you gone out looking for a horse, Perón would be bringing you one, already saddled. If you found a shelter in the snow, Perón would be inside waiting for you. While staring into space, he displayed no hate, no sadness nor joy, no weariness, no enthusiasm. His emptiness was evident. When not abstracted, the feelings of others were then reflected in him, as though he were a mirror instead of a body.

2. DIARY ENTRIES

(Christmas Eve, Tucumán, 1971. Somebody passing me on the street called me by my father's nickname, Nucho, instead of Tomás. I wonder if one's name changes as one grows older.)

265

Today I came across somebody who knew Perón a long time ago, when he was not yet part of history and still behaved without regard for who might be watching. I feel certain that this person saw in the past what the present could not reveal to us; that in 1941 he had deciphered the enigma the Argentines were unable to solve thirty years later.

He is a friend of my parents. I talked with him one afternoon in the patio. His name is Augusto Maidana. He turned his words over and over when he talked, as though turning a hat in his hands.

After he left, I kept thinking of Kurt Gödel's theorem. How to translate Gödel's formulas into words? Let us undertake the impossible. Something like this.

In any system of mathematical logic . . .

No, that's not the way.

In every truth, obvious as it may be, there is always something that may not have been proven.

Better. That a man has ears, nails, a nose, and walks does not necessarily mean he has ears and walks. However, what Gödel means is even more complex.

After thinking it over carefully, I mentioned the theorem to Perón in April of last year. I said to him, General, have you ever considered what history might have been like without you? Imagine it. Everything the same as now: Madrid, the sky, the death of García Elorrio under the wheels of a car, Franco expressing disappointment in his former minister, Fraga, the poodles, the pigeon lofts. All of this happening without you ever having happened.

He answered: Any man who thinks that would have to leave himself and jump out the window.

Gödel's theorem, precisely.

3. NOTES FOR A NOTE

When he arrived in Merano at the end of May, 1939, Perón moved into a little house on the Via dei Portici that had three rooms, a hall, and a foyer with a fireplace. The windows looked out on the Duomo.

Spring was late in coming. The Benedetto mountain still showed traces of snow, and the Pasirio River carried frozen dogs and birds. Milan radio broadcast alarming news. Chamberlain had stated in Birmingham that England must prepare for the worst. In Berlin, Ciano signed the steel agreement with Germany. Inspector Ottavio Zoppi ordered a proclamation posted for the Tridentine Division that the officers interpreted as an advance declaration of war:

IN ACCORDANCE WITH THE BILATERAL AGREEMENTS, ITALY'S FATE FROM THIS MOMENT ON IS LINKED TO THAT OF THE THIRD REICH.

Lieutenant Colonel Perón decided to prepare himself intellectually and sharpen his reactions. He would come to the shooting ranges half an hour early to practice manipulating the heavy Hotchkiss machine guns and to test the effectiveness of Brandt mortars on fixed targets.

Captain Maidana appeared in the middle of June. Perón gave him the room farthest away from the hubbub of the street. His new companion helped ease the pain of his widowerhood that had so depressed him at the outset of his trip. Loneliness had always lurked about the house to some degree but now it was less assertive.

The weather turned mild. Perón began using the white silk uniform worn by the officers of the mountain troops. He took pleasure in following the Duce's project for transforming the beaches of wretched Albania into a showcase for displaying the new image of imperial grandeur. "The time of the utopians has come," Perón predicted in a lecture before the General Staff of the Tridentine Division. "An ordinary man accepts his fate. The utopian creates his own and then makes it obey his will."

All at once, Merano filled up with tourists and Tyrolean musicians roistering in the squares until daylight. Sensing war in the air, everyone strove to live life to the hilt. Maidana and Perón would stroll Corso del Principe Umberto in the evenings, not returning till the hour when matriarchs, grown drowsy, started abandoning their balconies to digest their skeins of spaghetti indoors, next to the radio.

They became inseparable. The lieutenant colonel instructed the captain in the wiles of diplomacy, recounting for his benefit how he had evaded intelligence officers on his trail.

"I sprinkled sand on the terrace of my apartment and at the front door of my office," Perón said. "I would leave a bit of thread, always a different color, on top of my papers to check on whether, despite my precautions, anybody had gone through them. Two intruders tried to get in one morning to search the house. My wife heard the footsteps in the sand and drove them off with a broom. I sent my reports to Buenos Aires in a diplomatic pouch with a false bottom. One time, in a confidential letter addressed to our Minister of War, I wrote that the commander-in-chief of the Chilean Army was thicker than a Galician stew. I had always been on friendly terms with this general but, after that letter, I noticed that he avoided me whenever possible. I assumed he had gone through my correspondence and decided to confront him. The next time I saw him at a reception, I said to him, "My opinion of you in the pouch was a lie, General. I sent the truth to Buenos Aires under separate cover." The man looked at me, speechless.

Things happened so fast no one could follow them. In July, the two friends traveled to Rome to find out what new turn their destinies had taken. Although the embassy had promised them an audience with the Duce, they had to accept a collective interview with Count Ciano, who arrived late and with his mind elsewhere. They listened to a few inconsequential observations on the coming war, now inevitable, a trap into which (he said) Italy would not fall. Then, before they knew it, Ciano had slipped away amidst magnesium flashes, and there was no opportunity to question him.

The lieutenant colonel did not put his uniform on even once during the ten days he spent in Rome. He went about in golf trousers fastened at the ankle and gray woolen stockings thoroughly inappropriate for the warm weather they were enjoying. After much hesitation, Maidana finally ventured to ask why he was doing such a strange thing.

"So I'll be taken for an Englishman," he explained. "I get much more accurate information that way."

"But, how, if you don't speak English?"

"No, I don't speak it, but I gesticulate it, and nobody catches on."

They were separated after that. Perón returned to Merano, and Maidana was stationed in Bassano del Grappa, nineteen miles north of Venice. No sooner were they getting oxygenated in one city than they were shunted off to absorb the local color of another, as if the brink of war meant nothing but junketing about. At the end of November, 1939, Perón had to go to Penerolo near Turin. Three months later, he crossed the peninsula and settled in at Chietti. Those irrational kangaroo jumps over unknown territory served for nothing but training to move around, pure and simple. He translated regulations from Italian into Spanish and back into Italian again just to retranslate them later. He committed crass errors in both languages, confusing the *ardor* of the Arditi and the *ardimiento* of the Alpini. He was interested not in accuracy but in keeping his senses sharp.

In the middle of spring he was transferred to a battalion in Aosta. That gloomy city, dotted with ruins, gave him the feeling that it was the last crossroads before the end of the world. At times, when he walked from the Emperor Augustus arch to the Collegiata de San Orso, he would stop at Count Tomaso de Saboya's tomb and reflect that all this bucolic tranquility would be dismantled and blown away by the storm. The victorious howitzers of the Reich were completing the encirclements at lightning speed. To be in tune with the times, he returned to *The Nation in Arms*, rereading it tirelessly.

Von der Goltz's book now spoke to him in the Duce's voice, repeating that a nation divided, ill-disposed to sacrifice, misgoverned by miserable hack politicians, incapable of forging a war industry of its own, is a nation of vassals. Only the strength of the father, the soldier, the leader can save it; only the power of the chief trained to wield power, the leadership of him who knows how to lead, the providential forethought of him who is far-seeing.

When he received the summons to Rome, he assumed that the hand of God had come to rest on his shoulder. The European night was now closing in. Soon there would be no time to breathe and all foreigners would have to leave. On May 14, 1940, Hitler's armies crossed the Meuse and advanced on Amiens. France fell apart like a rotten fruit. Exultant, the Duce wanted to occupy the provinces of the Midi at once. Various of his generals tried to restrain him, saying, "We're not ready. The Italian people don't want this war."

The Duce was to demonstrate that one single will was

enough to push thousands to the edge of any abyss. It happened on June 10. Maidana and Perón in their Argentine officer's uniforms mingled with the multitude in the Piazza Venezia, watching in disbelief an almost religious ceremony take place. As evening fell, the Duce appeared on a balcony of the Palace. He looked to the left and he looked to the right, the imperious jaw mesmerizing the uncertain crowd. He infused it with a sense of security, setting it aglow. He began a dialogue with it and, little by little, quelled the fear and shock his words produced. He spoke of death and the mass responded *Viva!* Maidana felt his friend levitate, drinking in the spectacle with all his senses, learning once and for all that the art of leadership lay not only in what is said but how it is said; the plain and simple seemed more powerful than all other reasoning combined. They remained in Rome for nearly three months. Food was being rationed but, having diplomatic status, they were given double cards. Occasionally, they ventured into the maze of the black market for cigarettes and liquor. The better part of their day was spent poring over maps, figuring out safe routes for crossing the border to a neutral country and returning to Buenos Aires by ship across an Atlantic infested with warring navies.

Italian troops invaded Greece and Libya. They advanced, humbled, with no solace but their continual defeat. Perón learned in November that his friends in the Tridentine Division had been decimated. There was no time for condolences. He had to flee the war, without even a chance to see it. He set out in a cavalcade from Genoa, armed with open-sesames and safe-conducts. He crossed the border at Ventimiglia and followed the arc of the Côte d'Azur to Marseilles. Perón went through two weeks of suspense and anxiety until he reached Barcelona on the morning of the first day in December.

"That was Perón's entire European experience except for the flight, about which I have not yet told," Maidana summed up.

And what about the descriptions of Berlin he gave to at least three visitors? And the trip to the Masurian Lakes of which he gave a complete account to two other people. And his audience with the Duce that he bragged so much about to Pérez Jiménez and Trujillo?

None of it took place, according to Maidana. Yet, Perón was not lying when he told those stories. Of course, they were lies, but he repeated them so many times that he ended up believing them.

STUCK IN EZEIZA

We're not going to get anywhere, groans Zamora when the taxi comes to a stop, bottled up at an access road of the freeway, unable, finally, to move ahead. The shield of trucks in formation ahead of them has stopped at the Workers' Home housing development: protective phalanx on strike, in eternal delay, motors in cardiac arrest.

De orders dey give us is to stand here, and dis is where we gonna stand, informs one of the truck drivers at the center of the caravan, asserting his authority, unassailable in his *pocho* cap à la Perón.

Change the station, will you? clamors Zamora, overcome by the driver's eternal tangos. Colonia, Rivadivia. See if there's news on Belgrano. Maybe Perón's already hit the ground and we're missing the speech. Listen! The anthem! The anthem's coming over the loudspeakers.

An apotheosis of tangos to the left on the dial, a chorus of national and popular welcomes for the Great Man on the right. And in the center, Leonardo Favio sobbing out "One Summer You Were Mine." Suddenly a deep voice cuts across the entire band: ". . . and in view of the seriousness of what has happened at the appointed place for the reception of our greatest leader, top government authorities are studying the possibility of detouring the plane in which General Perón will arrive to an alternate military airfield. More news in a moment . . ."

Zamora lights another cigarette.

Should I look for a detour? the driver asks.

Stay here. It ought to open up any minute. We're not the only ones who aren't getting anywhere today.

It's all the same to me. Either way, you're paying.

A gray light falls over the final pages recovered by Zamora.

4. THE FLIGHT ACCORDING TO MAIDANA

(Transcription. Literal. Correct treacherous grammar.)

Finally, we went to pick up our baggage. I had to go along

with Perón. What a tedious job, phew! I didn't get around to explaining that we traveled by train, bus, and truck, but our luggage didn't. It went by ship, direct from Genoa. We spent the whole day there. Perón said, "A crate is falling!" And then we heard the crash of breaking glass. "Now it's your turn, Maidana!" And the crane disemboweled the trunk with my clothing.

We must have been in Barcelona less than a week. From there on we could do as we pleased. I latched onto Perón who proved himself knowledgeable and sharp in dealing with travel problems. On the way to Madrid by train via Zaragoza, we saw nothing but ruins and pock-marked church steeples left by the war. And hunger. We had to hide when we ate to avoid contending with the people's voracity. In Guadalajara, a gang of armless beggars, heads shaved, their wounds crawling with flies, tried to storm the train. The Guardia Civil came and had to fire their rifles to drive them off. Perón said, "What we saw in Italy was terrible but the conflict that just ended in Spain must have been much worse. No hatred is as vicious as that between brothers."

From Madrid we headed for Lisbon where it was sit and wait. Two, three weeks, whatever Fortune decided. In time of war, it's all a matter of patience and death. Death to assuage patience or patience to disembark for death. We were finally able to get out on a small Portuguese boat, *The Spotted Claw*. There were musicians aboard but the high seas never gave them a chance to play. It took two days to get to Madeira and nobody saw anybody during the whole trip. They were all below fighting seasickness. Suddenly it calmed and the people came up on deck, rings under their eyes. Not Perón. He was dapper as usual. What storm? he wanted to know. Didn't even notice it. Too busy working.

Sly fox! They told us in the infirmary that even his brains had probably turned green from the pitching of the boat. That his liver was a disaster area and his stomach in a knot from all his vomiting.

I met up with him again in Mendoza at the end of the summer of 1941. He was a General Staff officer at the Mountain Troops Training Center. He had been rejuvenated by all the fresh air and I felt a change in him. He seemed less tense, more disposed to enjoy life. He had led an ascetic existence in Europe but was now making up for it. He could be found at the Colón sweetshop in the afternoons, surrounded by girls, drinking orangeade. He would describe secret cities built by Hitler—according to him—in the occupied countries. He alluded to private meetings with Mussolini at which the Duce would ask for his advice. I believe that his twisting of reality goes back to those years when he was going about with his imagination overheated. I hear that now he tells everybody who visits him in Madrid that the only truth is reality. But in those days he liked to say there was one truth for every man and that he knew of no two truths alike.

At one point, an old mountaineer from near Upsallata turned a daughter of his over to him to be raised. The girl was maybe fourteen years old and according to malicious tongues, Perón simply cohabited with her. She might even have been the same girl he turned up with in Buenos Aires whom he introduced as his goddaughter. I can't swear to it, but I do remember that both this one and the other were called Piraña.

I know all about that angle because as early as '42 he would ask me to go along with him to the Tibidabo cabaret. The owner had taken a liking to him. He would walk in like through his own front door, size up the girls, pick out two or three that suited his fancy, and say to him, How do these fillies whinny? He liked nothing better than to sleep with a woman's toes in his ear.

He made me his confidant. He dreamt of reviving the General San Martín Lodge, which had once been very powerful, but Justo had the army in his pocket then and nothing was done without his okay. If Justo had lasted a few years more there wouldn't have been any Perón. And who knows where we'd all be today? But fate forgets what we might have been. It goes by what we were. Now a colonel, Perón began to feel his oats. We were working together in the Mountain Troops Inspection Unit. He never stopped talking from the moment he opened his eyes. He was a word machine.

We had fallings-out over trifles, foolish things. He took it into his head that nobody could pay a check while he was around. That gave him a hold over us. One night in the Tibidabo, I rebelled. I'd had enough of that kind of extortion for a miserable couple of drinks. I'll pay, I said. You can't pay! And he wouldn't let me. He was giving the orders. Nobody foots the bill for Colonel Perón's vices. For Major Maidana's, even less, I said, turning my back on him. I put my money on the bar and left. I never went back to the Tibidabo again. I preferred to go my way and, as now, to be my own man.

ZAMORA'S FINAL OBSERVATION

This damn Zen poem won't let me be. It keeps buzzing round and round in my head:

> *The moon is the same old moon,*
> *The flowers are as they always were.*
> *I have come to be*
> *What's left of all the things I see.*

That's my Gödel's theorem, now. The only possible movement is for me to leave myself and jump out a window. Out of the taxi and into life. But even that way I won't arrive.

16
THE FACE OF THE ENEMY

I wonder what the Old Man was like in bed, Diana Bronstein said as she and Noon were settling in at the gloomy villa on the Camino de Cintura soon after they arrived around midnight on June 3. They threw a mattress stuffed with cotton waste on the floor, Noon lit the stove, Diana spread the yellow flowered sheets, and looking at each other's defenseless body, they felt love and pity, sought warmth at the little fires that burst from every pore, embraced and drank of one another until dawn. Outside, for a change, the trees exuded fog.

(Now, the cocks crow the day in with another voice. Diana and Noon, leading the southern column, advance hand in hand among the eucalyptus trees. The excited crowd following them left the last houses of Monte Grande behind and spills out covering the broad river of Route 205 at the mouth of which is the altar of the ceremonial platform at Ezeiza. They are 20,000 and the number swells. At the crossroads, they meet mud, islets, springs, tributaries of all sorts. They sing, fly by grace of the bass drums, letting their joy flower everywhere. And you are someone else, Diana. Not the one who was wondering:)

What do you suppose Perón was like in bed? Naturally, I'm not talking about these last years, *che*, dummox, fathead, and just to show you what I think of you, I'm sticking my tongue in your belly button. I'm talking about before, when he was in his prime. Who was he shacking up with then? Was it the one, Noon, that had the terrifically sexy nickname? That's it, Piraña! Imagine why they called her Piraña! Her appetite between the legs must have been voracious.

But that doesn't give you the right to touch me. Stay still, now! I'm going to smear you with cold chocolate and melt it on you. My, look at the condition you're in! A person can't even talk to you. Hold off a bit. Could you ever imagine the Old Man like that, stiff, petting, doing stuff with his tongue? That's the way it goes. Those are luxuries that can be enjoyed by the down-and-outest humans in the world, but not historical characters. Only virtues are ascribed to them. The books don't take Freud into account on that point, as though sex were shit, Noon. Mistaken, mistaken. Without a libido you can't get anywhere.

That's it, frustrated soldier boy. Fondle me slow. Thank God, a frustrated one. If you were a soldier who'd made it, I'd already be dying of boredom. When I dreamed of hell, I was a soldier's wife. I polished sabers all day . . . during the entire dream, I mean . . . just to console myself. Or, I was married to a historian wearing a toga, who scratched at ultimate truth with his fingernail. I was a little mouse wearing a Phrygian cap and I sat in the doorway of truth shouting "Nobody can come in because my husband is inside and truth cannot be shared!" And I who share everything but you, woke up in a cold sweat. That's it, touch me there. Don't move from that place. Come. Now.

At three in the morning, the scent of sex again aroused Noon and since Diana was already lying back in the languor of her red lava, curling into a ball within the long, long strands of that lava, Noon licked at her ear and lured her, whispering craftily, I don't think

276

anything special would happen in bed with the Old Man. That was enough to put Diana immediately into a mood for love, senses aroused, her desire opening to Noon's ever more tender importuning. That's it, be sweet to me. All right, now go crazy. Don't leave me, yet. Not so soon. Stay in till tomorrow.

Diana was determined to remain alert to recall just how pleasure grew in her but when she reached port she had nothing to remember; the frontier of joy was a river, an unconsciousness of self, a shore of oblivion, a levitation to the very depths. And when she began to recover, all that she could feel were saccharine little verses and tango lyrics that came to her mind. Inanities, such as:

> *May the sun never rise again,*
> *The moon not shine anymore,*
> *If a tyrant like this*
> *Brings new misery to our door.*

She licked like a cat at her evil thoughts and sitting back against the wall, arms folded across her breast, scowling menacingly, charged again. "But you told me that feet turned the Old Man on, which, I would say, is a sign of imagination. That he would sleep with Piraña's feet in his face and vice versa. I wonder if he did the same with Evita. *Che,* wake up!

How should I know? It depends. Maybe Evita didn't have pretty feet.

They were perfect, Diana decided. There wasn't anything about Evita that wasn't!

They stayed awake, navigating all night, the sails of their caravel filled, entering and leaving their common seas, bemoaning that so much still remained for them to explore, that Noon will have missed Diana's Seven Cities and Diana, Noon's White Caesar, that you didn't touch my El Dorado a little more, that I didn't drink up your Fountain of Youth.

When day broke, they took a bath together. Noon soaped Diana's feet and when he raised his head there was a bubble on the end of his nose. She sighed, combing her copper hair fused by the water: What luck we aren't national heroes. What would happen to us if the history books condemned us to angel sexuality, like Manuel Belgrano, to die virgins like Paso and Moreno, to have children by an accident of nature like poor San Martín . . .

(In the distance, Vicki Pertini and Ox Iriarte appear, banners flying, at the head of a fleet of Leyland vans. Behind, across dry Las Ortegas Creek, the roaring of another tempestuous multitude can be heard, the sky remains blue, the purity of the truth has not been corrupted by the perfidy of documents, life begins and I feel such a zest that even the urge to smoke is gone from me. Everything is gone except you, Noon, you big dummy, you alley cat.)

Let'th have a look at the fathe of the enemy.

Two helicopters, motors warmed up, are ready at the military section of the Ezeiza airfield. All around it, army guards march back and forth beneath the sun. The orders coming through the walkie-talkies overlap and tangle in the atmosphere into which gasoline rains intermittently and smoke blurs understanding.

"Tholdier, announthe that we're going to take off."

The lieutenant colonel climbs into the more heavily armed of the helicopters. The guards fan out. The blades begin to rotate. Lito Coba enters at a bound to occupy the position beside the chief. Behind the seats there are boxes of tear-gas grenades, ammunition, several Itakas, two Magnums.

War, whispers Lito.

The helicopter lifts off.

They're the oneth looking for it. There'th no room in a lefty'th head for anything but war.

As soon as they are airborne, the wind swings them toward the platform. The lieutenant colonel is already wearing his ceremonial clothes: a suit with wide lapels and necktie decorated with horse motifs. His brilliantined casque is plastered down so tight that even the slipstream of the propellers does not ruffle it.

At the sight of the multitude, the pilot is unable to repress a gasp. My God, there's millions of them!

A river of pilgrims floods across the fields. What a fever! Never have this many people been seen pouring over the vast bed of the freeway, fording the streams, shoes held on their heads. The lieutenant colonel is not yet disturbed by the slogans on the banners; when all are raised they will blend and cancel one another out. From his armored tabernacle, Perón won't see anything but eddies of letters. And the master of ceremonies Leonardo Favio and his melodious baton will drown out the shouted catchphrases. At the

278

moment, the voice of the emcee can be heard through the loud-speakers above, and from below, all overlapping, the words, chanted and sung: *You were mine . . . (The boys . . .) . . . one summer . . . (. . . together we will triumph . . .).*

The few tents not yet taken down dance, bellying in the wind. The stands emit blotches of smoke, and the fragrance of sausages rises body and soul to the heavens. A fleet of trucks on the horizon blocks the way. Behind, caravans of despairing taxis seek an opening. It is impossible to move.

Through his field glasses Lito has been checking every suspicious buzz in the swarm. Beneath the placards of the Montoneros he recognizes the Blue Sewer, a seditious vocal group, that disrupts the harmony of the concentration by chanting slogans attacking General Aramburu. And he knows that at the foot of the platform, next to the music stands of the symphony orchestra, the Golden Throat, a vocal group from Lanús, has been heckling the Union Youth for some time. Let them sing their heads off. They're doomed before they begin. It's their swan song. Hemmed in from all sides, their slogans sink into an acoustical pocket. Nobody can hear them. This isn't the opposition that worries Lito. The enemy he fears is the enemy that can't be seen, the lefties in ambush behind the culverts, the ones who must be digging trenches between the roots of the eucalyptus trees, ready to spring onto the platform from who knows what strategic holes.

Now, they are flying over stubby, blank little houses that border the fields from Tapiales to Llavalol. Nothing seems to be out of order, nothing detectable but random clumps of innocent trudging people, flying balloons, carrying children on their shoulders and radios. Yet (Lito thinks), the invisible ones must be very close by, now. It is almost 1:30. The General will be landing shortly after four. They have only a couple of hours in which to cut off the first thousand feet and get a toehold inside the captured bastions. If they're allowed to. Because the instant they set foot in the problem zone, within the cordons, they'll be crushed in a steel girdle. The problem is going to be what to do with them. Simply dissuade them? Threaten them so they'll leave? Not possible any longer. It's been too late for that for several days now. There's no other way (Lito thinks) but annihilation. Throw everything at them and aim for the head, like the General says.

Inside the helicopter, the vibrato of the motor drills into their ears. They talk in signs, using thumbs and forefingers. Their hearing dead, all they have left as human beings is sight. They are eagles, seagulls, rapacious craws. Flying over the platform, Lito makes a quick survey of forces. The ambulances, the armored Dodge, the cordons of ponchoed sluggers, the paramilitary guards with sawed-off shotguns. All in place, beaks sharpened, claws raised. To the left, he spots the wicker baskets containing the 18,000 doves on the verge of their fabulous release, a thousand at a time for each of the years of the Great Man's exile. Leonardo Favio is now saying what he is supposed to say at this very moment: "Never in the entire history of the human race has there been a tribute like this. Not for Julius Caesar, not for Alexander the Great, not for Pedro de Mendoza when he discovered Buenos Aires. Not for anyone. Only for Perón!" A shadow, neckless, outlines blurred, separates from the rest of the anthill on the platform. They see it waving at the helicopter with an Itaka. Lito recognizes it through the field glasses. Arcángelo Gobbi. How reckless! The lieutenant colonel yells: That'th too bad!

The helicopter swings westward, combing the eucalyptus groves from the muddy shores of the Matanza River to the Atomic Commission buildings. No sign of the enemy. The growling of the motor splits the afternoon apart. Suddenly at the right, Lito spies a burst of darkness on the horizon. A menacing snake approaching over there. Snake? The leftieth, the lieutenant colonel indicates.

They watch a dense vapor, a hippopotamus, advancing. The brown beast sways ahead from Avenida Fair, pointing its maw toward the Esteban Echeverría barrio. It has now passed all surveillance cordons and is approaching the little school where double barriers block the way. But before getting there, the jaws turn aside, the feet sink into the mud flats, the hindquarters camouflaged against the dry fields. There are over 20,000, not as many as the lieutenant colonel had expected. But nonetheless: Watch out! Lito spots three or four thousand more coming up along the edges of the Olympic swimming pools, the sides of the hotel and the youth hostels, where the steel workers have posted reserve troops. Keep on coming, then, Lito says, clenching his fists, right into the meat grinder.

That'th them! exults the lieutenant colonel. Watch. They're marching in thilenth, thneaky, like weathelth, all nerved up. They've got their bannerth flying. They know we're following them and they think they can fool uth with their ditharmament.

The thocialitht fatherland . . . Here they come. The lieutenant colonel picks them out one by one through his binoculars: Noon, Iriarte, the Redhead, Juárez, the Pertini woman. He sinks back into his seat: They're ready for a fight. I can thmell it. I know them. We'll accommodate them. Fatht, let'th go down! The thocialitht fatherland.

He rubs his eyes. He throws his head back and roars with laughter, the turtle shell of brilliantine breaking apart with the guffaws. The pilot laughs, too, not knowing why. And Lito, his teeth clenched, nostrils dilating, becomes tense. He shouts: Look at them, Colonel! They're walking into the trap.

Yeth, right thraight in. Five againtht one. Not a lefty'll come out alive.

Che, look! It's incredible! Diana rejoices. It is completely credible that Pepe Juárez and Ox Iriarte should be showing up there in the shadow of the water tower on Calle Almafuerte but she chooses to grace it with incredibility. She lets go of Noon's hand and runs to kiss them as if she hadn't seen them in ages. Where the hell have you been? Look at yourselves! What a sorry-looking pair! She ruffles Pepe's hair, and trying unsuccessfully to encompass Ox's girth, says, I never can make it, kid. You're a baobab. Vicki Pertini's Egyptian profile pokes out of the window of the Leyland, tics racing one another over it. Let's get moving! What are we waiting for? She claps her hands. The revolution begins now or never. Much thought has been devoted to this slogan. Vicki Pertini's flashes of acumen are always surprising.

She gets skinnier every day. She wakes up wrinkled and diminutive. Diana, in her moments of malevolent humor, says that Vicki sleeps in a bottle of nicotine and kerosene. By now, being nothing but skin and bone, her nerves are on the outside of her together with her hair. Her nose is sharp, her lips always puckered around a cigarette. She can breathe only when in motion. Repose asphyxiates her. She is out of the Leyland in a bound to assist the shantytown volunteers in the feverish preparation of the banners. She bites off her words. Easy, boys! Careful unfolding the cloth. When the General sees it, the lettering's got to look like it's been starched.

Diana, however, never stops kissing and hugging. She stirs up turbulence. The pilgrims take the water tower by assault, as in the

Crusades. It has battlements, mock cloisters, medieval aqueducts. The shantytowners are exhausted, stained with mustard and sausage from the trip. Leaning against the tower, Ox does not try to hide his letdown. He feels peculiar. Vicki's proximity, hopeless as it may be, is his only consolation. He looks at her with his dark, lachrymose, bovine eyes. Noon is the only star in her heaven. Fat men turn her off. And Ox Iriarte is irremediably fat.

In the spring of 1970, when Ox decided to join the group, Noon told him, Watch out with those depressions of yours, *che*. Depressives don't take well to this kind of life. And although seized by sudden onsets of melancholy, Ox hung on. He was always ready to take on any assignment. He would cure himself, holed up in the garage, working out his attack by fighting carburetors and transmissions. When he surfaced, there would be no sign of the scars of the struggle.

His father had been a barroom pianist in Bahía Blanca. A year after Evita's death, he was brought to Buenos Aires to entertain at a party in the presidential villa. He met Perón there and his life from then on was changed. At ten o'clock, just as he was playing "La Morocha," the General came over to say goodnight.

Iriarte, let me congratulate you, Perón said. I have never heard anybody beat out this music like you.

His father did not know how to thank him enough. In that case, General, in your honor, I'm going to break the world's record for playing "La Morocha" on the piano.

Perón took him at his word and offered him the Ice Palace for the ordeal. His father trained obsessively until, finally, one day in October, he said he was ready. He played "La Morocha" nonstop for 184 hours with rhythmic variations to keep from falling asleep. There were big audiences at the beginning. Women gave Ox lollipops and toys. By the fourth day, however, the public began to peter out until nobody but his mother and the inspectors were left. A cradle had been set up for Ox alongside the piano. News of the world record appeared in the press. One of the ministers received his father and presented him with a medal in Perón's name. That summer, they spent two weeks in Claromeco, gratis. They had a period of prosperity.

The General was ousted soon after and his father was no longer able to find work. Blacklisted by all the bars, he had to fall back on playing in whorehouses. The family lived for several years like nomads in the towns south of Buenos Aires. Ox was never able to go through an entire grade in one school. Finally, he was taken on as an apprentice in a garage. Cleaning carburetors gave him more than enough time to think. One day, it occurred to him that if he had been happy as a child during Perón's administration, then Perón alone could bring back that happiness. He saved everything he earned down to the last centavo so that he could get to Madrid to see him. He ate leftovers from the pizzerias and grew obese. One Saturday night he was knocked on the head and all his money —which he kept sewed into the lining of his trousers—taken. He spent a week in bed, disconsolate. When he got up, he resolved to find work in Buenos Aires.

He was lucky enough to get a job almost immediately near Retiro. A month later Pepe Juárez introduced him to Noon. After that he met Vicki. Ox, sluggish as a turtle, was fascinated at first sight by the giddiness of her beelike trajectory. He began dreaming about her and would awake, his shorts sopping with desire. Pepe advised skipping the formalities and getting into Vicki's bed forthwith. Vicki didn't much care what she did as long as it kept her from having to go to sleep. But Ox was shy and invited her to the movies. He tried to fondle her hands. Outraged, Vicki, without removing her eyes from the screen, pushed his hand away. On their way out of the theater, she said to him, Don't pull that stuff again, Ox. Next time, I'll wallop you.

When Diana entered the group and became its center of gravity, Vicki began to occupy her time scrubbing the organization's centers and sewing with the shantytown women. Ever persevering, Ox tried again. Useless. It was a matter of principle with her: Sleep with me whoever wants to but nobody better screw me around with love stories.

In one of the cassettes Noon brought back from Madrid, he had recorded the General telling the fable of the dogs and cats. Everybody found it ironic and amusing. Not Ox. The General said:

"Nations are made up of 90 percent materialists and 10 percent idealists. The materialists are like cats. When you want to hit one you can't catch him. And if you corner him, he'll face up to you and fight back. They react out of desperation. The idealists are like dogs. They react from instinct. If you fetch one a kick, he'll back away and then come over to you and lick your hand. The only way you can get rid of an idealist is to kill him. And even then, the dog is capable of thanking you. Consider the cat. The point is not that it is an animal with nine lives but that it cares deeply about the one it currently has. As for me, I like dogs better but I admire cats."

One Saturday when Vicki stayed up with him almost till morning drinking maté, Ox felt the fatalism of being a dog. It was cold. Cobwebs of dampness hung like gray flowers from the ceiling. They had one blanket and, covering him with it, she said, Come on, get in. The two of us together, but platonic, understand! He was ill at ease because his big body was a skein of tenderness and he didn't know how to separate one thing from another, in what corner to conceal the tenderness. She asked him what Noon's part was in the reorganization of the cadres in the popular government and Ox, licking at her with his bovine eyes, presented her with a detailed organization chart, trying to draw her closer to him with his use of pronouns. First it was "they," then, "you" in the familiar form and, finally, braiding her in with "we." But Vicki, logarithmic, kept her distance. She insisted on knowing how Noon would manage to dissolve the structures in the movement that were infiltrated with López-Regaism. The poor boa constrictor was inveigled with her toad spume, hedged in by her revolutionary-tract jargon, until at last it dawned on him that Vicki wasn't there in that squalid room to listen to him but so that she could pick up echos of Noon from his mouth, Noon's leftovers that remained stuck in Ox's memory. But, even though his outrage was infinite, even though he felt befouled and humiliated, the boa reproached her not at all. He stood up, saying that he was falling asleep and took his leave assuring her that his heart willed him to stay, but I can't, Vicki, this platonic angle just makes me suffer.

Now, they are together at the base of the water tower and on the shores of death, as if no history in common bound them and the last chance of that happening would be lost: Vicki, in the grip of her obsessive sense of order, a blue and white band across her forehead announcing her credo—Montonero—forms the shanty-town volunteers into squads of twelve, arms linked into a band of iron, now, let's hoist those banners and . . . march!

The helicopter of ill omen makes another pass. In the church tower a few blocks away, the wind elicits a few fitful strokes of the bell. Noon orders all hardware to be hidden in backpacks and Forward march, boys! Diana, beside him, eyes clear and ardent, bobs about like a kayak. There's no knowing to what lengths she will go, how many deaths will now be saved from life.

284

On detouring toward the little square of the barrio, they come to a big, crumbling old house where a string of expressionless children in gray uniforms fill the balconies. Orphans, murmurs Ox, and he remembers the mouldy flowers that fell from the ceiling the night he was drinking maté with Vicki. Orphans, says Diana. I wonder who brought them here. The children wave little Argentine flags. Several nuns peep out from behind, in the refuge of shadows. This all makes me very leery, she complains to Noon.

The helicopter has disappeared. The sky is covered with splotches, however. Balloons, smoke, sparrows: a bit of night passing somewhere. Let's go, boys. Let's start singing, Noon exhorts. The shouting in the distance reassures him. Nobody could guess that the hippopotamus's tongue would split in two when it reaches the platform. That the columns headed by Pepe Juárez and Vicki will lap the right kidney, Noon's and Diana's the liver on the left. Ox, leading the squads of shantytowners, will hold back, at the tonsils, as protection in case of an eventual withdrawal, displaying over the freeway an immense banner of Montonero welcome.

May the Lord enlighten us! The time is near. From the platform railing, Arcángelo Gobbi sees the face of the enemy approaching in slow motion. And he feels invincible, historic, thirsting to become right now what he will be tomorrow, hero or martyr. Behind him, a squad of the Elect stands guard, Itakas and a variety of sharp-pointed chains in hand, at the foot of the armored tabernacle. Above like a new bird, Isabel's jubilant photograph pours the flood of her protection upon the Ark. She is nearing. They are all coming. And this time it is no dream.

17

IF EVITA WERE ALIVE

Fate is unfair, Perón says. Eva
spent only a week in Madrid and was showered with honors. I
stayed thirteen years and all I have to show for it is a street they
named after me.

Camouflaged between chests that block out the windows of the
Mercedes, the General has managed to slip out of the villa in the
grayness of the twilight. What he had expected to find difficult
turned out to be quite simple. He found Lucas, the Moroccan gardener, in the dining room and said to him: I want to go out. Would
you be game to drive the car? That's all there was to it. The swarm
of reporters and photographers outside ignored them. Who would
have foreseen the obvious? It was unthinkable that the General,

officially ill, would be venturing out. Even to Lucas, who, disconcerted by the request, wanted López's authorization but could not find him anywhere.

At the crossroads of the road to El Pardo and La Coruña freeway, Lucas stopped to put the chests away. There being no need now to hide, Perón is free to bid Madrid good-bye as he sees fit.

The streets smell of sanctimonious churchwomen. An oily dew falls like an effusion from spermaceti candles. Several old men in black, wearing hats, reverently bear cemetery angels on a platform, through the mazes leading to the reservoir. The Mercedes turns northward on Espronceda Street. The summer darkness, like a fly, descends heavily.

Two binders of Memoirs lie on the seat beside the General. He knows he will not even glance through them but nonetheless he does not want to be separated from them.

> *I felt the need of a revolution since the time I returned from Europe. I was impatient to get it under way. Nobody was better prepared to command in Argentina than I was, yet, instinct told me that the grapes were still green and that my harvest would have to wait. I needed one of the generals to give the orders for me. I thought of my immediate superior, Edelmiro J. Farrell, with whom I had worked in the Mountain Troops Inspection Unit. He was a good man, a bit timid, who played the guitar and was fond of animals. Not long on culture, not too intelligent. Made to order for me. After a few chats together, I more or less briefed him on the responsibilities that would be in the offing for him but without giving any advance information, so as not to alarm him.*

How sluggish memory has become! Not the memory that's in the binders, which, having been put into words, is his no longer, but intimate, personal memory that he needs in order to know what he sent someone or promised another. That memory has gone lax and torpid, like his prostate. And he can find no doctor who knows how to bring it back with warm baths or to clear the soot out of his chimney. His memory has always been faithful to him but now it becomes distracted and, at times, he loses it entirely. It would have been better to train it, break it to the leash. But can that be done with such an erratic little animal? When the remembrance is old,

287

yes, because it leaves deep tracks. The General's head is a lattice of mildewed recollections. The cells of the honeycomb are still open and even odors keep within their same slots for years and years. But not so with what happened a moment ago. That memory flies away. Somebody arrives from Buenos Aires and embraces him: Thanks for what you did yesterday, General. And he hasn't the slightest idea who he is clasping to his bosom: You're quite welcome, son, quite welcome. He always says the same thing in order to avoid mistakes. Immediate memories are bare, a desert; the distant ones, on the contrary, adhere. Eva, for example. He did not go along on Eva's trip to Spain; nevertheless, it is always there in his imagination. What a nuisance the way other people's memories stick to one!

I sent her here as my messenger, Lucas, twenty-five years ago. The Madrilenians still can't forget her. It was June, like now. She went out in furs under the scorching sun. And, even so out of season and all, they fell in love with her.

But I ask myself: Isn't that glory really mine? When I came looking for her, as an exile, the Spaniards didn't want to give her to me. I waited thirteen years. For nothing. I had my street: Avenida del General Perón. But I didn't exist as a person. Franco never answered my letters. The ministers refused to receive me. Am I a pariah? That was what I wanted to know. Nothing doing . . . deafness in the palaces. I kept taking on more substance in my country, where I no longer was, while right here, where I lived, I became more and more of a ghost. As López says, I lived longer because I was a ghost. That, being a phantom here in Madrid, disease and disaster couldn't get me.

Imagine, Lucas, this is the street they gave me! Scruffy, unfriendly, alongside a soccer field. Just so that the howling of the fans will torment me in the other world and the gassy crowds can befoul my name when they come pouring out of the gates. Nasty tricks played on me by Franco, an irresistible demonstration of his ingratitude and envy. Did you notice what barrio they put me in? Chamartín! A mockery of our sainted liberator and my exiled person. They call you *che* San Martín. It's wicked. I am the only Argentine of importance who has resigned himself to vegetating here in this backwater of Europe. The Liberator had the good sense to retire to the Straits of Dover to die. And the last poverty-stricken years of our glorious Rosas were more bearable for him because he didn't budge out of Southampton Bay. Back in 1940, when I passed through this uncapital city, they brought me to Chamartín. There was nothing here but whorehouses and swamps. Franco put the two together and made the convents out of them that now clog my avenue. Just listen hard, now. All you can hear in this heat is the belly-rumbling of the novenas. I predicted it in my Memoirs: that we Argentines should have turned out the lights in Madrid and not returned. But I did. We all did. Even poor Eva followed my footsteps.

> *War changed human nature. It made people anxious and jumpy. I was one of the few who kept a cool head. In 1942, the water wasn't warm enough yet to go in. General Justo wanted to succeed Castillo as constitutional president, and to keep his ambition from being sidetracked he stymied all conspiratorial moves by the army. Most of the officers wanted Argentina neutral in the war but Justo was an ardent supporter of the Allies for reasons of political expedience. As far as the people were concerned, it was all the same to them which side won.*
>
> *The outlook was gloomy during those early months of autumn, 1942. The army fell into disrepute. There had been irregularities in the Office of Procurement. A summary court martial was instituted which exposed frauds of disastrous proportions. Then came the scandal of the homosexual cadets. I felt a need to join up with any lodge of colonels capable of healing our wounded morale. We had to prepare ourselves. The country needed a leader with an iron hand who would compel the landlords to plow their profits back into industry. We were eager to have peace but in order to preserve it we had to be ready for war. The next president could only be a soldier. The boys were insisting that it be me. But what hope was there in a country where two greedy sharks were wrangling over the shoal of fish? But, as usual, providence sent me signs. The first came at the end of March, 1942: the death of Don Marcelo de Alvear. The other was on January 11, 1943, when General Agustín P. Justo was struck down by a cerebral hemorrhage. President Castillo lost no time in baring his teeth in support of the candidacy of Robustiano Patrón Costas, a feudal chief from the Northwest whose tongue stank of British asses. Aha! I said to myself, I'm not letting this character through. And I*

got in touch with the boys who had been after me. Do you want a revolution? I asked them. Well, the time has come. Let's contact the officers and anyone who doesn't string along or plays dumb, overboard with him. Right? That's how it all started.

At the end of February, we began holding secret meetings in my house. By March, we were already organized and had drawn up strict covenants that committed us to a new military doctrine against traditional politicians and communism. There were nineteen of us and we referred to ourselves in private as brothers of the GOU, the United Officers Group. It is now well known that as many different meanings were assigned to the acronym as the intentions attributed to the organization. Just "GOU" was enough for me. It is an onomatopoeia for strength, like the "eia, eia, alalà" of the mountain troops.

I continued to keep our plans from Farrell, holding him in reserve. The one who did come in with us was the Minister of War, General Pedro Pablo Ramírez, whom we nicknamed Palito because he was thin and fond of whisky. In the preliminary stages of the revolution, he released our men from administrative duty and moved them into command positions.

We decided not to take the plunge until September, before Patrón Costas could be made President through a fraudulent election. Then, a way out occurred to me that would avoid bloodshed. If Ramírez were to be the army's candidate, he would have to be called in and told straight from the shoulder that he must present a platform of his own as well. When word reached the Radicals, who were running around like dogs on a bowling green, they latched on to my lapels and said that if Ramírez was the man, they would back him. We had several meetings. The Minister of War hedged. He didn't know what to do. He polished off all the whisky I had in the house and still kept flirting with us like a nervous virgin.

The one who brought things to a head (unintentionally) was Castillo. Somebody leaked the story that Ramírez was going to muck up the stew for Patrón Costas. The President got upset and asked for his resignation. We sensed the danger and forbade him to sign anything. "Okay," Palito said, "I won't come out in opposition to you, but I won't come out in favor. Find yourselves another general." One of our boys, ambitious and inexperienced, brought in Arturo Rawson, the cavalry commander. I didn't care for Rawson, but let him go ahead, telling myself that it wouldn't be for long.

It was drizzling when I woke up on the morning of June 4, extremely tired. I had been working hard during the entire day before trying to bring indecisive officers around to committing themselves to the coup. The best part was that civilians didn't have even a toe in the door this time. It was a pure movement: The Nation in Arms.

At about 5 a.m., I went to the Army Club and got Farrell out of bed. "You mustn't miss this revolution," I told him. "What revolution?" The poor fellow had no idea what was going on. "Yours, General." "Oh," he said, surprised. "Then, I'll get dressed right away."

The march started out at seven o'clock from the intersection of Avenida San Martín and Avenida General Paz. We advanced without incident as far as the Army Mechanics School. They opened fire on us from there and we retaliated with artillery and mortars. The head of the guard and several soldiers were killed. They surrendered immediately.

As soon as he saw that it was turning out to be easy, Rawson put on his musketeer's cape and plumed hat and stepped to the head of the troops. At six in the afternoon, he slipped in ahead of us and had already installed himself in the presidential seat. And that same night we were betrayed. He had supper with two civilians and offered them cabinet posts.

The revolution was the work of the colonels and since I was the one who was sticking his neck out, my comrades threw it up to me, and with full justification. "Che, what are we going to do about Rawson?" I reassured them. "This won't be hard to square away, boys. I'll go over to his office and ask for his resignation. If he refuses, overboard he goes."

And that's how it was. Various colonels, six or seven of us, I believe, went to the Pink House each with a .45 under his overcoat. We found him in the presidential office, doodling. "Get out of here, right now," I told him. Rawson tried to stall us off by appealing to his friendship with General Ramírez. "Let me think it over until tomorrow, boys. It will be to your benefit, as well as mine." I stood fast. "It won't benefit us for shit. This presidential chair is ours and we'll decide who sits in it. In any case, it won't be you." He backed down. "What do I do, now? Where do I go?" It occurred to me that it would be best to send him off as an ambassador. "What country would you like?" I asked. "The closest one possible." "Start packing. Next week you'll be on your way to Brazil," I promised him.

The boys tried to convince me to be President. But I was no fool. I handed them a history lesson. "Every revolution devours its children. But I'm too raw. I don't want the revolution getting bellyache. Let's put in Palito Ramírez." I sent for him and draped the sash across his chest. We'll go with you tomorrow when you take the oath." "Under what conditions?" he wanted to know. I answered that he could appoint only one civilian minister and that he had to turn over the Ministry of War to Farrell immediately. He lost no time in accepting.

I had to deal with a few threats from hidden enemies jealous of the influence the GOU was gaining inside the government. They tried to oust me several times but weren't able to. On the contrary, the GOU's patriotic ideals were winning new partisans every day among the young officers. Finally, in September, 1943, fed up with intrigue, I asked Ramírez to appoint me Director of Labor.

He was surprised. "What, Perón? That's not for a man of your stature." It was an insignificant office at the time with almost exclusively bureaucratic functions that channeled timid union demands to government ears, invariably deaf to them.

"You're mistaken, General," I told him. "It's a spot from where I can bring Communist agitators into line and establish a broader base of support for the revolution."

When I came into the Department, I had to contend with a bunch of hacks who didn't even know labor law. I put them to work straightening out the files and dusting off the dossiers. I brought a statistician along with me who was worth his weight in gold, a Catalonian by the name of José Figuerola. He was an expert who had made an in-depth analysis of Italian corporative organizations and had been case-hardened in such revolutionary governments as Primo de Rivera's. "Let's see, now, Figuerola," I told him, "make me a study of the previous

government's economic and labor programs and let me know
what changes are needed." A week later he was back. "There
aren't any programs," he exclaimed.

That was another sign from providence. I had started a
revolution but in a country that had no identity, no form, with
too many paths and no goals. Fourteen million Argentines
were living adrift. So, I said to myself, "I will give a destiny
to this land without destiny. I! Is it nothing but cartilage?
Then, I will give it my bones. I will be its chance, its necessity,
its prophecy."

And after all this time, Lucas, I end up with these memory
lapses! Stop the car. Just look at those broken-down balconies,
blacked out. And those railings to the left. Everything shrouded in
darkness, in permanent agony. That's what Madrid has meant to
me, Lucas. A cloistered, incense-burning little capital. God rescued me from the dampness but at the same time he suffocates me
with the smoke of old age. I have had more than my share of
droughts. My prostate's dried up, my feet are like ice, and I have
asthma of the brain. My fingers cramp up. And not a single one of
Franco's officials has shown interest in the state of my health. They
shot off all the salvos due me for Eva. Do you know what that was
like, Lucas?

The gardener shakes his curls: No, sir. And he keeps his olive-
shaped eyes on the monument to Cybele. In Morocco, young people make a habit of forgetfulness.

It was the opposite with Eva, Lucas. I trained her not to forget.
When she came to Madrid in 1947, she found this gloomy Calle
José Antonio all decked out. Cheers and carnations poured from
the balconies. It was nearly ten at night, like now. Dead Spain
came to life. They hid away all the religious ladies in black. The
fountains played and there was gaiety in the squares. As Eva
passed beneath the Alcalá arch, the mayor drew up alongside and
covered her with flowers. She received two decorations that night,
to say nothing of the keys to the city, presentation of arms by the
Moorish Guard, hand-kissing crowds prostrating themselves before
her in thanks . . . for favors that I, the absent one, had granted.
The celebration had been so extravagant that Eva considered it
prudent to speak over the radio before retiring to her princess's
suite in the Pardo. She described herself as overwhelmed and

drunk with happiness. At the end, out of the blue, she suddenly mentioned me. "I am no more than a messenger," she said. The next day, she telephoned me to beg my pardon. "I don't deserve you . . . I don't deserve you," she repeated. I didn't give it a second thought. But, now, it bothers me. Why should Eva be upsetting this farewell today, which is mine alone. I feel like everything is turned around. I don't know if I'm leaving or arriving. If I am the one she's sending off or the one staying on with her.

I met her in the midst of the madness of the San Juan earthquake. The catastrophe occurred on January 15, 1944, a Saturday. The next day, I mobilized the entire country behind the devastated city. By then, my office had become a powerful ministry. I was Minister of Labor and Welfare.

I sent out planes and railroad cars with supplies, chartered trucks with food and tents, organized committees that toured the country raising funds. It was a colossal disaster. There were 8,000 dead among the ruins.

People from the entertainment world offered their support from the very first. Many, just to be seen; others, in all sincerity to stay and work. Eva was the most devoted of them all. There was a benefit at Luna Park for the victims on the Saturday following the earthquake. Somebody took the seat beside me. It was Eva, who looked at me with those dark-brown eyes of hers and said, sweetly, "Colonel . . ."

"What is it, my dear?"

"Thank you for existing."

Thank you for existing. That sentence shook me to the soul. I wanted to continue talking to her but all the excitement at the moment made it impossible. For the first time, I looked at her intently. Libertad Lamarque was onstage singing "Madreselva." Eva was pale and nervous. She lived without sleep, in constant tension. I was struck by her delicate, tapering hands. Her feet were the same, like filigree work. She had long hair and burning eyes. Her figure wasn't good; she was one of those typically skinny criollas with straight legs and thick ankles. It wasn't her physical qualities that attracted me, it was her generosity.

I asked her where she worked.

"At the Yankelevich station. Radio Belgrano. That's where I am, with a group of ham actors."

She always belittled herself with that word: "I'm not an artist, I'm a ham." But the truth of the matter is that she did a very worthwhile educational job. Her program told the story of the lives of famous women like Lola Montes and Madame Lynch. Eva identified very deeply in her portrayals of those characters as though foreseeing that she was to outdo them all in real life.

I stopped by the radio station the following week. I called the magazines and asked that they take a few photos of us together. The Russian Yankelevich wasn't very nice to her and I wanted him to get it through his head that if he didn't behave himself he would have to answer to me.

Evita was very grateful. She came to see me at the Ministry of Labor about continuing her work for the San Juan victims. I gave her carte blanche. Accordingly, she took off in an ambulance plane for the devastated city, made a survey of conditions, and returned with a list of needs that I immediately took care of.

She was so intelligent and sensitive that I couldn't get her out of my mind. She radiated strength in torrents. There was nobody to equal her even among the men who assisted me. I said to myself, "This diamond in the rough must be polished into a fine jewel."

And so it was. Eva Perón was my handiwork. She had a great heart and a noble imagination. When a man knows how to cultivate such qualities, the woman learns to serve him better than the most sophisticated of instruments. Naturally, it was also necessary to instill a little culture in her but that wasn't so easy with Eva. She rejected anything that didn't ring true to her.

When we had become friends, I said to her, "Why don't you come over to the Ministry of Labor and give us a hand?"

She accepted at once, without pay or conditions. I gave her a little office and appointed her Secretary for Women. Although we began to be intimate very soon, the two of us had an understanding that the political and social would come first. The rest when there was time left over. Her new mission was a matter of life and death to Eva. She didn't fuss much over her appearance. But when we had a party for poor people, she would spend hours before the mirror and put on her finery. "I want to demonstrate that a woman of the people also has a right to dress elegantly," she explained. It wasn't out of vanity that she did it; she wanted to look good so that others could feel proud.

I was concerned with cleaning the Communists out of the labor movement. The Communists had infested everything. Eva turned out to be an invaluable collaborator. At one point, a banker who professed to being a Socialist came to see us. It was just a disguise. As soon as he opened his mouth the hammer and sickle flashed onto his teeth. Eva happened to be the one to receive him. The man thought she was a pushover and made a pass at her. She drove him through the door bashing him with her purse. I came running out of my office, startled. I had never heard a string of profanity of that caliber before. Eva could be sweet as honey when she wanted to but anybody who provoked her, beware! Stirring up that hornet's nest brought out insects with a very nasty sting.

Eva was something special. It would have been impossible to achieve as much with any other kind of woman. With her I practiced the art of leadership to its utmost. I became discouraged at times because given that ungovernable spirit of hers, it was impossible for her to accept halfway measures or to be headed off once she got under way. If Evita had been alive on June 16, 1955, when the first gorilla sedition occurred, she would have shown them no mercy. A rebel, in her book, deserved nothing but the firing squad. She was like that in everything: a sectarian Peronist, incapable of coming to terms with anything that wasn't Peronist. Cooling her down cost me a lot of agony. In politics, sectarianism is negative. It alienates sympathy. That didn't bother her. Eva was Eva and let the chips fall where they may.

Not long after we had met there was no reason to dissimulate anymore. We started living together. Ramírez turned out to be a failure and I had to replace him with Farrell. Since the army didn't think much of the new chief's style, I was obliged to take on the Vice Presidency of the Republic and the Ministry of War. I was more interested in the Ministry of Labor, so I hung on to that, too.

It didn't take long for envy to get its claws into us. The military are frightened by women on the loose. They like them shut up and nailed down. Eva wasn't that kind. They started *in with their stupid complaints. An army man of my standing mustn't get involved with a cheap vaudevillean! And they kept filling my head with all kinds of nasty gossip. Finally, I had to stop them cold. One day I called a meeting at the ministry and said: "I'm not a hypocrite. I have always liked women and I will go on liking them. I don't see what's immoral about that. Immoral if I liked men!"*

Fate is unfair, says Perón. I made her what she was and she stole most of my glory. The disadvantage of not dying young, Lucas. Eva will always be on her way up in the people's memory. They remember her for what she could have done not for what she did. But look at me. I'm on the way down. Time passing is time losing me. Get me out of here, now. Take me to the Palacio de Oriente. Eva was received there like a queen but I could never even get into the place.

I don't know if I really fell in love. In my day, men didn't lower themselves by saying "I love you." Intimacy happened or it didn't, without need for sugary words. All I know is that when women love us very much, the way Eva loved me, there's no way to resist.

In the hectic weeks of the San Juan earthquake, I was living in a three-room apartment across from the Palermo Brewery. My work kept me out until midnight. Eva was always standing there when I got home, leaning against the door, waiting for me. What could I say? I would invite her in, we'd have a glass of vermouth, and stay up talking.

Then she began little by little to leave jars of ladies' creams in the bathroom. One night, she brought a toothbrush, another night she filled my medicine cabinet with Le Sancy makeup. A week later, I had to give her a closet to hang up her silk dressing gowns, sequined costumes, and gauze dresses that actresses used in those days.

A girl from Mendoza had been cooking for me and doing my laundry for a couple of years. Piraña? Yes, I guess I was the one who gave her the nickname, because of the two huge front teeth that disfigured her face. But that story about my having relations with her isn't true. It wasn't possible. She was my goddaughter. Her father was a poor cowhand from Upsallata

297

who put her in my care when the little creature was still wet-ting her bed. Yes, I am a man of strong instincts, but within bounds. Depravities don't fit in with my character. It's true that I sometimes took the Piraña along with me to Luna Park. We enjoyed watching the fights of the Negro, Lowell. Just seeing us having a good time together was enough for the nastiest gossip to come out in the papers. I couldn't care less. I was beyond good and evil. The Piraña had no idea. What would a wild little kid from the hills care, who hadn't had even two years of schooling? Yet such lies get into the history books. One lives his life without getting bogged down by his every little act and he forgets about them. But suddenly the future comes along and there they all are again, lined up, waiting for us.

One evening when I got back from the Ministry, I didn't see the Piraña around. I went to her little room and not even the bed was there. Her clothes, her dolls, the Columbine costume I bought her . . . all gone. There was nothing there.

"I shipped her off to Mendoza," Eva told me. "One woman is more than enough to take care of one man."

For better or for worse, Eva was headstrong, ungovernable. When she took an idea into her head she pursued it to the end with no concern for consequences. That's probably why lots of men were frightened of her. I wasn't because she was docile with me.

There was more phosphorus than flesh in that puny, ivory body. Anybody who didn't know how to touch her got burned.

The waning moon blacked out behind heavy clouds, Oriente Square was rarely as dark as on this evening before summer's onset. Irregularities of weather have always been harbingers of bad luck in the General's life. It was raining the night Lonardi swore vengeance against him. There was cloudburst the morning he was ousted. How did that go?: "The sky of Buenos Aires, low and dark, pressed down upon the roofs of the houses. There was no sign of life . . ." Like now in Madrid.

"Shall we turn back?" asks Lucas, the Moroccan, who is falling asleep at the wheel of the Mercedes.

"Don't be in a hurry, son. Let me ramble."

They are at the arcade of the Royal Palace in the languor of the night. Eva once described the magnificence of its staircase decorated with lions and castles on which she had herself photographed with Franco's ministers. She was overwhelmed by the marble, Colmenar stone, Venetian glass. She walked as in a dream through the palace's thirty salons, asking to have the stories of Trajan, Hercules, and the Good Angel that were woven into the tapestries, repeated to her again and again. Then in the west gallery, she suddenly turned to Doña Carmen Polo, the Caudillo's wife and, addressing her in the familiar form, said, "Say, tell me something, how many war orphans do you still have in Spain, anyhow?"

"Two hundred thousand, I would estimate. Perhaps a few more."

"Then, why, with all the rooms like these you have here, don't you give them a decent place to live?"

Doña Carmen's tongue froze.

"Don't lose any more time, woman! Remodel the place once and for all into a children's home. Otherwise, what's the point of our being presidents?"

When Eva came to Spain—was it told to the General or did he see it in the movies twenty-five years ago?—there was a frenzied throng in that square, now so murky and deserted. Franco, in dress uniform, offered her his arm as she stepped out of the gilded carriage. He decorated her in the throne room with the Great Cross of Isabel la Católica. The heat was incandescent as lava, adhesive. Eva, possessed by her majesty, poured sweat under a sable coat and ostrich-feather hat, without batting an eye. After the speeches were over, she removed her coat and stepped out onto the balcony. A storm of applause ripped through the square. The men knelt. Children from the orphan asylums waved little flags. Eva greeted the crowd, bowing her head as in the theater. Hysterical cheers erupted. Some peasant women, in black, burst into tears. "Never have I seen such a demonstration," said Franco into her ear. Eva paid no attention to him. "Thank you," she shouted into the microphone. "Thank you, my people of Madrid . . ." She stiffened, stretched out her right arm in the Falangist salute. Then, she disappeared from the balcony.

It was two months before she returned to Buenos Aires. Her triumphant likeness appeared on *Time* magazine's cover of July 14, 1947, and the next day, the Argentine press, rejoicing, spread the good news: "Not for her alone. It's for him, too."

"It is for me," the General admitted. Now, among the lugubrious statues of Oriente Square, he knows it was for her, not him. And the chill of jealousy bites into his soul.

Early one Sunday morning, midway in her trip, Eva telephoned him from Lisbon and between sobs told him she needed him, missed him, that without him happiness had no meaning. The General was thoughtful after hanging up and, finally, decided to have a look at what *Time* had to say. He read the translation prepared for him by a secretary:

> Last week, on broad, imposing Alvear Avenue in Buenos Aires municipal workers were setting up an enormous stage. "What's that for?" a reporter asked. "Independence Day or the visit of the President of Chile?"
>
> "It's for the señora's reception," one of the workers answered. "The whole world is impressed with her trip. She's the talk of Europe. A miracle, isn't it?" Yes, it's a miracle.

We can't let ourselves be outdone by the outside, the General decided. We'll give her a mythological welcome. And I said to the ministers: My wife's glory is for us all. She is Argentina.

Although it was winter, Buenos Aires made ready to receive Evita with a downpour of flowers. As the ship bringing her from Montevideo approached the dock, all the other vessels opened their whistles full blast. At about 3 p.m., the General was able to make her out in the fog. She stood on the deck, bejeweled and imposing.

She waved her handkerchief, as in the movies, and blew kisses. Impatiently, she jumped to the pier before the sailors had finished setting the gangplank in place. She was immediately engulfed by the throng. She felt them lift her bodily and carry her back and forth. The General was nowhere to be seen, gone. Where are you, Perón? she called, weeping. Finally she saw him. Dizzy, she fell into his arms. The photographers climbed on top of one another to capture the image of the immortal queen suddenly turned adolescent, helpless.

Without you, I am nothing, Perón, Evita said to him when night had fallen and they were finally alone in the residence on Calle Austria. Without you, I'm incomplete, no matter where I go.

The General sat at a distance from her. He was ill at ease, stiff.

300

He wore the waistband of his trousers higher than usual. Having his wife about the house once more, talking a blue streak, disconcerted him. She's another person, everybody was saying. She's come back a goddess. Smoking incessantly, he put off going to bed.

"Now, you must rest, Eva," he said. "All this turmoil will kill you."

"How can I rest if I am the only one able to help you?"

Subjugated by the rage of her insatiable love, the General was unable to find what to do with his body to appease Evita's frenzy.

You're holding something against me, Perón. Have I hurt you in some way? What could it be if I haven't separated you from me for a single second. Come to me, don't hold yourself off. What is it that bothers you? Tell me. What I once was? You shouldn't lose trust in me, now. I don't deserve that. I'm yours. You made me. I'm yours.

That was true. I made her. I rescued her. Evita had been through much suffering in her family life. When she was a year old, her father, a cattleman by the name of Juan Duarte abandoned his five children and went to live with another woman in Chivilcoy. He was killed in an automobile accident before Eva entered school. The abandoned children appeared at the wake, where they were met with hostility. That snub left its mark on Eva. I'm just a waif, she would say to me, just a poor little country waif. Whenever those experiences came to her mind, she broke into the most terrible sobbing. She would have nightmares and wake up with chills, soaked in sweat. I calmed her down. Don't talk about that, anymore. Bury your past forever. Yes, yes, she would promise me. But at any moment . . . she could be putting on a dress or opening a drawer . . . those memories would come back to haunt her.

Eva finished sixth grade in 1935 when she was fifteen years old. Her mother, an enterprising woman, had opened a pension in her house in Junín to support the family. The older daughters were married off one by one to respectable lawyers and government employees who boarded there. Eva, however, did not care for the ordinary life. She wanted to be an actress. One time, she described how she put on a circus in a grove of tall trees next to the house in Junín. She swung from the branches as though they were trapezes and recited speeches from movies to the other children. Norma Shearer was her favorite actress. She saw Marie Antoinette *at least ten times and left the theater weeping every time.*

She was so determined to be an actress that her mother had no choice but to let her apply to a radio station in Buenos Aires. The tryout consisted of declamations. Eva moved everyone with her recitation of poems by Amado Nervo. She would repeat those same verses when she was married to me, as she took her bath: "Where do the dead go, Lord, where do they go?"

But that was only the beginning. She went through very difficult years. There was no lack of scoundrels waiting to take advantage of her inexperience and trust. Eva dodged them adroitly and filed away the affronts in her memory for future retaliation. Just the opposite of me, she held grudges and never forgave people.

The first time she stayed at my house, she looked at me intently with her great brown eyes.

"You are going to hear ugly stories about me," she said. "None of them are true. Everything they tell you will be dirty lies."

"Those things don't concern me in the slightest, little one," I told her.

She had attacks of melancholia at the beginning. She would curl up with her head on my chest, weeping, and ask my forgiveness.

"I will go on loving you even after I die," she would say to me. "All I am, even the bad part, is yours." Then, she would smile sadly and enfold me again with the tenderness of her most unforgettable words: "Colonel, thank you for existing."

Now, behind the old Teatro Real, next to the equestrian statue of Philip IV, Perón sees her once again as she was when they awoke together that first time, her dark hair in ringlets, transparent hands laced with veins. Evita did not like her body. I have a disobedient body, she would say. My nerves are rebellious. They kick up terrible rows underneath my skin. Don't look at me in the mornings, Perón. The circles under my eyes show without makeup. I'm prettier inside. And happier. It's not fair for one woman to have so much happiness.

One night, when they had moved into adjoining apartments on Calle Posadas, she whispered in the General's ear what she proclaimed to the heavens in public squares and on the radio: "There was a time when I didn't notice misery, misfortune, poverty. The more injustice around me, the blinder I was. Finally, you came along, Perón, and opened my eyes. I have loved you since that day, so much that I don't even know how to tell you. You are here at my side, my knight in shining armor, and I think I must be dreaming. And having nothing to offer you but my soul, I give it all to you. Belonging to you is a gift of God."

She was so anxious to black out her past that even before the General could say, "I made her," she said, "Perón made me." It wasn't true. Everybody is at each moment another person. But how can they be another if, basically, they do not go on being the same one. Eva was already Eva when Perón met her.

She was living at the time on Calle Carlos Pellegrini, near Avenida Libertador. When she came out in the mornings on her way to the radio station, she would see a line of monstrous children, runaways from institutions, on the stairs of the Seaver arcade. She would pat their heads and look at them sadly.

One day she spoke to them. "Don't you have homes? What do you eat?" And she discovered that they were mutes. She was to play Lola Montes that afternoon. Her performance was listless, unconvincing. A nervous cough made her lose her voice in the middle of a love scene. She almost ran from the station to find her friend Pierina Dealessi.

"I want to rent a room for those poor creatures," she told her, "and to pay for their food. I can't sleep in peace when I think of the condition they live in."

Pierina knew of a boardinghouse in the waterfront section where musicians from the provinces stopped when they came to the city. She assumed, correctly, that the proprietress would look after the orphans for a modest sum. That afternoon, Evita completed the arrangements. When Pierina came to the Seaver arcade with her friend and saw them on the stairs picking lice off one another, she could not control her nausea. They were not children but wizened albino dwarves dressed in burlap bags and covered with scabies.

She tried to dissuade Eva. She argued that they would be happier out in the open than at the boardinghouse. It was no use. With the samaritan's unshakable stubbornness, Eva spent almost half her earnings on salves for their scabies, mattresses, and dwarves' outfits, and did not let a day go by without visiting them in their new home. She treated their sores, checked their weight, taught them to eat with a spoon, and to shout. Most important of all: to shout. She held on to the hope that their voices would emerge at any moment. She went out on the balcony with them and ordered: "Yell, kids! Come on, now, yell so Evita can hear you! A e i o u! A a a a a!!" They tensed their necks, squeezed their throats, got red in the face but nothing happened. They were born without vocal chords.

She was so proud of the slight progress made by her charges that soon after she got to know the General, Eva brought him to the attic of the boardinghouse to see them. It was a disaster. On entering the room, they found them on the clean, newly starched white bedspreads, naked from the waist down, smearing the walls with streaks of fresh excrement.

The General gagged.

"With so many orphans needing care, Evita, why waste time on people who are incurable?"

An army truck picked up the mutes that night and took them to the Tandil asylum. On the way, the noncom driver stopped off at a roadside eating place in Las Flores to have a pizza and when he came out there wasn't a sign of them. That was where they probably had disappeared. The cornfields were dense and although several search parties tried to find them, they were lost for good.

Eva was impossible. She overdid everything. No sooner did she begin working at the Social Welfare Foundation than she slipped from my grasp. We would see each other every now and then for a short time. It was as though we were living in different cities. Preferring to work at night, she would get home at daybreak. I, an old soldier, used to living the other way around, left for the Pink House at six in the morning. Sometimes, we met at the front door. She always bragged about her exhaustion.

Two of the many exploits for which she was known still move me. One is like a tango. It happened in the winter. It was raining in Buenos Aires for a change. Day had just dawned. Haggard from lack of sleep, dissatisfied with herself, Evita was on her way through the deserted streets. At the entrance to the Güemes arcade, she spied an emaciated woman with three little girls clutching at her skirts, barely managing to keep from being drenched by the downpour. She had the driver pull over to the curb and leaning out of the window, called to her, "Where would you like me to take you, señora?"

In the darkness and fog, the woman did not realize who was talking to her. Picking up the little girls she got into the front seat of the car. Her head hanging, she unburdened the story of her misfortunes. Her husband was in prison, the few possessions left to her had been taken by creditors, and her only hope now was to get to see the señora and trust in her mercy. She sobbed into a dirty handkerchief. The little girls coughed. No soap-opera writer could have imagined a more pathetic story.

The miracle then happened. Eva tapped the driver on the shoulder and ordered, "Turn around and go back to the Foundation. I must take care of this."

The woman then recognized the unmistakable voice. Stupefied and transported, she let fall her handkerchief.

"Oh, my God!" she exclaimed, embracing the children.

Eva immediately appointed her caretaker of a school for orphans where she was able to save enough money to buy herself a little house.

The other story also took place in the early morning. For months, Eva did not spend more than a couple of hours out of the twenty-four in bed. When her assistants pressed her to rest, she rebuffed them, offended. The endless lines of poor people at her office door kept her from sleeping. It was as though the time slipping by burned her. Toward four o'clock, a woman out of a nightmare, her head projecting from a notched, primordial hump, crawled in, dragging herself along the floor. If that were not enough, she also had, hanging from her armpits, two very short vestigial arms ending in webbed fingers. Even Eva, always so in command of herself, was disconcerted by this monstrous apparition. One of her assistants heard her whisper, "It's them . . . Them, coming back . . . !"

She hesitated, wondering, no doubt, who would be capable of caring for this monstrosity, could bear its presence. Feeling herself incapable, she took off her magnificent diamond earrings and holding them out to her, said, "Here. Begin another life. They're yours."

That's why she was so loved.

I sent her off to Europe to give her a little distraction. That was the origin of her famous tour. I wanted to pull her out of the exhausting spiral that was dragging her down. The invitation from the Spanish Government was for me, not her. Soon after, Italy also wanted me to visit. Both countries owed me important favors. At the end of the Second War, the Allies decided to ostracize Spain and there was only one ambassador left there—mine. I saved the Italians from starvation in 1947 with a present of half a million tons of cereals. Why shouldn't they urge me to visit? But I couldn't. Government problems required me to be in Buenos Aires. So, I figured that by sending Eva I would be killing two birds with one stone: fulfilling my obligation to the countries that wanted to receive me and compelling her to take the vacation she needed so urgently. And that's what I did. Eva was an able woman and played her role as my representative to perfection. She sent me a touching letter from Rome, I think it was, or maybe Lisbon, thanking me. She never stopped thanking me.

"Now, we can go back, Lucas," the General murmurs, suddenly feeling desolate. "I don't want them missing me at home."

In an effort to avoid the traffic in the Plaza de España, they unexpectedly find themselves deep in the shadows of Rosaleda. It is midnight and Madrid smells, as always, of fritters. A torchlight parade can be seen moving slowly in the distance. Several knights dressed in black habits with ruffs stroll through the trees flanked by a guard of halberdiers. Once again the city has reverted to its past and were it not for the verdant presence of the black poplar trees, if living faces were not to be seen framed in the blurry windows, the General would feel Madrid, the last refuge of his old age, moving backwards into the caverns of history, disappearing into the maelstrom of time, carrying him off with it. This city is me, says Perón. All at once, vultures of cold envelop him. He presses the binders of the Memoirs to his breast but they impart barely any warmth.

This last night but one before departure, the General again dreams of the Polar expedition. He is uneasy in the dream because thanks to the anchor of rationality that keeps him moored to reality—

306

always, even when asleep—he knows that conquest of the heart of this frozen waste is now a senseless exploit. Other Argentine soldiers did it before he could, in the summer of '65. They advanced —he had read—over plateaus bristling with towers and caverns, hearing at every step the groans of their dead ancestors. They saw no sign of a volcano at the entrance to the Pole but tricks of nature: swarms of fiery white flies buzzing over blinding pampas.

Nonetheless, the General sets out, coughing, in his dream, over the Weddell Sea. He walks and walks. Once again, his body floats through the stiffened foam of the passes and is torn by stalactites. Finally, sticky with blood and amniotic slime, he makes out the volcano of the Pole in the distance, the sign only he knows. Suddenly, the instruments rebel against him. Compass and theodolites indicate that not a volcano, but an immense vagina is there, erect. His mother stands guard at its apex, her hair unbraided, a man's poncho over her house dress. But who is that beside her? It's López, wearing the grosgrain-and-lace dress Grandmother Dominga used to put on for opera parties. The General's mother assenting, López turns him away, saying, "Go back, Perón. Take to the Weddell Sea. You may not enter here."

Gasping for breath, he tries to protest, "Please, *mamita*, just for a moment . . ."

But his secretary-grandmother drives him away with psalms from the nether world: *Pe pe orupandé/Oxum maré coroo Ogum te* (He scatters his bones along the perimeter of those chill penances), *Salve Shango, Salve Oshalá.*

Sweating, the General opens his eyes. It is now day. At the foot of the bed, López, in kimono and slippers, is holding out a glass of water and aspirins to him. For a change, he has anticipated the General's wishes: he will be releasing him from the iron bands that grip his skull. Now, he helps him get up. He tests the water in the tub to see if it is lukewarm as should be. Then, from outside the curtain, he hands him the bath sheet.

"What would I do without you, López," says the General appreciatively.

"And without the señora, who looks out for us both."

"That's right. What would become of us without Chabela?"

After he has finished his breakfast of strong coffee and a water biscuit, the General feels better, eager to get to work. The memories he is now looking forward to reading trace themselves over his face: a past that slipped away before he was able to enjoy it, like that of children, spun of the fleeting threads of "tomorrow I shall do, tomorrow I shall be."

"We'll be leaving here without having corrected even half the Memoirs, López. Do you realize that?" he says, puffing, as he slowly mounts the stairs to the sanctum. "That makes me uneasy . . . What are we going to do later on in Buenos Aires to manage an hour or two to ourselves?"

"You put in the soul, General, I'll give it the body. There will be time for everything. You'll see."

Upstairs, López has laid out copies of "Projects for the Nation," which he had roughed out thirty years ago. One contains the amendments to Labor Law and List of Appropriate Persons to implement them; another, maps with the changes in Nomenclature, and the Almanac of New National Holidays; hanging on the wall, the Schedule of Objectives and Time Frames; on the side table, amid photographs of Eva, scrolls of Mnemonic Devices for schools. The General is moved at the sight of those herbariums turned to dust before ever having been put to use.

"Treat these mementos with much care, López. However scorched and covered with ashes they may be on the outside, they are alive inside. Incredible, all that one leaves undone! Frightening. Better not to stir them up. Open that other folder, rather. What's in it? Is it damp? Can the dew be filtering in on us even at the top of the house . . . ? Read to me. Let's hear what it has to tell us."

> *In Argentina, the people are what they are but rarely what they seem. Our country is not knowable on the basis of the forces that meet the eye but through the sources—always disguised and underground—that feed those forces. In 1943, the revolution that ousted Castillo was embodied in a lodge, the GOU. And the GOU was the army. Of its 3,000 officers, no more than an insignificant little group of unconditional supporters of the Allies was willing to mortgage the country's future by going to war. The rest of us were neutral. We felt bound by a blood pact. One of the cornerstones of the GOU was the requirement that on joining our ranks, every officer sign an undated, unconditional resignation as a guarantee of his conduct and loyalty. I, the Undersecretary, kept those res-*

ignations in my office at the Ministry of War at the disposal of the Minister and the President. It is well known that the owner of Paradise is not God but the one who holds the keys, Saint Peter. I was the Saint Peter of the army at the time. In October, 1943, before the revolution had really jelled, the Minister of the Treasury, Jorge Santamarina, made some indiscreet statements that threatened our neutrality. I was indignant and telephoned President Ramírez to warn him that if he didn't take immediate action to kick Santamarina out, the army would not find the task at all distasteful. Ramírez not only heeded the complaint but asked me to choose the replacement.

I turned several names around in my mind but had reservations about each. I put the problem aside for the moment and went to dinner with some newspapermen at Scafidi's restaurant on Calle 25 de Mayo. The light suddenly dawned when I was in the middle of my steak. How many Argentines do you know who have built up fortunes starting from scratch? I asked them. They had no idea. One of the reporters dug out a list from the morgue at La Razón *and was curious to know what I wanted it for. Very simple, I told him. Anybody who knows how to make money for himself couldn't fail to do the same for the nation.*

I was startled by the name at the head of the list. I know that fellow very well! I laughed. I was responsible for his making the first thousand pesos of his life. How? Let me go back twenty years. One Sunday in 1924, walking along Calle Viamonte on the way to my grandmother's house, I passed by a woebegone, dirty little shop, obviously one step this side of ruin. An odor emanated from it that was at the same time so sweet and so fierce that it seemed like a hawk poised to swoop down upon the olfactory nerves of the passersby. It was a surprise to me to see behind the counter not the typical elderly couple of Sunday shopkeepers but a dark, anxious-looking young fellow with bright, penetrating eyes. I stopped out of curiosity and compassion and bought fifty centavos' worth of loose tobacco from him. I examined the mixture and made a diagnosis. "Turkish?" I asked.

"Greek, from Smyrna."

One didn't have to possess the attributes of a Sherlock

Holmes to deduce the young man's life story on the basis of those three words. From his accent, he was a Greek; from the geographical reference, a patriot, since Smyrna had come under Turkish control a year before; from his expression of anxiety, a refugee without papers; from his behavior, a tradesman of good family. I told him all this. Since I had gotten everything right, he wanted to fill in the rest of the story for me.

He was twenty-three years old. A fugitive from the atrocities of Mustafa Kemal, he had made his way from Trieste to Naples and from there to Buenos Aires using a false passport. He was a part-time worker for the River Plate telephone company. He was on a starvation diet. His father, in an effort to help him out, had sent him a shipment of tobacco at great sacrifice, one would imagine, and the young man had to spend a year's savings to get it out of customs. And now, he had no idea of how to dispose of it.

"In this country, nobody can do business without connections," I told him. "I'll give you a recommendation."

One of the managers of the Picardo factory owed me a favor. Then and there I wrote him a little note on a piece of wrapping paper.

"What's your name, young fellow?" I asked him.

It was Aristotle Onassis.

Months later, he came to the post to see me and thank me. He was wearing a wing collar and spats. He had taken out Argentine citizenship. The factory was buying thousands of dollars' worth of tobacco through him at prices set directly with the owner of Picardo.

My telegram in 1943 offering him the post of Minister of the Treasury took him by surprise in New York. He sent me a warm and generous reply. "Count on me for anything but to govern. I, Argentine. Ari." He was destined for business, not politics.

I thought I had lost contact with him for good, but that was not the case. In 1946, he telephoned me to ask who in Buenos Aires could sell him ships. I put him in touch with Alberto Dodero, who owned a huge fleet, and Fritz Mandl, an Austrian armaments manufacturer who had taken refuge in Argentina, in flight from his wife, Hedy Lamarr. I don't believe they came to any agreement but a close friendship sprang up between the

310

three of them. On that occasion, Onassis came to see me at the Pink House. I reminded him of the brushoff he had given me in 1943.

"Who did you finally appoint instead of me?" he wanted to know.

"Nobody. I put in a philosophy. All the ministers I now have came up out of nothing, like you did."

He looked gloomy and had dark rings under his eyes. Wealth had turned him into a celebrity collector. Historical personages came and went in his life as a matter of course. When Eva arrived in Europe, Dodero was in her entourage. Through him Onassis sought her out with such persistence that my wife finally invited him to dinner at the villa on the Italian Riviera where she had gone to escape protocol.

Onassis arrived punctually, impeccably attired, with a bouquet of orchids. Eva, in a house coat, showed him into the kitchen. She was frying veal cutlets.

"A person who gives as you do, señora, has a right to ask for much more," said the Greek, with ceremonious gallantry. "Tell me what you want and it is yours. I am at your feet."

My wife, who told me the story soon after, was afraid he would make passes and stopped him cold with an elegant riposte. "It's easy to get on the good side of me. Write me out a check for ten thousand dollars for the Argentine orphans."

I can't help laughing every time I think of Onassis's face when he heard that.

You see, López, I still laugh at it. We were talking about the GOU and who knows how we got involved in these trivialities. Mischief of the memory. I wonder if it wouldn't be better to cut them. What do you think? Do they tarnish my image? No, leave them in. If it weren't for the little things of life, its pathos would do us in. It's cold at the top and a man has no choice but to be constantly fighting his feelings. One enjoys the power but that's about all. And life slips away like water through our fingers. By the time one wants to find out about other things, it's all over with. There's not time enough to get to know them. That's why it's a good thing to dwell on one's unimportant remembrances and let himself get engrossed in them. Before, I never used to rise in the morning without doing a few memory exercises to clear my brain. Now, I can't even remember the exercises.

One of the clocks in the sanctum, which strikes the hour only occasionally, now emits a single dull stroke of ill portent. It is 9:30.

"Cámpora is already at the desk waiting for us, General. He has come to get final instructions for the government. After that, as you instructed me, I will have to accompany him to the wreath-laying ceremonies they've involved him in for this morning: flowers for San Martín in the West Park, for Columbus in the Museum of America, for the victims of the 1808 executions. What a chore! It will be days before I get rid of the pollen."

"Send him up, López. Tell him to come ahead."

"Here, to the sanctum?" The secretary is surprised.

"Yes. He should see these old ornaments of government. If he didn't understand them when Eva was his teacher, perhaps he will now. Dense as he is, maybe the sanctum will open the pores of his noodle."

President Cámpora arrives more highly polished than usual. Before he has even set foot on the first step, his shoeshine, the crease in his trousers, his brilliantined casque, the Paco Rabanne perfume are already upstairs. He appears, arms thrown open but reverent, signaling submission rather than the imminence of an embrace.

"What a treat you gave the reporters this morning, General! After holding vigil for so many days, waiting to see you, concerned about your health, and suddenly without previous warning you appear at the door twice, hale and hearty . . ."

The General is intrigued. "I came to the door?"

"Yes," López reassures him. "Your body . . . They saw it and so they had material to write about."

"The boys from the cable office have asked me to show you today's news bulletins. They want your okay before transmitting them to Buenos Aires. Here they go. See what you think, General:

"7:30 After rising, Peron had his usual breakfast of black coffee and a water biscuit."

"That's not how it was this time," López interrupts. "Correct it to read: 'Feeling better, the General had tea, toast, and marmalade today.' "

312

"8:00 The Peronist caudillo appears at the rear of the chalet, some fifty feet from the entrance gate (beyond which correspondents may not pass). He sits, pensive, in a rocking chair, where he remains for a short time. He is wearing a tan shirt, yellow vest, light-gray trousers, and sport shoes. And on his head a red pochito cap with black stripes (like the ones he popularized during his administration)."

The General, still in pajamas and dressing gown, is nonplussed. "Wasn't that the outfit I wore last night, López?"

The secretary's beady eyes spy signs of unrest in the atmosphere of the sanctum. The early morning bustle has unrigged his intelligence. His defenses are low. He feels himself. His toes, sticking partway out of his sandals, have turned aggressive. His kimono is open wider than it should be. Even his hair, always so manageable, has sprouted unruly tufts.

"You know how bodies are, General. One can dress them in other clothes, but they always keep on the ones they want. And, now"—he lowers his head—"if you will excuse me . . . I must dress to accompany the President and be back by noon. The señora will be asking for me when she gets up . . ."

Relaxing, Cámpora shuts the door. "The news agencies and television channels want to photograph us among the boxes and trunks you will be traveling with, General, so that people can see us in Spain as though we were in Ezeiza. Doesn't sound like a bad idea. It would be a lift for the million people who have started out for the airport."

"Now, stop worrying yourself so much about people's problems, man! Worry about yourself." The General lets himself drop into an armchair, as though blanking out from lack of air. "Come closer. Have you been training your memory these days? How many speeches can you repeat without having to read?"

"Just snatches, sir. I'm not gifted by nature like you."

"What about the Peronist Doctrine, have you been saying it over every night?"

"Haven't missed one, General, except when we were in prison in the South and the freedom-revolution boys were reading our lips even when we were asleep. I know the Peronist Doctrine backwards and forwards."

"That's the bad part, Cámpora. Some of your boys say it back-

313

wards. Sit down here. Open those scrolls. Aha. The Mnemonic Exercises. What do you see there?"

"A face, General. I think it's Figuerola's face. Wavy, like in the movies. And a caption underneath. Yes, that's him: 'The people will always remember Perón, not because he governed well but because the others governed worse than he did. Signed, José Miguel Figuerola.' "

The General lets out a guffaw. "The remark of a genius. Do you remember Figuerola?"

"How could I forget him, sir. The Galician. He was a whiz."

"The world's greatest statistician. He invented the Five-Year Plan, the Mnemonic Scrolls, a Die that predicts revolutions, the New Calendar of National Holidays, the Military Promotions Roster. If I had kept him alongside me, nobody would ever have been able to turn me out . . ."

"Exactly, General. I'll never forget how his Galician accent dripped from his teeth as he read the Five-Year Plan in the Congress."

"Gums, Cámpora. You, as a dentist, should have noted the difference. Figuerola was using false teeth by then. He got his plates at the same time I did, so as not to be outdone . . . Look, man, I want to ask a favor of you."

"I don't do you favors, General. I do as you order me."

"Close your eyes and recite the Peronist Doctrine, as it should be done. Do you recall that according to Figuerola's advice, the best way to learn the doctrine is to find a simile for each principle: an object, an image? Tell me, what did you use to practice with?"

The President has lowered his heavy lids. He bites at his thumb.

"Me, sir? Radio jingles. I picked out the most popular ones."

"Then repeat the first principle. Everybody knows it."

Cámpora covers his forehead with his two hands. He hesitates.

"Forgot it, did you?"

"No, General. I say it at least once a day . . . But I've never been able to separate it from the jingle I learned it with back in those times."

"Say it, then, man."

"I'm embarrassed."

"Say it."

" 'Don't miss pleasure. Smoke Treasure . . .' 'Our party is a mass party, the indestructible union of Argentines, which acts as an institution ready to sacrifice everything in order to be useful to General Perón.' "

"Nothing to it. Let's see how you do with Principle Number Sixteen."

Cámpora blinks and smiles. " 'Don't say hola. Say *O-la-vi-na.*' 'General Perón is the supreme chief. Inspirer, creator, executor, and leader. He may change or annul the decisions of partisan authorities, just as he may also examine, regulate, and replace them . . .' "

The General nods, fatigued. The morning, which is now only beginning, suddenly drops with its entire weight upon his shoulders.

"You can rest easy, Cámpora. You did very well. You had the stuff, but we didn't see it in you at the time. We didn't recognize it until later. One never knows when the precise moment has come. Not the opportune moment, the precise moment. For a representative of mine, as in your case, the most important principles are the first and the sixteenth. But, for your boys, call their attention to seventy-seven."

"That's the one I keep uppermost in mind, General. Shall I tell you how I remember it? 'The clothing fits if you buy it at The Ritz.' 'The clothing fits . . .' and automatically the rule comes to mind: 'In every circumstance, a Peronist must maintain that every decision of a Peronist government is the best. He shall never accept the slightest criticism of it nor permit the slightest doubt to enter.' "

"Do you sense the difference in style? The others came from Figuerola, a civilian. This last one could have been produced only by a soldier. It's mine." The General pulls his robe around him and makes a tentative effort to stand. All at once, he puts his arms down. "Pay close attention, Cámpora. Before we lose track of one another in Buenos Aires . . ."

"How can you imagine such an idea, sir? I'll come to see you daily. I'll be at your disposal twenty-four hours . . ."

"But I don't know if I will be available. I have many matters to consider . . ."

"You're not thinking of leaving me alone with the government, are you, General? If you resign power, I will resign, too."

Perón looks at the President in dismay. He is unable to comprehend that he does not comprehend.

"What an idea, man! I couldn't give it up even if I wanted to. The power is part of me, like these legs. Relax, and listen to me. I want you to have a monument erected to Figuerola."

"Yes, sir."

"With this inscription below: 'The World's Greatest Statistician. Not because he was so good, but because the others were worse.' "

"Got it, sir. I'll have it engraved in the marble."

"And have the doctrine taught every day in the basic courses for Peronist youth, but using the Galician's exercises."

"Right."

"One last instruction. Hand me those calendars."

Reverently, careful not to brush against the prie-dieu, Cámpora unrolls the huge maps of the cities not yet founded in Argentina, which Figuerola had named after defeats.

"Which one shall we begin with, General?"

"It makes no difference. What counts in this case is philosophy of history. Figuerola once called it to my attention that the Argentines are death-oriented. He used a strange word: 'thanatophiles.' That San Martín isn't honored in February when he was born, but on August 17. The same with Belgrano, Sarmiento, Evita, and Gardel, too. We celebrate their end. We have the little ones in first grade repeat the forefathers' last words. We are cadaver cultists. Figuerola believed that defects should not just be suffered but turned to advantage. He was right. I want you to change the names of the streets, Cámpora. You used to dream of naming them Perón. Call them: Vilcapugio, Ayohuma, Cancha Rayada, Curupaytí. Let us feel the constant sting of failure! Have the Malvinas marked in black on the maps. If we lost them, let them wear mourning. And put up a huge statue to Lonardi. Have it say on the base: 'Honor to the man who defeated Perón.' "

Cámpora feels himself being dragged toward the edge of he knows not what abyss by a brutal will that smells of death. "Is that what you want, General?" he quavers.

"Nobody has ever been surer of anything."

At that same moment, Omar Sívori, a soccer player, and Goyo Peralta, a boxer, are approaching the gate of the villa. For years they have partaken of the Sunday barbecues with the General and sung tangos out of tune together. A Guardia Civil officer bars their way. "No, gentlemen. There's a do-not-disturb order. The General cannot see anybody, now."

316

Then, a door opens and peering through the swarm of photographers Peralta spies Perón, in a yellow vest, sitting on the porch in a rocking chair, lost in thought. Standing on tiptoe, he shouts, "It's Sívori and Goyo, General! We came to say good-bye!"

A sad, vacant face turns toward them. And smiling at them with a smile that seems to take an age to appear, Perón says (or they believe he is saying) in his unmistakable hollow voice: "Thanks, boys. *Adiós.*"

18
THE PAST THAT RETURNS

I'm afraid to meet the past that
comes back to face me with my life.
Alfredo Le Pera, Volver

Their places have now been oc-
cupied by other people, taking over even the dregs of air and invad-
ing the very confusion of their thoughts. The General's seven
childhood companions no longer have even the illusion that there
is any purpose at all in their having returned to Ezeiza. Nobody
pays any attention to them. The man with the lizard's head who
drove them around the hangars and runways of the airport, going
nowhere, has disappeared, a pistol in his hand. Zamora, the newspaperman who coaxed them all the way out here with flattery and
false promises, is lost in a lair of silence. Señorita Tizón and Benita
de Toledo have been tracking him down by telephone, indignant at
first, then anxious. At home, his wife knows nothing. At the *Hori-*

zonte office, a compassionate woman reassures them: Be patient. Zamora will be coming. It's odd that nobody from the magazine is there. Not the editor, either? Don't be alarmed. How could they have disappeared right now when the General's plane is about to land?

But nobody comes. Not even the witnesses themselves feel that they are getting anywhere.

Outdoors,the passageways of the airport are being taken over by grim-faced, big-bellied men, armed as though for war. They wear white armbands, and when a few stray mules wander onto the parking area, they drive them off with spike-studded clubs.

Artemio and Captain Trafelatti have tried several times to use the first-floor toilets. No, gentlemen, not permitted. They wouldn't allow even Cousin Julio, whose need is quite obvious, to relieve himself. An important lieutenant colonel is holding a council of war up there and has ordered all access closed off. María Tizón has snooped around in search of a powder room to freshen her makeup. No use. The security cordons include the rest rooms. Only a foul toilet in the hallway is available and it is almost never free.

They are shocked when they see themselves in the lobby mirrors blurry with mold, looking like phantoms. Benita's fox coat, one of the shoulders of which rebels, slipping stubbornly down to her elbow, is bedraggled. Don Alberto Robert's quid of tobacco has dribbled onto his shirt, and to make matters worse, his cloudy blue eyes are beginning to hurt. Señorita Tizón's pink party dress is stained with grease and mud, mementos of the outing to the hangars. But Cousin Julio is bearing the heaviest cross of the morning. Lack of sleep has thrown his sphincters completely out of kilter and María Amelia's solicitude notwithstanding, his trousers now saturated, are dripping and the moisture has already soaked into his stockings.

Shortly before two, shouting and applause are heard. Squads of soldiers run to the military section of the airport and the big-bellies with the white armbands close ranks in the passageways, weapons at port. José Artemio pokes his head out and finds to his disappointment that it was not the General's arrival but that of welcoming dignitaries that had set off the commotion. He identifies three of them: the Papal Nuncio, Monsignor Lino Zanini, bejeweled as for a wedding; Solano Lima, to whom Cámpora had entrusted the reins of government, who walks with athletic stride, proud of the military salute; and, one step behind, the monkish form of Don Arturo Frondizi, anointed President by Perón fifteen years ago, somber now, with his seminarian's smile, coming to pay tribute. Following them, the ministers whom José Artemio, hemmed in by a new contingent of guards, is unable to see.

He hears Benita clucking excitedly: They are saying on the radio that the entourage of notables has just had lunch at an air base. What about us? It's now nearly two o'clock and nobody has offered us even a sandwich. The big-bellies with armbands don't deal with complaints. They pass them by as though the seven oldsters were ghosts, cloacas, of the General's past.

José Artemio then announces a heroic determination: "All these secret-service men have eaten here. They smell of chicken. There must be chicken and sodas somewhere about. I am going to look around upstairs."

Cousin Julio's voice, floating up from the depths of an easy chair, quavers: "And on the way, please see if there isn't a men's room."

Removing his beret, José Artemio improvises a white armband, which Benita fastens to his sleeve with a couple of pins. Señorita Tizón approves the metamorphosis: standing, minus his scarf, chest puffed out, Señor Toledo takes on the aspect of a matinee idol past his prime and might even resemble Henry Fonda. The best part of the transformation is the sneering expression that poisons his face. With his vacuous look he could pass for one of the big-bellies.

Summoning up courage, José Artemio makes straight for the elevators, the only entrances not under guard. He goes up to the first floor. Impossible to exit there. Men are sitting lined up in the hallway between machine guns, rolls of barbed wire, chains, and cartridge clips. José Artemio shakes his head. This is a hotel but it looks more like a rundown stable. A painful spasm of fear grips his neck. He continues on up to the second floor. There are guards at the stairways but not in the hall. Accordingly, he steps out of the elevator and walks as though he sees nobody. And so it is. As a small boy, he used to think that one who does not see cannot be seen, either. It rarely failed. He proceeds through the dark shadows, his mind a blank. All he feels is the protection of a strange mantle of dampness that impregnates the hotel, foot by foot. How is this possible with the blazing sun and crisp autumn breeze outdoors?

320

Ahead of him, he sees a door guarded by three burly, olive-skinned figures with tattooed hands. Turks or offspring of Turks. He must immediately wipe them out of his consciousness, become a body they ignore. He takes in the hardware on the doors with a rapid glance. One is unlocked on the side where the Turks are posted. He heads for it unhurriedly, as though it were his destination, and enters.

He is in luck. No one is inside. The room is small and very plain. The light is on, the venetian blinds down. There are two blunt pencils and an open notebook with writing on a little table. Scattered on the double bed are nylon stockings, an Itaka, several ammunition clips, and a Magnum of the type that takes both hands to fire. Next to the window, a door open on a clean bathroom with a supply of soap and toilet paper. Smiling, he imagines how relieved Cousin Julio would be.

The smell of food and cigarette smoke drifts in from a neighboring room. José Artemio puts his ear to the wall. He hears the faint sound of distant voices. Perhaps they are coming from the citadel guarded by the Turks at the end of the hallway. His intuition tells him there is no one in the adjoining rooms. He tiptoes to the communicating door and cautiously slips the blade of his penknife into the crack. The bolt has not been thrown. He turns the knob. It is open. He enters.

A billiard-table lighting fixture illuminates the remains of a banquet. His hound-dog's olfactory sense has not misled him. As he moves to pounce on a platter of cold cuts, the voices he heard before suddenly sound closer. He freezes. He has miscalculated. They were close by, only one room away. And there is a door on that side. He is overcome by a frightening sense of helplessness. As if he were naked under the light and, all at once, somebody were coming at him with a knife. Now, he is too terrified to move. He has tempted fate too far. He backs up, scarcely moving the air, until, against his will, against the warnings of his instinct bidding him to get away from there as fast as he can, he hears what is being said with perfect clarity.

"Let'th thtop the crapping around, Lito. The General can't . . . muthn't . . . land here. If he doeth, the leftieth'll take him over. Without realithing it, the Old Man'll get pulled in by the thloganth, and he'll do whatever they want him to. If that happenth, we'll have to thtorm the ship. There'th more of them, lot'th more."

Now, a chilly voice comes through which José Artemio instantly identifies. It belongs to the oily, brown-haired man who came out to meet Arcángelo Gobbi when they returned from the bus ride. The one who said: "We mustn't lose any more time. The lieutenant colonel needs you."

Now, he repeats, "We mustn't lose any more time . . . I agree. But look at the whole picture. We're waiting for them but they don't know it. Even if they're carrying hardware, they won't dare use it. If they did, they're risking that the General will blame them afterwards for ruining his party. You have to take into account the mentality of those people, lieutenant colonel. The lefties think of politics as moral. They suffer from the sickness of scruples. That's what defeats them. If we intend to have the first thousand feet secure, then the concentration can be held. Those thousand feet are assured beforehand."

"Don't be a jerk, Lito," cut in a woman's hoarse cigarette voice.

"You're the jerk. What about all the oneth who'll be yelling behind the thouthand feet? Who'th going to control thothe people? There'th millionth. How're you going to convinthe them not to call Cámpora 'Uncle'?"

"And what about poor Isabelita?" says the woman.

"Right. They thtill have Eva on the brain. They'll give the the-ñora the cold shoulder. That'th for sure! The problem ithn't the leftieth, Lito. The leftieth' thloganth are for the punkth and the green tholdierth there to muthle them. The mob ith the problem. You have to know who you're hooking up with, the math or the mathter-mindth. And make no mithtake about it. Daniel ith the mathter-mind. Thay Daniel and you're thaying Perón."

Holding his breath as he moves, José Artemio has found a crack through which he can see the three shadows. The woman gesticulates. She is angular, hysterical. The lisper is smoking, his hands on the desk in front of him. He can make Lito out from the waist up, standing.

"Then there's no more to discuss," Lito says. "All we need is a provocation to light the fuse with."

"I better get out of here," José Artemio says to himself. And he repeats it a hundred times: "I better get out of here! Better stop listening in! Better put this bad dream out of my mind!" His hunger has fled, the food in front of him poison and smoke.

"A lefty fink," the woman laughs.

322

"The one we got. The thame kid that thquealed to you. The one that thpilled that the thouth column wath going to try and do a pinther and cut uth off from the platform. Thend word to that one that when the shit thtartth to fly, to pull his piethe and fire a thingle shot. Jutht one. That'll give uth the excuthe to pull the thwitch."

"It has to be right away," the woman says.

"Right away," repeats Lito.

José Artemio takes the gamble: all or nothing. Cautiously, he backs up to the door of the room at which the nightmare began, pushes it open and enters. He sees with relief the same cartridge clips, Itaka, and nylons on the bed, and waits. He hears Lito give orders and run down the stairs, the Turks after him. He hears the lieutenant colonel arguing with the woman, but he no longer understands anything . . . doesn't want to. Taking a deep breath he plunges into the hall, again without looking, as if going through a lifelong routine. The elevator is still there. He enters and descends the two floors in an eternity.

The picture in the lobby has changed. It is swarming with police and soldiers wearing armbands of different colors. There are two impassable cordons at the hotel entrance. The copies of *Horizonte*, the tables, and easy chairs have all been removed.

"Did you find food?" gasps Benita.

"There's no food. There's nothing." José Artemio's muscles are in knots, his eyes glassy. "Let's plead with them to get somebody to take us back to Buenos Aires. This is all over with."

"What do you mean? The General will be landing in an hour." Captain Trafelatti has awakened. "They said so over the radio."

The elevator doors open with a bang. A woman, followed by two guards, strides out looking about. Tension or irritation pull her thin lips down at the corners.

"Coba!" she calls out. "Lito Coba!"

All at once she fixes on the seven childhood companions, standing, stranded, out of place in the pandemonium of the lobby. José Artemio feels a chill run down his spine. "The tobacco voice of the second floor! I was seen," he says to himself.

"What are these old people doing here?" she yells. "Get them out!"

"I am Julio Perón," the cousin says, drawing himself up in a surge of dignity. He did not say: "I am the cousin."

"I am the General's first cousin," says María Amelia.

In the hubbub and hysteria, the woman cannot hear what they are saying and shouts,"Who brought them, anyway? Get them the hell out of here. Throw them out in the field."

A horde of big-bellies descends upon the old folks. Incredulous, Benita watches them pick Señorita María up bodily and dump her on the asphalt of the parking lot, the daintiness of her pink dress violated and torn. She sees Don Alberto dragged away and María Amelia's skirt stripped off her. She then feels brazen hands seizing her, and in a flash of lucidity, hears her body hit the floor of a bus.

". . . far away from here, in the middle of the field!" the woman growls.

"Right! Señora Norma," says one of the big-bellies, saluting.

Benita ends up in the rearmost seats next to María Tizón. One of the guards holds his pistol on them.

The sun is still beating down. There is a breeze but it is hot. The people filter through the woods, singing. Once again,the witnesses pass the hangars, the runways now teeming with trucks and soldiers, the barbed wire fences, the eucalyptuses. Benita and María recognize, at the same time, that they are in the same bus that took them on their morning tour. Benita picks up the soiled and tattered remains of a copy of *Horizonte* from under a seat. She comes upon the photograph of herself as an adolescent on one of the torn pages. Regarding it with melancholy, she collects the shreds of the story to shelter them in her lap.

The bus jerks to a stop in a burned-out field.

"Here we are!" bawls one of the big-bellies. "This is as far as your ticket takes you."

They get out. All at once, they are engulfed by the forlornness of the open fields and the infinite emptiness of their lives. And they move on. Captain Trafelatti hurries along. After fording a stream, he leaves them behind. Cousin Julio, his fists clenched, sobs. Benita and María Amelia pause to soak their swollen feet, raked with thistle scratches. To shed her illusions of the past, Benita reads:

> Evita Duarte, who was always fascinated by the parallelism fated for certain lives, came from a background as murky as Juan Perón's. Her parents were unmarried when she was born in Los Toldos on May 7, 1919. And they never married. Before Eva was a year old, Don Juan Duarte, at the behest of his legitimate wife in Chivilcoy, left Los Toldos. Eva and her

four older brothers and sisters grew up on their own, waifs as she would say later.

Her mother, Doña Juana Ibarguren, was a proud and beautiful peasant woman. In her family, too, the surnames were as intermingled and relationships as apparently incestuous as those on Perón's maternal side. Instead of Toledo and Sosa, there were combinations of Nuñez and Valenti, which the ladies of the village never were able to disentangle.

Both fathers were at one time justices of the peace. The mothers were enterprising women, strong-willed, indifferent to the malicious finger-pointing of neighbors. But, contrary to Juan Domingo's case, Don Juan Duarte never recognized Eva. She had to create herself, to invent a past, to be the beginning and end of her own lineage . . .

(Ripped-out page. Photograph of Evita as a little girl, torn and mud-stained.)

. . . the data are confusing at this point in the story. Did Evita leave Junín with the tango singer Agustín Magaldi when she was fifteen years old? Seems unlikely. Probably untrue.

Magaldi sang in Junín at the end of 1934. Eva traveled to Buenos Aires on January 3, 1935 with two letters of recommendation and the express permission of her mother. Had one of the letters been from the singer, it would have been of no use to her. On March 28, 1935, when she began working as a bit player in a company that belonged to a friend who had the same given name as she, Eva was living in a boarding house in the Congreso barrio and Magaldi had taken off on another tour in Santiago del Estero . . .

(The darkness is hurting Benita's eyes. The letters shrink in size. The wind blows the page out of her hand.)

8. Grac   por   xist r

The festival organized by Colonel Perón in Luna Park was scheduled to start at 9 p.m., but President Ramírez's wife was delayed by household problems and they didn't arrive at the stadium until 10:30.

It was one of those humid, suffocating nights that only a Buenos Aires summer is capable of producing. The San Juan earthquake had taken place only a week before; grief and euphoria merged at the festival.

The stands were packed. Evita was radiant, her mother-of-pearl skin, black dress, elbow-length gloves, and hat with a white feather made a beautiful ensemble. A friend, Colonel Aníbal Imbert, had gotten her a ringside seat in the second row, behind the President. How Eva managed to move into the place beside Colonel Perón, nobody knows.

At eleven o'clock, she was seen to weep when the Colonel spoke, standing straight, imperious, glowing in his chalk-colored uniform. Eva was already in love with him by the time she heard him saying: *It is the poor who have suffered the most in San Juan. It is the poor who have suffered and sacrificed the most in this wonderful country. And while the working class expresses its solidarity by giving unstintingly, as it has done here tonight, there are many big moguls who are living the good life at the nation's expense and turning their backs on our grief.*

The Colonel left the platform, drying his forehead with a handkerchief. The stands shouted their acclaim. He was obliged to stand up at his seat several times, his arms held high, asking for silence. Finally, he sat motionless for a moment beside Evita, his eagle's eyes staring off into space. She, plucking up her courage, ventured to brush his uniform sleeve with her fingertips.

"Colonel . . . ," she said.

Perón looked at her for the first time. Until that moment he had seen nothing but a tiny, emotionally stirred body, nothing more than another throat amidst that multitude.

"What is it, my dear?" he asked.

Evita, then, said the words that changed both their lives forever.

"Thank you for existing. That's all: thank you for existing."

(Cousin Julio is walking along on a muddy shoulder, his feet wet, chilled to the bone. A fine drizzle begins to fall, transparent at first, then tinged with the shades of night as the light wanes. He has kept some pages of *Horizonte* in his pants pocket, he has no idea why. Now the paper is a soggy mass against his damp leg. Much of the print is blurred and illegible:)

. . . not even the core of seven officers who, together with Colonel Perón, created the lodge in December, 1942, know the meaning of the acronym GOU. The history books decode it as *Grupo de Obra y Unificación* or *Grupo Organizador y Unificador*. What difference does it make?

They agreed that there should be no head, to renounce personal ambition, declared that they would serve no interests other than those of the army and the fatherland . . .

. . . erlinger stood up. He was in a frenzy. Perón did not move a muscle.

"Have you ever stopped to consider Severo Toranzo's letter to Uriburu? Have you had the guts to read it? It was written in 1932 and could be written again tomorrow. Look at it."

"I have no patience with it. There's no time. That's enough!" said Perón.

"Listen to it!" said Perlinger, blocking the way out with his body. "I'm going to make it heard if it's the last thing in my life I do!"

With trembling fingers he puts on his glasses. Perón, infinitely patient, looked up at the ceiling.

"Until September 6, 1930, we had an army that was idolized by the Argentine people. Nobody, among even the worst of our leaders, would have dared use it as an oppressive instrument against the peop— You and your henchmen have undermined its discipline by corrupting it with benefits and privileges . . . Now, the army of Argentina is despised by the true people . . ."

(The field has now finally merged with the horizon. It is pitch dark. Not even animals are visible. Señorita María, leveled by exhaustion, sits on the edge of the culvert. In the distance, the throng continues on its way down the highway in never-ending rivers. But not arriving. Returning, now.)

. . . strange, but both stories happened on the same day and to the same person. The train, coated with dust, fled the salt flats of Córdoba and plunged into the deserts of Santiago. It was daybreak. The compartments were filled with women: secretaries, census takers, heads of basic units. Unexpectedly, all of them suddenly felt that Evita was there. Nobody had to say so. They felt it. She was passing through the aisles, dressed in a long negligee of white tulle, her hair loose. A satin shawl over her shoulders.

"Am I or am I not a goddess? Am I or am I not?"

The train stopped at the Frías station at about nine o'clock in the morning. *Les misérables* were there in a swarm, bent over, like sad small animals. All they wanted was to touch her. Eva flung a shower of banknotes over them. The people did not move to pick them up but kept their eyes riveted upon that beautiful presence, like white moths held by her light.

A tiny old woman, a bundle upon her head, managed to reach her. She approached Eva and held out an offering . . . a dish of fried chicken covered with a napkin. Eva touched the woman's head, and blessed her. Then, she lifted a piece of the chicken to her mouth. One of the secretaries, speaking in a low, urgent tone, stopped her.

"Señora, you mustn't eat that!"

Eva ate with violent haste. She then disappeared momentarily inside the train. She could be heard at the rear of the car giving the secretary a dressing down.

"A woman of the people prepared it for me. Don't you realize that? God alone knows what love and respect went into that dish. Do you want me to throw her love into the garbage? Finished! I never want to lay eyes on you again! Do you understand? I don't ever want to see you again."

Central Intelligence Agency
Report No. FIR DB - 312/04751 - 73

. . . from the time Eva became bedridden, Perón never entered her room again. Apparently, he would stand in the doorway and, from there, ask her how she was feeling. He made sure to keep far away. He was afraid that cancer was contagious.

(The childhood companions have stopped again to catch their breath. Clutching herself to José Artemio's breast, Benita weeps: short, disheartened sobs that die like the flames of little matches. Cousin Julio, fortunately, has fallen asleep, his head on his sister María's lap. Could there be a telephone anywhere in this backwash of Ezeiza, any little first-aid station, a compassionate nurse who would see to this old man who has begun to breathe with death stertors?

(Don Alberto Robert, who had trailed behind, has walked into a barbed-wire fence in the dark. Groping for support, reaching into nothingness, he again lacerates his hands. His fingers touch some fluttering papers, freeing them from their wire prison to fly away into the night. It is conceivable that Don Alberto, poised at the abyss of his blindness, his senses in perpetual alert, is divining the obscure thought now borne by the wind that none of the other witnesses will ever read. The statement made by Perón [when, before whom, in what tone?] that sums him up totally: a river of a statement that could hold an ocean.)

"I do not know what it means to hesitate. A leader may not hesitate. Can you imagine God ever hesitating? If God were to hesitate, we would all disappear."

19
DON'T LET THE
SPARROWS LIGHT

When the Chinese want to kill sparrows, they keep them from settling
on the trees. They chase them off
with poles, not letting them light,
and so, leave them breathless, until
their hearts finally burst. That is
what I do with those who try to fly
too high. I let them fly. Sooner or
later they all fall, like the sparrows.
Perón to the author,
June 29, 1966

H̲e has taken in so much liquid
that he feels his body flooded, yet fear has lodged in his throat with
a dryness that oppresses its membranes, his saliva like cork. He
should have no reason to be nervous. After all, he has gotten the
easiest assignment—waiting.

As the column led by Noon and Diana advances, banners raised,
it opens cracks in the left flank of the concentration, entering,
suffusing, and while Vicki Pertini, at the head of another long
tongue of militants, tears the security cordons to shreds on the
right flank, he, Ox Iriarte, baobab, bovine-eyed, has remained behind covering the rear, in back of the platform, in the no-man's-
land that keeps the mob isolated from the airport.

He would have preferred it if Diana or Noon had not been so ready to accept the easy success of the maneuver . . . if they had questioned why no gang of killers had appeared to block off the march when it swung from the water tower to the forbidden highway where only police vehicles were permitted to pass; why no helicopter had tried to check the column's advance when it split into two around the supports of the platform and, in a pincers movement, drove the points of the tongs into the temples of the crowd. How could they, always so alert, not suspect anything? The sight of their goal was enough to blind them.

Ox Iriarte takes in the field at a glance. Behind him in no-man's-land, the hosts of shantytown volunteers are lined up in double file to unfurl the gigantic welcome banner as soon as Perón nears. In front, Diana and Vicki dig their elbows into the ribs of the concentration and, at the rear end of the platform, a line of ambulances and buses stands dozing, apparently empty, their motors shut off. As though nothing were happening.

He has drunk quarts of water. His tongue is nevertheless a dead piece of rag. He is choking. On top of the metal scaffolding of the platform, some thirty feet from the ground, shadows spring, swaying, between the pipes. Will this fragile skeleton resist when the General appears? How many of the millions now roaring on the other side of the bridge will be able to withstand the urge to run toward him and embrace him, squashing him? Although the intensity of the uproar confuses all sounds, Ox can hear the pipes of the platform groan. A house of cards! The wind blows. The banners flutter at the flanks.

He turns around and observes the empty field: the tiled church they have just passed, the big orphan asylum, the crenelated tower. Three Ford Falcons snake through the empty streets at top speed. They come toward him. He hears the screech of the tires with his stomach, not his eardrums. Torsos emerging from the windows, hands on the roof, men in black display Itakas, Beretta carbines. They point them at him.

The cars cross a wooden bridge, ford a ditch. They are now upon him. In the last of the three, Ox distinguishes Lito Coba's icy smile.

A trombonist who arrived late had to be lifted bodily by the crowd onto the orchestra stand, built in the shape of a gigantic piano, at the base of the platform. A path is opened to let two violinists through, walking sideways, but without room for them to carry their instruments. From time to time, scraps of bologna casing, sausage coloring matter, bird droppings, splatter down upon the music stands. Even with the mess being made of their notes the orchestra manages to keep in tune.

The miasma emanating from the mash of bodies grows ever denser. It is now past two o'clock. Nobody has moved for the last half hour. There is no return for anyone who leaves. Families with babies have been pushed back to the open spaces behind. The first few yards are occupied only by those with elbows of steel, feet of cement, and anesthetized sphincters.

Several bass-drum corps are practicing their thunder at the foot of the stand. Fireworks explode in the sky. A sweaty stout woman, armpits in the air, tries to push her way through. A blowsy counterpart slides a foot under her as she looks off in the other direction, tumbling her to the ground. Threats ensue followed by a hair-pulling match. Easy, girls. Cool the polenta. This is Peronism Day.

A blue and white balloon belonging to the State Gas Company suddenly appears between the patrolling helicopters that come and go overhead. Two aerialists activated by a spring are shot out of the basket into the void. A cable breaks their fall in midair. They are dummies. This brief moment of illusion was sufficient to afford the pickpockets a field day to remember.

The booming voice of the official announcer, Edgardo Suárez, overrides. "We are now more than two and a half million Argentines here waiting for the General." Leonardo Favio takes over the microphone and corrects him: "Keep counting! *Compañeros*, we have already reached the three-million mark!"

Favio tries to dissimulate his concern. He is watching fleeting outbreaks take place at the sides of the platform. "Let's rehearse, *compañeros!*" he shouts, pushing back the pompon of his woolen cap. "Let's warm up our throats in tribute to our beloved General . . ."

Nothing doing. The cordons of Union Youth close ranks, right arms locked to companions' left arms, shoulders pressed together, driving back with heads and knees the tide rolling upon them. Only the first charge is stopped. The second wave immediately forms and rolls in again. Diana and Noon have broken through several wire fences. They are pouring with sweat. The irresistible force behind them contracts momentarily, then pushes anew. Bodies are crushed, stripped, leap in a cataract. A wooden wall topples in splinters. One of the Elect on the platform blows his whistle, the signal for the men of the cordons to give way and take their places behind the ambulances on the flanks.

At the head of the column, all hold their breath and then begin to pant like a woman in labor. And they plow ahead. When the two long tongues of the column finally join in front of the platform, a great shout bursts forth. Pepe Juárez and Noon raise their banners high.

The huge bulk of the concentraton has given ground and pours over the culverts. The gorillas with the green armbands, clinging to the union trucks, regroup four deep. They make ready, pulling out their lead-filled hoses and, in plain view, adjusting brass knuckles.

People are still struggling, but only to free their legs. The Golden Throat has jumped the gun and started chanting:

> *Like Vandor, the traitor,*
> *Rucci'll get his later.*

Meanwhile, the chorus of the Blue Sewer, tossed by the avalanche, can be heard in the distance shouting as they dance around the trucks, challenging them:

> *They've got to go, they've got to go,*
> *The union bosses have got to go.*

One of the trucks, its motor roaring, spitting smoke, threatens to run them over. All the bass-drum corps thunder in unison. Vicki, who doesn't know which way to move first, jumps up and down, screaming Perón's nickname: "Come on, Pocho! Come on, Pocho!" as if that would hasten his arrival. The confusion of clashing noises saturates the atmosphere.

Then, the sound of a shot is heard, crisp and different. In that vortex where nobody can hear even his own breathing, everyone hears it: the first shot, and with it, silence.

———

Did we have to bust our guts that way to end up slipping through like on a greased slide? But what are you talking about, Diana Bronstein? The worst hasn't started yet. The fascists have enough stuff for a war up there on the platform. I should have covered my head. With this red mane of mine, I'm a traffic signal. Let's get those signs up there, now, boys! Hey, you, *che*, don't you have some piece of rag you could give me?

(They rock them. They pull and push them. Once in a while they find an opening. We have only one body, and this kind of turmoil wears it out. But what would become of the body otherwise; what should wear out if not the body?)

Still, it's peculiar that it should have been so easy. Peculiar? You're a paranoid Jew, Diana. Centuries of concentration camps have squelched your hope. This isn't the Warsaw ghetto. Or, maybe it's worse. Dig that platform. *Mamma mia*, what mugs! A rogues' gallery mural. The capos have skipped from Auschwitz and Dachau but they're alive and kicking here. Look at that Rigoletto there, Noon. See him? The one in the sweater, rubbing his hands. No, the one without hair, the bald hunchback moving around in back of the box. That one! Did you get a good look? He's been giving me the heavy eye for quite a while.

Able to catch her breath, finally, shielded by the signs, Diana discovers that there are hundreds of people nesting in the trees. Opposite the little school swarming with López Rega's goons, several families have set up platforms between the branches of the cedar and walnut trees: aerial settlements, like in Jules Verne. One old woman has lit a brazier up above and is steeping maté. Doña Luisa? Isn't that the matriarch of Villa Insuperable who said to her only two days ago: If you're going to be there, Diana, I won't miss it? And the man next to her singing or talking to himself, with the cigarette in his mouth . . . isn't he her rheumatic husband? Doña Luisa! It's Diana! she shouts. And the woman looks up from the brazier, waving in all directions.

A pair of twins from Lanús, wearing Montonero headbands, yell to her from the top of a walnut tree. They have come because of her . . . following her. What a burgeoning in the trees!

Further away, in an ashy eucalyptus, a dark-skinned woman with a sweet face is nursing her baby. Three men, tuning their guitars, are covering her. They, too, wave handkerchiefs and smile. From time to time, they all raise their heads and search out signals in the sky, the vapor trails of planes, the growling of the helicopters. The General will be landing at any moment, now. An eclogue, Diana thinks: the people one has chosen to be near, earth figures like oneself.

(We have only one body and there are times, flashes, when we wish we could love with two bodies, eternities in which we wish we could forget about this body that is afraid.) And, still . . .

Crossing the fence, now on the grounds of the school, some twenty men carrying light rifles have climbed up to squat on platforms installed at two levels on telegraph poles. They are pointing their weapons in all directions, as though preparing to blow up the world.

The louder we shout the slogans, the more it will be felt that we are here because we want to go along with a rejuvenated country, and the easier it will be for the General to open his arms and accept: As the people wish! National socialism? If that's what the people want! I mustn't make myself hoarse before time. Come on, kids, let's sing. Here goes:

> *We'll make our country Peronist,*
> *But it must be Montonero and Socialist.*

Yes, yes? Let's sing it again! *Che*, what's with you all? Let's open up those voice boxes and let out some sound!

"*Compañeros*, lower your signs for a moment!" Leonardo Favio calls out over the platform microphones. "Only for a moment. Here beside me are cameramen and news photographers who have come from the farthest corners of the globe to make a record of this glorious spectacle. Nothing like it has ever been seen, *compañeros*. Never in the history of America has enthusiasm been demonstrated that could compare with this . . ." Every word must be calculated. Call out the General's name as many times as possible. He is immortal as the Andes, sacred as Pericles, great as Napoleon. And link his image with Isabelita's. But don't mention Eva. Or the Uncle. The scenario is clear. Watch that!

"Lower the signs just for a moment so that the photographers can get some shots of this laurel wreath that we are going to place on the brow of our Great Leader, General Perón!" Nobody pays

335

any attention. At each word of Favio's, the signs are raised higher, beating wings. No one listens any longer. The sky covers the earth with its mouth.

Arcángelo Gobbi waits for the signal behind the booth where the General will take his place on the platform. He paces. When he passes close to one of the Elect, he repeats: Keep a sharp ear. Wait for the first shot. His hands are sweating. He is afraid that after being still and tense for so long, his hands will turn to jelly the moment he needs them. His nerves bother him. His back is torture. An unexpected sense of strangulation runs in waves down his insides to remain in his gut, pulsating. It is like the chill of masturbation when he can no longer withstand it and must run to the toilet to relieve himself.

Something has fallen onto the platform. A bottle? A wire? No, it is a violin bow, it's hairs torn. All his senses are keyed up.

He puts on his dark glasses. And although he has told himself repeatedly not to do it, he fixes his eyes again on the woman with the flaming hair. He presses his gun with his damp hands. As soon as he hears the signal, he will wipe that image from his mind that is so painful, will tear this woman to pieces in the depths of his thoughts. Those green eyes, freckles, that red hair of the enemy woman shouting under the Montonero banner, are the same ones that torment him in his dream: the Virgin who comes looking for him every night has at last arrived. Now, he must get rid of her. He must. What more fitting offering for Isabel Perón, the true possessor of that sacred countenance.

Rarely does anything happen in the lapse between two thoughts. But there is an interval now—Noon thinks—as the incredible Ox climbs up the pipes of the platform, a drawn Colt in his hand, in which reality can be sensed: on the right, inside the Social Welfare food truck, he feels the throb of shotguns; on the embankment, he has discovered the web of wires and cables about to descend on him; behind, he smells the lightning of clubs brandished by the killers with the green armbands. He would like to be able to tell whether it is he or someone else who is hearing this silence. The bass drums have stopped, the musicians have disappeared into thin air, the loudspeakers have clamped shut, Favio is no longer there. The balloon passes into a cloud. And precisely in that desert where things do not happen, Ox pulls the trigger.

———

As Lito Coba draws away from the scaffolding of the platform, zigzagging over the no-man's-land of the freeway, toward the airport, between the bewildered shantytowners who are still trying to fathom how it was possible for Ox Iriarte to walk over to such bigshot fascists and shake their hands without gagging, how a people's militant could have stepped to one side to talk privately for four or five minutes to one of the bloodthirstiest of the henchmen of López-Regaism. And then, the shantytowners see him leave his post in the rear guard to race madly, clumsily, to the platform, climb up the pipes, draw the Colt 45 Lito had just given him, aim at one of the guards, shout "Perón or death!" and shoot, but into the air, at random, the Montonero headband glowing on his huge head like a lantern. Then, instantly trying to escape, he dashes like a madman in the direction of the Olympic swimming pool. Vicki Pertini, trying to catch up with him, manages only to hurl a curse after him. What are you doing to us, Ox? Oh, what mess are you getting us into? But there was no time for the terrified baobab to hear her. At the same instant, a bullet from the rifle of one of the sharpshooters on the telegraph poles has torn through the nape of his neck. Has ended forever Ox's dark and solitary dreams. Has left him dying without leaving any clue as to how it was possible for his loyalty to have crumbled so suddenly, to the resentments he had to swallow, to what death he has had to go now, to what darkness of the sky he will be bringing the bad luck of his tenderness.

You needed a cigarette desperately, Vicki Pertini. After all that agonizing, you wanted to wet your head in any puddle, catch your breath, and warm your soul with a butt. Then, the shot. A door opened that you were not expecting and *ciao*, you're through it now, exhaling the smoke of the cigarette you will puff on tomorrow. The shot. You run, for a change. You yell something. And, without knowing how, you are back at the center of the whirlwind, the maelstrom sucks you under, your puny little body marked for nothingness and atomization is no longer you, Vicki. Now, all you feel is that Pepe Juárez lets go of your hand, that you have lost sight of the Golden Throat, and that the strength of a beast lifts you by the hair to the platform, drags you beneath the General's effigy, while other claws asphyxiate you with black plastic. And you don't know in what corner of nothingness to hide your body, the wisp of person that you are, how to get out of yourself so that you will no longer feel the blows of the chain smashing into your flesh.

The instant Ox has fallen, a contingent of stretcher bearers runs toward him, but none is concerned with the hole in his neck, the last bloody petal to drop from him. Rather, they surround the body with stretchers and take refuge behind the parapet.

The rear guard of the Blue Sewer is still singing next to the embankment where he was brought down. Only the crack of the telescopic rifle was heard there. One knows, of course, what one sees: that a comrade lies wounded at one side, shot from behind, his headband bloody. One of the tenors, red handkerchief around his neck, is horrified, and goes to pick up the dead man.

He is stopped by a volley of shots. The stretcher bearers have opened first-aid kits, exposing among the bandages flat Barettas that sting before they can be heard. If skillfully triggered, the bursts of three to five shots never miss. The fingers of the tenor with the red handkerchief were blown off. The jaw of the contralto who tried to cover him was splintered.

On being separated from Vicki, Pepe Juárez feels that all instincts have left him except that of survival. If he does not retreat immediately, his men will be endangered. With Pepe in the lead, the mass, banners waving, zigzags, fanning out in an ever-widening arc, and manages to reach the eucalyptus woods. As soon as they are safe in this providential refuge, he orders the weapons to be taken out: .22's, cat-killers, birdshot. Anything capable of making a noise will help save the necks of his bewildered followers when they disband.

Juárez is squat, very dark-skinned, with eyebrows grown together. He has never considered himself brave, but now he discovers that blindness of the muscles, the sudden disdain for the future in any aspect, is just that—bravery. He is gripped by an impulse to jump toward the trenches of the culvert, get around to the flank, crawling, and attack the stretcher bearers who savaged the Blue Sewer. How many might he save before they killed him? Although, thinking it over carefully, he isn't concerned about them killing him. From what he has heard of these fascists, what worries him is having his tongue torn out after having been made to talk under torture.

He will have to hold out in the woods, then. López Rega's gorillas control the field: the ambulances, the platform, the little school, the union trucks, the Olympic pools. The only escape route is behind him, through the Matanza River.

The concentration is finally split apart by the chunks being constantly bitten out of it by the bullets. The throng spills out, feeling its way through the tall grass, hoping to see no more, hear no more, until the hurricane subsides. The balloons have been let loose from the platform. The sky turns idiotically festive. Hugging the deck, the musicians of the symphony orchestra shield themselves in the jungle of the music stands.

Only the column headed by Noon and Diana has held the positions won, chanting slogans as though nothing were happening, their signs raised high. When the shooting gets heavier and two of the marchers behind Noon are wounded, the brave ones of the column draw their weapons. In a hard, flat tone, Diana orders them: Put away your guns, comrades! Don't answer provocation.

They stay there a few minutes longer in the hope that strength of numbers will be enough to protect them. They hear Favio's voice again over the loudspeakers: "Peace, *compañeros*, peace! Everybody stay where they are. There is no reason for panic." But the bursts of gunfire come closer and closer and even the veteran photographers get far away from the line of fire.

> *Hang in, hang in,*
> *The General's on the way . . .*

chants Diana, keeping spirits up. She gets no further. Two ambulances, coming out of nowhere rip the guts of the column with the fury of a wounded whale, crushing bodies, tearing banners. The worst are the sirens that freeze the blood.

Shots now spray the entire field. Decimated, the column crumbles and scatters. Noon runs. He manages to slip under the platform, between the pipes. He waits. Closing his eyes, he keeps breathing in deeply.

When he opens them again, a way through the maze of the scaffolding comes miraculously into focus. He squeezes through, emerging finally in the no-man's-land behind the area, crosses a bridge, and comes to the edge of the Echeverría barrio. Not until then does he make an unreal discovery, an emptiness in his hand, like a memory that has taken leave. He realizes that Diana is not at his side. That he has lost Diana in the eternity of this frenzy.

Arcángelo had Diana in the sights of his Beretta several times, even during the wildest moments of confusion. And each time the pleasure of feeling her at his mercy caused him to lower the weapon. But he didn't consider the pleasure. What he said to himself was: If I blast her from here, I won't see her anymore. The lefties will take her away and she'll be gone for good. She won't give me any peace. When I dream, I will have her above me.

A ferocious determination unsettles his being. His movements, until then controlled, deliberate, become frenetic and jerky as a cockroach's.

"Bring the ambulances, fast!" he orders. "I want three men with me, armed."

Not three, but seven men start out. Obeying the blasts on a whistle by an invisible member of the Elect, the cordons of green armbands open a swath at once between the columns of Montoneros. At the same moment, the ambulances leap from the embankment, sirens open, and charge into the mass. The flanks of the column give way almost immediately but others, crazed at the sight of the outrage, counterattack, suicidally trying to slash the tires, to smash the vehicle, but they are ineffectual. Arcángelo clearly indicated before leaving whom he was after.

The prey is in the densest knot of the turmoil, which is chanting defiantly: "Hang in, hang in!" She is protected by a swarm of Indian-looking women and burly boys with heavy beards, yellow with mud. In the fever of the hunt, one of the ambulances gives full voice to the siren's shrillest screech. And it attacks. Diana has unerringly deciphered the signal. The frenzy is directed at her. She tears herself away from the swarm and tries to take cover next to the platform. Cornered there, she confronts the fascists, with the pole of a banner. She tries to jam it into the radiator, the windows, until her fingers break. Then she waits for them. Let them run her over! Let them dare to kill her!

But the hunters play with her. They back off and then hem her in. Three men get out, engulf her, immobilize her. Inside the ambulance, the doors are slammed shut, and a gag forced into her mouth.

Arcángelo has been waiting for her in the ambulance. Greedily, he is able finally to examine his prey. Could she be an insect from another world? He scans the arch of the red eyebrows, the desperation of the green eyes, the spots on Diana's breast. And, with infinite precaution, as though about to plunge his hands in a brazier, he touches her. He feels the strange warmth of the perspiration on her lips, the fluttering of the nostrils, the rage of the temples.

The ambulances, their sirens hoarse, speed around the embankment into the freeway and on to the airport.

Arcángelo observes the shadows outside that are gradually darkening. He sees the outlines of houses, a tower with battlements, a church that should be blue and is now black. He rests a damp claw on the driver's shoulder.

"Turn back," he orders. "I want to put the woman in there. In the church."

20

THE SHORTEST DAY
OF THE YEAR

At close to three o'clock in the afternoon, when the skirmish had finally died down, Norma called a press conference at one of the offices at the international hotel and gave a less neurasthenic briefing than usual. The day's tensions had left marks on her that would take some time to fade. Her shoulders sagged like a toboggan slide and her skinny, muscular legs trembled uncontrollably.

The telex beside her desk chattered spasmodically and a retinue of radio operators and corpulent policemen kept arriving with photographs of the situation and reports from the General's plane, now in a holding pattern over Porto Alegre. The lieutenant colonel peeked in at one point, plucked up courage, and approached Norma to whisper in her ear.

"The leftieth threw the firtht thtoneth and now they're playing innothent. They're leaving the platform. Anybody who'th not in Etheitha, it'th becauthe he doethn't want to welcome the General. Do you get my meaning?"

Norma, who hated to look straight ahead, withered this officer with a glare of fury. She has expressed herself scornfully on his political acumen on more than one occasion.

"I know what I'm doing. I know what I should say."

She has tried for a long time to emulate the General, coming out with the words others expected of her, but she is much too nervous to tune in accurately on the direction of their desires. This made her seem peevish but it was unfair to attribute that peevishness to her words since it was a quality that stemmed rather from her very nature.

She sent out for coffee, forbade photographs, and spoke so differently from her usual manner, so diffidently, that she was asked to repeat her opening words several times:

"Some of you already know that the platform on which we were expecting to receive our great leader was attacked a few minutes ago. Those who gave the order to fire have now been identified. They are tools of the sinarchist, imperialist, and monopoly interests that are opposed to the General's presence in our country. Those hired assassins are being dissuaded by the people's security forces . . ."

With a start, noticing that she had left her 9 mm Walther on the desk, she picked it up and put it into her briefcase.

". . . people's forces," she insisted. "The infiltrators have no choice but to leave. Only the true people will remain, then, to welcome the General. Our slogan for this glorious day, is to fight for a Peronist fatherland. Perón is the fatherland."

She stood up. One of the correspondents stopped her.

"Do you think, señora, that the General will go to the platform even in the awareness of these serious incidents?"

"Yes, he will go."

"In case he should decide against going, have alternate airports been alerted?"

An uncontrollable grimace darkened her face. She asked one of the big-bellies in a whisper whether the press conference was being broadcast live. He nodded that it was.

"There is no reason to be concerned about alternative airports. The General will land at Ezeiza. That is a fact."

"You are asserting, then, that the situation has been brought under control?"

"Absolutely."

"What is the estimated time of arrival?"

"After dark. The flight is an hour behind schedule. It should be kept in mind that today, June twentieth, is the shortest day of the year."

As anticipated, the news of the press conference produced a furious attack by the south column. When Lito Coba returned to the area of the platform, now in a heavily armed Torino, he saw the banners of the lefties alive again in the trees. A frenetic clamor advanced in seismic waves from the most distant borders of the concentration toward where the pilgrims from the Northwest had retreated:

> *What gives, what gives, what gives, General?*
> *The Fatherland is socialist,*
> *And now they want to change it!*

Pitiless volleys from the ambulances and the platform rained down on the column, breaking up the chanting, but it kept regrouping miraculously with incredible strategic ingenuity: first, all the bass-drum corps led off with their maddening thunder, immediately followed by squadrons of disabled pushing their wheelchairs with one hand and waving flags of truce with the other. The barricades of the eucalyptus woods had been dismembered long since by the Dodges and Falcons crashing into them, and the ditches alongside the roads had been swept clear by sappers with wax-tipped mustaches like Turks, but nobody knew by what prodigies of will this crowd, without leaders or a previous plan of concerted action, was able to pick up its wounded after each repulse and persist in congregating before the platform to keep chorusing the same phrase: *What gives, what gives?*

Lito noticed that a few armed men had found refuge on tree platforms and were supporting the advancing columns from there. That was one of the problems solved by the generals of olden times with a few words. He climbed to the platform, took firm possession of the microphone, and blew into it. It was operating. He ordered the Elect to slacken fire and aim their rifles at the trees.

"I will now communicate a final decision," he announced, passing his hand over his hair. "All persons who have taken the cowardly action of hiding themselves in the trees must come down immediately. I am giving you five minutes to do so."

There was a spark of silence which was extinguished by somebody cocking a pistol. A tremendous whistling and hooting was then set off.

"You heard," shouted Lito. "You now have four and a half minutes left."

Defiantly, he jumped from the platform and ran toward the little wood of walnut trees and cedars that plumed the ramp leading from the embankment. The order had struck home and terrified women were climbing down, carrying their children. The snipers were nowhere to be seen. They had now vanished into the mirages of the afternoon. Maté kettles, braziers, soiled diapers, and guitars, however, rained from the branches. While several of the shantytown women from Villa Insuperable were reaching up to help Doña Luisa's rheumatic husband to the ground, she, the old wife, slid gracefully down the trunk holding on to the stumps of the branches, and just as her slipper finally touched the hump of a root, her eyes met Lito Coba's.

This was the only instant in that short day of June that was measured not by watches but with the savor of eternity in the present . . . Doña Luisa, who covered her gray hair with a white kerchief and had lost count of her wrinkles many years before, was now confounding the logic of time with a splendid, unconcealable pregnancy. She carried her belly with such serenity, with an assurance of her sweet expectation so contagious, that the other elderly ladies of Villa Insuperable had also begun to tempt fate and all became pregnant, became medieval women. Her lips were graced with a gentle smile like that of the saintly knights on antique playing cards. And that smile could not but stab so deep into Lito's soul that he turned his back on them and strode off to the platform.

He had taken no more than a couple of steps when Leonardo Favio's voice came through the loudspeakers greeting the flight of the 18,000 doves, liberated from their baskets, now rising into the ashen sky.

The release of the birds triggered an immediate conditioned reflex in Lito, imprinted in him at the camp in Canuelas by Inspector Almirón, and drawing his Beretta, he kicked at a crowd barrier, yelled, "Now!" and with one unerring burst brought down several doves.

Until the moment he emerged on the little square of the Echeverría barrio, Noon Antezana had respected as a divine truth the General's favorite maxim: *Situate yourself in the center as you walk on the flank*. But, now, after the law of gravity had forced him irresistibly to the side, he realized how dangerous it was for anybody other than the General to tread the center.

He refreshed his face in the little fountain and was shocked at the image in the water of his scratched, mud-stained face. He had to find a hiding place until dark. With the distraction of the massacre over, López Rega's men were anxiously beating the fields in search of him. He felt time, racing, escaping him. In front of him he saw the absurd hulk of the church with its tiled façade and roof, arched portal, and bell tower with four clocks, each showing a different hour.

He crossed the atrium on the run, tried the door, found it open, and entered. A dim light filtered through the romanesque stained-glass windows. At the altar, a sacristan was polishing the crown of one of the images. Two neon-lighted crosses were on and the votive candles were melting at the feet of the saints. No one else was there. Outside, dusk descended slowly.

He realized that he had to think but there was no room left in his body for thoughts. He could only feel and even that, not fully, as though a part of him were feeling in secret.

The agonizing shriek of a siren returned sensation to his numbed nerves. He heard curses, orders. His first impulse was to crawl along under the benches and hide between the narrow planks, covering his eyes like an animal. On his right, he saw a confessional in a niche in the wall. He managed to climb into it just as a death squad burst into the church, their behavior a demented combination of savagery and reverence. He peered at them through the grille. He immediately recognized the humpbacked movements of Arcángelo Gobbi. Incredulously, he watched him cross himself before the main altar. What followed seemed to have the substance of a dream but the voices were real and the men acted with a force that occurs only in reality.

One of the killers struck the sacristan on the head with the butt of his gun, smashing him to the ground, then pulled him by the legs to the atrium where two others picked him up like a side of beef and threw him into the ambulance. Arcángelo took no notice of them. He moved swiftly from one side to the other among the images of the Way of the Cross, as though disappointed by the church's tawdry decorations. Suddenly, he stopped next to the confessional, where he appeared to find something. Noon held his breath. Through the grille he could see him kneel, disappear, come back into view holding an effigy of a little Virgin, a toy, carrying a plaster Child Jesus. He put the image back in its place gingerly as one cleansing a wound, and remained there for a moment, his hands together, worshipping it.

He then unbuckled his belt and began divesting himself of his weapons. He left the Beretta on a prie-dieu, removed a Walther fitted with a silencer and two hand grenades hidden under his armpits, and piled up the thirty-cartridge clips that bulged out of his coat between his knees. Finally, he turned up one leg of his trousers. He then took out a pair of tailor's shears which he opened, contemplating the gleam of its blade against the light. A frozen smile disfigured his face.

Not until then did Noon Antezana make out the bundle that Arcángelo had left under the holy-water font when he came in. He saw the hunchback drag the bundle, permitting nobody to help, and, panting, dump it under the flickering candles that surrounded the miniature Virgin. A single flash of light was sufficient. Under the seams of dried blood, the gag, and the tattered blouse, he recognized Diana's body. Her eyes were frozen in an expression of horror. Black scratches striped her breast. And her lips, always chapped by the first chill of winter, instead of cracks now had holes in them.

Noon heard the clicking of the shears. Then he saw Diana Bronstein's flaming curls fall, still warm, and felt himself nailed to the darkness of the confessional by the bloodied whiteness of that head he had felt pulsating so often between his hands, and with one of those remote feelings of surprise that belong only to childhood, Noon found that his face was wet, that a tide of tears covered it, remaining there as though forever.

He waited a long time until his senses quieted and his body returned to being his again. Then, stealthily, he left the place. He walked hugging the walls, between the gloomy houses where television sets flickered from time to time. The night was becoming soaked with dampness. The grass smelled of rot. Suddenly he saw Leonardo Favio gesticulating on one of those screens, his face distorted. He heard him saying:

"A boy begged me to come quickly to the international hotel because they were torturing people there. I went up. A goon tried to stop me. I pulled away from him. I said to him, 'Don't you try to stop me because I will start yelling my head off.' I knocked at a door. They let me in. An officer took me by the arm. 'You can relax, Leonardo. Everything is in order here.' But I'm no fool. There were a lot of people lying around on the floor, all smashed up. The walls were covered with blood. Imagine what it must have been like! These walls were spattered up to the ceiling! I began to cry. I fell to my knees. Maybe I'm chicken, but I don't care! 'I'm not going to denounce you, but I want you to guarantee the lives of these people,' I begged them. They promised to call a doctor and that they would stop the torture. So, I left. I noted down the names of the wounded so that their families could rest easier: José Tomás Almada, Alberto Formingo, Vicki Pertini, Luis Ernesto Pellizón . . ."

Later, Noon watched images of the General, Isabel, and López Rega, arms upraised, coming down the steps of the plane, and Noon's soul became a desert of rancor so measureless in an emptiness so irremediable, that he abandoned the cover of the houses and plunged into the darkness like a sleepwalker.

At 3 a.m. on June 21, a police patrol car found Noon Antezana, out in the open, motionless, staring at a eucalyptus tree with three men hanging from it whom nobody knew.

The General had anticipated sadness but not in this form, with the delirium of so many people. When the Betelgeuse finally landed at the Morón military airport at five o'clock in the evening, the first thing he saw through the windows was the menacing threads of dampness that hung in the air like ghosts.

He heard applause at the back of the plane, a hoarse voice shouting, "Long live the fatherland!" and, at the same time, discovered that outside, ministers, commanders-in-chief, archbishops, and bankers were also applauding.

López leaned toward him and said, "See how much better it was this way, General . . . safer. No rumpus, no pushing and shoving, no torches . . . There will be more than enough occasions for all that."

"Yes," admitted the General. "The people, poor things, will be wanting to see me, too."

The señora arranged her hair. She opened her compact, dusted the shine on her nose, and said, "Am I all right like this? Seeing the women out there with all that jewelry on, now I'm sorry I didn't keep my black suit handy."

"You'll feel fine in your coat," the General reassured her. "With a rosette on the lapel. Today is Flag Day."

"They should have brought the dogs to us," the señora complained. "They've been vomiting the whole trip, the poor things. They're sick."

"Daniel will get them for you, Chabela. Daniel is taking care of everything."

They had to stay aboard until the Vice President completed the formality of reversion of power to Cámpora. Then they walked down into the darkness. They were lit up by flashes from the cameras of a few photographers some distance away. The General was upset that the Betelgeuse should have dropped so brusquely into the uncertainties of the night. They had been flying in daylight for eighteen hours, the same number as the years of his exile, and, suddenly, on looking through the window, he found a horizon without twilight: there were only stars and a thin sliver of a waning moon.

He was received by a salute of honor with drawn swords. The same people who had once decreed the mere mention of his name in public to be punishable by imprisonment and who had outlawed his party in all elections, were there once more, embracing him, thanking God for having kept him in good health and strong enough to rescue the fatherland.

The General was impatient to return to the respite of his routine as soon as possible. His body felt the urgent need of a house. He said so. But López Rega took him by the arm and diverted him toward an office where the commanders-in-chief were waiting for him.

Again he listened absently to the details of the recent massacre. They repeated the names to him of some of those responsible. The General immediately forgot them, exhaustion having turned the names to water.

"We'll teach them a lesson Argentina will never forget!" he said with all the severity he could muster. Then, turning to López, he asked, "Did you bring the binders of the Memoirs in your briefcase, my boy? Tomorrow, when we get up, we must continue with the correction. Everything begun must end someday."

One of the commanders insisted on reading the official reports on the dead and wounded in Ezeiza. The General interrupted him. He wanted to know where the pilgrims who had come from distant provinces to see him were being lodged so that flowers and blankets could be sent to them.

"There are no flowers, General. It's winter," said President Cámpora, separating each syllable. "What they would appreciate most is if you could speak to them."

The señora stood up. Her gaze was always uneasy, as if she might lose it at any moment. Now, the uneasiness was gone. The lost gaze alone remained.

"What about my doggies?" she asked. "Why don't you bring them to me right now, Daniel? Where have they taken my poor little rascals?"

My fate is sealed, Zamora said to himself once again. I see history through a keyhole. The only reality I know is what appears on television.

At six in the evening, the wall of trucks blocking passage of his taxi in front of the Workers' Home development broke open without warning and the vehicles immobilized at the entrance to the freeway returned to the depths of the city in an incomprehensible, unanimous inversion of the migrations that had ruled the day. The thunder of the bass drums started up again but without rolls now, beating out only a single funereal cadence. A silent multitude wandered back, retracing in a few hours the way over the shoulders of the road that had cost them eighteen years to get to.

Zamora was struck by the immobility of the silence that floated like a planet over the interminable lines. He could not have imagined that it was possible for a throng to walk in silence like that, all together, without it or the silence giving way, above all under the tremendous weight of the backpacks and the sorrow.

Once again, he felt separated by glass from what was happening and determined to get out into the open air. He paid the driver triple the fare and at the moment of opening the door was afraid. It is easy to write history. Plunging headlong into it could relocate the meridian of feelings. He got out. It surprised him that the night should have neither odor nor sounds but only the same myriad silences he had discerned from inside the car. A light frost was beginning to appear.

He walked against the current. He did not care how he would get back to Buenos Aires because now the center was here in this blind spot of fog. He forced his way through foot by foot, fighting the crowd, but the effort slid off his body as though instead of advancing him it was being absorbed by the others. At least, I know where I am going, he said to himself. But he didn't know.

Finally, he came to a house with a pock-marked façade, of many rooms, where people were entering and leaving. In one of the yards, he saw a line of men urinating and he urinated, too. He then prowled around empty spaces until he reached what appeared to be an eating place. Dogs and saddled horses without owners wandered about in the darkness.

He came out into another yard. There was a rustic kitchen made of planks. People were warming their hands at the fires. The walls were cracked and dusty. Some peasants in tattered gray ponchos sat on the ground, resting. Nobody spoke. Everybody's eyes would focus on whatever happened to gleam in the air, and if anything was being said, it was just for themselves.

In the darkness, television screens at the houses in the background, glimmering like fireflies, multiplied the parade of downcast pilgrims along the highway, the national dejection, the depression of death that filtered down on the city like the heaviness of fog.

Suddenly, Zamora heard a few stray phrases that came out of the silence. He recognized the General's voice, cracked, flat, as though issuing from a throat that was not his:

"I don't know what dark turn of fate brought me back to Buenos Aires after eighteen years of absence without affording me the opportunity to give the Argentine people a symbolic embrace from the deepest recesses of my heart . . ."

The men woke up. Even the horses turned their heads toward the lights of the television screens. The volume rose.

". . . first, because we left Madrid a little late, to begin with. And then, because today, June twentieth, is the shortest day of the year. It was a routine trip but we arrived behind schedule . . ."

Zamora approached the knots of listeners that grew larger and larger. Finally, he was able to catch glimpses of the General who held himself erect, was healthy-looking, and showed no signs of strain from the long trip. His hair was neatly in place under a layer of brilliantine. Seated in a thronelike armchair, he scarcely moved. López Rega stood a step behind, his hands resting on the back of the chair. President Cámpora, in the seat beside him, sat listening, enthralled. The national shield decorated the scene.

Although it was an improvised speech, López Rega seemed to be following it easily with his lips. The General said, ". . . to avoid disorder, I did not want a night concentration in a zone as dark as the airport. I did this in fullest consideration of the poor people who had come to Ezeiza from so far away to welcome me."

However, there was something about the image that went against nature, like seeing rain pouring upward. The peasants and the horses became nervous. Zamora sharpened his attention. The General said, "Later on, I will have to make a tour of the entire Republic . . ."

One of the men looking on realized that López's lips were forming the words before the General said them.

"Watch close!" he muttered. "They're herding the General!"

It happened again. The secretary's lips could be seen saying: ". . . and I look forward to seeing the Jujeños in Jujuy," a fraction of a second before the General's voice did.

". . . and the Salteños in Salta," dictated the lips.

". . . Salta," repeated Peron.

Dismay settled over the people like an instantaneous sickness. One of the women walked away from the television set, weeping, and lay down next to the braziers. Others began to warm the children's food. The whole house remained suspended in that chasm that exists between indifference and explosion, until one of the peasants finally stood up and said, serenely, irrefutably, "That man can't be Perón."

"Can't be," the women agreed.

"When Perón finds out what's going on, he'll come back," said the peasant.

On the screen, the General produced a final, melancholy smile. Zamora turned away and sought a moment's respite in watching the children romp. And, as was said at the time, the shortest day of the year passed into eternity. It came to its end. Zamora stood up.

"Even if he comes back, it's too late. We shall never be as we were."

352

EPILOGUE

Standing on the chair, haranguing,
he shook hands with the dead, one
by one. Nobody knows whether it is
better if he welcomes us or spurns
us.

José Lezama Lima,
Slow Curtain for Short Arias

The shantytown women of Villa
Insuperable descended on the yellow hulk of the Teatro Colón with
the foreboding that they wouldn't be able to see the General this
time, either. They put up improvised shelters of plastic and broom-
sticks that were constantly being blown apart by the wind and took
turns heating bottles for their infants in the neighboring lunch-
rooms in front of which the funeral wreaths were piled.

They had been in the columns of mourners for some fifteen hours
during which they covered a little over twenty blocks, walking from
west to east. It wasn't easy to calculate the time because they were
already in the beyond, in the eternity of funeral rites, where the
General's vast depth spread its contagion without limit or discrim-
ination.

From time to time, the radio stations went on national hookup and enumerated the telegrams of condolence or transmitted the sobbing of the people who lined the streets. Houses were left with the doors ajar and the newspapers concerned themselves with nothing but the mourning.

In the early hours of Wednesday, July 3, 1974, the media unloosed a barrage of information and opinion for the historical record that placed the General even further out of reach of the shantytown women, as though he had been carried off in a mirage.

The Great Man's casket was already in the Blue Room of the Congress. A congressman proposed that it be left on the dais of the main hall for an indefinite period so that his immortality might inspire the laws and decrees of the future.

The body was dressed in military uniform. A mother-of-pearl rosary encircled the interlaced fingers. The presidential sash crossed his breast. The Radio Rivadavia commentator observed that the uniform seemed inappropriate on the body that had been unable to wear it for eighteen years and finally adapted to the freedom of civilian dress. Eight administrations had prohibited him from using the symbol of the sun on the epaulettes, the saber, or the cap with golden palms that now lay on his chest.

There must have been over 400,000 persons in the throng waiting to see him. No more than 2,000 per hour could pass. Radio Belgrano announced that, as in Evita's case, nobody would be allowed to touch the General. This was an old man's wake at which philosophizing outweighed tears. A railing with a blue cloth over it separated the casket from the people. The cloth was soiled with tears, mud, the backup of detritus from the streets, but the pilgrims kissed it nonetheless. The Elite Guards replaced it every fifteen minutes.

Isabelita, the widow, was at last President of the Republic. She acted befittingly, with studied solemnity. She visited the chapel every two or three hours, escorted by military aides-de-camp, said a paternoster, arranged the dead man's hair, and dried his saliva with a little black handkerchief.

The Radio Mitre commentator was surprised to see that each time Isabelita came out of the chapel, López Rega went in, leaned over the deceased to recite prayers in his ear. "You can follow him on your screens," he said, "and watch how the General's secretary brushes his chief's forehead with the tips of his ring finger and little finger. Observe the reverence with which he performs the ritual. He touches him once, twice, three times. Now, he takes one pace back."

Before day dawned, the Radio Continental news broadcast announced that the Reverend Martin Luther King's mother had been murdered in Alabama or Kentucky as she was playing the organ in church. Doña Luisa, the old woman of Villa Insuperable whose pregnancy had driven Lito Coba off at Ezeiza, was nursing her infant when she heard the news. It gave her such a shock that she withdrew her breast in fear that her milk would sour.

"The General has laid the death egg," she told her husband. "Once these misfortunes begin, nobody can stop them."

She suspected that the radio stations were thinking the same because they were being extremely reticent about mentioning the word "death." When they reported how many had fallen by the wayside, they said, "Seven thousand fainted and are now back. One hundred and fourteen have been hospitalized. Twelve had heart problems and will not be returning."

Because of the dampness, Doña Luisa's bunions were giving her a very bad time. The pain was shooting out in waves that sometimes caught her in the pit of the stomach. Like the other Villa women, she wore a shawl over her shoulders and a white kerchief on her head but in a rainy winter like this clothing was more of a burden than a protection. The husbands were brewing maté. With the dawn, the rain eased and the column of mourners was gradually leaving the theater behind them. Some construction workers brought wicker chairs for the shantytown women so that they could nurse their babies in comfort. Different radio stations could be heard at the various segments of the queue, but the voices were equally lugubrious and ceremonious. The music that came on was always church music.

The Radio de la Plata remote-control unit reported that the Pergamino textile workers had decided to hold a wake in the union hall meeting room using a poster of the General. In a voice charged with emotion, the announcer said, "It is a most moving experience to see how these women of the people have placed the venerated likeness of the General on a lace pillow bound with crape so that all can share in the feeling that the General, lying in state, is here in person in Pergamino, too, like our Lord in every Host." After this, they reported that the inhabitants of San Luis and Catamara were enshrouding busts of Perón in order to offer up requiems to him.

"If that's the idea, then we can hold our own wake in the Villa," Doña Luisa decided.

All were in agreement. It took them some time to make their way back through the muddy alleys of Bajo Belgrano with their packs on their heads. When they were finally nearing home and caught the aroma of hot soup, they felt that the General would be better off there than out in the open, together with people like himself rather than surrounded by the pomp of the authorities.

Doña Luisa's house consisted of one room. The husbands moved back the cots, the dining table, the new infant's cradle, and put up an altar of fruit crates. It came out in the form of a pyramid. They covered it with a cretonne bedspread and set up the television set on top. The image on the screen was being transmitted by a stationary camera focused on the body at the chapel. From time to time a closeup was shown of the General's rigid face between the placentas of his shroud. The people could be seen as they passed by, almost at a run, and when anyone tried to linger a second longer, the soldiers dragged the person away.

"You see what I'm saying?" repeated Doña Luisa. "The General is better off here than there."

They lit two large candles on either side of the television set and from the ceiling hung a cross put together with scaffolding planks. They decorated the walls with black bows, and Doña Luisa made a lovely floral arrangement at the foot of the pyramid with plastic carnations. The news of the wake spread through all of Bajo Belgrano and a long line formed at the entrance to Villa Insuperable. On reaching the television set, each mourner knelt, passed his fingers over the screen, and left silently. Every once in a while, Doña Luisa wiped off the General's image with a little black handkerchief and stroked his hair through the glass.

They saw Noon Antezana come to attention before the dead man and salute him with upraised fist. They watched how Arcángelo Gobbi supported the señora by her elbows when at daybreak on July 4, she was overcome by a fit of weeping and seemed about to faint.

Doña Luisa never left the television set until the doors of the Congress were shut. The cameras moved in on the General for a last closeup showing his face shrouded in the gauze uterus. Then there was interference of some kind and snow began to fall over the image. The dead man gradually sank into the depths of whiteness until nothing was left on the screen but blizzards and volcanoes of ice, like those at the Pole.

A voice over the snowy image mentioned that 200,000 people had been left outside the Congress without saying good-bye. The columns of disappointed faithful stretched for ninety-four blocks, from Calle Paraguay on the north to Avenida San Juan on the south, from Carlos Pellegrini on the east to Calle Jujuy on the west.

At 9:30 on July 4, the funeral cortège left for the chapel of Nuestra Señora de la Merced at the presidential residence of Olivos. The women of the Villa knelt before the image in the casket mounted upon an army gun carriage, wrapped in the flag. It was getting soaked in the drizzle. Thousands of flowers, carnations, gladioluses, jasmines, orchids, fell from the balconies, delicate summer insects that had left their hothouses to live that one instant. The Presidential Guards beat their drums.

The shantytown women broke into tears. In that desolation of the end Doña Luisa felt as though they too were dying. A lump formed in her throat. She realized that the instant the casket disappeared from the screen they would all be left orphans forever. But she was not a woman given to resignation. She climbed the altar of fruit crates, put her arms around the television set, and hugged it tightly. The General's smile enveloped her in its omnipotent warmth and Doña Luisa believed that anything was possible, that it only had to be said for it to happen:

"Resurrect, big man! What's to stop you?"

ABOUT THE AUTHOR

A journalist and author of novels, short stories, and two collections of essays, Tomás Eloy Martínez left Argentina in 1975 after a bomb was found in his office. He lived in Venezuela from 1975 through 1983, and in 1983–84 was a Fellow at the Woodrow Wilson Center in Washington. He now divides his time between Argentina and the United States, where he is a professor of Latin American literature at the University of Maryland.